Saga Across the Atlantic

Shefqet Meko

Arbjon Press—Minneapolis, MN
ISBN: 979-8-218-39892-7
Library of Congress Control Number: 2024906115
Title: *Saga Across the Atlantic*
Author: Shefqet Meko
Digital distribution | 2024
Paperback | 2024

Saga across the Atlantic is a work of fiction. All names, characters, places, dialogue and incidents within are products of the author's imagination or are used fictitiously. Any resemblance to real persons, living or deceased, or actual events or locales is entirely coincidental.

Translated from Albanian by Jon Meko
Editor: Amanda Ziebell

Published in the United States by New Book Authors Publishing

Dedication

This novel is dedicated to my only brother, Çelnik Feim Meko, who lost his battle with Covid-19, in Torino, Italy, March 26, 2020. He was my first teacher and first reader of my writings. My brother was an exceptional man, with great passion, courage, and a lovely spirit. He always believed and inspired me to be a writer.

Dedication

Chapter One

It had been a quarter of a century since Xhelo Lakrori first set foot in America, but he still found himself straddling that elusive divide between his homeland and the "vast expanse" across the Atlantic. This land of liberty unfurled before him like a sprawling canvas, inviting him to paint the portrait of his life with bold strokes of toil, pleasure, freedom, escapades, idiosyncrasies, camaraderie, adversaries, mysteries, and, above all, the quest to understand himself—a journey of existential proportions for every soul in pursuit of purpose. In this land, he reveled in the freedom to shape his destiny as he saw fit and, most importantly, to safeguard his individuality. He'd often muse to himself, "Nowhere else on Earth can you find the same level of intimacy and familiarity as you do here in America."

Xhelo Lakrori found himself amid a vast wave of Albanian refugees, a stream of souls seeking new horizons on American soil. They were not alone in their quest; countless others had embarked on similar journeys, long before and during Xhelo's own arrival in the land of opportunity. It irked him to no end when he heard the political rhetoric in Albania claiming that "the homeland was losing its population."

"Politicians, they're nothin' but 'dog tails,'" Xhelo Lakrori grumbled in a hushed tone, his whiskey glass in hand as he observed the pre-election spectacle of American Democrats parading for the White House 2020 on the television screen. The lineup seemed never-ending, reminiscent of the political bureau gatherings during the May 1st parades back in his homeland. "Ah, it's like those 'milk lines' from decades ago, but this here's a top-notch line up, not like our pitiful ones that drove us to the brink of madness," he muttered to himself.

The campaign for the highest office in America was in full swing. People of all genders, races, ideologies, and alternatives clamored for attention, waiting for their moment in the spotlight. Only one of them would emerge victorious, while the rest would be brushed aside, fading into obscurity, swallowed up by the masses. Xhelo listened to their impassioned speeches and grandiose promises. They radiated self-assuredness, showered themselves with praise, and bragged about their prowess to "dethrone Trump." They pledged solutions, innovations, and necessities, all while emphasizing that their triumph was the linchpin for the Democrats. "I champion the cause of America and the ideals of democracy because I am the best among you... I am the one who can prevail," seemed to be the mantra of every candidate. The moment of reckoning had arrived. These candidates, akin to political predators vying for the same ideological territory, pounced on each other's stumbles, inadequacies, and falsehoods. With quintessential American confidence, they laid out their visions before the cameras, proclaiming, "Only I can unseat the incumbent President Trump. Only I can restore our homeland..."

Xhelo suppressed the notion that whispered in his mind: "I am the best." It made him ponder whether this sentiment had its roots in Albanian ideals, even in the days of "Socialist Albania." Weren't they once celebrated as a "beacon of hope"? Wasn't Albania hailed as the "communist paradise and the future of the world"? Now, they proclaimed themselves as a "splendor beyond the Atlantic," deeming themselves "world leaders." But who had bestowed upon them such a grand title? Wasn't it a manifestation of extreme egoism? If America upheld the principle of voting, why hadn't it subjected its "leadership role" to a vote instead of claiming it as an exclusive privilege? Who had elected the "world's leading nation"? Why hadn't the United Nations determined it? American politicians, in championing the idea that every facet of leadership should be earned through democratic processes, frequently referred to America as a "global leader" on the world stage. With an unusual naivety, he posed a series of probing questions: "Who cast their votes? What percentage of the world voted? How many dissented? Who oversaw this global vote? Were the voices of the working class suppressed?" He became immersed in contemplation and analysis, his thoughts shifting like the sands of the Sahara Desert.

This was his intellectual rumination, a mental exercise he privately indulged in. It allowed him to delve into ideas, hypotheses, reminisce about quotations, and arrive at conclusions that had lingered in his mind from days gone by. Thanks to the freedom he now relished in the present, he could think without fear, anxiety, or trepidation. In the past, such musings could have led to a dark path. Being in America afforded him a different brand of courage, a sense of judgment that seemed to have descended from the heavens, as freely as sunlight bathes the land.

"Don't forget, Xhelo," an inner voice of history reminded him, and Xhelo listened intently. "For over two centuries and more, the American experiment has not only withstood challenges but has thrived. It has displayed unparalleled resilience, vitality, and remarkable adaptability to the ever-evolving dynamics of life and human nature. This adaptability is the key to its success on this continent. Pay no heed to the politicians; politicians are cut from the same cloth everywhere, but America itself stands apart. Can you name another system that rivals the American way? Why do nearly all those who find themselves unfortunate in their own lands look to America with hope? Consider your own journey. Why did you leave Albania and come here? Why do people dream of reaching this 'promised land'? It's because here, you encounter a realm of boundless possibilities, just as you did, sir, arriving with only three suitcases..." This inner voice whispered, rekindling a profound philosophical fervor within him.

He longed to heed his inner voice in silence: "That's why you err in criticizing America's prominent role, Xhelo. It has earned its position; it's as if it's summoned by a higher power, even if you don't believe in it. While you're within its embrace, you experience freedom every single day. You only think of the state when taxes come due, often forgetting those beyond its borders, far away. Ask them for their opinions. Their gaze is fixed on America; they yearn for it to remain a symbol and leader of freedom. They place their trust in this nation as a beacon of democracy..."

"Well, alright, perhaps I got carried away with all that American self-praise," Xhelo mused, though he couldn't help but feel that living in the land of the free did give off that impression. Gradually, he began to see the justification for America's entitlement to such praise. It had opened its arms to all nations, offering refuge to the oppressed souls from across the globe. This was precisely why monarchs from every corner harbored a deep disdain for America like no other.

"If it were up to kings and dictators, there would be no America," he pondered. "Even the King of England, had he foreseen how radically different America would become from his own kingdom, would never have dispatched that initial group of pilgrims on the 'Mayflower.' Reflect on it, Xhelo Lakrori! Take a moment to compare and don't forget so easily… Name another country in the world with such a diverse mix of nations, tribes, languages, beliefs, ideologies, theories, inventions, conflicts, and eccentricities as this vast continent. There's none. It's this influx of nations from every corner of the globe that makes this nation a true melting pot, a fusion of nations. Do you grasp where the unwavering American spirit stems from? It's woven into the very fabric of this nation, composed of hundreds of nations and all the races of the earthly globe, do you see?" Xhelo engaged in this internal dialogue with himself. "So, it's this freedom to critique that truly defines you as an American. Freedom of speech is the true monument of America, do you comprehend?" he'd whisper to himself, not out of fear, but with a sense of reverence. He often found himself ensnared in this contemplative "trap," especially when pondering matters related to politics and politicians.

Ah, the world of politicians. These individuals, belonging to the human species, all shared a common trait: political opportunism. They rose above the masses, capitalizing on the unthinking fervor of the crowd, for politics was a ruthless arena that manipulated the emotions of the masses. "The crowd, it's a relic from medieval times," he reflected. "Back then, the crowd represented power, a tempest, a ringing sword... The crowd could hang, maim, burn at the stake, or crucify you... Today, the crowd should yield to expertise because everyone possesses a voice, a microphone, and a camera; every individual has their own 'television channel' through which they can address the world, marking the greatest revolution of the 21st century... Power has descended to the individual, to the human being. This is the era of human explosions, but 'everyone in their own little box'..." His thoughts became entangled in this changing landscape.

Xhelo held a deep admiration for socialism, a system he knew well. He had once held hopes of progressing towards communism, envisioning a society where the principle was to "work as much as you can and take as much as you need." What an enticing ideal it was! It resembled a vision of pure Christianity. Was there anything better for our planet? What a dream it was...He fondly remembered his partisan uncle, who, like Americans on Memorial Day, paid tribute every May 5th to those Albanian fallen in WWII. Following the ceremonies, his uncle would deliver similar speeches in Vërnik, and every village in Devoll. During these speeches before the pioneers, he would be impassioned and principled, but when they gathered around the campfire, he would speak from the heart, without notes. "My dear nephew, when we first took up arms as partisans in the mountains, we were promised great things. 'When Albania is liberated, we will all dine with golden spoons.' How could you not be swayed by such promises?!!... Think about it. I deserted from the Italian gendarmerie post to become a partisan. I don't regret that decision but look at us now. We even must stand in line for a piece of bread, silently. We eat our bread with our heads lowered. This is what they want... Power blinds you, nephew! Look, Comrade Pilo fought alongside me; we were comrades, he was the commissar of our partisan squad, and we slept under the open sky in the mountains and bushes together... Look at him now, living in a big villa in the capital city, while I struggle just to get some bread... We fought together, but our fates diverged," his uncle, Ferit Lakrori, who was renowned for his honesty, would say in silence. That grand promise of *"Work as much as you can, take as much as you need"* turned out to be the colossal lie of communism that engulfed half the world... It triggered a major upheaval. The world was split in two... Some bourgeois children in the West conceived notions of a profound transformation, with the proletariat governing the world. These ideas spread to the Russian steppes, leading to revolutions, violent changes, and the overthrowing of tsars and kings... A grand illusion had conquered the world's most impoverished populations, while the philosophers of the era, offspring of capitalism, had anticipated these changes in London, Paris, or America. But they unfolded far from these places, in lands marked by poverty and ignorance... "Man is a creature with many enigmas," Xhelo Lakrori, the veterinarian, would often remark.

He would muse about life, friends, loved ones, and it seemed that everyone affirmed the well-established theory: "It's me, without them." Our criticism of the idealists had been in vain. They had been right all along, and the fact that at this very moment, I, Xhelo

Lakrori, found myself echoing the thoughts of Hegel from nearly two centuries earlier, served as confirmation of the validity of his philosophy. "It's me, without the others. It's me, without the world," he quietly murmured, and the triumphant egos of the Democratic presidential candidates suddenly appeared justifiable. If a person doesn't value themselves, why should they extol someone else? Doesn't the world originate from the self? We Albanians deemed self-praise disgraceful; we reserved it for eulogies at funerals because during life, self-praise was deemed a "great shame." So, let death come, and we would speak a few kind words before laying you to rest in the grave... That was the society he had left behind, far to the east of the Adriatic Sea. Whereas here, in the embrace of capitalism, even though the blend of sweetness and saltiness was different, savagery seemed to have acquired a more palatable flavor. In a society where freedom and the free individual were paramount, madness was more pronounced. Here, madness was at your disposal; here, you went mad because you chose to. He recalled a poem by a late poet who, despite holding high-ranking positions in the Albanian state police, would suddenly sit down and author a book of poetry. In one of his sincere poems, unlike any police chief, he wrote... *"In birth and death, we are so human. In death and birth, we are not hypocrites..."*

A person enters the world with a cry, a primal announcement of existence that reverberates through the universe. Amidst the cries of birth, concealed behind stoic facades, mothers often moan in pain, contemplating the mysteries of life and love. They may wonder, "Why did I engage in that act of love...? See, the very act of passion leads to this agonizing pain, accompanied by a lament: 'To be born or to die...'" When we are born, we confront a paradoxical human reality that lingers with us until our final breath—a Hamletian dilemma: "To be or not to be..." soon fades from memory. Once a person returns to normalcy, when a woman recovers from the pain of childbirth, she readily indulges in the passion of love with a man, momentarily dismissing the impending challenges... "You've lost your mind, Xhelo," his inner voice echoed. But without such experiences, how would you have come into this world, or even to America? Life is an unpredictable adventure, promising both light and darkness...

In America, European philosophical and existential principles take on a different hue, seen through a unique lens, and the cult of individualism assumes a distinct character. Consequently, Americans, before praising others, primarily, indulge in self-praise. Such self-affirmation is a natural facet of the human ego: "It's me, without the world...." It's a fascinating phenomenon. A person is a complex tapestry of ideas and peculiar contradictions. In this context, American society itself mirrors humanity, akin to an individual... Here, no one polices your thoughts. This place is a "paradise for philosophers." Say what you want, write what you want, criticize the government, condemn the party, express your anger, and vent your frustration at the president... Your thoughts and the turmoil within your soul are your own property, requiring no authorization.

For Xhelo, this wasn't his first encounter with this authentic facet of American life. "America is distinct, 'everyone in its own right...' Thank the heavens for bringing me here... Thank God," he'd mutter to himself, reminiscing about numerous occasions when, back in Albania, infamous collective gatherings would commence with the phrase "With the teachings of the party and Comrade Enver... As the party and Comrade Enver instruct..." When the notorious red books were distributed in Tirana and handed out at cultural centers in villages, everyone would meticulously peruse them with a pencil in hand. Decades spent laboring, volumes in hand, notebooks filled with summaries, newspapers cast in lead, and radios brimming with propaganda and speeches, yet true education remained elusive... In America, no one compels you to switch on the television and follow debates as was the norm in their earlier forms of education... If you wish, you can simply tune it all out. This is called freedom... He harbored an insatiable curiosity about the interplay between American reality and his experiences in the "different era" of Albania. Certain aspects seemed familiar, but the crucial distinction lay in the space occupied by the power of the individual. The tangible result of this difference was that the brilliance of American society appeared to him as the "product of individualism," where power and governance represented the "final layer." "Thank goodness I haven't departed this world without experiencing this unique reality," he often reminded himself. He eagerly anticipated the next day at his clinic, where he'd share the joke of the day with his clients: "Did you follow last night's debate? That's how socialism was—endless talk, yet every sentence had to invoke the party and its leader... It was unclear who would emerge victorious..."

The ringing phone snapped him out of his contemplations. It was his schoolmate, Pirro Maloku, who had resided in America for years. Xhelo promptly answered the call and listened to his friend from hundreds of miles away.

"Do you see how democracy functions, Xhelo? Make sure to take notes!" his friend exclaimed.

Xhelo took a sip of whiskey and responded without delay:

"We're learning, every day, from this imperialist democracy. Just make sure not to forget to cast your vote. Your vote is a 'bullet for the enemy'... Do you hear me?"

The two engaged in a spirited discussion about the ideas being disseminated via microphones and TV screens, reaching millions of viewers.

"I won't vote for those individuals anymore!" Xhelo interjected. "I'll vote differently. I'll cast my vote with a raised fist..."

"Xhelo!... Have you gone mad!? Have you forgotten the teachings of our party? How can you, the son of a humble peasant, do this?" his friend challenged him over the phone.

"America opened our eyes! I'm not destitute anymore, I'm not like you. I've ascended to the middle class, achieved it through my own labor..." he began to jest.

Then, as the political discourse waned, Pirro sought Xhelo's opinion on a business idea that had sprung to mind. He envisioned importing Albanian brandy, known as raki, to America, and even Kallmeti wine. Pirro hoped to enlist Xhelo, who possessed substantial financial resources, in this venture. However, Xhelo regarded this as a challenging endeavor. He was aware that numerous dedicated farmers in Albania were producing pure raki from grapes, without any additives or chemicals, reminiscent of the early days of the free market. They could brand it as "organic raki" and even market it as "raki mani"—a remedy for all. They might even tout it as a "cure for Covid-19." In this free land, they could shape the narrative to their liking. According to Pirro, once the market was open, they could also import "organic olive oil" from olives crushed the traditional way, resulting in genuine oil. Pirro spoke fervently from Dallas, Texas, as though seeking Xhelo's blessing and hoping to embark on this venture together.

"There are thousands of tons of olive oil lying dormant in the homes of Albanian farmers. They're seeking a market, and we can assist them, all while turning a profit," he asserted, transitioning seamlessly from raki to organic oil.

Listening intently to his friend's enthusiasm, Xhelo couldn't help but draw parallels between the spirited discussions on television and the business proposals put forth by the Albanian American residing in Texas, the largest state in America. Xhelo believed that when people witness the open and candid expression of political ideas, they are often inspired to delve into their own entrepreneurial ventures, fueled by a common ambition: profit. And what's wrong with profit? Humans are inherently wired to thrive, not to falter. Profit serves as a catalyst for development, refusing to let one rest; it stirs energy, ignites passions, births projects, nurtures ideas, and propels progress. However, based on the observations Xhelo had made, he couldn't help but notice that the alcoholic beverage market was oversaturated, and competition was teetering on the edge of self-destruction.

"No, Pirro, business in America isn't quite as they say back in Albania, '*the grape sees the grape and ripens.*' It demands innovative ideas that set you apart from the rest. What you're proposing seems like a futile endeavor, doomed before it even begins... You know, the Greeks have mastered this line of business. Don't count on my involvement. You're a clever person; put your mind to it..." Xhelo remarked.

Pirro didn't take kindly to the response and abruptly ended the call. While Xhelo found the behavior impolite, he understood his friend's temperament and chose not to make a fuss. He knew that if the line was disconnected, Pirro wouldn't call back immediately; he preferred to wait until tempers had cooled, allowing them to restart their conversation from scratch. This wasn't the first time such an incident had occurred with Pirro Maloku. Having lived in America for years, Pirro often came up with borrowed ideas, rarely originating something with true originality. He opted for ventures that seemed easy, managing accounts, buying here, and selling there. He devised plans on paper but seldom made substantial investments. Pirro worked as an agronomist at the large corporation Cargill, earning over $95,000 annually, but he lacked significant ambitions. He was married to Teuta, an animal husbandry specialist from

Shkodra, who worked for City Group in Dallas. The couple enjoyed a comfortable income, but a sizable portion went toward their children's education. Two of them had already graduated as general practitioners, while the other two were still in college. "Life passed by working for the kids," Xhelo often remarked when talking to Shano, comforting himself with the thought that his earnings were now solely for him and his beloved wife.

"I'll never vote for them again, never!" Xhelo Lakrori exclaimed, downing another glass of whiskey since the Albanian raki had run out months ago.

"What's gotten into you, Xhelo? I left you in good spirits!" Shano, his wife, responded after returning from the women's hairdresser.

Xhelo, lost in his thoughts, had momentarily forgotten about her, as this had become a weekly routine. He addressed her affectionately, "Oh, my beautiful bride! Let me give you a kiss!" and reveled in the warmth of her lips. Shano informed him that after her hair appointment, she had gone to the mall with Moza, Sabah Makutllari's wife, and purchased some lovely items. She had also indulged in a 45-minute special massage by a Chinese therapist. Following their shopping excursion, she and Moza had watched a movie at the cinema. This rapid account overwhelmed Xhelo, who had politics on his mind.

"That's wonderful, my dear. Now, relax," he said, diverting his attention back to the TV screen.

Chapter Two

They had been married for thirty-five years. His wife, Shano, loved him unconditionally and endlessly. Although she hadn't given him the long-desired heir, she had bestowed upon him something else—a gift that thousands in Albania and millions worldwide could only dream of. One day, she approached him with news that promised to transform their lives. Their journey had been laden with emotional burdens, but they had loved, dreamed, and served, not only benefiting themselves but also those around them. Life involves traversing dreams and offering service, alongside grappling with pain and unrealized desires. Who can depart from this world without experiencing suffering? Driven by his dreams, Xhelo always found ways to transcend his ego and distinguish himself. Hence, any news from Shano was akin to a beacon of joy, akin to their intimate exchanges.

One day, she rushed into their yard, her eyes brighter than ever, her arms extended as if they were wings. Leaping into his arms, she exclaimed: "Discover the surprise... It's an astonishing announcement... We're saved, Xhelo!" What could this news be? A letter from his political associates in Tirana? The rediscovery of his great-grandfather's long-lost will in Istanbul? While he had dared to dream that she might be pregnant, the rational part of him knew that was a fading utopia. Without prolonging the suspense, she handed him an envelope sealed with the American emblem. Shano Lakrori had won the first round of the visa lottery—a sensation that swept through half of Korça and its neighboring villages. Xhelo nearly fainted. The day was unforgettable. At last, they could escape the oppressive rumors and embark on their journey to what Xhelo affectionately referred to as 'the empire of the world,' despite propaganda depicting it as a hellish, exploitative place. The arduous process of gathering documents and meeting various legal requirements had commenced—and they emerged triumphant.

In the heart of Chicago, they were welcomed by a distant cousin from Xhelo's father's side, marking an unforgettable initiation into the American West. The Lakroris embraced this fresh start every 4th of July and Thanksgiving, akin to their annual pilgrimages up the sacred Tomorr Mountain in their homeland of Albania. Here in the United States, they left behind the complexities of inheritance disputes and reveled in the newfound freedom and normalcy, free from the prying eyes and endless inquiries of their Albanian neighbors. "Why should anyone else be concerned? Inheritance is a private matter," Xhelo would often grumble back in Albania.

In America, Shano often found herself comforting Xhelo, who had been the subject of idle gossip regarding his fertility or lack thereof. "Why do they care about whether I have children? Why meddle in my personal life?" he'd exclaim in frustration. In the United States, no one ever questioned their childless status, and Xhelo took solace in this privacy. Here, every individual was a sovereign entity, as significant as a president and as unpredictable as a gangster. While engrossed in a Democratic presidential debate, Xhelo's mind would wander, and he'd imagine himself on the debate stage, posing audacious questions to the lone gay candidate: "How many children do you have? Did your husband become pregnant?"

"Xhelo... Are you talking to yourself?" Shano's voice jolted him out of his reverie.

Startled from his nostalgic musings, Xhelo Lakrori rose from his khaki-colored leather armchair and turned to kiss her. His mind drifted back to their first kiss near the promenade in Bilisht, as Shano extended her cheek, adorned with those familiar Korçë dimples. His body tingled with electricity, reminiscing about that unforgettable kiss. Sliding his arm around his wife's neck, he launched into a political discussion.

"Do you hear these Democrats, huh? They promise 'paradise for all'... Sweet lies, my dear Shano. America offers 'opportunities for all,' not 'paradise for all.' It's a public deception. Understand? Deception. Even God doesn't promise 'paradise for all,' but suggests 'some in paradise and some in hell.' I've read the Bible line by line, despite being a born Muslim. Do you follow, Shano?"

Shano, a well-mannered woman accustomed to her husband's peculiarities, listened attentively without a hint of argument. She adhered to the old Korçë principle that "Men are right," recognizing that decisions were often influenced by the "veto vote" of their wives. Shano's interests leaned more toward fashion, cooking, and crafts. She often surprised Xhelo with novel dishes inspired by recent cooking shows.

"Oh, what a creative star I ended up with!" he would exclaim whenever he sat down to eat.

On this evening of the American political debates, Shano had prepared a plate of meze to his liking: a small salad, feta cheese, olives, and roasted meat. Whiskey served as a "warm-up" for him; his true love was red wine. She selected a bottle of Argentine wine, "Alma Andina," and returned to find Xhelo already savoring the aroma of the sumptuous meal before him. Looking at the spread, he couldn't help but think that a couple's true love began and ended in the kitchen.

"You remain sweet, dear, innocent," he said softly. "Life would be much harsher without you."

Shano retreated to the laundry room, leaving Xhelo alone with his political musings. Back in Albania, where Xhelo had worked as a veterinarian, politics were often seen as a "matter from above," and discussions primarily revolved around love and cooperative endeavors. However, once people started expressing their opinions, Xhelo was among the first to speak up, criticizing socialism and dictatorship. His fervor was such that he'd even disturb Shano's sleep, shouting slogans as if he were at a political rally: "Freedom! Democracy!"

Eventually, Xhelo became the head of the opposition party in Devoll district. He began to see the crowds as his own children, a form of spiritual consolation for not having any of his own. What was lineage but a fleeting pleasure leading to unending expectations? "These people resemble me, so I shouldn't feel bad about not having children," he thought. "Look, I have an army; it doesn't matter that they don't carry my genes. They are people who eat, drink, and excrete—just a crowd." This amalgam of psycho-emotional thoughts both troubled and comforted Xhelo Lakrori. An elderly man from the neighboring village of Bitincka, Halil Karagjozi, had once told him, "Don't worry about not having children. They only exploit you when they need you, but you realize it too late. Try to understand this in time to be happy." Halil was considered the wisest man in the area. Despite having raised nine sons, he found himself alone following the accidental death of his wife. Nine sons and still alone? This paradox offered Xhelo some consolation. The experiences of his friends seemed to confirm Halil's wisdom. Niko Noksani from Menkulas had three sons who had all moved to Greece; one even married in America and never returned. Oliver Kashari, from the village of Tren, had five daughters: two married in Turkey and three in England, never visiting him again. "Stay calm and consider yourself fortunate that you don't have children. They bring joy, but they can also bring sorrow," Xhelo often reminded himself.

In the vast expanse of Colorado, another event would come to grip Xhelo's heart, reinforcing the profound emotions tied to his childless state. It unfolded as a chilling tale involving a man named Chris, who had committed an unfathomable act of brutality, forever etching his name into the annals of infamy. Chris had not only ended the life of his pregnant wife but also mercilessly snuffed out the innocent lives of their two daughters. The shockwaves from this grotesque act reverberated across the United States, shattering the collective conscience of the nation. The grim details were chilling—Chris, this so-called "prolific father," had strangled his daughters, leaving their lifeless bodies to rest in an oil cistern. Meanwhile, the body of his pregnant wife was discovered in a nearby fallow land, cold and lifeless. Chris, devoid of remorse, had uttered a chilling statement explaining his actions: "I buried her near the girls so they wouldn't be alone." The sheer brutality of the crime was beyond comprehension.

Xhelo, appalled by the attention that the media showered on this heinous act, couldn't help but feel a deep sense of outrage. He saw how this tragedy dominated headlines, overshadowing the sacrifice of hundreds of American soldiers who had lost their lives overseas. To him, the media's treatment of these soldiers as faceless statistics was nothing short of a disgrace—a sinister propaganda machine at work. He couldn't contain his fury, and he fumed at the exploitation of such a horrific tragedy for profit, exemplified by the production of a movie about the murderous father.

"What worth does such a 'fertile' man have?" he pondered, his mind spiraling into a tumultuous sea of questions and emotions. The chilling acts of violence had shaken him to his core, prompting introspection. He wondered if fatherhood, with its responsibilities and burdens, could potentially lead a man down such a dark path. As tears welled up in his eyes, he questioned the depths of his own soul, contemplating the unthinkable. In moments of solitude, when Shano was away, he'd allow himself to release muffled sobs, tasting the saltiness of his own tears on his trembling fingers. "Ah, God, why have you punished me so?" he cried out, his voice echoing in the empty room. "I am a good man, the best man in Devoll. Why subject me to such suffering?" His heartache was palpable, though he harbored no illusions of receiving an answer.

Shano, however, remained a pillar of strength in the face of their childlessness. Her resilience set her apart. She admired the words of the Albanian writer Jakov Xoxa, particularly from his novel, "The Salted Flower," which masterfully depicted the emotional turmoil of a barren woman. Yet, even in despair, Xoxa offered solace with the timeless wisdom that "a bridge connects two banks, a kiss merges two paths." Shano embraced this philosophy, finding solace in the bond she shared with Xhelo. Their love story was one of complexity and contradiction. From their very first kiss near the picturesque promenade in Bilisht town, Shano had issued a warning to Xhelo that would reverberate through the course of their lives: "Try to hate me, Xhelo. I'm not for you."

Xhelo, smitten beyond measure, had responded with fervor that only love could evoke, whispering words of devotion: "Why are you saying this? I love you. I would die for you."

But Shano, with a burdened heart, pleaded with him, "Please, hate me. What must I do to make you hate me? I'm not for you. Please, don't love me like this."

Despite her impassioned pleas, Xhelo had fallen headlong into the abyss of love, unable to sever the emotional ties that bound him to Shano. She was the captivating girl from the vibrant village of Hoçisht, a place where the echoes of youthful laughter filled the air during weekly dance nights that had endured since the era of agricultural cooperatives. Shano was his oasis, his guiding star, a radiant sun that warmed him every time their eyes locked.

"How could such a miracle have been hidden from me?" Xhelo would often wonder, unable to find a comparison for Shano among the beautiful girls he had encountered during his university years. There was one such girl from Tirana, graced with rare beauty and impressive intellect. Yet, none could ignite the same spark that seemed to reside in Shano's eyes. Shano was the embodiment of innocence and purity, her sincerity transcending the boundaries of ordinary human connection.

As the most beautiful girl in her village, Shano had known the capricious nature of love. She had trusted men before, ensnared by youthful naivety and the relentless waves of adolescent emotions. Her only mistake had been placing her trust in men, allowing them to chart the course of her heart. She was young, innocent, sincere, and undeniably beautiful—a combination of qualities that rendered her both innocent and culpable in the unpredictable realm of love.

"Try to hate me, Xhelo, you'll be happier. I'm not meant for you. Hate me, please," she had implored repeatedly, her heart heavy with the knowledge of their fate.

Xhelo's response was unwavering: "No and never."

She had given up on other men after the traumatic experience with Ben Kapshtica, whom she had met at a village dance. Love at first sight had ensnared her in its tantalizing web, causing her to fall head over heels for a man she had known for mere moments—a nobody who had suddenly become her entire world. This man, Ben, was unlike anyone else, with his crooked nose and squinting eyes. Yet, he possessed an uncanny ability to pierce the fragile hearts of women with his poetry, words of love, and undeniable charm. Shano had been captivated by the allure of the unknown, and she had surrendered herself to him, believing that he reciprocated her deep affection.

But reality had dealt her a harsh blow. She realized too late that Ben had merely used her to satisfy his own desires, shattering her innocence and trust. In the end, she found herself pregnant—a situation she had hoped would bring joy and fulfillment into her life. Yet, Ben's reaction was far from what she had anticipated. Instead of embracing the news with love and support, he recoiled at the prospect of fatherhood. "Never with me," he declared, a crushing rejection that shattered her dreams of a happy family.

The man who had once recited love poems, which had cast a spell over her and painted the world in shades of enchantment, had now transformed into the embodiment of deceit and betrayal. Shano's heartache began with Ben, and it would continue to shape the course of her life.He was resolute in his decision; he didn't want to become a father. With a litany of excuses, he finally delivered the ultimatum in a voice devoid of emotion or empathy, "You must abort it, or I will deny it!" The tears streamed down the face of the beautiful girl, leaving her utterly bewildered. She was utterly clueless about pregnancy and couldn't fathom what "failure" meant in the cruel terms Ben Kapshtica had laid out. She felt herself on the verge of fainting in his arms.

He brushed her lightly with a kiss, uttering the words, "I love you, Shano, but you're too young to become a mother. Let's abort it."

"No! No!" Shano screamed, her heart yearning for escape into the wilderness. He firmly clasped her arm, persisting, "We can both meet the fate of Romeo and Juliet, or, if you value our lives, let's sacrifice this invisible embryo. It's not tragic; our deaths would be. The whole region would mourn for days and weeks. Think about it, Shano."

The man whose words once wove sweet tapestries of love and kisses had now turned into a monster. He tightly gripped her arms, pulling her close, his lips descending, and his hands sliding down her sides. But Shano Gërsheta, repulsed by his words, his actions, and his lack of emotion, reacted with a desperate head-butt to his nose, leaving it bloodied. She could never have imagined that the beautiful symphony of love could deteriorate into screams and hatred. If she had possessed a knife, she might well have thrust it into his cold heart.

In response, he seized her head with both hands, yanking at her beautiful hair as if to assert his dominance, decision-making power, and authority. He had left her pregnant, and in Ben Kapshtica's world, his word was the final word. His voice was authoritarian, decisive, unyielding, and irrevocable. With a trembling voice and bloodied lips, where Shano saw words intertwined with droplets of blood for the first time, he said, "The end will come swiftly if you don't heed my words. Abortion is your salvation, and I pardon you for the nosebleed you've inflicted. Do you hear me, Shano?"

She couldn't reconcile the transformation of the man she had loved. She had imagined countless scenarios, but none had prepared her for this. She felt powerless, condemned, and terribly unfortunate. Thus, with no other recourse, she reluctantly acquiesced to Ben Kapshtica's scheme.

In the world of women, often shrouded beneath the stern dominion of male authority, Shano yielded to Ben's will, clinging to the hope that one day he might feel remorse. But that day never dawned. She endured unbearable torment. The saying "luck of a whore" did not befit her. She loathed the phrase; she had never been that kind of woman. She was merely a radiant beauty misplaced in the world.

The procedures for abortion were barbaric, conducted under the primitive conditions of her village. Infections escalated, nearly claiming her life, but she managed to survive. However, the consequences were irreversible. Inflammatory reactions had sealed off the pathways where eggs would embark on their "magical journey" to meet sperm, the starting point of a potential baby. This gate was now forever shut. The doctor who had examined her after the horrors of the abortion delivered the bitter truth with brutal honesty: "I'm sorry, but you should know you've lost the chance to become a mother. It's bitter, but some truths are better acknowledged than left to haunt you like a phantom."

His words were like a dagger in her heart, causing her to break out in a cold sweat, trembling as if stranded in the frigid expanses of the North Pole. The world spun around her, and shadows of babies orbited her, just out of her grasp. She reached out to touch them, but they always slipped away, dissolving into a boundless cosmic abyss. "Just one, just one, that's all I want," she screamed silently to herself, but her pleas were ignored. Her existence felt purposeless. If she had possessed a weapon nearby, she might have used it on herself, disappearing like those shadowy babies with their unformed bones, nameless and devoid of consciousness. The torment and bitterness within a woman's soul were indescribable. Tears flowed like rain, and through them, she yearned to drown herself in the waters of Devoll's river or the depths of Prespa's lake. She longed to vanish, to dissolve as an entity and as Shano, transforming into cold marble and lifeless artificial flowers. "Why should I continue living pointlessly now? Why do I live? Why can't those baby shadows take me with them so I can vanish alongside them?"

A tempest of anguish raged inside her, and she couldn't even bring herself to look at the doctor who had delivered the news with such chilling equanimity. She didn't know how she had left the clinic or where she had wandered. Dizziness overcame her in a way she had never experienced before. How would her parents receive her? What about her siblings? And the village? Shano was living through the most surreal and devastating moment of her life. She sought solace within herself.

She remembered the words of the renowned Albanian writer Ismail Kadare from his famous novella "The Moonlit Night." She yearned to read it again, but where could she find it? Within its pages, she knew the "elegy of virginity" was described as the absurd notion of a society devoid of empathy, sensitivity, imagination, and love. But what was virginity? Why did people obsess over it? How foolish could Albanian men be? Why did they deify something they themselves ruthlessly extinguished on the first night of marriage or the first day of engagement? Whose validation mattered in the end? In this world, a heartless soul stole my innocence, so why should I bear the punishment? When Shano was younger, she couldn't fully grasp the emotional weight of that traumatic experience. Despite being captivated by every line each time she read "The Moonlit Night," the depth of the heroine's pain remained beyond her comprehension. Perhaps it was because she still considered herself a virgin, unable to relate. Yet, Shano, a real victim, couldn't help but feel as though Ismail Kadare had somehow foreseen her destiny. Resting her head on her clenched fists, she whispered, "I must live for myself and for those who love me. Infertility is a drama I don't face alone. Let's be practical—where there is fertility, there will also be infertility. Fate has chosen me."

Shano possessed a captivating beauty, but it felt like a double-edged sword, often strangling her. Her intelligence was undeniable, but in her community, a woman's intellect was frequently overshadowed. She despised apathy and was willing to sacrifice herself for the sake of "women who become mothers." Her selfless spirit ached when she thought of the heartless women who bore children and inherited, unlike her, the beautiful girl from Hoçisht. The mere idea of standing beside Albanian women who were both mothers and involved in politics, kowtowing to powerful men, filled her with revulsion. "May the day never come when I have to stand beside these 'fruitful mothers!'" Shano had vehemently declared.

She harbored a deep aversion to politics, viewing it as a venomous serpent in human society. For her, the apex of human existence was the human spirit. While some perceived this zenith as rooted in physical pleasure and fleeting indulgence, Shano Gërsheta regarded it as the "star of the human spirit." This was precisely how the poet of the lakes, Lasgushi Poradeci, had depicted this sentiment—a man she had never met but admired for verses that resonated like the gentle undulations of the human heart. Poradeci was the embodiment of love, encapsulated in verses adorned with the essence of the Albanian language. He was the torchbearer for loving souls who found solace in poetic solitude and the companionship of his faithful dog.

It was rumored that Enver Hoxha, the Albanian dictator, was incensed upon discovering that Lasgushi Poradeci's sole friend was a small dog. Hoxha had long anticipated a poem dedicated to himself, likening him to the waves and abundance, set against the backdrop of the Drilon River and Dry Mountain, but that tribute never came. A state security officer reported that Lasgushi would first recite his new poems to his dog. In fact, he had penned an extraordinary poem about a dog's unwavering loyalty to a man. This revelation was deeply unsettling for Hoxha, who couldn't tolerate the company of animals or people who surpassed him in any way. While vacationing in Pogradec city, his first directive was clear: "I do not want to see the poet walking with a dog!" And his orders were carried out without question. The security detail ensured that upon Hoxha's arrival from Tirana, Lasgushi would either be napping or engrossed in deep poetic contemplation. They both, Lasgushi and Hoxha represented two diametrically opposed poles, entirely incomparable. If love could be distilled into genuine words, it would serve as a universal remedy for all of humanity. Shano Gërsheta's imagination transcended boundaries and politics; she embodied the essence of feminine virtue that few understood.

Suddenly, she found solace. She hadn't been violated like thousands of girls in India and beyond. She had read that in India, between 50 and 80 cases of rape were reported daily. Imagining the horrors that unfolded each day, she felt as though a soothing balm had been applied to her wounded soul. She had simply been in love. She hadn't engaged in physical intimacy under the shadow of terror, anxiety, violence, or threat. No. The truth was that she had shared in consensual intimacy, driven by her own desires, and had willingly given herself to the man she loved, cherishing his masculine presence within the tender fortress of her feminine world. This was the undeniable truth she couldn't overlook. Love was not a sin; male infidelity was. She was a woman of integrity and desired to live. "Let me live without love until the day of reckoning ordained by God," Shano whispered, her gaze fixed upon the rugged slopes of

Dry Mountain. The unyielding rocks seemed to console and embolden her. "Live, Shano. Live. There is nothing quite like life, even if it's laden with pain and devoid of progeny. Live."

As she embraced this soothing inner voice and newfound optimism for life, she felt transformed. Through wild fantasies, she envisioned a world resembling a jungle, where male dominance prevailed and evil reigned. What would the world be like in a hundred or two hundred years from now? Everything would fade into oblivion: the births, the sterile, the presidents, and the peasants distilling special rakija for the ruling class. Imagination was the most potent antidote for the spirit. "Do you see those women who bear two or three children, residing in villas, adorned with fashion, chauffeured cars, and servants? A hundred or two hundred years from now, they will be nothing more than forgotten shadows. But you will endure as a monument of virtue, even if you could not bring forth life. Every living thing reproduces; the miracle lies in your choice not to. In this way, you become the final seal of your own legacy. It's historical, even if you fail to realize it. Just stay clear of the flames, so you won't be consumed by the fire."From that moment onward, Shano couldn't bear to cast her gaze upon men.

"They are savages. Men are our affliction," she confided to Liza, her friend from Bitincka, who had also endured a similar ordeal but remained fertile.

"Shano, there's no need to despair without cause. The one who genuinely loves you won't be bothered in the least. You can still find happiness, even if it's tinged with pain. Life and marriage are preordained. Think of how many girls have taken their own lives or vanished due to such heartaches. You're still fortunate, dear Shano," Liza offered her reassurance. Liza had faced even greater challenges, having married, and given birth to a son with autism, a source of ceaseless heartache. She couldn't explain why such a fate had befallen her—whether it was Leko's fault or "divine retribution"— but she accepted it with unwavering resolve. In comparison to her daily struggles, Shano's infertility seemed like a bed of roses. Shano had to concede. In the Devoll district, countless dramas often spiraled into tragedies, frequently driven by male arrogance. So, when she saw the depth of Xhelo Lakrori's love for her, she attempted every conceivable means to dissuade his affections, but it was a futile endeavor. He was her true Romeo, and she longed to join him in death, even though she understood that she could never experience the joyous moments of motherhood.

Shano Gërsheta was a woman of indomitable fortitude. Following her harrowing experience, she distanced herself from the ceaseless gossip that pervaded the region. With unwavering determination, she told her parents, "Forgive me for the pain, but I shall never succumb to malevolence. I shall remain your proud daughter, and you shall remain my unwavering monument." Thus, she earned the moniker "The Iron Lady" of Lakrori. This steely resolve made her a legend throughout the area. Even though people were aware of her painful past, she remained impervious to every suitor, debunking all predictions and assumptions. She never yielded to anyone, no matter how charming or persistent. Only Xhelo Lakrori had the power to break through her defenses. Despite her confessions, despite his full knowledge of her history, despite her daily pleas, urging him to "curse me, please," he remained the healer of her wounded soul. "It's either you or I that will perish. I have no use for the tales of yesteryears; all I need is you, Shano. Do not let me wither away. I love you, and that's all that matters!"

In the end, Shano Gërsheta wedded the finest young man in the region: Xhelo Lakrori, the gifted veterinarian. He possessed not only rugged handsomeness but also towering stature, a chiseled physique, piercing sapphire eyes, tousled blonde locks, an aquiline nose, and, above all, a heart as boundless as the horizon. Shano Gërsheta became the luckiest woman in the entire district. Although malevolent tongues wagged ceaselessly, the two lovers, unlike any other couple in the expanse of the Devoll district, exemplified in the most exquisite manner the true essence of love, sincerity, devotion, self-sacrifice, loyalty, nobility, ardor, and illumination in the realm of lovers. They became an enduring pair, an archetype by which no other could be measured. They disregarded the mindless prattle of others, proving that love was a destiny that held them in its unbreakable grip until the end of days.

Chapter Three

The childless couple eventually found solace in America, far removed from the prying eyes of judgmental gossip, and reveled in the liberating embrace of their new homeland. Weekends became their canvas, painting adventures across the vibrant tapestry of Los Angeles, the enchantment of Hollywood, the eclectic charm of San Francisco, or the dazzling lights of Las Vegas. They ventured to the tranquil shores of Honolulu, traced the Great Wall of China with their footsteps, and sailed the azure waters off the coasts of New Zealand.

"The world belongs to us, my love, even though we bear no heirs. Fear not. I cherish you, and you are my universe. We weren't shackled by the world's opinions; we defied it because we possessed each other's love. Many couples, even those blessed with fertility wither away like blades of grass. But not you, Shano; in my eyes and heart, you remain an unparalleled spectacle. Do you grasp the depth of my sentiment?" These words wove a beguiling spell around Shano. They were not mere flirtations, but rather the delicate petals of Xhelo's soul, unfurled for her alone. Their lives had been marked by the unwavering dedication to their work, both in Albania and now in America. Life had a way of unfolding as it willed.

In the beginning, the frosty American embrace felt formidable, but they swiftly adapted. They embraced every opportunity that came their way, unflinchingly. Xhelo's passion for veterinary medicine presented a formidable challenge when it came to having his diploma recognized, an arduous journey marked by agonizing waits, unforeseen obstacles, and unanticipated twists. He surmounted numerous tests and diligently attended university courses, ultimately attaining certification as a veterinarian. Through tremendous toil, he secured a substantial half-million-dollar loan, acquiring a private clinic, and after years of unwavering perseverance, they both ascended to the ranks of the American middle class. Their journey had been fraught with anxieties, dramatic twists, unexpected turns, and moments of adversity, but they emerged triumphant, finding contentment in one another.

Xhelo would forever carry the memories of their humble beginnings, working as an assistant in a company overseeing wastewater drainage systems in the environs of Chicago. Never had he envisioned that a veterinary graduate would find himself in such a role. His mind teemed with ideas, yet he struggled to carve a niche in America. It was the defining challenge of his life. On this continent, everything commenced and culminated. He had heard myriad tales of the travails of immigrants, particularly those who arrived bearing university degrees, anticipating a utopia with an office ready and waiting. Nestur Oboti, who had extended an official invitation replete with financial particulars, had written, "Your departure from Albania is in vain. There, you hold significance as an intellectual; even the streets and elders know your name. Here, nobody questions your identity. University professors might be tasked with carrying bricks, mixing mortar, or even tending to horses. Some who escaped communism sell their minds and look down upon others with five dollars less. America is a hellish realm for intellectual dreamers. Stay where you are. Do not come. Your journey is in vain, dear Xhelo. I'm telling you this so you are forewarned, and you cannot say I didn't caution you. The decision is yours; I'm simply sharing the wisdom I've gained while striving to become an American, and it is no easy feat. Decide as you see fit; I'm sending you the invitation."

Nestur was neither deceptive nor peddling illusions, unlike some who had not experienced life in the West. They would return after a mere two or three years of labor in America, bedecked in fine attire, lavishing exorbitant sums during each visit, even while mired in the clutches of capitalist debt. That was the cycle.

Xhelo arrived unafraid, but not without trials. He had never fathomed that behind America's grandeur lay a labyrinth of polluted waters. Failure to manage these waters would spell catastrophe for the populace, the public image, and even the reputation of America itself. The job might have been no less remunerative than a deputy position in Albania, but it was hardly the life Xhelo had envisioned. During those adventurous months, as he delved beneath the grand villas and towering skyscrapers, he unearthed another facet of reality: a veritable human cesspool. Some treated it as refuse, a byproduct of human existence, as was the American custom, while others turned a blind eye, eventually becoming indistinguishable from the waste that every living being inevitably generates. The continent of boundless consumption accorded the waste product of human existence the same degree of solemnity as it did to sustenance, and perhaps even more. To undermine the management of this final destination for everything consumed by every individual, citizen, and senator alike could unleash a nightmare akin to an African cholera outbreak. "Behold it as a plate, not as human waste," the company's supervisor would intone during the first hour of orientation.

He had never fathomed that this line of work could be so lucrative. It was a multi-billion-dollar industry, with waste coursing through the veins of plastic pipelines deep beneath the Earth's surface every single day, every fleeting second. This wasn't just a Chicago affair; it was an all-American phenomenon. As he pondered the stark contrast to his life back in Albania, he realized that you could gauge a nation's culture by how responsibly it managed its waste. In Albanian culture, there had been a dearth of serious attention to this fundamental necessity. In fact, the only reference to waste was often a derogatory one, equating it to the "lowest of the low." Albanian villages often lacked the most basic amenities, such as running water, and sanitation was often relegated to the back burner when it should have been a paramount concern. He recalled a feeble attempt to introduce biological recycling in the agricultural cooperative, a directive from the capital city of Tirana. However, it had been a primitive and ineffective endeavor, resulting in waste littering the village streets.

In the land across the Atlantic, an entirely different experiment was unfolding: Your destiny rested squarely in your own hands. As an individual, as a free soul, you charted the course of your life with the time that God had bestowed upon you. Xhelo felt as if he had been snapped back into reality from these reflections. Never had he imagined that he, a former party leader in Devoll, would find himself contemplating such matters in the underground catacombs of Chicago. It was vastly different from the idealistic dreams of his youth. In the real world, Xhelo Lakrori had confronted an America rife with grime and squalor yet managed with exacting technological precision and unwavering discipline. It was often said that America boasted more pipelines and channels for wastewater than there were highways spanning the entire globe. These infrastructures were indispensable for a healthy existence and the smooth operation of civic life. When Xhelo recounted the intricacies of his initial job to Kristo Kovaçi, a fellow immigrant he had met on the flight to America during their early months of adaptation, Kristo was taken aback.

Kristo, once a physical education teacher in Albania and a published poet, struggled to acclimate to life in the United States. To him, the vast expanse of the country had dwindled into something small, arduous, and distant, thrusting him into an unprecedented crisis. Although they had settled in different states, they maintained contact through phone calls. Kristo and his family had made their new home in Alabama, thanks to the warm welcome of a friend. They often reminisced about their transatlantic flight to America, where they had sipped wine in the comfortable seats of Delta Airlines and discussed their dreams for their new homeland. That journey had forged a profound bond between them, offering solace and encouragement.

Kristo Kovaçi, a father of two in the prime of their youth, had aspirations of pursuing a career in education or sports. He was younger than Xhelo but was drawn to him due to Xhelo's enduring optimism, something Kristo struggled to find within himself. When he heard Xhelo passionately describe his work with wastewater, he couldn't help but be incredulous.

"Faith and optimism can move mountains," Kristo remarked during one of their conversations.

However, one day, Kristo made a somber call to Xhelo, expressing his mounting frustrations.

"Xhelo, we were deceived about America! It's incredibly challenging here, especially for us intellectuals. I'm deeply disheartened. I'm contemplating returning to Albania." Kristo, a talented individual from Kolonja who had spent decades in Tirana, sounded thoroughly dispirited.

Xhelo did his best to uplift his friend.

"Patience, Kristo. Good things take time. We must endure. We chose to come here; no one forced us. Consider the generations that endured internment in the crucible of communism. Compare your situation for a moment to theirs, and you might find a glimmer of optimism. Be patient, my friend. I work on the streets where cwastewater flows, and I still find it worthwhile. But I don't intend to remain there forever. I'm biding my time, searching for my path."

"Good on you, Xhelo! I could never do what you're doing. Back in Tirana, I was a respected educator, surrounded by eager students and supportive parents. In short, I was somebody, Xhelo. Here, no one cares about me. America might not be the right fit for Kristo. I can make do in Albania; nobody there is going hungry. Lili and I are considering packing our bags."

"Don't rush into this, Kristo... Exercise patience, my dear friend. Don't merely see America as a means of survival; view it as a realm of enlightenment. Ponder it, Kristo. I'm patient, and you should be too. If the leaders of the National Movement could send messages filled with hope from Istanbul, imagine, Kristo, what they could do here, beyond the Atlantic. Exercise patience, my friend, exercise patience!" Xhelo had made every effort to dissuade Kristo Kovaçi from returning, but his efforts were in vain.

Two weeks later, Kristo rang him from Tirana, saying, "I'm back in our homeland, Xhelo! I'm sorry I left you there, but your friend from Shkodra was right: '*Hedgehog has its place in bushes.*'"

"Not like this, Kristo. If you had only held out a little longer," Xhelo responded from the depths of Chicago, ending the call abruptly as he was at work, sealing off a water flow deep beneath America's tallest tower, the Sears Tower.

Those were years of labor reminiscent of what Victor Hugo described in his Paris's catacombs; it might not have been the prestigious work that Albanians may have aspired to, but it was indispensable. Jim Clown, the seasoned technician who worked with efficiency, fetching the necessary equipment from the junkyard's cars, seemed to discern Xhelo's despondency. Making eye contact with Xhelo, he remarked, "This might not be a white-collar gig, but somebody's got to do it. What you're seeing here, we produce day in and day out, just like clockwork. You know, our toilets are the great equalizers, where we all dispose of our biological waste the same way—whether it's me, a congressman, the president, or even dictators from around the world. This is the one physiological act that makes us all equal. Without these thousands of sewage channels carrying away human waste, there'd be no life, no joy, no happiness; in short, no rich or poor. Somebody's got to take care of this job. It fell to you and me, my friend."

Xhimi was a maestro at unclogging blocked pipes. He diagnosed the issues with pinpoint accuracy and offered equally precise, enthusiastic solutions. Surprisingly, after the initial stress, Xhelo began to find satisfaction not only in the handsome paychecks, but also in the appreciative reactions of clients. Upon witnessing their dire situations resolved, they were willing to embrace both Xhimi and Xhelo, despite their work overalls, rubber gloves, and masks. Xhelo started to view this transitional occupation as a unique challenge, understanding that one day's work in America equaled two months of salary in Albania. This was more than just "cleaning up filth," as some Albanians might put it; it was a true mastery, channeling even the most repugnant human waste into clean conduits without any fuss. If given the opportunity, he would perform the same role at the White House or in the grand halls of the American Congress without a second thought.

Xhelo Lakrori couldn't find sleep on the day he learned of his compatriot Kristo's return to Albania, a return marred by bitterness. If Kristo had been nearby, Xhelo would have been willing to chain him down just to keep him from leaving. His heart ached for Kristo's wonderful children, who had seen their cherished dream crumble before their eyes. Checking the time and realizing it was still early morning, Xhelo decided against making a call. Instead, he opted to pen a letter, laying bare all his thoughts and feelings, and allowing Kristo to reach his own decision. Xhelo knew that America was magnanimous in this regard; it didn't slam its doors shut on those in distress but rather welcomed them back with open arms, free from prejudice.

In accordance with laws passed by the American Congress, green card holders who reconsidered, experienced homesickness, or longed for their homeland were free to return and could do so within six months to reignite their American journey. The laws were even more accommodating: if you wished to remain and work in your home country yet retain the right to return, all you had to do was cross the American border twice a year.

"Let me try to change his mind. America needs good people like Kristo Kovaçi and his family," Xhelo mused, his resolve driving him to compose a letter. It was a missive resembling a declaration of faith, chronicling his personal tribulations and fervently beseeching Kristo to reconsider his departure, offering assurance that fate would eventually bestow its blessings upon him. He sealed it with these words:

"Kristo, my dear friend,

We all grapple with despair at times, but succumbing to this corrosive moment within you is akin to surrendering your dreams to the abyss. Your family holds a future here; do not trample upon the fortune that has come knocking at your door. Ponder it. In the annals of history, future generations look back upon your odyssey and raise monuments in your honor. Recall the words etched onto the Statue of Liberty, that welcoming beacon for weary souls who arrived after arduous months confined in the bowels of ships. Think back to how you and I embarked on this journey, my enlightened companion: by airplane, savoring wine, with a television before us. Contrast our experience with that of the pioneers who forged this colossal America.

Never forget those words chiseled into that statue bearing the torch aloft: 'Give me your tired, your poor, your huddled masses yearning to breathe free...' Can you fathom the foresight of those early settlers? Come now, Kristo, success awaits you! I hold unwavering faith in this, but it requires your patience, my dearest friend. Recall the wisdom of our Albanian heritage: 'Good things take time.' Trust me and return as soon as you can.

With sincerity,

Xhelo Lakrori, Chicago, October 10, 1997."

The very next day, he dispatched the letter, affixing a simple stamp bearing the address of Tirana, trusting it would find its way to an Albanian whose fortune had taken an unkind turn. Xhelo possessed an innate drive to do good when the opportunity presented itself, believing that kindness and love among people formed an inexhaustible ocean in which one could never drown. He recognized that emigration marked a profound physical and psychological transformation that imbued life with a different significance. He never saw this human migration as an act of betrayal, but as a unique adventure to be embraced with nobility and grace. While he acknowledged the initial hardships, he never perceived them as insurmountable.

Shano, his wife, had initially harbored expectations of America molded by movies, but she swiftly confronted the reality. She embarked on her journey by working as a custodian for the state of Illinois before enrolling in school. With unyielding courage, she pursued a career as a certified nurse, attaining a level of financial stability beyond her wildest dreams. Xhelo encountered his own set of challenges but remained resolute in his pursuit of aspirations. Over the course of a decade, they transformed their dreams into reality, enjoying a life free of want and characterized by boundless freedom. As a couple, they made a solemn pact: "We shall not adopt children. Instead, we shall dedicate our lives to the care of pets, the most innocent creatures that God has created." In fact, they had formalized this commitment through legal means, detailing their posthumous wishes with a lawyer.

Certain nieces and nephews who sought to curry favor soon found themselves rebuffed by Xhelo: "Feel free to cozy up to your uncle, but don't expect anything from the will," he would curtly inform them. They departed in the same manner they had arrived, their hopes of inheriting the "meatballs," as they say in Albania, dashed.

For Xhelo, what held significance wasn't family avarice but rather the profound value of American freedom, which he regarded as unparalleled and irreplaceable. He fretted that American liberals risked compromising this essence by peddling a utopian vision. Although Xhelo considered himself left leaning, he struggled to comprehend Albanians who exhibited fanatical devotion to leaders like Berisha. He'd often quip to his friends, "How can someone fresh out of a dictatorship still be willing to 'die' for a leader, especially the very first one? Does that even make sense?"

Xhelo's social circle boasted diversity, with friends and acquaintances representing various political parties that had sprung up like mushrooms following the advent of pluralism. Among his acquaintances was Rako Sinica, who had evolved into a close confidant of Berisha. When Xhelo playfully remarked, "Your devotion to the great one reminds me of our reverence for Comrade Enver," Rako chuckled heartily. "Oh, Xhelo, this is democracy. I love the one who loves me, and I serve with unwavering dedication. Berisha is our towering figure. He rescued Albania from the clutches of communism. Without him, there would be no democracy!"

Thanks to his unwavering commitment to the Socialist Party, Xhelo Lakrori had ascended to the position of regional head. However, the electoral shenanigans in Albania now appeared as ludicrous jests to him. Memories of a heated debate with a university friend during an agricultural fair in Thessaloniki and a disagreement with a journalist acquaintance at Radio-Tirana still lingered. The latter had criticized the party leader for failing to fulfill post-prison promises. In response, Xhelo, displaying that Balkan tenacity, had declared, "If you badmouth Fatos Nano one more time, I'll end you right here in Thessaloniki. I am a socialist, and Fatos Nano is our symbol of triumph." His friend had been visibly shaken. After regaining composure, he'd said to Xhelo, "I know Nano better than you do. You've only seen him at podiums and party meetings, while I've shared drinks with him. But if you must put an end to me, do it in Tirana, not here in Greece. Down with Fatos Nano!" Xhelo was fuming but found himself rendered speechless.

Chapter Four

America, unlike any other Western country, invests a substantial amount of time in the electoral process. It's a public marathon, but Americans have long grown accustomed to this selective political method. Here, the clamor for the next president begins almost two years before the incumbent's term legally ends. Naturally, the primary beneficiary of this dizzying electoral noise is the media. Tasked with reflecting debates and alternatives, they provide a significant service to the public. They broadcast all proposed ideas, but of course, this service comes at a cost. Someone pays, and someone profits.

The American game is a colossal vortex where ideas and media become intertwined, thereby augmenting the pursuit of profit. They call it "the American dream." The real dream of this continent is profit, freedom through the power of the dollar. Just tell me, when has a destitute American ever competed for the presidency? Never. It can't happen. Because the might of the continent resides in the freedom to succeed, not in a destiny of destitution. The defeated remain nameless, anonymous, and crushed. Here, the question for an individual is: What is the worth of their wealth? How much does it translate to in dollars? Thus, there's no human wisdom without passing through the dollar's yoke. Nobody asks how many books you've published or how many titles you hold. The dollar is the sole measure of a person's abilities in America.

Thus, the media, often labeled as the "enemy of the people," as Trump put it, orbits those with financial power. As for the others—the less fortunate, the financially feeble, those without sway over American society—they remain nameless, mere "media extras," just votes on a ballot. It's a primitive play of human instincts, a relentless pursuit of domination and control over the masses who are less fortunate. The media only descends to the level of the ordinary individual or the crowd when a murder, crime, rape, robbery, or accident unfolds; otherwise, the common person remains faceless, simply another voter.

In this swirl of interests, where the rule was "pay to play," staggering sums were squandered, like water from an endless well. Xhelo Lakrori, a man who harbored doubts about this extravagant spectacle, couldn't help but ponder the situation. To him, it all felt like a twisted story from a child's fairytale, where the media was a voracious beast, consuming every resource, and dominating the collective consciousness.

"Is there not a more direct, affordable, and perhaps even more graceful way?" Xhelo mused, his thoughts flowing like the Mississippi river. Deep within his soul, an inner voice prodded him with persistent questions. "But can you, my friend, offer a better path? Wasn't the socialist society back in your homeland just as stifling as the media frenzy in this land of the free? There, only one voice held sway, while here, at least everyone has a chance at making their voice heard. Can you discern the fallacy in your thinking? The American experiment, dear Comrade Lakrori, has shown its mettle, its ability to adapt. It's the experiment of those who had lost hope in their own land. Look at yourself; your homeland granted you nothing but Shano. You arrived with three suitcases, and now you're worth millions. Can you not appreciate the allure of America? Focus on yourself, not on distant horizons. Interrogate every idea that crosses your mind." Xhelo remained silent, for he could not challenge this voice; he had no successful alternative to offer. The mad model had obliterated the Communist East of Europe. People rose against the "political bureaus" not because America commanded them, but because "the pilaf couldn't hold water anymore" as the saying in Albanian goes.

Whose voice was this, speaking in a language that reverberated through Xhelo Lakrori's psyche? It was a voice that resonated like the whisper of a tempter, one who counted every cent earned and never squandered a single dime. Strangely, the journalists seemed to avoid any debate about the exorbitant cost of elections, a burden that weighed on every citizen like an anchor. "Where does this boundless wealth come from, and why isn't there a movement to curtail these expenses?" Xhelo pondered. Despite countless hours in front of the screen, he had never witnessed a serious discussion about the astronomical sums of money being "burned" before his eyes, while the homeless and less fortunate shivered in the unforgiving cold, beneath towering bridges and on the city streets. The irony of it all was palpable. In the old Albanian saying, they would say, "The village is burning, and the harlot is preening herself." Where, Xhelo wondered, was the humanity, the generosity, the Christian values that America claimed to cherish?

"You're all hypocrites, whether leaning left or right. You, who beg for votes, care only for yourselves! You politicians are shameless," muttered Xhelo Lakrori, the Albanian American. There seemed to be no outlet for his burning frustration. He had come to America from a "granite rock on the Adriatic coast," where it was common for two families to share an apartment with just one room, a kitchen, and a bathroom, and let's not forget the luxury of scheduled water. It was harsh, but people didn't sleep on the streets. When he heard reports of American homelessness on the old Albanian TV, he would purse his lips and declare, "It's propaganda. That's how the spin doctors like it. They're lying. There are no homeless people in the free world." But when he arrived and saw the misery of the unfortunate homeless in America firsthand, he was rendered speechless. If he spoke out, they'd label him a communist, and if he remained silent, he felt guilty.

The years of the Trump administration were tumultuous, marked by seismic shifts and unparalleled diversity that had never before been experienced in American or global society. While Xhelo was taken aback by the unfiltered candor of a president who strayed far from any conventional protocol, he couldn't help but notice that the leader of the White House was, indeed, a representative of the American people. This notion was reinforced when a claim that had been propagated in Albanian communist propaganda for four decades—the influence of the war industry on American politics and policies—was echoed by the president himself. "Many generals don't like me because they want wars, and the war industry wants wars that I haven't started," President Trump had boldly declared during his campaign. "Bless your words, Mr. President!" Xhelo Lakrori had exclaimed.

He was captivated by the rhetoric of the Commander-in-Chief. The president stood firmly against anyone who dared to oppose him publicly, berating and attacking even his own wife if she disagreed with him. "The world needs a leader like this, and we need him for another four years," Xhelo Lakrori contemplated. In fact, the four years of the Trump administration had brought unparalleled prosperity to Xhelo's business. He had earned such a substantial amount of money that he had managed to clear all the debts of his clinic.

"Why do I need carefully crafted or contrived political statements?" Xhelo Lakrori pondered. "Trump is unfiltered and spares no one, not even his own wife if she disagrees with him." The thought brought a chuckle. Would he do the same? No, he was different. To him, the political arena was a battleground of wolves and sycophants. He held disdain for most of the senators who made grandiose declarations in the media, astonished at how men could contort themselves so disgracefully against the truth and facts, all for the sake of appeasing those in power at the White House.

Though he endeavored to remain rational, with each passing day, Xhelo understood more vividly that political games were the greatest affront to humanity, civilization, and, in particular, intellectuals. "There's no better model, so let's fight to improve this one," a philosophy professor had told him while bringing his dog for a check-up at his clinic. "Professor, the world has its eyes on America. The world expects to learn more," Xhelo had responded. "Don't worry, Mr. Lakrori, America learns even through failure, but remember, we, whether on the left or the right, self-correct, and this is a process and a challenge. We, as Americans, never claim to be perfect, but we strive for it every day."

With the eloquence of the philosophy professor's words still ringing in his ears, Xhelo Lakrori contemplated the November 2020 elections as more than just a political event. They embodied a profound process and an audacious challenge. While politicians trumpeted them as "historic elections," the true essence lay beneath these lofty narratives, hidden in the intricate machinery of democracy.

The backdrop to these elections was the relentless battle against the COVID-19 pandemic, a seismic struggle that threatened to unseat President Trump from his perch of power. Yet, in Xhelo's eyes, Trump deserved a second term, not merely due to being a "family victim" of the "Chinese virus," as the president often quipped, but because, amidst the cacophony of criticism and opposition from the media, the left, the Democrats, and myriad other detractors, Trump tenaciously led the charge in the quest for a vaccine—a beacon of hope to save not only the nation but the entire world.

Day by day, Xhelo found himself immersed in the narratives of Fox TV and Infowars, drawn to the speeches of astute orators and conservative philosophers. These voices resonated within him, stoking his conviction that, in the tumultuous landscape of American politics, only President Trump could serve as the vanguard, the guardian of America's future, and the savior of humanity itself. Trump, a political outsider who had emerged from the world of business, wielded his words like a legendary blade, reminiscent of the "sword of Skanderbeg." He dismantled entrenched senators and silenced eloquent speakers, defying expectations.

Notably, Trump's audacious journey had led him to secure the Republican candidacy, a remarkable feat given his past donations to politicians spanning the ideological spectrum, from both Clintons and Obamas to the Bushes and others. Trump's mastery of the political game, his ability to straddle both sides of the field, culminated in his triumphant rallying cry: "Make America Great Again" (MAGA), resonating with millions. Thus, he ascended to the highest office in the land, becoming the 45th President of the United States.

During his tenure, the White House remained free of war. America, under Trump's leadership, had all but eradicated terrorist threats, including the formidable Islamic State, ISIS. Trump's administration even engaged in discussions with Afghan Islamic fundamentalists, proposing solutions that once appeared as sheer madness. Negotiating with the Taliban? Only Trump possessed the audacity and strategic acumen to navigate such treacherous waters. Moreover, he etched his name in history as the president who ventured into communist North Korea, extending a hand of friendship to its enigmatic leader.

As Xhelo reflected on these unprecedented events, he couldn't help but draw parallels with his homeland, Albania. He imagined a scenario where a figure like "Trump" had graced the political stage in the '70s and '80s, forging a bond with Enver Hoxha and "Socialist Albania." In his reverie, this dynamic leader would have extended a hand of friendship, with Albania eventually becoming the 51st American state, nestled in the heart of Europe—a beacon of power and influence. "How unfortunate we Albanians are," he mused, lamenting decades spent under the sway of "Old Brussels," or the 'Brussels of harlots.'

These thoughts ignited within him a torrent of ideas, as wild and audacious as the proclamations of the "Balkan Son-in-law," a moniker he sometimes affectionately bestowed upon President Trump during his contemplative moments. The controversies that swirled around Trump's every appearance only deepened Xhelo's yearning to see him occupy the White House for another four years.

Suddenly, Xhelo found himself volunteering for the Trump campaign, fervently advocating for "Four more years." While he couldn't bring himself to part with a single cent, he invested his time, engaging in impassioned conversations and offering his undivided attention to the cause. Whenever he encountered the question on his tax form, "Do you wish to donate $1 to the presidential campaign?" he resolutely struck through it, declaring to himself, "Whoever aspires to that position should reach into their own pocket. I won't part with a single cent. My money is safest right here, in my own pocket."

Amid the fervor surrounding Trump's re-election bid, Xhelo Lakrori had become consumed by the political spectacle, yet his support didn't take the form of monetary contributions or ostentatious merchandise. He opted for a quieter brand of advocacy, nurturing his intellectual support for Trump, eschewing the ubiquitous caps and Trump-branded shirts that had flooded the market. Suspicion gnawed at him regarding such merchandise, and he chose to trust his own methods instead.

His approach was subtle yet effective, honed over time. Xhelo had an innate understanding of how delicate Americans could be when it came to their political affiliations. He had learned to navigate this terrain cautiously. When he sensed that a client was navigating the murky waters of political ambiguity, he would skillfully steer the conversation toward his own experiences with socialism and the opportunities he had discovered in America. His opening salvo often consisted of, "America is so vast; there's no room for socialism here." Though he grappled with the accusations of socialism leveled against American Democrats—a group he perceived as no more socialist than their Republican counterparts—he held firm in his belief that a less intrusive government and fewer regulatory norms would be to everyone's benefit.

Xhelo was no stranger to sparking lively debates, and he wielded his experiences in socialist Albania as a vivid backdrop. He painted a picture of it as a "lustrous beacon," "the future of the world," and "the path of development." But then he'd delve into the dark side, recounting the societal hardships that had emerged under the rule of high-ranking officials. He described the orchestrated unity of party congresses, where enthusiastic voices echoed with chants of "Party-Enver, we are ready anytime..." He narrated how unanimous support for leadership led to imprisonment, denouncement as enemies of the party and people, and brutal executions of even the highest-ranking officials.

The pinnacle of this brutality arrived in 1981 when Enver Hoxha spared not even his steadfast Prime Minister Mehmet Shehu, making him a tragic victim along with most of his family. Xhelo infused these stories with fervor, knowing exactly when to pause for maximum impact, holding his listeners in rapt attention until he dropped the emotional hammer: "May humanity never experience socialism. It's a form of collective suicide."

His clinic in Chicago became a hub of discussion, the most frequented in town. It wasn't long before Republicans themselves declared, "Go take lessons from an immigrant from Albania!" Xhelo relished his newfound sense of importance, recognizing that in America, armed with a modicum of wealth and original ideas, one could attain fame.

One day, a daring idea took hold of him. "What if," he thought, "I display a slogan at the entrance of the clinic that says, 'Even Pets Would Vote for Trump 2020'?" The prospect intrigued him.

When he shared this idea with Shano, she responded with caution: "Xhelo, don't be foolish! Do you really think that slogan will resonate when Trump has never been seen petting a cat or a dog? He's a political animal, as the journalists say; he doesn't need pets. Do you understand?"

In response, Xhelo assured her, "No, my dear, it's not that harsh. He's an important figure, the head of the White House. Please, be careful. With him in charge, we will earn more money, open more clinics, and employ more staff for Xhelo Lakrori. Long live President Trump!" Shano Lakrori chose not to continue the debate. She knew of her husband's ever-shifting political nature and decided that silence was the wisest course. Xhelo felt her reticence acutely.

"Speak up, Shano; share your thoughts," he implored gently, wanting her to engage in the conversation.

"I choose to remain silent, as is my right under the law and the Constitution," she responded. "In Devoll, they say, 'Silence is golden.' It's this Albanian wisdom that Americans have adopted and incorporated as the Fifth Amendment to their Constitution," she added, smiling faintly as she met his gaze.

"'Silence is golden?' America is in turmoil, teetering on the precipice of collapse, and you wish to remain silent? Look at the protests unfolding in Minneapolis following George Floyd's death! Observe what is happening in Portland, where a 'free republic' has been declared within the city! Can you fathom the magnitude of the crisis engulfing this nation? We are in the midst of an unparalleled crisis in history. It's terrifying, but I believe things will improve," he vented. "We're at a pivotal moment, Shano, where public opinion, anger, dissatisfaction, and rebellion are breeding false heroes. They emerge from the streets, rising from obscurity, reminiscent of the Gavroches of old Paris. The American majority may remain silent, but the rest are screaming, protesting vehemently, setting fire to police stations and private businesses, looting, and inflicting profound societal trauma. They may not represent the majority, but they make an incredible racket. Witnessing all of this unfold in this land of freedom distresses me deeply. And while America burns, Democratic senators and congressmen 'kneel down.' It's abnormal, unscrupulous, and purely for the sake of votes. This uprising and the audacity of these senators could one day bring the Capitol, the cradle of freedom in DC, to its knees. Do you hear me, Shano?!"

His voice rose, as if he stood before a vast assembly, only to quickly realize he'd crossed a line. It struck him then that he had started to view Shano through an unusual prism, oscillating between seeing her as a multitude or a mere droplet, a curious parallel to the way Albanian-Canadian writer Kurt Bitola—a friend settled in Toronto—often portrayed the masses in his writings. Inwardly, he contemplated his own political transformation, oblivious to the fact that he had evolved into a fervent Trump supporter, perhaps more zealous than Trump himself, or even Trump's own kin.

In the annals of American political history, it was an anomaly for children to publicly declare, "Long live our father, the President! He alone shall safeguard democracy and the true essence of the

Republican spirit." When Barack Obama had embarked on his presidential journey, his teenage daughters remained conspicuously absent from television screens, their presence more restrained. Even Chelsea Clinton had simply urged, "My mother is the best candidate; I encourage you to vote for her." In stark contrast, Trump's offspring boldly proclaimed before captivated crowds, "The Republican Party is Trump's domain. There's no GOP without Trump. Republicans exist only because of President Trump."

"We never spoke in such terms even during the era of communism," Xhelo muttered to himself. "Where have America's values vanished? What happened to Lincoln's Republican humility? We pledge our allegiance to the Constitution, not to a monarch." For the first time, America seemed to groan under the weight of a royal diadem, where phrases like, "The first one said, the grave is burning," held sway.

His sympathy deepened, both for America and for himself. Never had he borne witness to such a confounding, tumultuous, unprincipled, and vicious election campaign. The magnitude of deceit, character assassination, and blatant public audacity was unprecedented. Often, he felt ensnared amidst a raging conflagration—fire on the left, fire on the right. Which way to turn? As the ominous November 3rd deadline approached, his sense of entrapment only intensified. He couldn't help but think that if Trump were to lose on November 4th, America itself might crumble.

His mailbox brimmed with a deluge of entreaties from Democrats. Even the former President, Barack Obama, had penned a personalized email addressed to him, beginning with "Dear Xhelo Lakrori..." and proceeding to enumerate reasons why he should throw his support behind his former deputy.

"All politicians are mad; Obama and Trump, they're no different. They're all mad," Xhelo grumbled in frustration. Sensing that Shano's spirits were also sagging, he slid into his car and drove towards the Serbian club, where he could order a bracing shot of plum brandy—or as it was commonly known, slivovitz.

"This time, I'll opt for Czech plum brandy. Not Croatian, not Serbian. Somewhere far from all of that," he muttered to himself as the ML550 seemed to take flight.

Chapter Five

For the first time, there was someone waiting for him right outside the clinic. Xhelo Lakrori had a routine of arriving a full hour before opening time. It was a cherished period of solitude in his well-appointed office, where he reviewed the charts of the patients scheduled for that day while sipping his coffee. As he refreshed his memory about each canine or feline visitor, he couldn't help but reflect on the unique bond between humans and animals.

"These animals are truly man's best friends. The Albanian who coined the curse 'dog, son of a dog' never understood the companionship they bring," he quietly mused. Memories of the mockery directed at Western lifestyles during his country's socialist years came to mind. Back then, the propaganda machine often spouted, "People there live alone... They only have dogs and cats. A pitiful existence." These messages were widespread, painting a dismal picture of a life confined to the company of pets.

"In capitalist societies, they even sell water to people. The proletariat stands ready to cast off the chains of enslavement. The momentous day of global revolution is drawing near," the Albanian radio and television would proclaim. Propaganda was as common as bread and cheese, and the people, wearied and fearful of government "Agitation and Propaganda," would listen in silence, awaiting a wedding or some other occasion to momentarily forget their woes.

The client waiting outside, however, made a profound impression on him. Approaching the man, Xhelo greeted him warmly and inquired how he could be of assistance.

"Dr. Lakrori, I don't have a dog or a cat, not because I dislike them, but because I can't afford them," the man explained apologetically.

"I'm very sorry to hear that," Xhelo responded. "How can I assist you in this situation?"

The man, middle-aged with red curls cascading around his face and tired eyes, introduced himself as Jack Lake and revealed his affiliation with the Biden-Harris electoral camp. Despite his slightly disheartened appearance, there was an air of sincerity in his voice as he stood by his beliefs.

"Do me a favor, doctor. Don't cast your vote for Trump. He's going to lose in Chicago and throughout Illinois. I came here to tell you that you're missing an opportunity. The entire city knows you're a skilled doctor, but your vote for Trump is short-sighted. I'm sorry, doctor, but—"

"What?! How dare you try to dictate my electoral choice?" Xhelo interjected. "I came here to vote freely, not to be coerced. I apologize, but the days when party comrades told me how to vote are long gone. You've come to the wrong person."

"Mr. Xhelo Lakrori, I didn't come here to convince you to vote for the Democrats; I simply wanted to advise you against voting for Trump. I'm sorry, but he's the only president who didn't bring a pet to the White House—no cat, no dog, not even a snake. This fact alone should deter you from supporting him. Do you understand, sir? That's all I wanted to say."

With that, the enigmatic visitor disappeared as swiftly as he had appeared. Xhelo Lakrori caught a whiff of gasoline from the man's Malibu Chevy, a scent that seemed to symbolize resistance against Trump. He remained silent, pondering the one undeniable truth the man had shared: During Trump's presidency, the only living creatures to grace the White House were the turkeys spared from execution on Thanksgiving Day. Shano had mentioned this as well. While it was indeed a fact, Xhelo couldn't bring himself to believe that it was reason enough to withhold his vote for Trump for another four years. To him, Trump represented the embodiment of conservative ideals, especially evident in how he had stacked the courts, including the Supreme Court, with conservative judges. It signaled a resurgence of American conservatism in his eyes. The liberal agenda, with its intricate ideas about equality, same-sex marriage, abortion rights, and global economics, left Xhelo feeling torn. For the first time, he felt like the old saying from his hometown of Devoll applied to him: neither fish nor fowl—an individual without a firm stance.

Yet, he couldn't deny the allure of the opposing candidate. The rival, in many ways, appeared tailor-made for the role: dignified, enthusiastic, compassionate, experienced, possessing vision and finesse, and deeply committed to family values. Battle-hardened, with decades of government service and various roles under his belt. Nevertheless, he had ridden the political rollercoaster for forty years with little substantial achievement, as Trump had ruthlessly pointed out in one of the most scandalous debates the nation had ever witnessed. Why would he attempt another run at the presidency? Wasn't it Trump's candidacy that had shattered the twenty-year dynasty in the White House: Bush-Clinton-Bush-Obama-Clinton... and Clinton again? A dynasty that desperately needed breaking, that shouldn't be perpetuated. Trump had effectively blocked that dynasty's path. In many instances, Obama seemed like a more polished version of the pleasure-seeking Clinton, though he had managed to avoid a sex scandal like the one involving Clinton and Monica Lewinsky. For this reason alone, Trump could be considered a champion in his own right. Xhelo admired and voted for him, despite his reservations about the man's character.

"Have you forgotten about Trump's sexual scandals?" a voice echoed in his mind. Xhelo shot back mentally, "He didn't engage in those scandals in the White House. They happened in hotels and private settings because we are men, and allure has a way of tempting and corrupting us. He simply did what many do behind closed doors." Never had he experienced such inner turmoil. Often, he would sit at his clinic computer, reflecting on his life's journey— the challenges, the dedication, the unwavering principles that had guided him. In these aspects, neither Clinton nor Trump surpassed Xhelo in character. "I've only ever been with Shano," he thought.

The encounter at the clinic left him with a firm decision not to display any campaign advertisements on his premises. His patients neither had awareness nor voting rights—why should he involve himself in this political melee? But the stranger's words continued to echo in his head: "Trump doesn't have any pets to pet." It was an indisputable fact, and for some inexplicable reason, he attributed it to Trump's Slovenian wife, Melania, who had presumably been drawn to Trump's wealth. "Perhaps she doesn't have an affinity for pets—it could be a cultural trait from the Balkans. We, in the Balkans, are known for curses like 'Dog, son of a dog,' or 'Wicked cat'... It's a Balkan idiosyncrasy that the elegant Melania from Slovenia must have picked up," Xhelo chuckled softly as he sipped his coffee, savoring the rich aroma that invigorated him. He decided to reframe his musings: "The more I acquaint myself with American senators, the more I appreciate the company of animals."

One brisk October morning, his phone broke the tranquility. Xhelo Lakrori wished that his secretary could manage the call, but when he saw it was Kurt Bitola from Toronto, he hesitated before answering—his thoughts preoccupied by the day's list of scheduled clients.

"Hello, Kurt, what's so urgent that you're calling this early? You're usually an evening caller, like Lasgushi by the lake," he quipped, stifling a yawn. The voice on the other end carried an unusual tone, indicating that the Albanian-Canadian writer from Toronto had something out of the ordinary to share.

"Good morning! I tried calling you on your cell phone, but you didn't pick up, so I decided to reach out to your office. I have some news... Bilal Eshka has passed away." "To Tirana?!" Xhelo asked instinctively. "No, he's gone... Covid-19 took him from us... He couldn't beat it. I know you two were close, so I wanted to offer my condolences," his friend spoke on the phone, his voice filled with sorrow.

Xhelo Lakrori's smile froze. Another loss! His heart skipped a beat. Bilal Eshka had been a dear friend, residing in Denver, Colorado, for 24 years. They had been college buddies and maintained their friendship for decades. Although Bilal had graduated as an agronomist, he was a man full of dreams and hope. Xhelo had taken English lessons from him. They used to share morning coffee at the Institute's cinema in Kamëz. Bilal was optimistic, adept at sharp criticism, voicing his discontent with the system and its rules, yet he remained a loyal friend. Xhelo had often advised him, "Only confide in me, not in anyone else. Even the walls have ears..." But Bilal couldn't hold back. "If I tell you, those comrades at the office, those idiots leading us, will find out... They're all good-for-nothings, oh Xhelo, because at least a fool is sincere... We have no choice... what can we do?" Bilal would conclude with a rhyming jest: "Silly, silly, oh you fool..." They would share a laugh and then head off to their respective lectures.

"What did you say, Kurt?!... I spoke with him not too long ago, and he mentioned he was working on a poetry collection. According to him, it might even compete for the Nobel Prize, giving Kadare a run for his money... What a tragedy."

Kurt Bitola fell silent on the other end of the line. He was a rare gem in the world of Albanian prose and storytelling. Despite his communist leanings, much like Xhelo's unchanging, genial demeanor, Kurt Bitola was an Albanian exception. His oft-repeated phrase was, "I love all people, but not communists." In truth, Kurt Bitola epitomized the idealistic fool of the Albanian transition. He was among the few in Berisha's "inner circle" who, in the end, gave in to emigration, as he refused to partake in the corruption that ensnared most of his peers. Thus, Kurt Bitola remained a symbol of honesty and idealism during and after the Albanian communist era. He preserved his integrity in journalism and literature, akin to a flawless crystal.

A lengthy silence enveloped the conversation that October morning, much like a whirlwind. Xhelo Lakrori couldn't help but recall his last chat with Bilal Eshka, who, after a fiery discussion about the American election campaign, had pledged to vote for President Trump. Not because he idolized Trump or believed he was the best choice, but because the alternative candidate, in Bilal Eshka's view, represented a "shadow of the past" or a "white Obama."

The death of his close friend saddened him deeply, but curiously, beyond the sorrow of losing a life, he felt a twinge of regret that candidate Trump would now receive one less vote due to Bilal's eternal slumber. But he quickly scolded himself, as if awakened from a dream. "Fool. You've become a fool, Xhelo! Snap out of it."

"Enough! How can you think like this when you've just lost a friend?" he seemed to berate himself.

He recalled a particular debate with Bilal Eshka that had preoccupied his thoughts for an entire day at the faculty. But why do we insult people by calling them worms when worms are noble and clean creatures? That question had taken him aback. Once, Bilal Eshka had wanted to share a powerful poem about worms: "We give birth to worms, we produce worms, and we crawl, crawl over everything." Those lines had left him sleepless. Who was his friend referring to? The worms in power or those who had lost it? "Don't show it to anyone. They'll imprison you if they find out. Please," Xhelo Lakrori had pleaded.

Bilal Eshka had responded, "You and the editor-in-chief of the 'Agriculture Student' newspaper are the first and last to read this masterpiece. If I go to prison, I'll have both of you to blame!" Over the decades of his life in America, he often paraphrased this "gem in verse" by Bilal Eshka differently. "We give birth to congressmen, we produce senators, and crawl, crawl toward whoever holds the power."

"Xhelo, are you still there?" the gentle voice of the Canadian writer echoed.

"I'm sorry, writer, I apologize. The news shook me, and I got lost in the memories the departed left behind. It hit me hard," Xhelo Lakrori responded.

"I understand, that's life. But hey, don't forget to cast your vote," Kurt Bitola interrupted with a touch of irony.

"I'll be voting for President Trump!" Xhelo retorted. "Even Bilali, if he were here, would do the same."

The Albanian-Canadian writer couldn't believe his ears. Here was another left-leaning individual supporting the right, a spectacle he had never witnessed before. Kurt Bitola was witnessing one of the most significant shifts in the Western electorate. Devolliu Xhelo Lakrori, whom the writer considered a product of freedom, was the latest example. Meanwhile, in Toronto, numerous individuals who had proudly represented the extreme left in Albania were undergoing a metaphorical transformation, turning into fervent Trump enthusiasts. The 21st century was demonstrating that the political beliefs of people had adapted seamlessly, complicating expectations based on facts and visions of the future. He wasn't sure if this reaction and the cacophony of opinions were the results of freedom or deception, truth or the blinding passion that had engulfed a modern society believing it was founded on truth and the human mission of progress and well-being. Under these circumstances, all he could do was observe patiently and quietly the American process that was shaking the world and emancipated societies. With a voice as soft as silk thread, he continued:

"Oh Xhelo, so you're voting the same way as Minosh Samiti, the former journalist from 'Voice of the People' newspaper? How is it possible that all Albanian ex-communists, in both Canada and America, are supporting Trump, even in little Albania?" the caller from Toronto asked sharply.

"He reminds us of a man who stood against everyone; that's why we're voting for him. A fearless man who is never afraid to speak his mind and voice what the common people think," Xhelo responded with a hint of mockery. "Don't forget, I've never worked in Tirana, and I've never been a member of the Labor Party. Remember these truths, Kurt Bitola! As a veterinarian, I've wandered from one stable to another, and I wear that as a badge of honor and dignity!" Xhelo retorted.

"I'm well-acquainted with your biography; that's why I'm surprised by your 'bullet for the enemy' vote. You've joined the not-so-small camp of Americans enchanted by Trump. Only they would vote for Don! My condolences, Xhelo! You've lost one vote," Kurt Bitola said before hanging up the phone.

Xhelo was taken aback by the abrupt ending of the call. Kurt Bitola was usually gentle, composed, and consistently ironic. He seldom got angry. His laughter had carried a hint of mockery, even as it resounded wisely. They had debated American politics and freedom at length, argued and reconciled, and exchanged various ideas. Xhelo had even stated bluntly, "Writer, you can't be right-wing with your gentle soul. The right-wing lacks a soul, it only possesses dollars, tradition, custom, and profit. One doesn't become left-wing without reason. You speak and philosophize like a right-winger, but you are honest and idealistic to an unbelievable degree. In that respect, you are the antithesis of right-wingers. I've vacated my spot in the leftist camp. Go and take my place. I'm no longer a leftist!"

"Never ever," Kurt Bitola would respond. It seemed that abrupt phone hang-up was another "never ever."

Xhelo felt guilty about the tunnel vision he was experiencing. His admiration for Trump had evolved into the same blind allegiance he had once shown for Enver Hoxha. Blindly believing in and loving every word, every press statement, every screen appearance, every tweet, every absurd paragraph seemed reminiscent of "Enver's quotes." With such blindness, he failed to comprehend what he truly admired about his candidate. Trump often appeared as a formidable leader, taking on the entire world, the media, journalists, generals, NATO, China, mocking Brussels, while maintaining a somewhat congenial stance with Moscow. Yet, his speeches never resonated with Xhelo, which was equally puzzling. "How can America elect a president incapable of expressing human emotion and feeling? How can the majority vote for someone who simply repeats the same fifty words and turns every rumor into intrigue?" Xhelo would question himself, especially after Trump's victory in 2016.

At that time, he had cast his vote for "Clinton's wife," as he referred to the Democratic candidate. He had given her his vote because he had arrived in the USA during Clinton's presidency, and according to him, Clinton was intelligent and had brought prosperity to America. As a recent immigrant, he had witnessed firsthand the conditions fostered by the Clinton administration. It took a mere 30 days for him to secure gainful employment. Jobs were plentiful, prices were reasonable, societal peace prevailed, gasoline was virtually free, and the media lacked propagandistic fodder. For half a year, they had been preoccupied with a Cuban named Gonzales, debating whether he should return to Cuba or remain in America. But during those years, millions were spent on television and print media, along with endless debates in Congress and the Senate over whether President Clinton kissed or didn't kiss a beauty of Polish origin. Did he or didn't he have sex in the White House? Did Clinton lie or not, this champion of the Albanian cause in the Balkans? For Albanians in the Balkans and around the world, he was a hero, but the Republicans were ready to roast him like "meat on a skewer," as the Albanian saying goes. What a wonderful era that was! How starkly it contrasted with today! Society now seemed unhinged, and the fight for power was bare-knuckled. The media and big screens served as the arena where verbal and metaphorical "swords" clashed in the battle for power. "The media, this 'stumbling block' we must endure. It muddles your thoughts and makes you foolish," the veterinarian from Devolli would murmur to himself each time. Xhelo was aware that he had fallen victim to "communist brainwashing." He knew of the domino effect of communist propaganda. "What's happening to me?" he mumbled. "Am I the real Xhelo?" His mind was in turmoil as never before.

Quite shocked by himself he kept thinking: "Am I real? Am I right? How can I cast my vote for the Democrats, who allowed the city of Minneapolis to descend into chaos and then championed 'Defund the police'? How do I support those who encourage the crowd to 'lick, spit, and kneel,' disrespecting the flag? No, never. Trump is on the mark. The crowd doesn't lead; it's a faceless entity devoid of identity. Democrats manipulate the masses; they ignore destructive mobs and riots. I can't back them any longer. American

Democrats remind me of that Albanian saying, 'Out of spite for my mother-in-law, I go and sleep with the miller.' No, humanity deserves noble principles and standards, not 'anything for power.' Protests have their place; every American citizen has the right to demonstrate, but wise politicians don't pander to the masses—they uphold principles and rules. That's why we vote and elect senators and congressmen. Consistency in politics is a hallmark of nobility. These folks lack nobility; they're neither left nor right. They're all cut from the same cloth. Power-hungry scoundrels, just like in that poem by Bilal Eshka. Period..." Xhelo Lakrori muttered to himself.

During his morning contemplation, he recalled a comment from his millionaire friend, the Serbian American Aleks Petrović. A successful real estate agent who had helped him purchases the clinic; they often shared a glass of raki. "Xhelo, all these pre-election events are just an attempt to oust Trump. Keep in mind, after the elections, there won't be any more fires and riots in Minneapolis or anywhere else. Democrats are like 'Balkan communists'; they exploit any form of rebellion and circumstance for power. I assure you; Trump will lose..." Xhelo didn't appreciate this prediction from his "Serbian adversary," even though the evidence seemed to point in that direction.

He retorted sharply, "Impossible. I'll vote for him because I don't condone this cunning pursuit of power."

It was the most mentally tumultuous morning he had experienced, and this situation became a daily occurrence, growing more chaotic as the day drew nearer—alongside the news of thousands of dead from the virus—November 3rd of the ominous year 2020, which was approaching like a "political cortège."

"The 9 o'clock meeting is ready," the secretary's voice echoed.

The workday had begun. Fortunately, he was distracted from politics by his profession, caring for pets more than people.

Chapter Six

The next day, he found himself on board a plane bound for Denver, a journey he hadn't originally planned. Shano didn't challenge his sudden decision. She knew that her objections often were ignored, given Xhelo's stubborn nature—a trait he readily owned up to. So, she didn't argue about this unexpected move but simply stated, "When you return from Denver, you'll only share a bed with me after you take the COVID-19 test. I love you, but I love myself more!"

This was the most peculiar declaration Xhelo, the veterinarian from Devoll, had ever heard. He gave her a teasing look and then inquired, "Am I really hearing this from my Shano?"

Shano remained silent. She held the "family veto." After 35 years of marriage, Xhelo found himself under his wife's command. He wasn't fond of it, but aware of the horror that many American couples—and others around the globe—were experiencing, he quietly acquiesced to her demand. Shano was wise. Why should she risk her life for the recklessness of her husband? The world was profoundly divided. Lovers were perishing beyond windows and screens without a last loving touch, so why should Xhelo undertake such a risk for a friend? But if he dared this adventure to honor a life now extinguished, didn't Shano have the right to protect her own life? These questions pummeled his mind like a hydraulic hammer, causing him distress. Deep within his conscience, he agreed with Shano, but outwardly and publicly, he believed such a visit during a crisis would enhance his stature. This is what he told himself because if he had agreed with Shano, she would have cast him out of bed. "Man is indeed a baffling creature," Xhelo mumbled and fell silent.

Shano was unaware that her husband's trip to picturesque Denver during pandemic times was not merely for a farewell, but also to fulfill a bequest she knew nothing about. It was locked within the enigmatic world of her husband from Devoll, who was utterly devoted to her.

As he flew, he remembered her disapproval, yet his thoughts veered in a different direction. For him, Bilal Eshka was a friend and ally to whom he owed a final honor, out of solemnity and a matter of conscience. They had been friends since college, comrades since the years of socialism. Back then, society was a type of relationship savored in emotions, honesty, trust, and profound debates. In those times, the essence of humanity was passed from one to another in the most magical way. He doubted any other generation could experience the camaraderie they had relished during socialism. Such friendships were simply inexplicable when compared to today's cold, digital pragmatism. Amidst the grandeur of America, their bond seemed to have paled in comparison to their frequent encounters in Albania.

However, Xhelo was a realist. America engulfs and assimilates nations, let alone societies like theirs. Bilal Eshka deserved a human farewell. He was the man who had provided so many intellectual stimuli back in Tirana, inviting him into his home several times and introducing him to his parents, a noble couple. Bilal's father, Bedri Eshka, had served in the army. He was a wise man, and every time he encountered Xhelo, he would say, "You folks from Devoll know how to honor friends and beauty, but the only boor remains the distinguish writer Dritëro Agolli." They would then discuss poetry, books, politics, patriotism, and war. One day Bedri Eshka warned him, "Be cautious with this Bilal, the poet; he often spills his soul into his poetry, not thoughts. I don't want anything to happen to him," he would express his concern whenever his friend moved from one room to another within the apartment.

As the plane reached cruising altitude, he pulled out his laptop from his bag, intending to review a few puzzling diagnoses. Perhaps the high altitude could provide him with the professional clarity needed to determine suitable treatments and therapies. He had left Tom Kreig, an exceptional American graduate, at the clinic, who possessed a near-magical ability to address any situation related to small animal diseases. Flights during a pandemic were akin to midnight train journeys—almost one passenger for each row of seats. Despite upgrading to business class for a few extra dollars, he noticed the plane was so sparsely occupied he could count the passengers on his fingers.

"Hello!" a voice to his right greeted him. "Starting work? I'm John River, a farmer from Lincoln's birthplace!"

A large, robust hand, encased in a faintly colored plastic glove, reached out to him. Xhelo was taken aback by the sudden interruption, but when he turned his head and spotted a burly man with thinning hair, a broad forehead, and black eyes resembling olive pits, his smile seemed to bubble up. Setting aside his laptop, he bumped fists with his seatmate. The man was wearing a mask adorned with symbols of the American flag.

"I am Xhelo Lakrori, from Chicago, a compatriot of Mother Teresa and Ismail Kadare," Xhelo introduced himself, not without a hint of pride. Although initially not in the mood for conversation, upon seeing the inherent nobility that radiated like a beam from the face of his fellow traveler, he reconsidered. Kindness deserves recognition, he thought, and offered a slight smile.

"Traveling to Denver?" the other man continued the conversation.

"Yes, I'm attending a friend's funeral," Xhelo confirmed, looking at the American beside him.

"I'm sorry," the other man responded. "I assume it's from COVID. This pandemic has turned into a worldwide massacre. You mentioned you're Albanian like Mother Teresa; I haven't heard of the other name, Ismail, as you said. The entire world knows Teresa and Lincoln," the American farmer continued.

Cheerfully, Xhelo replied, looking directly into his eyes, "That's right, Lincoln and Teresa are famous. However, this Ismail Kadare will be better known by your grandchildren and great-grandchildren because, as they say, immortal fame enshrouds you after death. Our writer is still alive, so you haven't heard much about him yet."

John River listened attentively, struck by the pride with which a man from such a small nation spoke. He found it admirable. After inquiring more about the writer and his works, the American shared that he had been aware of Albania since its breakaway from the Soviet bloc. At that time, he had anticipated that the small country would join America in the fight against the socialist bloc.

"Instead of growing closer to the West, however, you veered even further East," laughed his fellow passenger. Suddenly, his eyes lit up with recollection as he told Xhelo about how he had made a quick flyover of Albania in the 1960s—a mere "stroll in the sky"—while stationed at a nearby airbase.

Xhelo listened and felt as though he was speaking with a veteran of the Albanian war. The conversation seemed to take on a life of its own. To him, many Americans seemed insular, engrossed in their own problems and business affairs, with the majority uninterested in prolonged conversations during travel. If they did engage, it often lasted only as long as the plane's ascent or descent. To Xhelo, most American friendships were transactional, or "Craig list" affairs, as he liked to call them. These were akin to the relationships established when buying or selling something online, lively, and expressive until the "deal is closed," at which point each party forgets the other as if they never existed. It was a practical way to view fleeting acquaintances and connections in such a vast, free society. Only in Albania is it said, "A friend for life." Here, there was no equivalent.

"Your recollection of that flight brought back some of my own memories," Xhelo remarked. "When I was a child, I used to watch airplanes flying high in the sky; they seemed like UFOs to me. We were very isolated. We were a country of bunkers, but thankfully, that era is over, and we have America to thank for not backing down."

Xhelo's narrative took off like the roaring turbine of a plane. He didn't hesitate to laud America as the savior of the most beleaguered nation in the Balkans. He reminded his companion that only America had saved Albania from disintegration, a fate plotted in Berlin, Moscow, and Paris.

"America is the greatest friend to the smallest nation. You never forgot us! We used to say, 'we dance in the mouth of the wolf,' but without America, we would have been devoured by the Euro-Russian wolves." He recalled the broadcasts of the "Voice of America," which had been the only beacon of information. While the BBC shuttered its Albanian service due to a loss of interest, America never fell silent. He mentioned the Albanian American Elez Biberaj, who informed the masses and whose voice became a symbol of hope for an overthrow and change that eventually brought Xhelo here.

"You Americans are our real friends; I love this country where a man finds his freedom and his dreams," Xhelo said, looking the farmer straight in the eyes.

John River cast him a quick glance and, as if roused from his reverie, remarked, "The silence has fallen, and we travel in quietude. Have you read the American Southern writer, Garcia Marquez? We are living the fantasies he wrote! I am also traveling for a funeral. I am going to Salt Lake City. My son has died; he was the last one…"

Xhelo Lakrori wasn't sure how to console him. He set aside his computer and extended his hand, a gesture reminiscent of the days before 2019, giving it a firm squeeze.

"My condolences! I'm deeply sorry for your loss," Xhelo said with a steady voice.

Both men, as if on cue, reached for the bottles of disinfectant provided at each seat as a precautionary measure after shaking hands. Xhelo felt the hand he shook was heavy, like that of a robust farmer, yet it also felt comforting. He was surprised that they had both broken protocols to shake hands as they would have done in the past. Instinctively, they shared a look and laughed.

After a moment of silence, Xhelo found his fellow traveler intriguing. Setting aside his computer once more, he observed the man who held a version of the Bible in his hands, searching for something in that troubled face that seemed to have borne witness to both drama and tragedy.

"How did it happen, if I may ask?" Xhelo ventured.

John River chuckled lightly and, setting the Bible aside, continued, "That's life! We come into this world only to leave it, but we don't know how. Now, I'm left with nothing: just me and God."

Xhelo Lakrori shuddered at what he was hearing. He didn't know how to react.

"You're not alone, Mr. River! Look, at this moment you're with me; you will never be alone. Please, don't be upset," Xhelo stammered, trying to comprehend what had so greatly distressed his newly met fellow traveler.

"This pandemic claimed my third son, too. He was just 40 years old and unmarried. The wars in Afghanistan and Iraq took my other two sons! I'm destined to be the last to leave this world, severing the genealogy of my German Irish heritage. It's a fate I must accept. Where we're headed, it's more peaceful, better, devoid of the stress and pain of this earth... I'm eager to leave this unjust world, this barbaric and deceitful place..."

Xhelo could almost feel the other man's pain radiating onto him. His heart pounded fiercely, as if to remind him that he was not a digital device, but a human being with a soul and a heart. He felt an urge to tightly embrace the white-haired American, to show him that one day he too would close a "branch of inheritance," albeit not with such a dimension of pain as his fellow traveler. Xhelo felt compelled to follow the other man's story, observing the magical movement of human lips that expressed so much that had been overlooked when masks were worn. Now, the stories under the masks seemed akin to masked soldiers in the trenches and bunkers of Albanian socialism.

Quickly, Xhelo informed his newly met acquaintance about his own drama—about the Albanian fate, the brutal war in the country, the insatiable desire for democracy, and the numerous crimes committed in the name of freedom. He spoke of the great Albanian world, like that of Mother Teresa, whom he had mentioned at the start of their conversation. He also brought up acclaimed writers Dritëro Agolli and Ismail Kadare, and didn't forget to mention the Belushi brothers, with whom his fellow traveler was familiar. High up in the air, he seemed to skim through the pages of Albanian history for the stranger, illuminating that small country filled with so many remarkable people.

John listened. Then, John shared his own story, and Xhelo hung on to every word. He felt a profound sense of sorrow for the man's tragic solitude; he had lost two sons to war and another to the virus. Such bitter irony!

John River revealed that he had been a Republican for decades, but confidentially told Xhelo that this time he wouldn't cast his vote for the Republican Party, but for the other side. Briefly, he explained that the two major parties dominating American politics today had been birthed from the same political entity—the Democratic-Republican Party of the late 18th and early 19th centuries.

"This is the 'mother' of our two major parties," John explained. For the first time in his life, he saw America's most noble pursuit, like the business in the White House, becoming akin to private or corporate business, and this was neither traditional nor Republican. "For us, the Constitution and our freedom remain sacred, much like the Bible—not the parties," John River concluded their conversation.

Hearing such candid American sentiments, Xhelo Lakrori thought of the Albanian disputes in Michigan, where recent arrivals from Albania still spoke about spies, Serbian agents, Communist Democrats, and Soros-backed socialists. Blending what he heard from the American with his understanding of how Albanians offer advice, Xhelo felt a sense of discomfort. He didn't hesitate to tell his counterpart that he would vote for Trump, explaining his reasons, while John River had anticipated this:

"The vote is a personal decision, but everyone should vote for whom they prefer, not based on who the majority or minority likes or dislikes. Just remember, if you're voting for conservative values and Republican principles, these are exactly what's missing from the current president. I say this with full conviction as a staunch Republican."

These words stuck with Xhelo. "It's intriguing," he pondered. "We come from Albania and fervently support Trump, while these people, born into freedom, want nothing to do with him. Fascinating. Humanity is a boundless ocean. Countless waves rise from unknown origins, engulfing unsuspecting ships. This is freedom, not the contrived version back in Albania. Long live Shano, you hit the jackpot. We might have ended up dying as fools," Xhelo mused to himself.

They became friends and exchanged business cards. Shocked by his fellow traveler's predicament, Xhelo Lakrori planned to maintain contact after their farewell. He didn't receive many details about the upcoming burial ceremony, knowing only that it would be private. The writer in Toronto hadn't divulged information about the flight; he preferred it to remain a private tribute and felt no need to boast like the arrogant, since his friend in Canada had proven equally prideful. He came as much out of obligation as out of spiritual necessity. They had often joked about death, even preemptively paying respects to one another. He never believed it would be Bilal Eshka's turn, the man who laughed in the face of death.

After checking into a luxurious room at the Hilton in downtown Denver, Xhelo stepped out onto the expansive west-facing balcony overlooking the snow-capped mountains. He gazed at the majestic Rocky Mountain range that extended from British Columbia, Canada, to the state of New Mexico, spanning 4,500 km. It was a natural spectacle that only this continent could accommodate. His eyes scanned the horizon in search of Mount Elbert, the highest point in the state of Colorado, but his gaze seemed to wander into memories. For a moment, he imagined he was looking at Mount Dajti in Albania, a place he had visited several times with Bilal Eshka. Life is a segment of a journey that one must undertake until the last step. "Blessed is the one who departs without suffering,"

Xhelo seemed to tell himself before opening his computer to prepare "Bilal's Legacy." It was a pact they had made when they were incredibly young, one that Bilal might have forgotten, but Xhelo Lakrori had not.

Bilal's house was his largest investment in America. Constructed on a gentle hill near the city, it faced the sunrise on one side and the sunset on the other. With eight bedrooms and six bathrooms, two modern kitchens, and numerous spaces for relaxation and entertainment, it was surrounded by an expansive garden and a swimming pool, almost as vast as Little Prespa Lake in homeland. His sole dream when he left Albania was to own a large, beautiful house filled with "daisy milk." One couldn't blame him, considering he had lived with his parents and two other brothers in a two-room apartment with a kitchen until the age of twenty-five. When he reflected on those years, he felt constrained by the limited space and the inability to live a normal human life. Thus, as he once told Xhelo, his first aspiration upon emigrating was to establish a house as a sanctuary where his soul could find solace.

Linda and the children were deeply grieved. Each person, masked and visibly shaken, acknowledged Xhelo Lakrori as he appeared at the house's entrance. There was no time for customs or traditions. The hearse was almost ready to escort Bilal Eshka to his final resting place. He had initially desired cremation, to return to the dust, but he amended this last wish in the presence of the lawyer who drafted his will. As they were signing the documents, Linda had pleaded, "Let's be buried like the rest of the world, Bilal. I fear fire; I don't want to burn; it seems horrifying; I want to decompose..."

Bilal, taken aback by the fear in his wife's eyes, agreed. The lawyer revised the stipulation on the spot. Xhelo had been privy to all of this during their phone conversations. He felt a wave of sorrow at his friend's funeral. Only the family and a guest from Chicago were present. How many times they had engaged in passionate debates, both during their college days and in America, about the hypocrisy surrounding Albanian funeral customs. People attended the ceremonies not so much out of grief or respect, but to gauge the number of attendees. Hypocritical Albanians, he thought. "I don't want anyone at my funeral. No one, except my wife and children; others only come to spectate," Bilal had stated repeatedly to Xhelo Lakrori. And so, it was.

The burial unfolded at the city's oldest cemetery, Riverside, sprawling across some thirty-one hectares. This hallowed ground had been the final stop for souls for nearly two centuries, where crosses and statues cast somber gazes at each other. Bilal's casket was draped in the American flag, while the Albanian flag, folded with care like a peaceful pillow, rested at the head, imparting a blessing to his eternal slumber. Tears and grief hung in the air, a heavy cloud on the verge of releasing its pent-up rain. Words were scarce. A moment of farewell.

Linda stood in silence, her emotions too deep for words. Kujtim Eshka, the perfect likeness to his father Bilal, managed to speak a few words, but silence descended once more. It was a bewildering moment, an audience before a casket adorned with two flags. Xhelo Lakrori, present to honor a pact, stepped forward, his gaze fixed on his friend's casket. He turned his head slowly, as if sharing the family's grief.

No one mourned Bilal Eshka's passing more than his own family. No one. Xhelo realized this, leaving him at a loss for words. His lips trembled, his tongue heavy in his throat. He almost lost his breath, and for a moment, it seemed he might follow his friend into the great unknown. With tears in check and his throat cleared, he prepared to speak:

"I came here not just to offer condolences, but also to fulfill Bilal's final request."

Bilal Eshka departed without the blessing of a priest or imam, a reflection of his lack of religious beliefs, and this absence didn't perturb him. It was a unique funeral, devoid of the customary symbols—the cross and the holy book. Instead, Xhelo Lakrori felt like a priest in a black cassock, entrusted with delivering the last words for his lifelong friend, a role entirely new to him. Back in his village of Vërnik, Devoll, his father, the chairman of the village's democratic front, had always delivered speeches at open graves. Those speeches followed a predictable pattern, recounting the deceased's journey from humble beginnings to their dedication to socialism and the teachings of the party. Fists were raised high, shovels with broken handles awaited their turn, and hard candies that could break teeth were distributed. Attendees departed in silence.

Xhelo endeavored to pull himself from the melancholic past, to return to the somber present, standing before his departed friend.

Slowly, much like the words delivered at a funeral, he retrieved a small recorder from his pocket. Suddenly, Bilal's voice filled the air:

"I, Bilal Bedri Eshka, am dead today. I did not wish to die, but no one sought my opinion. I depart happily because I lived the life I desired. Do not cry. Tears will not revive me, while your laughter ensures my continuation in the afterlife. Celebrate my years on earth, for true homage is in honoring life. Ah, life, that never returns, how precious you have been! Now I love you, but you are beyond my reach. Now I seek you but cannot find you. Now I yearn to live but cannot. So, those of you who bear witness to my funeral, laugh, for laughter is the only 'cure' for death. Draw closer to each other as I depart, remember my jokes. Life, so beautiful, as light as a leaf, flies away like a butterfly and you are left alone. I confirm this is my original voice, today, October 10, 1983. Kamza, Tirana."

With a decisive click, Xhelo Lakrori shut off the recorder, like closing the lid of a coffin. Linda was overcome with tears, and the children, stunned by the voice they had heard, glanced at each other, as if questioning who had brought forth the voice they would forever miss. They were left speechless on this mournful day, yet it was their father himself who, though departed, had come to their aid by reciting his own eulogy. Such a thing had never been witnessed before, neither in America nor in Albania. Xhelo, hands trembling, touched the coffin where the two flags rested, silently intertwined, and said, "Farewell, Bilal. I did not forget your bequest. Farewell, my friend..."

Then, with a gaze that spanned the room like a rainbow's arc, he studied each family member one by one, swallowing back his tears. "May Bilal's memory be everlasting!" A grating noise filled the air, blending with the soundtrack of tearful sniffles, as the coffin descended into the patiently waiting earth. Clumps of soil slid like newly hatched birds into the grave's depths, rolling over the star-spangled American flag. In the end, only a bouquet of flowers remained the last sign of Bilal Eshka's existence.

Later, during the post-funeral meal, Xhelo Lakrori recounted the astonishing tale: "We made a pact that whoever passed away first would leave a recorded farewell to life. Surely Bilal, somewhere in his archives, also has my recording. But fate decreed that I would bid farewell to your father and Linda's husband in the way that he had desired. It was a promise from our reckless youth that I couldn't overlook. I apologize if this mode of farewell made the moment more difficult for you. We promised each other."

Linda remained silent. She had known her husband's penchant for surprises throughout his life, but she never imagined he would one day leave, turning her into the first widow among all her college friends. It was a death during a pandemic, a time of daily departures that marked an unprecedented period in human history.

The meal that followed echoed the quiet of the snow-blanketed mountain peaks to the west. Linda, caught in a whirlwind of emotions, struggled to find the right words. She had known Xhelo, Bilal's close friend, for decades and had shared countless unforgettable moments. She longed for the days of empty plates but hearts full of camaraderie. Those years when they were materially modest but rich in friendship and genuine happiness flooded her thoughts.

In America, they had achieved success, but the vibrancy of their youth remained elusive. Xhelo's presence on this farewell day touched Linda deeply, prompting her to confide in Bilal's friend. So, under the dim, heavy light of grief, she rose from her seat at the table and made her way toward Xhelo. Their children observed her silent approach with curiosity. Xhelo, his face etched with sorrow, met Linda's determined gaze as she drew near. With her striking yet melancholic visage, the mother of three remarkable children and the woman who had enhanced Bilal Eshka's enduring legacy took a seat beside Xhelo. It was as if she carried a secret, another legacy, another source of pain. Xhelo was taken aback. Linda, a captivating presence, approached him like a comet descending from the heavens. Wearied, her face bearing the wrinkles of time, she sat beside Xhelo. Their breaths seemed to synchronize, and the moment hung in the air like a scene from a dream. Linda's expression mirrored that of the actress in "The General of the Dead Army," hands outstretched as if to say, "General! Did you bring them, General?" For the first time, Xhelo questioned whether coming had been the right choice. Linda sat beside him, met his gaze, and shook his hand in the traditional Albanian manner, despite wearing gloves.

"Thank you, Xhelo! May you have a long life, along with Shano!" Linda said.

Xhelo clasped Linda's hand, feeling the smooth texture of her gloves. Memories of their college days flooded back—days spent at the cinema and the triangle, where she would arrive with Bilal, and they would share beer and order hot pork cracklings, fragrant with an aroma they could never find here. Memories, abundant for good people.

"That's life, Linda! Stay strong, ma'am! He left us, but his spirit and the house remain," Xhelo murmured, unable to contain his tears. Linda nearly leaned her head on his familiar, broad shoulder but held back. This was a post-funeral meal, a tribute to her husband, not those youthful gatherings from their college days. Linda felt a pressing need to share everything, and quickly. She couldn't hold back any longer:

"Xhelo, your presence was an honor and a surprise, and Bilal's recording was the most magical touch at the funeral, one I could never have imagined... But you should know, Xhelo..." Then she fell silent.

"What should I know, Linda?" Xhelo asked, exhaustion evident in his tear-streaked face as he looked at the children, enveloped in a mix of anguish and hope, a rainbow of hope for the future. His mind wandered to his own inevitable departure, one that would leave Shano alone, without a legacy, while Linda was surrounded by her family—albeit without the guiding light of her departed husband. His fate weighed on him as heavily as the pain of his friend's loss, but in a profoundly different way. It was a departure with a mission fulfilled. What about him? What about Shano? Why did life unfold this way? Xhelo was on the brink of vocalizing his frustration, a stark contrast to Bilal's recent serene passing. The differences loomed large... The sweeping view of the towering western mountains offered solace. He momentarily forgot that Linda had something to share, something that might be even more heartrending than his recent confusion, which had become more frequent in recent years.

"Linda, I'm sorry," he whispered, gazing into the eyes of his friend's widow. "This funeral seems to have juxtaposed two contrasting realities. Confused, I thought of Shano and what would have happened if I had passed before Bilal. Look, Linda, he left you a full house, do you see? If I go, Shano remains alone, abandoned, with only the cries of cats for company. Can you grasp the difference, dear Linda? It's like night and day, don't you see? Just consider this simple comparison to ease the pain that's cutting into your soul, even if just a little."

She met his gaze with unwavering intensity, her heart yearning to envelop him in a tight embrace, knowing he was the most vulnerable soul in this bitter chapter of her life. With her friend captured by her angelic gaze, she blinked back tears and began to speak:

"I understand your pain all too well, Xhelo, my dear friend. I know the battles you've fought, and I've heard countless stories from Bilal about your unwavering friendship," she said, hoping to steer her distant guest away from his own sorrow. For a moment, she contemplated keeping the rest of the story to herself, but it wouldn't be fair to her friend, the only one who had come to pay his respects at the funeral. He deserved to know the raw, unfiltered truth, for only the truth had the power to grant solace. With her voice trembling, Linda Eshka continued her account:

"Bilal's passing was marked by unprecedented terror, Xhelo. He isolated himself in his room, determined not to put us at risk. He was consumed by despair, and it wasn't just the illness itself that tormented him; it was the unintentional threat he posed to our lives. He held firm to strict safety measures, driven by his deep concern for my well-being and that of our children. He wept continuously, his tears turning into a relentless torrent in our home. We did everything we could to help him, to stay by his side, to care for him. But he never accepted the risk he posed to us. After just ten days in isolation, we'd leave his meals at his door, but he gradually stopped eating. He suffered from severe headaches and a relentless cough that would drive him to the brink of screaming in solitude. We clung to the hope that he'd recover, but on the thirteenth day of isolation, as I ascended the stairs to bring him his morning tea, I noticed that the door leading to the pool veranda was open. It was an unexpected sight that filled me with alarm. The children were always meticulous about keeping doors closed. I cautiously stepped outside, and as my eyes settled on the distant mountains, I silently promised that once Bilal recovered, we'd return to those peaks, ascending to the summit via cable car. However, what I witnessed froze me in my tracks. My heart pounded with terror as I saw Bilal's lifeless body at the bottom of the pool. He had thrown himself into the water, desperate to drown his torment, to escape the relentless grip of the virus. He'd jumped in with his feet bound, preventing his body's instinct to survive, weighed down by a cement block we used to anchor our tents against the wind. The horror of it is beyond imagination, even in the darkest of nightmares. Perhaps he could have outlived the virus, but the pain had become so unbearable that he chose to leave us. He departed. I know it's difficult to believe, but as his friend, you deserve to know the truth. This virus can drive a person to self-destruction. That's how Bilal left us, burdened by all that pain, my dear friend," Linda confessed, her words lost amidst her tears.

The pool nearby seemed to shudder, as if absorbing the weight of this harrowing tale, while all the tables appeared to be submerged in a torrent of tears, mourning the loss of Bilal Eshka. Xhelo found it almost impossible to believe what he had just heard, but it was Linda, the mother of Bilal's children, who had recounted the heart-wrenching story. It was a narrative that left no room for a suitable response.

He cast a glance at the grieving children and felt an overwhelming urge to dive into the pool, to follow his friend's tragic fate. After all, every individual is allotted just one death. Perhaps then, his departure would blend with the mourning for Bilal, allowing him to share in the pain of the next generation in a unique way. "I'll meet my end when the time comes," Xhelo told himself, eager to get into the limousine that would take him to the airport, where a flight to Chicago awaited him and his beloved Shano. He vowed silently that he would spare Shano the gruesome details of Bilal Eshka's departure.

During the flight from Denver to Chicago, Xhelo Lakrori found himself reminiscing about every shared joke and cherished memory with Bilal. Regret weighed heavily upon him, knowing that his dear friend would never live to witness the historic presidential election on November 3, 2020. The elections would unfold without Bilal Eshka and 250,000 other Americans who had fallen victim to Covid-19. Experts predicted that America would soon reach a death toll of half a million, a number equivalent to the casualties of several American wars combined.

Chapter Seven

Life and death engaged in a mesmerizing dance, a never-ending waltz that left Xhelo in awe. In this intricate choreography, life surged forth as an indomitable force, while death gradually receded, becoming a mere whisper in the shadows of memory.

The eternal question loomed: what held greater dominion, life, or death? What worth could one ascribe to life when death stood as an inevitable certainty? Faced with lifeless bodies, we all succumbed to solemn silence. It wasn't solely a tribute to the departed; it was an acknowledgment of our shared fate. One day, we too would embark on that quiet journey into the unknown, leaving behind the realm of pain. We yearned to witness that moment, that transition, but we were denied that privilege by the shroud of silence and the inertia of death. The fear of our mortality remained a construct of our minds, an unfathomable reality. Thus, we fell silent, not just out of reverence for the departed, but for our own sake, aware that in the afterlife, we would rest alone while others paid their respects.

For Xhelo, the defiance against death was encapsulated in the phrase: *"When I am here, death is not; when death comes, I am not."* This challenge epitomized the audacity of the human spirit, confronting death with deeds, crafting monuments and miraculous creations. These achievements, though they needn't accompany us beyond this life, endured as symbols of our existence. As we departed, we left behind our accomplishments as fragments of life and tokens of immortality. This was humanity's grandeur—a vision of non-existence juxtaposed with eternity, turning our world into a canvas where towering structures reached for the sky, and human exploration extended to the Moon and Mars.

Had the fear of death paralyzed humanity, they would have remained confined to caves, Xhelo Lakrori surmised. But history told a different tale. In the beginning, they constructed pyramids for pharaohs, and later, they journeyed across the globe, establishing civilizations, nurturing cultures, building religious institutions, raising grand churches, minarets, and pristine mosques, and envisioning and erecting towering skyscrapers. These structures became testaments to their defiance of death, encapsulating human creativity and magnificence, seeming almost immortal in their grandeur.

Xhelo yearned for a society that celebrated this remarkable human achievement instead of exploiting death in desperate ways. He was appalled by the media's penchant for sensationalizing tragedy—massacres, plane crashes, natural disasters, fires claiming lives, earthquakes, and epidemics. Headlines often fixated on death tolls rather than the number of survivors who had triumphed over adversity. Survivors were overshadowed because their stories failed to instill fear. Emphasizing survival contradicted the fear-driven narrative, yet governments and corporations thrived on a population gripped by fear, panic, and insecurity. Profiting from death had become a lucrative enterprise, a grave sin.

In times of such drama, politicians delivered impassioned speeches in the American Congress and Senate. Their words were carefully chosen, delivered with precision, and infused with a sense of urgency akin to a serpent's hiss. These speeches preyed on humanity's fear of mortality and oblivion. They were framed as saviors of humanity, but, in truth, they fueled fear and insecurity—two emotions politicians across the world exploited.

The pursuit of profit and control was humanity's creed. Everything else amounted to mere rhetoric, utopian dreams, and empty talk. Xhelo imagined a scenario where life was discovered on Mars, only to find it had perished; what would that revelation mean for humanity? Mars, with its Earth-like attributes, stood as a desolate wasteland, its reddish hue reminiscent of a mingling of seas and oceans with the blood of living beings. Could this truly be the case? Perhaps Martians, driven by insatiable desires for luxury, pleasure, and merriment, had depleted their planet, leaving it red and barren. Or maybe Martians had embraced communism, an ideal of collective existence, and their thirst for the color red, through revolutions and civil strife, had drained their planet dry, leaving behind a crimson monument in the cosmos. These were mere tales circulating on Earth. Mars undoubtedly harbored its own unique story, but Xhelo was haunted by the thought that he might not live long enough to witness the conclusions reached by Earth's scientists—conclusions that might only surface in the 22nd century. If only life were more enduring! On Mars, there were no monuments, pyramids, skyscrapers, museums, castles, or presidential buildings. Everything lay leveled in a red abyss. If Earth were to face such a fate one day, what words would be spoken in Congress?...

Engrossed in his thoughts, Xhelo lost all sense of time, his awareness drifting away from the fact that the clinic was ready to begin its day. The staff bustled about, and he found himself captivated by the morning's freshness, a welcome change after his exhausting flight from Denver. His gaze wandered out the window, only to be arrested by an unusual sight: a black limousine, measuring an extravagant five to six meters in length, parked just opposite the clinic. This was highly irregular; there were no unexpected appointments on the schedule. The last time he had witnessed such an arrival was fifteen years ago when Bilal Eshka had orchestrated a surprise. Could it be that everything he had recently experienced was just a haunting dream, and his dear friend had staged his own death to astound Xhelo with an unexpected visit? Would the tall, elegant, blonde-haired, blue-eyed figure of Bilal emerge from the vehicle? Would it be a resurrection akin to that of Christ, or something entirely different? Xhelo's anticipation hung thick in the air as he waited to see who would step out of the luxurious car. If it were indeed Bilal, he would forever doubt the permanence of death. But, alas, it wasn't. Instead, an exquisite woman emerged from the limousine, and her chauffeur held the door open with utmost courtesy. She was a vision in her autumn-hued dress, clutching a white box close to her chest, its contents visible even from a distance. She didn't wear a mask, but rather a translucent face shield that sparkled like a diamond.

"Julia, do you have any idea who this visitor might be?" Xhelo inquired, turning to his secretary as he made his way to the door.

"I'm not certain, Doctor. Our first appointment isn't until 10:30, and I haven't been made aware of..." the amiable secretary responded.

Suddenly, the door swung open, and the captivating woman entered the clinic. Xhelo, dazed by the unexpected arrival, retreated into his office. He couldn't spot any accompanying pets, and the purpose of her visit remained shrouded in mystery. She had specifically requested an appointment with Dr. Lakrori. Normally, Xhelo was not easily swayed emotionally, but after his recent philosophical contemplations on life and death, her visit felt oddly disconcerting. The tall, striking woman, bearing a rich chocolate complexion as though she had been basking on the shores of Shkozet in Albania, held a white box close to her chest. She introduced herself to Julia as Ana Parroti and declared that she was here for Dr. Lakrori, prompting Xhelo to step forward and invite her into his office.

Ana Parroti possessed an extraordinary height, her arresting presence capturing one's attention instantly. Xhelo had always been reserved and cautious, but her aura exuded a powerful, almost enchanting feminine energy that could easily ensnare anyone. He considered himself fortunate that such visits were rare, akin to a "once in a blue moon" phenomenon. Otherwise, he might have succumbed to temptation years ago. "Thank goodness Shano isn't around. I don't know how she would react," Xhelo mused silently as he extended his hand in greeting to his client, motioning for her to take a seat in a nearby armchair.

As their hands met in a handshake—a gesture he hadn't experienced since his first year in college—memories of a woman from his youth, someone with a similar face and bright eyes, resurfaced. She would grasp his hand and hold it until he'd politely request her to "move along." Could it be that this stunning woman had hit the jackpot and had come to surprise him? No, this was an entirely different situation from the peculiar encounters he'd had with college girls in Tirana. Instead of skin-to-skin contact, her velvet gloves seemed to glide delicately over his palm, which, surprisingly, appeared quite large beneath the soft fabric.

Xhelo couldn't help but notice that she was approximately six to seven months pregnant, though her height concealed the stage of her pregnancy, making her condition almost imperceptible.

"Dr. Lakrori, I'm Ana Parroti, and I'm delighted to make your acquaintance. I've heard many intriguing accounts of your services for pets," she announced.

After placing the white box on the nearby table, she bestowed upon him a look reminiscent of the one he used to receive during his botany exams from the unmarried teacher Drita Stafa, who was the sister of Albania's national hero, Qemal Stafa. Despite her pathological bias against female students, many had complained about her behavior to the dean's office. Their response was always the same: "We can't do anything! She's the sister of the national hero. She has connections." Drita Stafa would become utterly captivated by handsome, tall, and elegantly dressed young men, awarding them perfect scores in their record books and even forgoing questioning during exams in favor of offering a lingering gaze. Xhelo had experienced this himself. At the time, no one dared question her pedagogical practices, for she was the sister of the most celebrated hero of socialism. This memory from his past during the dictatorship and the prevailing ideology had returned to him suddenly, creating an unusual discomfort. However, Ana Parroti seemed to perceive Xhelo's confusion and swiftly continued her introduction.

"I've been a client of your competitor, Phil Schwartz, who operates a clinic on the other side of the Chicago River. I recently learned that he passed away due to COVID-19 last week," stated the elegant woman who had just entered his office.

"I'm truly sorry to hear that," Xhelo responded. "I've always respected his professionalism, and our competition has taught me a great deal."

When she mentioned "the other side of the Chicago River," it almost felt as if she were invoking the memory of the Devoll River. The river that flowed through the magnificent city where he lived and worked had a way of stirring nostalgia, an ache that never quite faded. Unlike the tumultuous and often menacing river of his birthplace, the one that divided the two rival clinics served as a tranquil reminder of both the Devoll and Buna rivers in Albania. Over its 251-kilometer course of Chicago River, Americans had constructed forty-five bridges and an equal number of protective bulwarks to tame any potential chaos, guiding its waters with a gentle hand toward Lake Michigan. The lake, like a natural mirror, faithfully reflected the city and its array of towering skyscrapers each morning.

As Xhelo got lost in these reminiscences and comparisons, he felt like a different person. During these moments, the captivating woman before him seemed reminiscent of Rozafa from Balkan legend—a tale still debated by the peninsula's inhabitants regarding its authorship, though they all knew it was an Albanian legend. Ana

Parroti stood before him as if she were the embodiment of Rozafa herself.

He struggled to grasp the purpose of her visit. For the first time, as he beheld Ana Parroti's beauty, he perceived the somber shadow of death as an inspiring halo, especially when he gazed into her stunning eyes, which held fragments of the sky. Even though she was pregnant, her body exuded an intriguing allure, gracefully revealing all its nuances as she sat. Ana Parroti was indeed captivating. She seemed to carry with her the mystical resonance of Luciano Pavarotti, a memory from a concert he had attended with Shano in Paris. Even her short name, reminiscent of Tolstoy's Anna Karenina, evoked an aura of feminine freshness akin to a newly blossomed peony. It reminded him of a beautiful girl from his university days, a pleasant coincidence in these trying times. Was she a doppelgänger from his past? This visitor, named Ana Parroti, was a magnetic enchantment. Every word she spoke seemed to create ripples across her face, a phenomenon Xhelo had never observed in any other woman. Simply put, he felt fortunate that such a creature had graced his office. Sensing the pet doctor's bewilderment, she attempted to act like a typical client, though it was clear she was anything but.

"I apologize, doctor, but I need your help. I believe you can assist me!" she pleaded.

"How can I assure something when I don't know what it is? I apologize, but I provide care for dogs and cats, and I don't see any of those nearby," Xhelo replied.

"Your patient is here, Dr. Lakrori. Open the box!" Ana instructed. She then gently picked up the white box, which was entirely made of ivory, and placed it closer to her swollen, warm chest.

"It's not moving at all. I want it to move and glide gently across my pregnant belly..." she said calmly, her concern evident.

Ana Parroti opened the box, revealing a lethargic yellow snake with dark red spots around its forehead and eyes. It gleamed as if its very essence had been condensed into its rounded body. Its flickering tongue, like threads of gold, startled Dr. Lakrori momentarily, but he quickly composed himself as an expert in animal care. To his surprise, Ana continued:

"The mother of my baby has a peculiar preference for the snake to massage the baby for 30 minutes, three times a day. It's her form of suggestive therapy, aimed at safeguarding the child from all of life's evils... It's a kind of psychological prophylaxis, doctor, and she insists it be practiced regularly until the moment of birth..."

"I don't understand," a bewildered Xhelo Lakrori admitted. "Which baby's mother are you referring to? You are the mother in this case. Am I mistaken, or am I dreaming?"

"Ah, Dr. Lakrori, you misunderstand me. I'm speaking of the baby's biological mother, Gina Miller, who is immensely invested in this birth... She's moving heaven and earth for this baby growing in my womb..." She spoke with a captivating laughter that triggered a vague memory in Xhelo's mind. Ana Parroti possessed a certain magnetism in her gaze that rendered him temporarily speechless. He remained perplexed, admiring this unique creation that God bestowed so sparingly.

"Miss Parroti, please be more specific. I appreciate your visit, but expressing yourself clearly will aid the process and allow me, as a veterinarian, to concentrate on diagnosis and the necessary treatment," Xhelo suggested.

Ana delicately lifted the drowsy snake, caressing it and lightly brushing her lips against its fiery tongue, which darted out like a miniature volcano from its formidable mouth. After this unusual display of affection, she returned the snake to its box, all the while casting a meaningful glance at the Albanian American from Devolli.

"Doctor, I'm a surrogate mother. This child isn't mine. I've simply become a biological vessel for this wealthy couple. It's my first time undertaking such a role, and it's making me anxious. I already have a daughter of my own from a past relationship that never led to marriage. There are many affluent individuals out there who have everything except children. This couple is certainly peculiar, but they're generous. I'm merely assisting them; they compensate me with 140 to 150 thousand dollars, in addition to covering all my living expenses during the pregnancy period," Ana explained.

Xhelo Lakrori was left astounded. How had this surrogate mother situation come about? Who had referred her? He reflected on his own challenging journey. America, he mused, remained a land of endless adventures.

Ana Parroti went on to share that the couple expecting the child in the upcoming months were among the most superstitious people she had ever encountered. They had suffered the loss of three pregnancies due to the wife's inability to provide the necessary nourishment for the embryos, which initially developed normally but then mysteriously ceased to progress—an enigma that had left doctors baffled. It was suspected that a hormonal imbalance within the uterus hindered further embryonic growth. After exploring numerous clinics and potential solutions, the couple had been left with no option but in vitro fertilization and transplantation to a healthy mother who could nurture and carry the fetus to full term. Ana had been chosen as the vessel for this unusual experiment.

Reportedly, the couple, traumatized by their recurrent losses, had become resolute in protecting the embryo at all costs. The biological mother had conducted extensive research and believed that if a snake were allowed to roam near the baby from the embryonic stages until full fetal development, it would shield the child from all evil and potential threats. Ana, despite her initial fear of the practice, had committed to it, even though she had contemplated fleeing in terror at first. As time passed, she had grown accustomed to it, and the once-terrifying snake had become her companion. Ana's adaptation to this cold-blooded creature seemed to evolve in tandem with the growing embryo within her, creating a bizarre yet factual coexistence.

Ana Parroti was essentially a hired womb. According to the extensive contract she had signed, she had effectively rented out her biological capabilities, becoming the exclusive property of the couple for the nine months of pregnancy. As a surrogate, she had to comply with whatever the biological parents, the genetic originators of the lab-created embryo, demanded. "I know it sounds insane, but to what lengths wouldn't one go for survival? At least, it's more dignified than resorting to prostitution," Ana remarked.

Xhelo Lakrori could hardly contain his astonishment. He candidly admitted that this was a unique case in his quarter-century-long career on the continent. Ana spoke ceaselessly, revealing more about the snake, the daily ritual, the wealthy couple's meticulousness, and their insistence on adhering to a strict routine during her pregnancy. Her presence felt like a provocation. Perhaps one of the local Democrats had sent her to challenge Dr. Lakrori's fate. It might even have been an Albanian who directed her to him, either to declare that he wasn't the only one without an inheritance or to assert that he hadn't fully exploited the opportunities that America had to offer.

He could have considered a surrogate mother years ago, even having a child by now, but he hadn't wanted to. He'd discussed it once with Shano, and she'd become markedly upset, refusing outright. "I want to feel the child in my belly, Xhelo, not in someone else's. It may carry my biological material, but it won't carry my feelings, my sensations, my creation. Tell me, Xhelo Lakrori, what feeling do you have for your great-grandfather? Do you even know his name? Does it stir your soul? You hardly consider that you had a great-grandfather, much like I do, much like your beloved president. Do you understand the difference, Xhelo? Life is about sensation, perception, electrifying moments that you must experience. I long to feel those baby kicks in my belly, just like I did a long time ago. I remember the exact moment when I first felt the movement of a baby in my belly. It was a biological tsunami. I was unlucky then, and I told you so during our first kiss. Have you forgotten?" Shano was the driving force. No matter the distance, she seemed to remotely control him, akin to how scientists navigate rockets in outer space. She appeared to scrutinize every one of his steps and fantasies.

"Doctor! What are you thinking about?" the beautiful Ana asked.

"Well, I don't know why this snake intimidates me, despite being my patient," he responded, requesting her to leave the snake at the clinic for some tests. The potential treatment could be determined by the afternoon.

After Ana Parroti had detailed the complaints of her new patient, who had just entered the clinic amidst a backdrop of President Trump dominating the town's conversations, she refrained from expressing any political leanings during her brief visit. With graceful strides, she made her way back to the black limousine, where a driver in a dark suit and red tie stood ready. Her farewell wave reminded Xhelo of the elegant departures of Princess Diana in the previous century.

Xhelo Lakrori had never been particularly fond of treating reptiles. His aversion wasn't solely because they generally struck fear into people, but also due to a traumatic childhood event involving a close friend who had succumbed to snakebite. That tragic scene had been etched into his memory, a horrifying incident that took place during a scorching summer when he and his friend, Gurali Rrëkeja, had been tasked with loading carts full of freshly harvested wheat sheaves. It was a primitive era, and the labor was backbreaking. Eager to outdo each other, the two friends had turned the day's work into a competition, racing to fill as many carts as possible. Xhelo had strived to keep up with Gurali, a natural when it came to agricultural tasks like plowing, hoeing, corn-picking, and tobacco-hanging. Gurali was undeniably an expert in these chores, and Xhelo often found himself trailing behind like a shadow, both envious of his friend's prowess and awestruck by his skill.

On that fateful morning, Xhelo had been eager to witness Gurali's next feat. In the blink of an eye, Gurali had loaded two carts with the sheer intensity of a bulldozer, gathering wheat sheaves at an astonishing pace. As Xhelo watched his friend's vigorous work with a tinge of envy and tried to keep up, he was jolted by a tremulous voice exclaiming, "Xhelo, the snake bit me!"

He turned to see Gurali a few meters away, his hand trembling in fear as he violently swung a scythe hanging from his left arm, the movement flinging the venomous snake away. Xhelo was horrified. He rushed over, and with no other recourse, used the scythe to cut the snake into pieces as it slithered away. It seemed that the venom had rapidly entered his childhood friend's bloodstream. Villagers quickly gathered, tying a scarf tightly around Gurka's forearm to slow the poison's spread, all the while offering words of encouragement. An ambulance from Korça arrived to rush him to the hospital, but he returned to the village the next day, lifeless. It was a harrowing day, Xhelo's first encounter with such a grim death. The horror didn't end there; Pandi and Drita lost their only child and never experienced the joy of another in their humble home. With Gurka's departure, a door had closed.

After conducting a series of tests, Xhelo determined that the snake, which had frequently crawled on the surrogate mother's belly, was suffering from a mild bacterial infection leading to dehydration. Personally, tending to this unusual patient, he administered an antibiotic injection and provided an oral saline solution via a syringe. Anxiously, he awaited the clinical outcome. Several hours later, the snake—an exotic species cherished by the biological mother— showed signs of renewed vitality. This improvement filled Xhelo with hope, and he anticipated delivering the good news to the beautiful woman who would soon arrive in the black limousine. He instantly sent her a message on her cell phone and resumed waiting in his office.

Ana was delighted that Dr. Lakrori's clinic had not only met her expectations but had exceeded them with its service and professional care for the reptile. The crawling creature had provided entertainment for both the biological mother and Ana herself, who was contractually obligated to endure the creature's cold trails on her chocolate-colored belly. As a token of appreciation, she arrived with a bouquet of flowers and a large tray of seafood and vegetables for the staff. After explaining the necessary care to prevent a recurrence of the infection and providing a prescription for reptile supplements, he didn't hesitate to ask the expecting beauty directly:

"Who referred you to my clinic? Is there more to this than mere coincidence and personal preference?"

Ana Parroti hesitated initially before answering. She was aware of the laws of the free market and could have easily used them as justification. However, after witnessing the thoughtful care provided by Xhelo Lakrori, she opted for honesty. She revealed that she had heard about the clinic's exceptional work from various clients, but there was another factor at play. One of the cleaners at the villa where she was currently serving as a surrogate was Albanian. Born in Vlora, where the Albanian flag was raised after five centuries of Turkish domination, the cleaner, known as Ela Shabani, was a mother of two. According to Ana, Ela had casually suggested she visit this clinic, mentioning that Xhelo, too, was childless, and perhaps Ana could offer her services to him.

This revelation unsettled Xhelo Lakrori. He had believed himself to be far removed from the chatter of Albanian society, but he was mistaken. In this vast continent, where gossip could only be silenced within the confines of one's own backyard, he remained a perpetual victim of Balkan words. Maybe Ela had good intentions, Xhelo began to ponder, abruptly turning back to Ana and asking, "How much would your services cost if my wife were to change her mind?"

Ana Parroti was taken aback by such a direct question. She was still in the preliminary stages of this business, a venture bounded by biological limitations. She was uncertain whether she would have the physical and emotional strength to embark on another contract. It was a complex, inexplicably sensory and biological experience. Her primary goal was to successfully complete her current contract and consider future opportunities. However, she knew that this type of work ultimately represented a modern form of human exploitation. If prostitution was the oldest and most primitive profession, this body leasing was the pinnacle of exploitation, a testament to the power of wealth and dollars. Confronted with this reality, the traditional slavery of the 19th century seemed almost benign. Humanity faced countless crises, but these non-massive crises were the first signs of moral decay, where money took precedence over the soul, effort, hope, and the instinct for continuity. Furthermore, modern technology now allowed couples to select their baby's gender, replacing the traditional anticipation of the baby's gender with scientific precision.

Ana harbored a long-held dream of aiding her fellow Albanians, a dream inspired by the tales she'd heard from her Italian great-grandfather, who had been a captive during the Battle of Vlora. Surprisingly, the Albanians had treated him in accordance with their code, showing restraint and avoiding torture or massacre. After his release, a Labëria family had rescued him from destitution and death, providing shelter for two months. This experience gave rise to a saying within their family: "The unfortunate Albanians, who save others." Gazing into Xhelo Lakrori's eyes with her captivating gaze, she remarked, "This is no simple endeavor, but it's a matter of survival for me. If you genuinely require my assistance, I can offer it next year. Beyond that, I intend to explore a different path."

Xhelo found himself taken aback by her response. Ana Parroti had just proposed something he hadn't even contemplated. Her unexpected offer added yet another layer of surprise to their encounter. He could predict his wife Shano's reaction to this unconventional proposition, but the very notion, the prospect of reshaping their lives, held a certain allure for him. With the weight of years settling on his shoulders, he was beginning to grasp that being a parent and leaving behind an heir wasn't merely a source of joy and pride, but a captivating and unpredictable facet of existence. And like life itself, where joy and happiness abounded, so too did their opposites. Startled by Ana's unexpected willingness, he gazed into her entrancing eyes and replied, not without emotion, "Ana, thank you. You are an extraordinary person. You know, we married folks always have a home base where we return each day. I'll speak with my wife, and if age and mindset align, I'll contact you directly."

Ana departed the clinic, content with her visit, leaving Xhelo Lakrori in a state of bewilderment. The angelic faces of his friend's children in Denver remained etched in his mind. The vibrant hues on their youthful, lovely faces seemed like symbolic farewell crowns. However, now that he was in his sixties, these thoughts appeared futile. He sensed a biological potential within himself to embark on this journey, but it all hinged on Shano's response. With newfound determination, he decided to return home and discuss the proposition with his wife while it was still fresh in his mind. He had nothing to lose. Informing his secretary of his imminent return, he hurried home. Shano had just had her hair styled that day and radiated the same beauty that had captured his heart. He kissed her passionately and got straight to the point, recounting the incident at the clinic.

"What do we stand to lose if we give it a try, my dear Shano?" he asked, eagerly awaiting her response. To him, Xhelo could live another 30 years, providing ample time to experience something that had haunted him all his life. He believed that history was replete with instances where an heir was conceived just as couples stood on the precipice of the grave. He felt ready to embrace the idea of passing away the day after receiving news of Shano's pregnancy, knowing a child was on the way. The intense preoccupation with ensuring one's lineage, securing continuity, baffled him. Sometimes, it seemed like the most senseless obsession, tormenting the soul. As Shano had once pointed out, he couldn't even recall his great-grandfather's name. So, what was the purpose of this frantic race for inheritance and continuity at this stage of life? Didn't all things, even the forgotten, revolve around the living? Worse yet, only the living who possessed wealth, influence, or power?

In his eyes, Shano represented a universe of wisdom, to which he humbly deferred, submitting himself and maintaining his silence. The sway women held over the capricious male ego bore an almost magical touch, nearly invisible, yet it bestowed true power upon women, despite men parading as undisputed rulers in society and within the family. "You men are fools," a voice seemed to chime in. Weren't men aware that even biologically they contributed merely one vote, one simple decision? Their biological potential pointed in one direction: male or female. That was the extent of their influence. The entire continuity of a baby rested in the hands of women. The true cradle of development, intelligence, the future, and perspective lay there. Were men cognizant of their limitations in biological continuity? Indeed, this simple observation cast light on the political charades men often attempted to impose on the opposite sex. The male ego, it seemed, was the greatest sin on earth. Shano Gërsheta grasped this concept thoroughly, starting from the day she first lay with a Devoll man. She bore hatred, curses even, for men, whose sole source of pride resided in something they utilized solely by chance, and never, ever permanently.

Unlike in the past, Shano remained steadfast this time. Witnessing the fervor with which Xhelo pleaded his case, she replied without much enthusiasm,

"The heat of August has passed, Xhelo! Spare yourself the trouble. We've had this discussion before. Don't forget, my dear, back in Bilisht almost 40 years ago, I practically begged you to hate me. I nearly shouted it in your ear, 'Hate me!' Are you finally ready to hate me now?"

He felt adrift, as if he were traversing another galaxy. Lost in his thoughts, he couldn't find the words to defend or explain himself. It was a well-established fact that Devoll men were mere reflections of their wives.Xhelo knew that lovers all underwent a spiritual transformation, while many married individuals changed so profoundly that even their parents failed to recognize them. "It's the power and magic of the woman you love," some wise elders from his village had advised, their words resonating in his mind as he stood before his wife, trembling.

"My dear, why do you speak this way? I've never held any grudge against you. I simply want us to give it a shot. It's not a demand, just a notion, a suggestion. We're fading away while still breathing. When I attended Bilal Eshka's funeral and saw those radiant children with the colorful rainbows illuminating their faces, it hit me how hollow our lives have become. One lives to die, like Bilali, surrounded by wreaths of every color. Those silent children, brimming with vividness in their souls and eyes, were like emblems of immortality, my dear Shano."

"Are you daydreaming or indulging in fantasies, Xhelo? What are you saying? Haven't I witnessed death firsthand? Thousands perish daily. It matters not if they're your friends or strangers, rich or poor, senators or presidents. Death claims us all impartially. The world is crumbling, and you're stuck on Devoll Bridge. How pitiable," Shano responded, leaving him utterly bewildered.

He wasn't sure how to reply, but he understood that a woman's influence over her husband was both mythical and real. "You'd exchange your trousers and your pride for a few scarves," Shano had once proclaimed so vehemently that the hefty chandelier suspended from their living room's ceiling had swayed. He felt humbled, like a deflated balloon. He didn't know how to retort to her, the woman he cherished so deeply. Observing his submission, akin to a man's ego deflated, Shano, with the assurance that the triumphant feminine spirit exudes, had remarked:

"What's to prevent us from ending up with some peculiar biological mutation? Did you know that instead of eyebrows, we might grow extra eyes?"

He fell silent. Shano was correct. Many times, he had found her perspective on life to be pragmatic. Often, he'd be carried away by the fervor of the moment, which frequently blinded him, much like many men from Devoll. When he had seen that striking woman who had arrived at his office in a limousine, accompanied by a snake adorning her chest, he had nearly forgotten Shano's expansive world and seemed to lose himself in the enchanting eyes of the surrogate mother. It was a fleeting transgression he dared not confess to Shano, but deep down, he acknowledged that men were often the most likely to betray their marital vows. In this later stage of his life, he noticed the erosion of his family's foundations as he indulged in rose-tinted fantasies. These were captivating moments, but they remained just that, and they could never replace Shano's essence. Despite not being a mother, she was a woman worth standing beside until the end.

Chapter Eight

Xhelo Lakrori had never imagined that, at his stage in life, he'd entertain the notion of marital infidelity. Two moments had profoundly stirred him: the beautiful children left behind by Bilal Eshka, and the glimpse of those blue eyes belonging to the surrogate mother with a snake on her breast. These two strange opposites coexisted side by side in his thoughts. Where had that remarkable woman with her extraordinary creature appeared at his clinic, carrying a snake in a box? Why hadn't she come a good ten years earlier?

"What would you have done ten years ago?" a voice asked him. "Would you have left Shano or...?"

"No, never. Who said that? If she had come ten years earlier, I would've convinced Shano to go through with the surrogacy, and we'd be parents by now. Do you understand what I mean? They call me Xhelo Lakrori. That's what I had in mind, not those other crazy ideas."

That night, sleep eluded him. As he gazed at his peacefully slumbering and devoted wife to his left, he reminisced about the many beautiful moments of life. He knew that life only came around once and should be lived, not weighed down by constant "what ifs" and "if onlys." Xhelo was a veterinarian, and his deep knowledge of animal physiology, reproductive processes, and the unashamed ways of the animal kingdom often led him to ponder over topics like embryos in test tubes. But he'd never acted upon these musings. It wasn't his fault that he was born in Devoll, where even in the face of liberal tendencies, tradition, custom, shame, opinion, and the weight of words held strong. Thus, Xhelo believed in the importance of personal freedom. He saw how American society allowed individuals to experiment freely, provided they dared and had the means. For instance, the wealthiest man in Chicago, having exhausted all other pleasures, yearned for an heir. If his wife couldn't bear children, he simply hired someone, and his dream came true. Who cared what the world thought? Did America concern itself with the world's opinions? In the quiet of the night, Xhelo often contemplated that human life was filled with an infinite array of ideas, dreams, and judgments, and in this world of pleasure and contemplation, getting involved in politics, political ideologies, or party programs, which amounted to little more than the pragmatic games of influential groups treating the majority as experimental subjects, seemed futile.

He'd wake up in a panic, relieved to find it was just a dream, understanding it was not reality. Yet, the same dream continued to haunt him. Surrounded by snakes of every kind, length, and girth, accompanied by a chilling, paralyzing, and deafening slithering sound, he found himself confronting a horde of reptiles unlike any other. He struggled to breathe, to escape from this horrifying biological population, but he couldn't. His hands felt locked, as if clasping onto a crucifix; his legs were almost paralyzed, ensnared by a labyrinth of snakes. Gasping for air, barely able to breathe, he fought to escape, to find his freedom, but it eluded him. He was held captive by the serpents of the world.

It was a terrifying dream, as if all the snakes on Earth had united to put Xhelo Lakrori on trial. He had committed no sin, so why this torment on that autumn night? He felt like he was on trial, surrounded by snakes from around the world. They were tightly coiled around his arms, legs, neck, and the base of his abdomen, as if reading him the indictment of the century. The snakes spoke in Albanian, judged him in Albanian, and accused him in Albanian. "English, please. English!" Xhelo shouted, trying to find salvation, but to no avail.

"Why do you humans view us with such contempt? Why do you attribute to us your fears, your twisted imaginations, and your uncommitted sins? Why do you portray us, the most unfortunate creatures on Earth, as symbols of evil? Why are you so afraid of us, and why do you link everything sinister in your lives to us, the snakes? Who gave you that right? We, the most persecuted beings on this planet, animals without legs, arms, or proper bodies, with cold blood, possess only a head, body, and tail. We lack the arms, neck, and ears you have; we can't even compare to your anatomical and bio motor excellence. We are not as venomous as they claim. We are not as ruthless as they depict us, nor as treacherous as they describe.

We simply slither through life in pursuit of our daily sustenance, using our tongues to taste chemicals, catching frogs, insects, mice, or other creatures to stay alive, all while trying to avoid your gaze. Yet you are everywhere. You humans, who have everything in abundance—arms, legs, beautiful bodies, lovely faces, ears, noses, symmetrical cheeks, and lips, extraordinary beauty, brains, ideas, imagination, expressive eyes of all hues—why do you make us the embodiment of evil?"

"I've never killed a snake except the one that bit my childhood friend Gurka! Just yesterday, I saved a snake. Please, free my hands and legs; let me breathe," Xhelo Lakrori mumbled, half-awake.

"We know that you healed one of our kin, which you've turned into a feather in your own cap. We're aware, but we can't fathom why you don't hold us in the same regard as dogs and cats, birds and rabbits, horses, and cows. They're all creatures, much like us. Why have you burdened us with the worst reputation in your human world? You only value our contributions after we've met our end; that's why you wear belts made from snake leather and ladies fancy bags and boots crafted from our hides. Yet very few among you welcome us into your homes. We're just like you, dear humans— living beings striving to survive. We seldom attack anyone. How many attacks have humans committed to this day? We don't engage in mass killings. Occasionally, we may bite someone, but not on the scale of humanity, which has devised nuclear, and hydrogen bombs capable of obliterating thousands and millions of its own kind. Can you comprehend the magnitude of human injustice and sin?"

"I'm a veterinarian. I'm the one who saves them from death and suffering. What issue do you have with me?"

"We know. Our concern isn't solely with you, Xhelo Lakrori. Our grievance extends to your entire human race. You must cease viewing snakes as symbols of evil, as bearers of fear and terror. These qualities belong to humans who kill, destroy, burn, flood, and maim others, condemning them to crawl like us, shackled by a sinful fate. You humans stand at the pinnacle of all evil among living beings on this planet. Like you, we have our own troublemakers— snakes that, much like your dictators, presidents, or prime ministers, seek to control and dominate us. However, most of us are creatures who merely seek to live. The rattlesnake may be a kind of monster among our kind, and we have other types that don't desire peace with humans, only conflict and strife. Most of us seek peace. We yearn for you to refrain from barbaric killings and to cease tarnishing our serpentine reputation. After all, it's not our fault; this is how God fashioned us."

"I hold no power. I left politics in Albania. Back there, I organized a few rallies, but committed no other wrongdoing. I have no children. I'm just one of the billions inhabiting this Earth. What do you want from me?" Xhelo asked, his brow drenched in sweat, his heart gripped by terror.

The snake charmer, as biological net, cold and colorful, continued to coil ever tighter around Xhelo Lakrori's towering frame. It felt as though, any moment now, a rattlesnake would appear to disturb Shano's peaceful slumber, injecting dread into their warm marital bed beneath the quilt adorned with knobs. Xhelo couldn't bear this for his beloved. He wanted to shoulder the burden himself, for he had sinned in numerous ways. He could have been more cordial to the yellow snake, which represented a blessing and salvation for the affluent couple expecting a child. Thus, he found himself pleading for forgiveness, vowing never to use the word 'snake' as a synonym for evil again. He promised to find another term—maybe even coin a word—that could serve as a substitute.

"No, we don't want that. We want you humans, when you intend to insult someone or describe your monstrous vices, to never employ the names of animals. It's all too effortless for you to curse someone as a snake, donkey, beast, pig, wolf, jackal, lizard, weasel, or sewer rat. Cease it, for each of these creatures harbors some positive quality—never as vile as what you possess. God has blessed you so much, yet you fail to appreciate it. So, when you wish to curse, to unleash your anger, hatred, passion, resentment, humiliating laughter, and deadly words, simply say: human. Do you comprehend our request? Otherwise, we will return to suffocate you, to witness you struggle for breath beside your slumbering wife. Unlike your friend Bilal Eshka, who was driven mad by a virus, we will elevate you to great heights in the sky. There, far from Earth, near the moon, a colossal whirlwind will slowly carry away your soul, leaving you as nothing, without a grave on Earth or the moon. Such is our wrath against humans, who, through some twist of fate, occupy the apex of living species but, in most cases, are consumed by ego, domination, control, violence, insatiability, jealousy, hatred, betrayal, bitterness, and all the other vices, as some of your philosophers describe them. Is there anything more venomous than your spiteful words directed at each other and across races? Do you comprehend our message? Do you promise to change?"

"Yes, I do!" Xhelo responded, quivering with fear.

"Speak in Albanian, Xhelo Lakrori! We've carried out this campaign against human brutality in your bed using the Albanian language. Albanian predates both English and Latin, as claimed by certain Albanian historians and linguists. You hold your heritage in high regard, yet you possess so little to truly be proud of. Speak in Albanian; it remains your sole identity, and you've even allowed it to become an international disgrace. You Albanians embody the true snakes, not us, the unfortunate inhabitants of Earth. Speak in Albanian, Xhelo!"

"Yes, I understand you clearly. Please, let me breathe," he responded, his words flowing in Albanian, as the serpents constricted their coils around him.

Suddenly, as if by some mystical sleight of hand, all the snakes vanished into thin air, leaving only one—the largest among them, black and elongated, adorned with a smattering of white spots resembling small flags of peace in the wars of humanity. It remained coiled around his neck, tightening its grip but abstaining from sinking its venomous fangs into his flesh. The pressure on his windpipe nearly choked the life out of him. Beads of cold sweat glistened on his forehead, and in a desperate plea, Xhelo shouted, "Let me breathe... I'm suffocating... I need air!"

He jolted awake from the nightmarish ordeal, discovering that the silk sheet Shano had meticulously spread just the day before was now wound around his neck. He gingerly touched his throat with trembling hands, a sensation of relief washing over him as he realized that the horrors had been nothing more than the fabric of a dream. Drawing a deep breath, he shifted his gaze to Shano, who still slumbered peacefully. The clock's hands indicated 6:00 in the morning. Silently, he slipped out of bed and tiptoed to the kitchen to prepare their morning coffee.

Dabbing the remnants of perspiration from his brow, Xhelo placed a tray with two cups of coffee at the head of the bed—an unusual gesture. Typically, it was Shano who would serve him coffee as if he were a lord from Devoll. This had become an ingrained routine in their married life, one that she took pleasure in executing.

The aroma and wisps of steam wafting from the coffee eventually roused her from her restful slumber. She blinked in mild astonishment upon seeing Xhelo standing there, a tray in his hands— an act that felt strangely foreboding. As she rubbed her eyes to clear away the haze of sleep, she inquired if something dreadful had occurred or if there was unsettling news from Albania.

"No, my love. Everything is fine. I had a distressing dream. But it was just that—a dream. Enjoy," he reassured her, gently stirring the Colombian coffee.

Shano possessed a remarkable sensitivity to dreams, often experiencing premonitions of events that would subsequently unfold exactly as they had appeared in her slumber. Of course, there were countless dreams she forgot, along with those that never came to fruition, but she clung tightly to the ones that manifested into reality.

"What did you dream about, my love? Was it me frolicking naked on the beaches of Pogradec?"

"No, Shano. It was unlike any dream I've ever had. I don't need dreams to see you because I have the genuine article right here with me. It was a torturous dream. I was ensnared by snakes, encircled by a vast crowd, reminiscent of the times we attended those iconic rallies, shouting, 'We want Albania to be like all of Europe.'"

"Snakes? What a nightmarish ordeal you've endured, my love! Did they bite you? Did you bleed? Snakes are emblematic of adversaries, Xhelo. We have our share of foes. Snakes are symbols of enemies, as my grandmother used to say. She dreamt of snakes when I faced hardships…" Shano said.

"Let's not commence the day on such a note," Xhelo interjected. "You, yourself, often refer to dreams as the whimsies of the mind. Let it go."

"Then let's light three candles!" She dashed to the table in the adjacent living room, swiftly igniting the candles she had prepared in advance.

"May the evil ones depart from us now!" Shano proclaimed, her arm encircling Xhelo's neck. In a moment of unity and solace, they shared a tender kiss on the lips, the aroma of coffee serving as a silent bond amidst a morning that had begun with disquiet for Xhelo Lakrori.

Chapter Nine

As he parked his car in front of the clinic early one morning, a police cruiser screeched to a halt beside his vehicle, sirens were wailing and lights flashing. Two officers swiftly emerged and swung open the rear door, a sense of alarm seizing Xhelo Lakrori. He hadn't committed any infractions; why were the police descending upon his clinic? His thoughts immediately darted to Ana Parroti. With her mysterious games and enigmatic allure, she must have been harboring secrets. She was an enigma, a captivating one that had left an indelible mark on him. Ana's beauty had etched itself into his mind so deeply that he had spent the entire night lost in contemplation, even dreaming of serpents. She was undoubtedly the most enigmatic woman he had ever encountered, and he couldn't decide whether he wanted her back at the clinic, offering her a different kind of friendship compared to his other clients, and, of course, assisting her with whatever she required.

"What in the world is happening to me? The police show up at my clinic, and here I am thinking about a surrogate mother. Get a grip, Xhelo! Control your impulses," he almost shouted at himself as the two officers approached him with brisk, military-like precision.

"We need urgent help! Please, Dr. Lakrori! Our dog's eye has been injured," one of the officers urgently pleaded.

A wave of relief washed over Xhelo. The police hadn't come for him. He swiftly unlocked the clinic door, and the two anxious officers carried a large dog inside, reminiscent of those once used at the Albanian border to prevent and neutralize escape attempts. In his early youth, Xhelo had read a book about an Albanian border dog named "Jurkani." He directed them immediately to the operating table. After stowing his bag in his office, he donned his white coat and headed to the animal treatment room.

"What happened?"

"A drug dealer and murder suspect shot our dog. We can't afford to lose him. He does the work of an entire police squad!" stated the officer who oversaw canine scent operations.

Xhelo swiftly administered a syringe with physiological saline to stabilize the dog's vital signs. He then took a white pad and gently applied it to the wounded eye. Profuse hemorrhaging flowed from the dog's left eye, hampering its breathing. The dog, displaying an almost human-like understanding, shed tears from its other eye while emitting a soft, plaintive whine as if to convey its endurance. The officer standing nearby watched every move of the veterinarian with a look of anxious concern, as if he, too, could feel the dog's pain, his own eyes welling up with tears. At that moment, Xhelo's primary objective was to stem the hemorrhage, which could prove fatal. The dog needed to be rushed to the hospital for further treatment.

"For now, I can only intervene to stop further blood loss," he explained to the two officers, who were observing his every action with anxious anticipation. "He needs immediate attention in the emergency room."

With haste, he affixed a pad to the wound on the dog's brow, securing it with transparent adhesive. Acting too quickly could risk further tearing of the wound, but he remembered the advice of his surgery professor from university: bullet wounds should be left open, not sutured. "How wise and practical those socialist teachers were," he mused. He was tempted to share that he had graduated in Albania, east of the Atlantic, where education was highly esteemed. However, he refrained. What would American police officers know about schooling under a dictatorship?

Next, he administered a drug to aid in blood clotting. After rechecking the pad on the wound, he recommended they seek additional help at the hospital. It was a swift, professional response performed under the watchful gaze of the police officers, and Xhelo felt a sense of pride, particularly following a night plagued by nightmares. The emergency was now under control. The officers, previously distraught, appeared to regain their courage and hope in Xhelo's capable hands.

"Rest assured! His life is not in immediate jeopardy, though the fate of his eye remains uncertain. That will depend on the outcome of the surgery," he assured the officers while soothing the dog, which expressed a human-like sense of relief in its eyes.

As Xhelo reflected, standing triumphantly beside the dog shot in the head, he was reminded of his disturbing dream from that morning. In the dream, a swarm of snakes had judged him. It was a bizarre creation of his imagination, yet it strangely foreshadowed the scene playing out before him. The man who had nearly killed the police dog had saved countless officers' lives in numerous operations against crime and criminals.

The wail of an approaching ambulance siren near the clinic's entrance brought him back from his introspection that often consumed him. After bidding farewell to the police, he retreated to his office in search of some tranquility. It was an autumn season rife with daily surprises, not unlike the American presidential campaign, which escalated the warlike rhetoric and public stress with each passing day. Immersed in the world of animals, even those that induced fear in humans, he felt a profound connection with every living being, especially for those unable to voice their pain or suffering, particularly those without limbs or arms. The tapestry of life was a marvel that humans understood little and seldom appreciated, while a significant minority displayed cruelty towards all living creatures.

Xhelo pondered that if his dream could be captured on film and presented as a movie, it would serve as a poignant prelude to the political campaign, where brutality and attacks on opponents had become commonplace. However, the fate of the injured dog in the battle against crime reminded him that life presented far weightier challenges than the soundbites of declarations the media featured from the rival camps in the quest for the White House. The destiny of the dog and the service of the snake during the surrogate mother's pregnancy transcended the ego-driven boundaries of individuals, especially politicians, ushering in a more genuine and humane reality.

As the clinic bustled with activity, his phone pinged, indicating a new message had arrived. It was from the police station, expressing gratitude for the service provided and requesting the invoice for payment as soon as possible. Xhelo responded promptly, "Our clinic was delighted to assist. As first-time clients, our service is complimentary this time." He sent a brief text to Shano, as if to reassure her that the day had begun well and considered sending Ana a message. He was curious about the effectiveness of the treatment administered to the reptile, and this would be a good indicator that the clinic cared for its patients.

Despite feeling shaken by her presence, he hesitated to continue this form of communication, which was typically the secretary's responsibility. However, since Ana had arrived with such fanfare and displayed a particular preference for Xhelo, she deserved at least a greeting and an intriguing query. With trembling hands, he selected Ana's number and, as if crafting a carefully worded essay, typed, "Hello Ana! This is Dr. Lakrori. I hope your special pet has recovered and is bringing joy to Mrs. Miller and yourself. Regards, Dr. Lakrori." He couldn't fathom why he experienced a surge of emotion while composing this message—a sensation he struggled to put into words. Perhaps it was because Ana was the sole client who had graced his clinic with such pomp and circumstance, and undoubtedly, she possessed a feminine allure unlike any he had encountered in decades.

Her response arrived the following day—short and seemingly disinterested. "Thank you, doctor. Everything is fine. Ana." It came as a surprise. He had expected a different reaction. During her visit to his office, Ana had radiated enthusiasm and vitality, even mentioning her willingness to potentially become a surrogate for his family. It had piqued Xhelo's curiosity, though he recognized it as a form of madness, an idea that Shano had dismissed. His thoughts had started to wander, daydreaming and concocting all sorts of scenarios—an imaginative realm that left him feeling disoriented. Yet every time he succumbed to these wild fancies, he pictured Shano standing before him, her arms crossed over her graceful chest—the same chest against which he had rested so many times, nurturing his dream of becoming a father. That pristine chest, however, had never cradled a baby. It was as if she were cautioning him, "What deludes you, Xhelo Lakrori? Haven't I warned you from the very first day you showed compassion for me? Beware! Aha, now it's too late. Now, I will dictate the rules against any intrigue you might fantasize about. Tread carefully, Xhelo! We women have tamed the devil. Be careful, my dear. I still love you..."

The silent authority of the woman he loved often filled him with trepidation. Before her, all his wildest inclinations crumbled. Xhelo was enticed by adventures yet haunted by the fear that, no matter how concealed they seemed, no matter how meticulously planned and detailed, they would invariably surface as clumsy secrets, exposing all forms of male duplicity. He yearned to distance himself from temptation, from any form of betrayal. In truth, Xhelo couldn't even entertain the thought of betrayal. His desires leaned more toward exploring the unknown, acquiring knowledge not yet within his grasp. He was an inquisitive man who restrained his instincts and tamed his Freudian passions.

He had perused Freud's writings repeatedly, both agreeing and disagreeing with his theories. While Xhelo found Freud's psycho-emotional analyses accurate, he couldn't bring himself to be a casualty of outrageous theories. According to Xhelo, mankind harbored a moral power within, a self-control of emotions that he saw as a transfer of divine power over male foibles. This self-regulation sometimes appeared as a divine force, at other times as the power of morality, a construct of human hypocrisy. Despite its often-violent nature, this self-control empowered man primarily over himself. Perhaps this innate self-control fueled human ambitions to dominate everything else—their desires, the people around them, those they encountered daily, even entire crowds, nations, and peoples, as leaders, rulers, presidents, and dictators did. It all began with self-control, leading to a relentless quest for control.

The power one person held over another remained an enigmatic puzzle, yet it found some semblance of understanding in Freudian perspectives. Humans governing humans... Humans then constructed cultures, theories, morals, codes, beliefs, idols, and customs... This was, in fact, the most hypocritical agreement that had unfolded over decades and centuries. Humans, these civilized primates blessed with consciousness and cunning, had struck a pact with their primitive instincts, dubbing it morality, behavior, character, integrity, or virtuousness. It was human absurdity.

When chemical reactions ignited, they mirrored the explosions on the sun—fiery, volcanic, chaotic, engulfing, and consuming. It was a law unto itself, with an irreversible cosmic trajectory. The only path was toward self-extinction, devoid of order, shame, morals, or judgment. Yet as the sun sets in the west, silently, gradually, often with a blush, tranquility descended without fanfare, known on Earth as night. And during this time, countless tumultuous events unfurled in disparate corners of the globe...

Earth, the sole planet known to harbor life, was a peculiar construct. When observed from the Moon, one would witness inequity and injustice wherever the meridians intersected the human-created parallels. One segment of the population initiated the night with amorous and carnal pursuits, with passionate encounters in bedrooms, lavish hotels, royal and presidential palaces, while another segment of the same human race awoke bleary-eyed, sipped coffee, exchanged the customary greeting of "good morning," and commenced another enslaving day, as if attempting to erase the transgressions of the previous night... "The world is unjust. The world is not level, not equitable, not sincere. The world is deception and a collective human disgrace... God, help me evade sin," Xhelo would mutter. The culmination of human hypocrisy. It was a silent collective consensus within human society. Those who championed this kind of morality were often the first to trample upon it, abandoning their commitment to social morality when confronted with beauty.

Her distant demeanor felt abrupt. He was disappointed, annoyed with himself for having nurtured affection for Ana, who, in the end, was just like any other woman. They would smile to your face, feign flirtation, but once they departed, they'd conveniently forget you. He felt ashamed for being naive, for believing in the feigned sincerity of that woman. She hadn't shown the slightest courtesy. At the very least, she should have initiated the first message, expressing her gratitude for the service, or offering constructive criticism if necessary—especially since, as he did with every first-time client, he hadn't charged her any service fees.

"You remain naive, Xhelo! Women deceive you with a smile. How many times has Shano warned you to be careful with women? She tells you she loves you, but you still get deceived by smiles, flirtation, and sweet words. Don't forget the Albanian wisdom: women are the power that controls men. Devilry resides in well-trampled bottles, but be careful, for when the devil escapes the bottle, it's unpredictable... As the Americans say, 'Fool me once, shame on you; fool me twice, shame on me.' Be cautious; there are some laughs whose origins you don't know," a voice from within cautioned. Xhelo had been naive when it came to those artfully crafted feminine laughs. He felt embarrassed, having openly shared everything with Shano, even entertaining the idea of hiring Ana as a surrogate mother. What folly.

Curiously, as he grew older, he found himself learning more from Shano. She was pragmatic, never placing her trust in anyone and putting herself above all else. Xhelo tried to console himself, reasoning that he hadn't done anything wrong; he had merely initiated contact and shown interest in a potential client, a professional attempt to expand his market with no room for ambiguity.

Yet, he couldn't shake off his lingering hesitancy. As much as he was disappointed with Ana's response, a part of him wanted to engage in a conversation that felt somewhat persistent. A thought crossed his mind: he could invite her for coffee to get to know her better, to inquire about her dreams, passions, and aspirations after her surrogate role was complete. Meanwhile, he would clarify that he and Shano had no intention of continuing with the service she offered. Of course, he would also convey his gratitude for her willingness. "I have nothing to lose," he reassured himself, and with his cellphone in hand, he began composing another message: "If you ever need my clinic again, please don't hesitate to call me and come by anytime. It was a pleasure to meet you."

This time, her reply came instantly: "OK. See you tomorrow, 4 PM at 'Koko' restaurant. Thank you."

Should he share this story with Shano, giving her all the details? It seemed futile. Every man had his secrets, some things remained concealed until death, akin to the credit cards one carried. His sole intent with this woman was to learn more about her mysterious service, a concept previously unexplored in Albania. He knew several couples in Devoll who were equally unfortunate, but the notion of a child being conceived in another woman's womb and still being considered one's own had never been broached. Shano was correct when she asserted, without a shred of doubt that a mother needed to feel the baby's kicks to truly love and cherish it; those kicks were the first signs of the infant's inclination to escape, to move away, and to yearn for the freedom that even a baby sought. Why would anyone want to remain within the confines of the placental dome, where every breath was a struggle? Creatures yearned for freedom, space, and independence. So, when a baby was successfully born, everyone celebrated, while the baby itself cried. Those who rejoiced did so knowing that the baby brought hope, joy, and continuity, while the baby cried because it understood that those celebrating were hypocrites, not revealing the truth about life and its behind-the-scenes reality, which could often be grim. Xhelo Lakrori couldn't easily escape this never-ending cycle of contemplation, so he decided to call Shano. In confiding in her, he found solace. He believed that an honest husband couldn't keep secrets from the one who shared his bed.

"Shano, tomorrow I'm meeting Ana, at 4 o'clock at the Greek place. At 'Koko,' where we had lamb together," he said.

"Be careful," Shano cautioned. "I don't place much trust in women who sell everything for money and luxury. Life can be simpler without money. Ana appears enigmatic to me, but perhaps I'm mistaken. From what you've told me, it seems she's primarily motivated by American greenbacks. I love dollars, but I love you more, Xhelo Lakrori! Do you understand?" Shano's voice carried a slight edge. She spoke as though she were an ocean of waves that kept him afloat, both as a man and a citizen. Without the support she provided, Xhelo might have become an American monster. He was aware of this danger, and he remained grateful to her until his last breath. To him, she was like an eternal sun that never set, shielding him from the darkness and the horrors of masculinity. So, when he spoke to her, he tried to choose his words with maturity and always spoke in Albanian.

"My love, I'm meeting her just to inform her that we don't require her services. You know I'm good with people, and I don't want to disappoint anyone," he assured Shano.

There was no immediate response, but after a prolonged silence, she finally spoke:

"I've always had faith in you, Xhelo, but remember, trust is relative. I don't want that to change between us."

"Shano! I'm as bound to you as flesh is to bone. Why are you saying this?"

"I didn't say anything, my dear Xhelo; I merely reminded you of a truth. It's not about you, but a lesson from life. Please be cautious. Let's work and savor the approaching retirement. The government hopes we never reach that day, but I wish and hope..."

In their conversations, she dispelled everything, leaving him in awe of the wisdom he had never encountered in other women who had taken everything from him—his soul, dreams, and passions. Yet they couldn't touch his primal instincts, which occasionally tormented him. He felt embarrassed, yet also at peace because these internal battles and quandaries were his alone. When someone could pry into and scrutinize the feelings and seductive doubts of another, it would be time to stop living. Everyone carried secrets and mysterious things, solely for themselves.

The next day, Xhelo secured a corner table at the Mediterranean eatery "Koko," situated far from the bustling city center. The atmosphere transported him back to Korça. The owner, Spiro Monikus, a Greek from Athens, was no stranger to Xhelo, as he occasionally brought his German Shepherd for visits. Spiro felt like a distant relative to Xhelo, and his restaurant served as a sanctuary for human emotions. It wasn't a bad place at all. People came here to unwind, escaping the monotony of home and work. Xhelo settled in calmly, waiting. The waitress, an Albanian with short hair and black eyes, approached him with a smile and addressed him in Greek. Her name, Xhefrije (Xhini), adorned her uniform, and Xhelo was pleased to see that she held onto her original name, using Xhini as a nickname. He didn't respond immediately but eventually spoke to her in Albanian and ordered a glass of water. As he observed the ongoing fusion of cultures in America, a prolonged process that had already culminated in Americanization, Xhelo reflected on the shifts taking place. Here was an Albanian girl working for a Greek owner, struggling with her boss's language despite not identifying as Greek. He didn't delve further into their conversation with the lovely girl from Përmet but looked into her eyes and remarked, "The Albanian language is so beautiful, sweet, and sublime..."

She remained silent and walked away, leaving behind a blush characteristic of Albanian women. "It's not her fault; it's the impact of the market," Xhelo muttered to himself as he sipped his water, which reminded him of a glass from the Cold Water in Tepelenë, south of Albania. He said nothing more and remained silent, eagerly awaiting the arrival of the pregnant Ana. He adjusted his mask and waited.

Ana Parroti entered through the door, and the entire room turned their heads to gaze upon her captivating figure. Even though the restaurant wasn't packed, half of the patrons couldn't help but shift their attention, checking their masks on their faces. Typically, pregnant women lost some of their feminine charm in the later stages, but Ana, at the end of her pregnancy, retained a remarkably fresh and captivating allure. This was precisely the quality that had captivated Xhelo. He envisioned himself married to Ana, with her being pregnant from the honeymoon month, and he observed the intriguing transformation in her charm. It was the most enchanting architectural transformation, where a woman, the conduit for human continuity, unconsciously metamorphosed in the eyes of her husband, who distorted her elegance with his masculine potential, resulting in this kind of anatomical alteration from which life, inheritance, and legacy were born.

Ah, luck had not favored him in this regard. He was eager to comprehend what drove Ana, who had ventured into this unique profession and managed to challenge deeply ingrained mentalities and doctrines in Albania. He saw in the beautiful Ana a potential source of healing for countless couples who were suffering, both the living and the departed. She confidently made her way towards him. He watched her with an unusual sense of reverie, as if everything in his memory and consciousness had been momentarily wiped clean. She appeared like a distant star, shining brightly despite being thousands of light-years away, distant yet dazzlingly brilliant. If he were unmarried, he would have whisked her away and disappeared somewhere with her, pregnancy notwithstanding. With her, he longed to embark on a cosmic journey, caressing a baby that cried and laughed. It didn't matter that the child wasn't biologically his; he would cherish those tiny tickles and tears that flowed from the innocent infant's eyes. He yearned to comprehend the true sensitivity of babies toward adults, whether they possessed consciousness from their very first cry, and how they perceived the world in its truest form. The adults, marveling at the infants' initial cries—what impression did such behavior leave on a newborn? This was a study that hadn't yet been conducted and perhaps wouldn't be for another five or ten centuries.

Ana arrived promptly, at the agreed-upon time. He rose from his seat and, in the manner of a Korça gentleman, offered her a chair. Once she was comfortably seated, he gently kissed her hand over her white gloves and took the seat across from her. Ana Parroti had never experienced such courtesy. She flashed a small smile and quickly launched into conversation, speaking rapidly as if presenting a report to her superior and not pausing to take a breath.

As she continued to speak, a man in his fifties entered the restaurant. Towering like an old Albanian elm, he fixed his gaze directly on the table where Xhelo and Ana were seated. Xhelo assumed it was a misunderstanding, but the man walked over and seated himself at their table. Ana interrupted her conversation, laughed at the man, and turned to Xhelo, saying:

"I apologize for the unexpected surprise! This is my boss, Mitch Miller," Ana said, introducing the tall man, who sported a mask with the American flag and 'MAGA' written on it, and seated himself across from Xhelo, creating a different dynamic for their anticipated conversation.

"Nice to meet you," Mitch said, extending a fist bump in compliance with epidemic guidelines.

Xhelo Lakrori found himself taken aback by this unforeseen turn of events. It seemed that Mitch, the father of Ana Parroti's unborn child, considered himself the one who had been invited to the meeting by Xhelo, rather than the other way around. Xhelo had envisioned a different course for their discussion, but Mitch's presence lent a new dimension to their conversation.

"Ana has spoken highly of you," Xhelo began, though his words caught in his throat. He had never encountered such a reversal of plans, and he had to adapt quickly to this unexpected situation. Mitch Miller seemed to grasp Xhelo's disorientation and promptly joined the conversation. He expressed his interest in meeting a professional veterinarian like Xhelo, motivated by Ana's enthusiastic description of her initial visit to his clinic. Mitch wished to understand more about Xhelo, the stranger, among other things. He then shared glimpses of his own life, businesses, and family, all while Xhelo cast sidelong glances at both Mitch and Ana, who stood between them. It was indeed an unusual meeting that brought together two disparate worlds.

Mitch Miller introduced himself as one of the wealthiest individuals in Chicago, with his business ventures rooted in the stock market and real estate investments. He briefly outlined his life, displaying a distinct curiosity about Xhelo's background. His speech was concise, and he seemed to be probing for the reason behind Ana's decision to arrange their meeting and what their shared interest might be. Apart from the fact that neither of them had children at the moment, drawing a minor parallel, there seemed to be little else linking them. Mitch was born in America; Xhelo in Devoll. Mitch was affluent, while Xhelo, despite possessing some wealth, could not compare. Xhelo was not a father, but Mitch Miller was expecting to become one soon, as he and Ana were anticipating the arrival of a childbearing their DNA. Under normal circumstances, it would have made more sense for him to remain indifferent but appreciative of the meeting. Nevertheless, Mitch conveyed that, based on Ana's description of the veterinarian, they were eager to meet him. To this, Xhelo modestly responded:

"I am like one of the millions who see this place as the final stop of life and hope. It hasn't been easy, but we are content with our accomplishments."

"You are just beginning your journey toward success and wealth, Dr. Lakrori. I would be pleased to assist you further," Mitch said, handing Xhelo a business card printed on a gold plate with embossed letters, reading "Golden Investments Group Inc., Mitch Miller, President and Founder."

Unfortunately, they couldn't share a meal together. An unexpected phone call forced Mitch Miller to leave, and he departed with Ana by his side. It was clear that the couple was careful to ensure Ana was always in their presence, either with them or protected by the yellow snake that encircled her pregnant belly, serving as a protective shield for their anticipated heir. It was the fear of a childless couple, a fear that Xhelo understood better than most.

It was the most peculiar meeting Xhelo Lakrori had experienced during his time in Chicago. Some unspoken factor played a role in the meeting and abrupt departure, leaving him with a sense of unease and a desire to confide in Shano and seek her advice. "A woman must be heard. She is the opposition that sustains a man in power until death," he reflected, pressing the button to locate his car's parking spot as quickly as possible.

Chapter Ten

Family dynamics in America can be compared to the enticing leaves near the Adriatic Sea at dusk. The gentle breeze arrives like a tender caress, both tantalizing and rejuvenating, reminding you of the day's hustle and bustle. It offers a momentary sense of revitalization, as if something bright might endure, but it often proves to be fleeting. This feeling had occurred to him several times with American friendships. They often begin with great enthusiasm and passion, only to fade rapidly over time. This was the case with his friendship with the Miller couple, which had been initiated by Ana. Despite the pandemic, they had met as couples several times, always with Ana in the middle, an irreplaceable presence.

Shano initially welcomed this type of friendship with interest, though the sight of the expectant woman, who changed shape every time they met, internally pained her. She viewed this relationship as a seasonal variation and kept her feelings in check. Shano was cordial and kind, occasionally engaging in discussions about the baby. "The day is approaching," she would gently say to Ana, directing her attention to Mrs. Miller, who possessed an aristocratic air. Shano held some resentment for not having naturally conceived but felt content to have outsourced her pain and worries to beautiful Ana. She observed every reaction and behavior keenly. To her, the affluent were no longer as distant as she had perceived them in the novels of her youth; they were normal people who simply possessed greater financial power than the majority around them.

She admired a journalist who, while discussing the American economic boom on a television show, stated that any one of us could walk alongside a millionaire every day or stroll next to them in a park or meadow without knowing it. Millionaires were growing in numbers daily and were just like us—simply people. This description resonated with Shano, who understood that all friendships in America often began swiftly and faded just as quickly. Given that both couples had somewhat similar stories, she always sought to find something useful in their dressing style, conversations, and life perspectives. They were indeed very wealthy, owning multiple houses and villas, including a luxurious palace and a three-bedroom, three-bathroom apartment in a high-rise building developed by Trump's company, located in the heart of Chicago where property prices were astronomical. Mitch was known for his shrewdness and reputation as a formidable player in the American stock market. He offered various ideas to Xhelo, but Xhelo brushed them aside without making any promises.

One day, while they were aboard a luxurious yacht in the heart of Lake Michigan in Chicago, and Shano and Ana were discussing the upcoming baby shower with Mrs. Miller, Mitch began to talk about the power of the dollar and the influence that came with it. Essentially, he asserted that America was driven solely by profit and the dollar, and everything else—whether ideals, principles, or even the constitution—were all imbued with the sense of profit, control, and the glorification of individual freedom.

"It doesn't quite appear that way to me," Xhelo responded. "In my opinion, America has a different kind of idealism, somewhat distinct from the pretentious European humanism, where hypocrisy often taints every conversation or promise. American idealism feels more genuine, youthful, and sincere. In short, here, the allure of money isn't hidden but is cloaked in an inspiring and motivating veil. I hope I've expressed myself clearly."

Mitch listened attentively, knowing that the perspectives of immigrants toward American reality often carried a unique scent, one that many who were born and raised within the system found difficult to discern and integrate into successfully. He relished challenging newcomers with thought-provoking questions and surprises. Looking Xhelo straight in the eye, he posed an unexpected query:

"Would you have voted for a candidate in Albania who expressed themselves as Donald Trump did in 2016 when he announced his candidacy? In my opinion, most Americans would still vote for me, even if I happened to shoot someone on 5th Avenue in New York..."

Xhelo was caught off guard by the question. It was quite surprising and reminded him of his friend, Muharrem Kodra from Pogradec, who had come to America after spending several years in political prison in Albania as a supporter of King Zog and the

Albanian monarchy. To Muharrem, that monarchy had been the only government that had made a significant impact on the impoverished society of early 20th-century Albania. Muharrem eagerly awaited the day he would be sworn in as an American citizen. However, during the preliminary exam, the immigration officer had asked him a pointed question: "If America attacks Albania and you have to fight, on which side of the war would you be?"

Muharrem Kodra came from a long line of patriots. His grandfather had been imprisoned for supporting the Albanian flag, and his family had been stigmatized by the communist regime as Zogists and enemies of the party and the people. In his view, the enemy had always been his Balkan neighbors, never America. How should he answer? The immigration officer was waiting for a response, staring at him with unsettling intensity. But the immigrant, who was eager to become an American citizen, knew how to navigate this moment. He responded, "America does not attack friends, for it is the nation of human friendship. If this were to happen, I would be a hero of peace, not war." This response had earned Muharrem Kodra the right to become an American citizen—an example of how love for what stimulates the mind and imagination can triumph overall.

Mitch's question seemed disqualifying, much like the one in the immigration office. At that moment, Xhelo didn't know how to respond. However, he recalled the Albanian resistance, their unwavering faith, and the resolute determination not to change or betray their principles, even in the face of adversity. So, he replied sincerely:

"He would have lost in Albania!"

"Exactly, Xhelo," Mitch responded, leaning in with an air of shared understanding, "he would have not only lost in Albania but also in Greece, considered the birthplace of democratic thought, and even in France and Germany. However, he won in America. Do you know why? Because he understood the power of the dollar he possessed and unsettled everyone with what he publicly stated. Do you understand what I mean? Here, the power of the dollar can elevate you to the skies. Donald Trump is the only president who served in the White House with a two-dollar salary. He never accepted a check from the government..."

Xhelo was hearing this from someone who was born and raised in

America. As Mitch had mentioned, he had inherited a symbolic amount from his parents, but most of his wealth was self-made. He had a brother, with whom he hadn't spoken in ten years due to a dispute where the brother had legally manipulated their father's will, taking almost 80% of the estate. This experience with his only brother had encouraged Mitch to be aggressive in the profit market. He had also experienced losses, much like Trump had with his casinos on the Atlantic City, but he had managed to bounce back. Resurrection in business, especially in America, was the greatest lesson a person could learn, according to Mitch.

For Xhelo, the insatiability for wealth and financial power was hard to understand. Not long ago, there was news on TV about a Democratic congressman from Louisiana who was investigated for corruption. During the legal raid, conducted with court approval, they had found $250,000 hidden in the freezer compartment of the refrigerator. It was the kind of news that made you both laugh and cry. He mentioned this to Mitch, who listened with interest. Xhelo had a unique way of storytelling, gazing directly into the eyes of his listener. The impact of his story was not solely through his words but also through the emotions conveyed in his eyes.

"That congressman was a Democrat, not a Republican. Did you know that?" Mitch asked.

"Indeed, I do. It's shocking because human insatiability for money knows no party or ideology. That's why I plan to vote for Trump this time," Xhelo replied.

"Good for you. We need him for another four years; then let the liberals can come to the White House," Mitch said.

As they ascended the stairs of the pier, adjusting their masks, their conversation continued. At one point, Mitch leaned in and asked:

"But in socialism, was there corruption or sexual abuse in Albania? I've heard all kinds of stories, but I'm interested in hearing your perspective, Dr. Lakrori."

Xhelo felt invigorated by this question. Although he had no nostalgia for the past and certainly not for Enver Hoxha, he believed that the truth must be told—without exaggeration, without blindness born from hatred, but simply the truth. During his time in America, he had interacted with various people from different strata of society, and he was struck by the fact that those who had suffered in the prisons of the communist system presented a credible and true narrative. In contrast, others who had not spent a day in prison but had worked in state or party offices appeared confused. They sought to secure a place in post-communist society not through merit, but through insults, lies, and occasionally hysterical propaganda.

According to Xhelo, the greatest sin of the years ruled by the Labor Party was the distortion of the truth about the kingdom and the pre-kingdom era. The regime not only concealed the truth but also falsified it, casting darkness to create a false light of glory by denying reality. This was evident in the stories of his uncle, who had served as a gendarme for ten years during King Zog's reign. His uncle recounted intriguing facts that were nowhere to be found in the history books of the time. Calmly and factually, his uncle explained the attempts to build a state and justice system in the impoverished and largely illiterate Albanian society. With a certain pride, he said, "The gendarme at that time was like a little king of the district where he served. Besides, that passport of Zog's era was one of the most coveted in the whole world, opening doors for Albanians everywhere." These truths had been suppressed to such an extent that even in the National Historical Museum, the regime's finest creation, the void and denial were clearly visible, erasing years and decades of history.

"Socialism had corruption; we called it bribery. But to tell the truth, in most cases, it was laughable when compared to what we see today," Xhelo began. "For instance, if someone held power in an office, the most popular form of bribery was lunch and dinner in the few luxury restaurants of that time or the gift of a bottle of rakia or some wine if you were invited to the boss's house. If such corruption were exposed, the state, controlled from above, had a terrifying striking power."

Mitch listened with curiosity; his eyes fixed on Xhelo. Immigrant stories often carried a unique flavor and a touch of profound sensitivity. They swept across the land like ocean waves, like whirlwinds of spirit and hope, and in this vast continent of America, they found fertile soil to take root. Mitch knew that many Americans, including himself, often took their good fortune and circumstances for granted, to the point where they struggled to find true inspiration. For them, the guiding light and motivation were often embodied by the almighty dollar, a magical elixir for all things beautiful. Xhelo's voice was sincere, carrying with it the weight of history and experience. He continued to share his narrative:

"I'd like to share an incident involving the brother of a communist named Todo Manço, who posthumously received the title of a hero after his death. Todo's brother, thanks to his commendable biography, assumed a directorial position within an enterprise. He had a distinct affinity for money, earning people like him the nickname 'money-lovers.' During that time, our society placed a strong emphasis on ideals over wealth. It was so ingrained that instead of swearing by God or something valuable, people would pledge 'For the ideal of the party...' It might sound amusing, but it's true. There was an active campaign against the worship of money. The irony, however, lay in the fact that the party's ideology, which dictated every aspect of the country's life, was itself treated with a sort of reverence. But this director, a 'money-lover,' cared little for the ideal. He pledged 'for the ideal' daily, yet by evening, he meticulously counted every bit of money that found its way to his house, exposing a blatant form of corruption during that era. Once the facts were gathered and verified, a thorough search was conducted in his residence. There, they uncovered several hundred thousand banknotes discreetly tucked within books bearing the name of the country's leader, Enver Hoxha. He had hidden 500-albanian banknotes within the pages of these leader's works. Personally, I would never have thought of hiding money in the pages of such a book, had I had the opportunity. In essence, socialism fostered an unappealing form of equality. However, given our lack of knowledge and ability, we yearned for a life beyond the system imposed from above, even though it was considered heretical to entertain such thoughts. That was socialism," Xhelo recounted.

Whenever Xhelo had the chance to speak about the past, he took great care to relay the truths he had either experienced himself or heard from reliable sources. He wasn't inclined to blindly follow everything published in the free press or stated on television, as it often included fabrications and scandalous lies. Even those imprisoned for crimes such as murder, theft, abuse, or sexual offenses claimed they were persecuted by the dictatorship because they supposedly fought for Western democracy. Their numbers had grown so much that they were overshadowing the genuine heroism of those who had truly opposed the system, ending up in political prisons.

"Regarding how that government treated sexual crimes, Mitch,"

Xhelo continued with a light chuckle, "Sexual activity was strictly prohibited in high school, and engaging in it would lead to expulsion. Furthermore, if you were caught having sexual relations with a girl, you were obligated to marry her, regardless of whether you loved her or not. Often, the village or neighborhood would arrange the marriage. It was far from the kind of freedom America allows."

Mitch expressed disbelief, saying, "Really?!"

Xhelo nodded and replied, "Yes, that was the society, and those were the laws. Sex was considered taboo and a form of degeneracy."

Mitch then asked, "I'd like to know more about the officials and high-ranking leaders you mentioned."

"In those circles, the situation was quite different. The general population was kept in the dark, tightly controlled by state security, and any confirmed cases of sexual misconduct, if they happened to reach the party offices, were met with severe and public punishments. However, beneath the surface, much was transpiring," Xhelo recounted. He went on to share a story from 40 years ago about a cleaner who worked in the Block. She had confided in him that a member of the political bureau had sexually assaulted her, but she was too afraid to file a complaint. She believed that she would be accused of trying to tarnish the image of the leaders, who were presented to the people as flawless, despite their many indiscretions.

Mitch Miller had not often heard such candid stories from the communist era, and he found them intriguing. While he hadn't invested in Eastern European countries, he had visited many of them and heard numerous stories like Xhelo's, each with its own unique nuances. Mitch knew that immigrants were among the most potent drivers of American society, arriving with boundless energy, unwavering determination, and a readiness to face the challenges of America head-on.

"Xhelo, your candid stories are truly captivating. It's as if your soul is speaking to me," Mitch said, prompting them to delve into a conversation about the pursuit of wealth. "It's not just America, a country notorious for its obsession with money, but it's human nature itself that's drawn to money and its power. You know, in ancient Egypt and early civilizations, the hunger for gold and precious stones were deeply ingrained in human nature. How many wars have been fought over these treasures? Countless. The truth is that in America, this thirst finds fertile ground to flourish, almost to infinity, as they say, 'the more you have, the more you want.' Have you experienced this, Xhelo?"

Xhelo was momentarily taken aback, reminiscing about the past. The millionaire was speaking the truth; his homeland had witnessed an unprecedented greed for money and fame in the 30 years since the fall of communism. While America was renowned on the global stage as the land of boundless opportunities for those hungry for wealth, Albania saw politicians who never seemed satisfied with their plundering and stealing. While in America, the sources of wealth were traceable, in Albania; corrupt politicians seemed to collectively shout in the Parliament, "Catch the thief..."

"I have experienced it, but I also know how to find contentment with little," Xhelo replied. "Because when you have all that, you need, and nothing is lacking, why be insatiable?" he pondered.

"Because Xhelo, the dollar has a way of whetting your appetite, especially when you see it multiplying, growing like fish in a pond or at the depths of the ocean. Let me ask you, my friend, do you want to become a millionaire?" Mitch suddenly inquired.

"I already consider myself one, and honestly, it's only America that provided me with this opportunity," Xhelo Lakrori modestly replied.

"Perfect!" Mitch eagerly jumped into the conversation, briefly removing his mask, and creating some distance from Xhelo. "I can teach you how to become a multimillionaire, and perhaps even a billionaire..."

"How? Why? I have enough," Xhelo Lakrori promptly responded.

"Some opportunities, Xhelo, are quite straightforward," Mitch Miller eagerly continued. "For instance, you own a clinic, along with other financial assets. You mentioned that you've paid off the clinic's market value. That's fantastic. You're positioned for a leap toward even greater wealth. You can go to the bank and request a loan using the clinic as collateral. The bank trusts you. Let's say you secure half a million or a million dollars. The bank becomes a co-owner of the property; you then invest that money elsewhere and sow the seeds of dollars... Or, if you need guidance, I can advise you on where to invest, or if you trust me for a year, this investment could double... Voila, Xhelo, there's more money, and you become even wealthier."

Listening to the millionaire, Xhelo felt like he was being lured into a financial snare. Now he understood why Mitch was so interested in their company; it seemed that one of his objectives was seduction with money, and seduction is the first step toward mistakes. He remembered the era of the pyramid schemes in Albania when people were obsessed with making massive amounts of money without working. He would never forget those peculiar scenes in Devoll, Korçë, and Pogradec, where the representatives of the pyramid schemes collected money in bags, often without even counting it, but weighing it by hand. "How much do you have? 100,000 drachmas? Ok," they'd jot it down in the notebook. "Next..." Or in Vlora, where if you had coffee with a local, they didn't serve Fernet or cognac; instead, whiskey and Campari were poured like water. People lost their minds until money drove everyone to madness.

Could it be that Mitch, the millionaire, was proposing a similar game? A few years earlier, he had heard about a prominent business owner in Minneapolis who also owned an airline company, Sun Country Airlines, but had constructed a secretive pyramid scheme right in the heart of the local metropolis. Tom Peters' fate ended in life imprisonment as a fraudster and counterfeiter. Another entrepreneur who had opened several car dealerships, a man named Deni Heker whose name frequently appeared in the press and on screens, had met the same fate. He would never entrust his money to someone else. Not ever. Of course, this was his decision, but he couldn't divulge that to his wealthy friend who had invited him for a leisurely cruise. In the meantime, he began to explain to the American how pyramid schemes had nearly buried Albania entirely.

"Mitch, you have some fantastic thoughts and ideas. I will ponder over this, but don't forget, my country was nearly buried by pyramid schemes. This should be taken into account."

"Don't worry, Xhelo, I just proposed an idea. You're intelligent yourself. I'll only intervene if you need me."

"Of course, I'll turn to you! Cheers!" Xhelo responded, and it seemed as if he could barely wait for that prolonged autumn walk along the vast Lake Michigan to conclude, where the brilliantly illuminated skyscrapers appeared to have plunged into its depths, hunting for the big fish.

Indeed, it was a beautiful evening, as autumn arrived with leaves that changed color and fell in increasing numbers with each passing day.

Chapter Eleven

He remained focused on the helm, while Shano recounted everything that had transpired as she found herself caught between the two mothers engrossed in conversation. Gina was the one who did most of the talking, deliberating, and making decisions. Ana and Shano were attentive listeners. Occasionally, Shano would share her thoughts, but often, Gina, with her gentle yet assertive tone, would guide the conversation, saying, "It's quite an interesting idea, but I believe it's better this way..." It was a matter primarily managed by women, and their attention was centered on the soon-to-arrive baby.

In Albanian tradition, organizing a pre-birth ceremony for an anticipated baby was unheard of and considered inappropriate. However, Americans, advanced in many ways, had a different approach. A baby shower was not just a sentimental gathering; it also served as a marketing event for the American childcare industry. Women would come together, bring gifts for the expected baby, and discuss various models, products, brands, innovations, and parenting experiences. It was akin to a preparatory course for both the mother and the yet-to-be-born baby, a tradition that was quite foreign to Shano.

Shano had avoided such gatherings on several occasions, primarily because she felt uncomfortable and disheartened in these situations. Why should she participate in such events when she hadn't been able to experience the pinnacle of womanhood herself? Of course, she couldn't outright decline the invitations, so she engaged in these consultations as a way to find reasons to avoid the upcoming party that would wound her soul.

"In America, they shower the baby with money," she confided in Xhelo. "But at this stage of life, I prefer to save those dollars for myself."

"Of course," Xhelo agreed, his grip on the helm tightening. He had no desire to discuss the conversation he had with Mitch. Although their conversation had been amicable, the proposition that

"Mitch knows where to invest" didn't sit well with him. He had already learned valuable lessons about fiscal responsibility from the pyramid schemes in Albania, which culminated in the turmoil and chaos of 1997.

Xhelo attributed the naivety of Albanians entrusting their money to others to the former system. "Money is safest in your pocket," his father had often reminded him. His father, an astute manager, had managed to send all three of his sons to college without them experiencing any financial hardships. This was partially because their father was an exceptional gardener who not only provided for the family but also sold various products, particularly apples and pears, directly to the collection company. He was the only one in the village that the state car would visit to purchase his apples.

Xhelo marveled at the financial stability of the past. There was a sort of serene yet astonishing security because there was no need for constant worry. Prices remained constant, wages were consistent, and employment was steady—a state of equilibrium that was accepted by everyone.

"It wasn't that bad," Xhelo murmured. "People didn't have these stresses, but perhaps stress makes you stronger..." The uniformity of that era struck him as its greatest drawback. "Why did we all have to be so equal, my dear? Why was the grandest dream a standard sofa and a standard mural? It felt like the system was trying to impose uniformity upon us all in the most forceful and deceitful way. It's incredible how ignorant we must have been, and how the state became a wicked stepmother to us. I can hardly believe it, even though I lived through those times..."

The past was gone, and it couldn't be blamed for the ignorance that many Albanians still clung to today. Xhelo often felt a sense of clarity and revitalization when reminiscing about that era. He had powerful reference points, like beautiful sparks, which led him to appreciate the present and American capitalism even more. As he closely followed the protests happening all over America—rebellions against injustice, inequality, exploitation, calls to defund the police, demands for an end to police violence, and calls for racial equality—he understood that the strength of American society lay in the freedom to protest and express one's opinions openly. He joined in voicing many of these concerns, but there was one point he disagreed with: the characterization of America as inherently racist.

To him, it was a more complex issue that couldn't be simplified into such an over-generalization.

"Those who make these accusations need to live six months under socialism to fully grasp what America and American opportunity mean," Xhelo Lakrori mused.

"But did you enjoy your time with Mitch, dear?" Shano asked.

Xhelo Lakrori was unsure where to begin. He admired Mitch's success, but he couldn't comprehend why the man was still so obsessed with money and resources. He briefly mentioned to Shano that Mitch was chasing after dollars wherever they could be found and that he had suspicions about the legitimacy of Mitch's wealth. Shano was taken aback by what she heard. She had witnessed the opulence, the luxurious lifestyle, the expensive art, and the jewelry—everything seemed almost regal. Xhelo didn't dispute her observations; he simply stated that he had doubts but lacked concrete evidence to refute what Shano described. They were among the wealthiest individuals Xhelo and Shano had encountered during their years in America. Their entry into the Lakroris' friendly circle had been entirely coincidental, initiated by a pet snake that required a veterinarian's attention.

Shano disagreed and emphasized that this was a kind of friendship that shouldn't be dismissed. Xhelo maintained that while the friendship was indeed valuable, it didn't mean they shouldn't remain cautious. For him, social gatherings were environments where opportunities came and went. From his life in America, he had learned that these events were merely forms of entertainment: modern dinners and lunches, strolls by lakes and oceans, deep-sea fishing trips all the way up to Alaska. But ultimately, any American friendship remained transient; you couldn't label anyone a "true friend." He sank into deep thought.

"Xhelo, you missed the exit for the house again!" Shano reminded him as he raced along the highway.

As if snapped out of a trance, he loathed this kind of distraction while driving but simultaneously knew that his driving instincts weren't affected by the thoughts and hypotheses swirling in his head, which seemed both overflowing and empty. He apologized and noted that he was driving too fast. Letting up on the accelerator, he made sure the car dropped to the permissible speed, then playfully asked Shano:

"Do you think, my dear, that we Albanians can be a bit over the top with our friendships? We alone put the friend first, surrender our entire homes to the friend, proclaim 'long live the friend,' even when we don't yet know them well. Only in Albanian do we lament that the darkest day was when 'the friend came, and I had nothing to give,' even while the children have been starving for days or subsisting on bread with sugar, cornbread with vinegar and oil. Aren't we slightly foolish, dear, in this regard as a people?"

Shano glanced at Xhelo, taken aback by the direction of the conversation he wanted to pursue. She was a superb cook, her hands skilled in preparing an array of special dishes, modern plates, and Mediterranean meals. She felt thrilled when guests gathered around her contemporary kitchen, where the dishes were elegantly arranged, and questioned each one in awe. Exhausted from a long day of cooking, she would explain the technical details about the type of meat used, the spices incorporated, and more. Watching them taste her creations and lick their fingers, she felt a sense of pride in the delicious meals she'd prepared. To her, friends were truly special, and she went to great lengths to surprise them with dishes they might not have encountered before. In short, these receptions and dinners were a stroll among friends, cultures, and flavors, where Shano, with her culinary prowess, became a star in her own world. This alone sufficed to make her happy. Among that circle of friends, she laughed, explained, and watched faces light up from the flavors she'd crafted. It was a dominant moment that allowed her to forget any kind of sorrow or despair. Friends were like a bouquet of flowers, bringing a different world and a refreshing air into their large, lifeless home. This truth sometimes hung like a gray curtain before her eyes, occasionally creating a void within her that she knew how to fill only with her optimistic fantasy.

"Xhelo, for all the receptions and dinners, I've prepared the menu you like, and you've always approved it," Shano responded.

"You've misunderstood me, dear. I'm not talking about you and me; it's a philosophical discussion. Why do Albanians overvalue friendships? Why do we corner our friends and even compel them to stay? We raise our glasses and demand they drink to the bottom. We often exhibit a kind of dictatorship with our generosity, don't you think?"

Shano was bemused by her conversation with Xhelo. He had shifted from politics—which she detested—to hospitality, which she considered a virtue of their nation. She passionately orchestrated Albanian-style feasts in her modern American kitchen, where she felt most at ease. She didn't entirely understand Xhelo's point but had observed many differences in American culture. Here, a friend was respected, yet given the freedom to choose and enjoy personal preferences. It was only in America that she noticed a friend could nonchalantly open the refrigerator and grab their preferred drink, beer or wine, or a piece of cheese. Despite the offered generosity, the host remained in control, guiding guests to the bathroom or deciding whether to offer a house tour. Only an Albanian would proclaim, "my house is your house," or "the house belongs to the guest and the Lord," welcoming everyone in. This was an exaggeration, and maybe Xhelo was correct.

He nearly leapt off the steering wheel, exhilarated to have finally engaged Shano in a discussion he relished. They reminisced about the beautiful times they had spent with friends, acquaintances, and colleagues who had enriched their lives. However, the boundaries were clear: the host remained the authoritative figure who laid down the rules of the house. No guest, not even someone as prominent as President Trump, could undermine the host's authority.

"I appreciate your perspective, Shano. You're a gem, but you prefer silence. Generally speaking, we Balkan people want to peddle our generosity and hospitality as something unique. I've noticed this among Serbs, Greeks, Bulgarians, Macedonians, Montenegrins, Turks. Do you remember when we were in Afghanistan, near the border with China? The hospitality in that village, with its neatly arranged tables—did it remind you of Albanian hospitality? Is hospitality solely the spiritual wealth of the poor, or is it something else?"

Xhelo seemed to have an endless appetite for discussing the subject, weaving allusions, comparisons, and deductions into his argument. This passion was born from having grown up where scarcity met hospitality. In his childhood home, they weren't impoverished, but he observed that the arrival of a guest—depending on the guest's importance—often led to the slaughtering of a chicken or a lamb. The visit would turn into a celebration featuring the finest dishes. Meanwhile, the children, hidden either behind a door or in another room, anxiously awaited the conclusion of the meal, knowing that whatever remained on the plates would be a windfall for them. It was a vivid snapshot of his past.

Taking an exit to circle back east towards their home, Xhelo leaned over the steering wheel, careful to mind his speed. He pondered the misfortune of the Albanian people, descendants of the ancient Illyrian and Pelasgian tribes. Some recent researchers even argued that these tribes' alphabet predated that of the Romans, who had plagiarized it. The Albanians had been humbled and confined to a small piece of land. Yet even within that geographical scar on the Adriatic coast, the entire nation, like a massive boulder, had their eyes fixed on their guests, interested in their opinions about life and politics in Albania.

"We suffer from guest syndrome," Xhelo whispered. "We forget our popular saying, 'The owner knows where his roof leaks.' If we continue like this, we'll never build a nation—never. A nation is a complex of laws and obligations required to combat evil. But if the state isn't recognized as a necessary force against its own oppressed people, we'll never form a nation. We'll keep floundering until we all drown in the Adriatic, like those unfortunate souls in the Otranto Channel."

The car eased into their large garage and slowed down smoothly. Shano, relieved, practically sprinted out of the car and exclaimed from the depths of her heart, "Oh, there's no place like home."

After an intense week, Dr. Xhelo Lakrori was taken aback the following day by a text message from veterinarian Klara Kavajska as he was opening the clinic: "Dr. Lakrori, I have been diagnosed with Covid-19. I need to stay home and isolate. I apologize if this affects your business and staff. Regards, Klara."

The news was shocking. He immediately called Klara to inquire about her health. Concurrently, he contacted Stiv Bordinan, the clinic manager, and instructed him to arrange for a professional disinfection of the entire clinic as a preliminary precaution. In an email to all staff, he mandated that everyone stay home and avoid coming to the clinic until further notice. He then reached out to his secretary, directing her to cancel all appointments for the day and reschedule them indefinitely. This was a sort of business calamity he wouldn't wish on even his competitors.

He called Shano to explain the situation, and she emphasized that the health of the staff and Xhelo himself was paramount. "My dear, we have weathered fiercer storms. Take care of yourself," she texted him, uncharacteristically. The silence in the clinic and the anticipation of its emptiness over the next few days filled him with anxiety. He placed a notice at the entrance: *"The clinic is not providing services today and until further notice. We apologize for any inconvenience."*

Xhelo secluded himself in his office, succumbing to a sense of emptiness. As he glanced out the window, he noticed the sparse traffic, a scene reminiscent of those he'd seen in Hollywood movies, scenarios that had been predicted years, even decades, earlier. Yet, when these scenes had unfolded from the comfort of plush armchairs in spacious American homes or cozy cinema halls—with viewers munching on aromatic popcorn or sipping a glass of beer or wine—people would dismissively say, "Movie stuff. Hollywood fantasy."

When the pandemic hit, Xhelo contacted the public health department, who advised him to employ a certified company for cleaning and disinfection to combat the virus and ensure business continuity. His establishment would need to remain closed for at least 48 hours. The pandemic had driven his business to new heights of service and profit. Confined to their homes and free from the oppressive presence of bosses, many Americans had discovered a newfound fondness for the companionship of small animals, primarily dogs and cats. Xhelo Lakrori found himself so swamped with work that he frequently had to bring in external veterinarians to help meet the demands of the numerous clients.

As the world grappled with the pandemic, businesses like Xhelo's weren't just busier than usual—their financial records reached unprecedented numbers. With financial liquidity that surpassed all predictions, he not only paid all his taxes in advance but also settled many of his financial obligations to banks. He had even dabbled in the Bitcoin market, which he viewed as an untapped gold mine. A mere $5,000 investment in that market a few years earlier had now swelled into an impressively considerable sum.

Shano, his wife, remained blissfully unaware of his financial maneuvers. She had blind faith in Xhelo and, since their marriage, had merely signed numerous documents without reading or verifying them. She was her husband's loyal satellite and was fortunate not to have crossed paths with a swindler or a gambler, as either would have ruined her. She never lacked for anything and could buy any clothing or jewelry she desired.

Surveying his financial growth during President Trump's tenure, Xhelo was convinced that another four years of a Trump presidency would usher in prosperity for all Americans. He even foresaw a possible federal surplus, despite being aware that the national debt had peaked. While Xhelo wasn't fond of Trump's unprecedented trade war against China, he knew that nobody cared about the opinion of a veterinarian like him. In his own personal sphere, both his prosperity and potential downfall resided, and he was more careful about it than anything else. In such contexts, he thought less about the course of political campaigns and more about exploring alternative avenues of investment and profit. In fact, the suggestions from millionaire Mitch Miller during a yacht ride on Lake Michigan had sparked the idea of opening a second clinic, in Lombard, northwest of Chicago.

"Valter Dima could be another treasure that might lead us to greater profits," Xhelo contemplated. He had known since their days in Devoll that Valter Dima was an exceptional professional in all aspects of veterinary work; they had worked together in the same agricultural cooperative. Considering these prospects seemed to invigorate him. Just as he was about to call Valter Dima, he realized incoming call from Mitch Miller, with whom he'd walked along Lake Michigan just a week earlier. He took the opportunity to express his gratitude to Mitch once again for the enjoyable and entertaining time they'd had.

"Don't mention it, my friend. I just called to say hello, and if you're up for it, we can take a ride in my private plane after lunch and head to Madison in the neighboring state, or St. Louis. The choice is yours. Do you have time? It's just for fun. Gina and Ana have their routine gynecologist visit, and I've taken the day off," Mitch's voice came through the phone. Xhelo was caught off guard. He wasn't fond of impromptu plans, but he also recognized that such opportunities didn't come along often. After confirming that all arrangements for the clinic's disinfection were in place, he felt an impulse to accept the invitation. He quickly texted Shano, grabbed his coat, and headed to the airfield where Mitch's plane awaited.

The aerial excursion over Chicago was breathtaking. Xhelo had never had the chance to fly so leisurely and so close to the city's skyscrapers. It felt like sailing at high altitude. Mitch seemed utterly at ease behind the plane's controls. The flight over half of Lake

Michigan and the bustling city below seemed to wipe away the morning's stress related to the Covid-19 situation at Xhelo's clinic. "One must occasionally leave stress behind," he mused, glancing at Mitch, who was also serving as an attentive pilot. Initially, he felt a slight unease, haunted by stories of small plane crashes. However, he quickly settled in, and his fear dissipated into the sparse clouds of the day.

The plane wasn't as lavish as Mitch's yacht, but it reaffirmed that Mitch wasn't an average American. Through their headphones, Mitch pointed out significant city landmarks and offered an aerial view of a large villa north of the city. He then suggested they head to St. Louis for lunch near the iconic arch on the banks of the Mississippi River. Xhelo, thoroughly enjoying the captivating altitude, nodded his agreement, letting the pilot take the lead. He trusted Mitch, who seemed to know exactly where he was going.

Having secured permission from the control tower, they flew southeast, gliding low over Springfield, the capital of their state, and over the historic residence of Lincoln—a figure Mitch often cited in his political discourse. The flight took an hour. They enjoyed lunch at an Italian restaurant by the Mississippi River before making their way back.

Mitch had little else to say, except to reiterate the perfect timing for investments.

"When most people are wondering who'll win, that's when we should invest. That's how the wealthy in this country operate, remember that," he stated during lunch. Xhelo wasn't greedy or fame hungry. He believed that fame was an illusion for those who yearned for it, as an individual's life unfolds regardless of fame and glory. Everyone experiences their own life, not the one others might boast about—those whom you've never met and who probably don't even know you exist. He knew that politicians and leaders worldwide go to sleep and wake up wondering, "What do people think of me?"—a preoccupation Xhelo considered the delusion of the deluded.

Upon their return, just as Xhelo was about to step into his Mercedes car, Mitch reiterated, "Investing in the Far East is the future of business and profit. China is on the verge of surprising everyone, so don't let your dollars sit idle in the bank. More millionaires are being created daily in China than anywhere else..."

He didn't explicitly state his intentions, but hinted that if Xhelo had any spare funds, they would be well-placed in Mitch's hands. However, this didn't sway Xhelo Lakrori's unwavering conviction. He responded with a gentle smile, expressing gratitude for the enjoyable day.

Suddenly, Mitch veered back from the road, gesturing for Xhelo to roll down the car window slightly. With an excited glint in his eyes, he said, "Xhelo, speaking of investments in China, I forgot to mention that I'm planning on selling this private airplane. If you're interested, I can offer you a special deal because I intend to sell it along with the hangar. Just let me know, my friend..." Mitch finished and awaited a reaction.

The proposition left Xhelo Lakrori stunned. Who would have imagined that one day, Xhelo, the small-town veterinarian who used to traverse the villages of Devoll with a medical bag containing a scalpel, two syringes, a trocar, and a few ampoules of adrenaline or caffeine, could suddenly be seen as a potential buyer in the airplane market? The very same Xhelo who had spent his childhood riding donkeys was now being offered an airplane in the heart of America! The tempting proposition cornered him. How could he respond to Mitch, a man who seemed to have everything and could even delegate the burden of pregnancy to a surrogate?

He recalled reading about the life of Steve Jobs, where a single paragraph encapsulated the quintessential American spirit. A shiver ran down his spine as he reflected on this excerpt: "On this continent, there's nothing one can't buy with dollars. Lack knowledge in economics? Hire an economist. Money lets you choose the best. Unsure about the intricacies of the internet? Employ and pay a specialist to handle it... Incapable of driving a car? Call a taxi or hire a driver... For every problem, there is a solution. However, when it comes to medical troubles that cause discomfort and pain, you cannot hire someone to go to the doctor for you... That is something only you can do..." Jobs, the man who changed humanity with his inventions, was unable to alter his own fate. Just like the Miller couple, who, unable to conceive naturally, had hired a surrogate to carry their child — the embodiment of American ingenuity.

The offer to purchase an airplane took Xhelo aback, nearly catapulting him into the very sky where such machines soared. He wondered why the millionaire would propose this to him. Why not advertise it on the internet, on Craigslist, or even on a large, colorful electronic billboard along the endless highways of Illinois, or beyond? Why had he chosen Xhelo specifically?

"Are you surprised by the offer, doctor?" Mitch's voice broke through Xhelo's reverie, returning him to the present moment.

"To be honest, yes. Why did you choose me? Why do you want to sell the airplane? It looks like new. Why? This surprises me, Mitch," Xhelo replied.

Mitch laughed. Glancing at the airplane that was roaring further down the runway with the swagger of the rich and the pride bestowed by the almighty dollar, he replied without hesitation,

"Because the more you have, the more you want. I've quoted this motto of the rich to you several times. When you have luxury, you crave super-luxury. When you have millions, you desire billions. Once you've seen the Moon, you aspire to see Mars... Haven't I told you that America runs on dollars and adventure? Why shouldn't I own an airplane with my name on it, just like Trump? What does he have that I don't?" he posed to Xhelo.

The doctor wasn't expecting such a question. He felt so cornered that he was tempted to start the car and escape from this ostentatious American conversation. Where else could one meet such an ambitious and self-absorbed American? This man aspired to own an airplane with his name on it? But who was he, beyond a man with a few more dollars and investments? He had never graced a television screen. Trump was a media star, a builder of skyscrapers bearing his name in New York, Chicago, Las Vegas, and countless other renowned cities. How could Mitch compare himself to President Trump? It was a moment when Xhelo felt the urge to confront Mitch's arrogant presumption.

"Trump is Trump, and he is our president. He has billions and serves in the White House voluntarily, for enjoyment, not for salary," Xhelo retorted.

"Perfect answer. But remember, Xhelo, those who have dream. I brought up the president merely as an example. I'm not jealous of him; I aspire to surpass him if I can. In America, we call it free competition. When you own a small private plane, you yearn for a bigger one, a supersonic one. When you're grounded, you desire the Moon. Do you understand this insatiability? That's human nature.

We humans are like volcanoes, Xhelo. We erupt and never extinguish. And forgive me, but this continent, as you call it too, Xhelo, nurtures such dreams that might seem fantastical anywhere else. If America didn't exist, people would be huddled together in small apartments or tents across Europe, awestruck by the pyramids of Egypt, the Great Wall of China, or the minarets of Istanbul. But God gifted humanity with America, a land without borders or coastlines, and it drove everyone mad. They came here, never returning to the antiquated Europe, Egypt, or China. Now, we have more Asian and Indian millionaires than native Americans. Not just that; in the next ten years, people will no longer aspire to vacation and travel around the globe as they do now, posting photos on Facebook. Instead, they'll take holidays on the Moon or in distant space hotels, which will be humanity's future business. You and I may have passed away by then, but true human vacations will take place on Mars. And sooner or later, there will be no more cemeteries on Earth, only the last mysteries of pain and loss."

Mitch Miller spoke with fervor, a near ecstasy, that Xhelo had never observed in him before—neither on the expanse of Lake Michigan nor in the heights of the sky above Chicago. Xhelo was witnessing a different Mitch, one teeming with bright fantasies, a peculiar transformation that he couldn't quite fathom. Engrossed in this monologue, he listened as Mitch unveiled his dreams, his face a mask of astonishment.

Mitch continued,

"In the future, people won't want to be buried on Earth, where worms and cold dampness consume them. Instead, they will choose to become ashes, released into the sun. Cemeteries will become tourist destinations, like the Great Wall of China or the Pyramids of the Sahara Desert. Do you understand why I'm considering selling this plane, Dr. Lakrori? You will come to share my thinking, my ambitions, but by then, I may be gone. Xhelo, don't be disheartened! We live in America, my friend," Mitch concluded, his monologue the most stunning discourse Xhelo had ever encountered.

"Embrace the normality here, where routine is boredom," Xhelo murmured in response.

For the first time, he had heard a version of Mitch distinct from the charming companion of their recent flight, which had just concluded. It was like a pinch of absurdity in the millionaire's usually predictable demeanor, a surprise rivaling Ana Parrot's snake in the ivory box.

Xhelo found himself bewildered by Mitch's soaring philosophies and his unexpected proposition to purchase the airplane—a concept that Xhelo could scarcely entertain, even if he were to live for two more centuries. Could this have been the true purpose of their flight? Why would Mitch impart this to Xhelo? Could it be that Mitch saw the Albanian American as a potential business prospect? Similarly, when on the yacht, noticing Xhelo's marvel at the luxurious vessel, Mitch had offhandedly mentioned, "If you like it, I could sell it to you at a favorable price."

In fact, Xhelo remembered Mitch casually suggesting during a dinner at their home that he might consider selling his opulent condominium at Trump Tower in downtown Chicago. A towering edifice with ninety-two floors, 486 residential units, and 1,000 parking spaces, the address at 401 North Wabash was one of Chicago's prime investments. Living there, in a spacious condo rather than a small studio, was indeed a dream that Xhelo harbored. It would also fuel his pride in being a Trump supporter, and he might be the first Albanian American resident in a building bearing the illustrious "Trump" name.

With all these thoughts running through his mind, Xhelo pressed the car button, intending to drive to Shano as soon as possible and discuss everything with her. His wife was increasingly becoming his confessional, where he unburdened himself like a devout Catholic speaking to a priest. Though he confessed all, there remained a specific secret tucked away in his "little pocket," akin to old coins hidden away in Albania.

Chapter Twelve

Following the implementation of preventive measures in his clinic, Xhelo observed an increase in clientele. Some clients came with dogs on leashes, others with cats in cages, and still others brought in frogs, turtles, hamsters, and various other animals. Each arrived brimming with peculiar questions about their pets' lives. All visitors were required to adhere to the protective measures as advised by the Public Health Protection Center in Washington, D.C. A large sign had been placed at the clinic's entrance, bearing an unambiguous message in capital letters: "Masks are Mandatory." As the owner, Xhelo felt responsible for ensuring the health and safety of his staff.

In the societal stress caused by lockdowns, restricted flights, travel bans, and the eerie silence of once-bustling city centers—where empty chairs now outnumbered people—many turned to the comforting companionship of the animal world. Some attempted to decipher the thoughts behind their cats' mesmerizing gaze, pondering their pets' mental processes as they licked their lips after a hearty meal. The clinic's answering service was flooded with an array of bizarre inquiries. Some questions were genuinely intriguing, while others were absolute nonsense—something far from scarce in Western American society.

Xhelo couldn't resist sharing an amusing message he'd received about a dog's barking habits with Shano. "Dr. Lakrori! Every time President Trump appears on screen, my dog barks twice and watches the news with me. When the Democratic candidate appears, he barks only once. Can you help me understand this animal language, please? How should I interpret this? I'm extremely curious." Meanwhile, another client had left an equally fascinating message regarding her cat: "My cat uses her litter box every time the presidential campaign chronicle begins. I've filmed her fifty-five times doing this. As soon as the 'White House campaign' is mentioned, she promptly heads to her litter box. How is this possible, Dr. Lakrori? What do these little animals mean by this offensive behavior? I eagerly await your explanation..."

Shano was usually the first to hear these amusing anecdotes, often laughing heartily at their absurdity. The couple, both intellectuals and childless, had not only keenly observed social dynamics in America over the years but had also read various books about the enigmas that make America a highly sought-after place to live, despite its occasional savage humanity.

Over the years, they had befriended many individuals now residing in Canada. While their friends were content in their new homeland, they often nostalgically exclaimed, "Ah, America!" According to Xhelo's notes, nearly 99% of these individuals had initially intended to immigrate to America. However, due to restricted avenues like the visa lottery or "family reunification," they had ultimately chosen Canada. Despite being under the reign of the Queen of England, Canada had established a social alliance that balanced American capitalism with the whisper of "God bless you." Unlike in many American cities, Canadians took measures to prevent their citizens from living under bridges and on the streets. The couple often spent their nights engaged in heated debates over the two faces of this North American coin.

"Canada is not America, my dear," Xhelo would tell Shano. "There is a different social spirit there, akin to a grandfather who keeps his grandchildren close. Of course, this proximity allows for better control. In America, the state seeks to maintain a certain distance from the individual, granting them the freedom to take responsibility for themselves—provided they don't forget to pay taxes. Failing to do so brings the government knocking on your door. At least, that's my understanding. Thus, America houses more wealthy individuals than Canada, but also more homeless people," Xhelo would elaborate, relishing these discussions. Indeed, juxtaposing the two countries presented two distinct models of human societies: one offering boundless freedom, the other providing 'restricted economic sovereignty.' Intriguingly, many Canadians dreamt of America, while numerous American citizens gravitated towards Canada, viewing it as a haven during their twilight years.

Xhelo Lakrori was a spirited debater when it came to social and political matters. He embodied the idea of the 'new man' as conceived in socialism. He had experienced the profound torment of the mass exodus of Albanians in the 1990s—a spectacle that drew international media attention as crowds flooded embassies and seaborne vessels. Xhelo had witnessed firsthand this outpouring of people toward Greece. There wasn't a hillside in Devoll district, a valley in Gramoz Mount, or any part of Konispol where one couldn't spot underdressed young men with bags in their hands and weariness in their eyes, abandoning Albania as if it were cursed, their destination unknown. Many didn't survive the journey, succumbing to the harsh terrain and elements. This marked a significant upheaval for a society mired in desolation and despair. Xhelo never desired to depart in such a manner. He loathed the system that forced people to scramble for their daily bread like hunted animals, but he was powerless to voice his thoughts or halt the human exodus.

Now, as time had soothed those wounds and as the world had moved beyond socialism and communism, Xhelo lived amidst the American drama, where southern borders were continually besieged by immigrants from South America. There was no socialism or communism there, only poverty and hopelessness. People fled toward America, perceived as a paradise and salvation. "They are right," Xhelo would think, "but this isn't the way. Entry must follow rules, laws, and be based on merit. Patience is required, not this." These thoughts, along with the sight of caravans journeying toward America, made him shudder. He couldn't comprehend how the world could undergo such a reconstruction.

Xhelo bore no resentment toward these unfortunate individuals, having once been in their shoes: impoverished and confined within his own country. But he didn't flee. He could have migrated to Greece like thousands of others, but he chose not to. Nor did he venture to Italy. He was all too aware of the ruthlessness of Enver Hoxha's regime. Touted as a beacon of human equality and justice, it actually drained those most loyal to the ideals that Enver espoused at congresses and public meetings.

"Anyone who didn't think like Comrade Enver was an enemy of the people," Xhelo remembered, contemplating a past that he couldn't despise merely because of his personal discontent and disagreement. It was a piece of Albanian history: voiceless, powerless, devoid of opportunity, and, fortunately for him, bereft of a lasting legacy. The painful past orbited him like a stubborn meteor refusing to fall. Xhelo had been among those who believed the leader was truthful, that he was fighting for the common man, for

Albania, and for a brighter future. He was the last to comprehend that these were grand deceptions, perpetuated by the government, society, and everyone who blindly placed their trust in the leader as their sole hope and salvation. What a tremendous disappointment.

He understood that many had a multitude of reasons to despise Enver. Still, amid the significant Albanian upheavals, Xhelo saw no one who could convincingly persuade him that Enver was the bane that had, thankfully, passed. Instead, he saw the same individuals who had been Enver's staunchest loyalists—those who scrutinized every red book published under his name, those who had frequented Enver's home, sharing meals and drinks, rowing boats with Enver's sons through Voloreka, visiting Paris, London, and Bonn, filling volumes with his name. They were the same writers who composed poems, poetry, and novels about the leader. These were the diplomats who quoted Enver in their UN speeches; the ambassadors who, like thieves, disseminated the works of the leader of the Party of Labour of Albania throughout world capitals. They enjoyed evenings of dance in the Block, partaking in Western delights and wearing sky-blue jeans, while Xhelo wore cotton trousers. The same people. None hailed from the faction of the great losers or critics. All of them, together in the chorus, simply filled Enver's shoes. These were the people who would slander and exile others from the party, reassign them from Tirana, and anathematize them with quotations from the red books. They claimed, "The world is inspired by our leader," "The world is enriched with the next revolution," and "Capitalism is dying." Such were the leaders Albania had to endure.

For Xhelo, who had lived through all this, the situation incited immeasurable anguish and disbelief. If he had the power, he would have silenced those who lectured using Comrade Enver's works. But Xhelo was merely Xhelo. He hadn't managed to reproduce himself, but he knew he possessed a spirit and worldview vaster and more unrestricted than those who had a multitude of children or a swarm of party members.

Xhelo possessed a virtue that few did. He believed that a nation was built by everyone, but primarily by good people—individuals with dreams and spirit like himself and Shano. A nation was not solely constructed by the illustrious, as the Albanians were deceived into thinking, not just by renowned writers, poets, philosophers, diplomats, journalists, politicians, or businesspeople. Rather, without a majority of simple, steadfast, and humane individuals unified in their values and ideals—people with passion and a benevolent spirit like Xhelo and Shano—a nation devoid of basic human substance would never fully form. These were people who worked, created, upheld the law, paid taxes, and respected others as they respected themselves. Consequently, Xhelo could no longer identify with any party, front, or ideology; each group seemed like a flock overseen by a shepherd dubbed the chairman. Initially, Xhelo had faith in political pluralism and the emerging parties and leaders, but his trust was swiftly shattered. To him, Albanian politicians had trampled like drunken marauders over those who dreamt of a just Albania when the bust was toppled in Skanderbeg Square. This was the subsequent betrayal inflicted on the common people. History repeated itself, mocking those who discerned the truth with a painful, ironic laugh.

Now living in America, Xhelo closely observed its politics and politicians. He noticed that those engaged in politics donned the same metaphorical suit. They were just as cunning and manipulative as their Albanian counterparts, but here, free votes would dig their political graves when the time came. The "political graveyard" in America is one of the largest in the world and human society. Here, votes lay you to rest, unlike the political landscape in Xhelo's homeland, where the same faces would apply fresh layers of metaphorical makeup with each election campaign. They remained the same—backward, striking deals amongst themselves. It was the same political quagmire that the Political Bureau had created with its own hands before its demise.

In America, politics often resembled a gigantic whirlwind, which might bring disappointment and disillusionment but also offered hope. The campaign for the White House included everything imaginable, and every promise fell from the sky like a comet. Surprises, attacks, accusations, and ambitions—an insatiable thirst for power and control over this unique union to the west of the Atlantic. Xhelo wished to vote for President Trump because he had vocalized some truths that the rest of the world had only murmured. True, Trump was not perfect, but he was different. He wasn't a genius, but he was wealthy and not a puppet of any party. He had as many merits as he had follies. For instance, he was clear about uncontrolled immigration, explicitly stating, "No borders, no homeland." Could it be any clearer? Xhelo was not a fan of the grand wall on America's southern border, into which millions of dollars were being poured. It reminded him of the constraints of Enver's era, though that wall sought to prevent people from leaving, while this massive one aimed to deter others from entering. Xhelo disagreed with the mass influx of people. They weren't escaping communism or dictatorship; they were fleeing poverty. But America couldn't make everyone wealthy, especially when their identities and origins were unknown.

He remembered his friend Bilal Eshka, a monumental example of free movement and legal immigration. Bilal had journeyed to America twice for training as a distinguished agronomist. He had visited and then returned to his home in Tirana. When people admonished him, saying, "You're a fool for going to America and not staying there to escape," he calmly replied, "I went to see, not to stay. Imagine you invite a friend for dinner, lunch, a wedding, or even a week's vacation at your house. You pay for everything: transportation, accommodation, food. Then, after enjoying his stay, he says, 'This is nice... I'm not leaving. I'm staying here...' How would you feel? Who's the fool: you, or the one who stays and exploits your hospitality? Can you see why you can't stay in America without papers, guys?"

Bilal Eshka epitomized the dignified immigrant who left Albania for the promise of America. He followed the law, fulfilled his obligations, returned to Albania, and left with a solemnity reserved for farewells to loved ones. This was legal immigration, not a chaotic mad dash. In fact, Trump's conservative stance on U.S. immigration policies was another reason Xhelo had chosen him in the vote. According to Xhelo, it was high time for America to quash any attempts at illegal entry into the continent. Xhelo knew very well that this was not merely a matter of human rights or a humanitarian crisis; nor was it truly about America's generosity. It was an underground economy—a mafia network of malicious individuals, criminals, soulless people who exploited everything and everyone for money, profit, smuggling, and human trafficking. For Xhelo, this was a new form of human enslavement, a depraved and foul use of people by other people. Lives of unfortunate children, distressed mothers, and desperate individuals were toyed with, sometimes even to the point of suicide, yet they refrained from such acts in the hope that America would save them. Everyone knew this, even the Democrats. That's why the caravans kept coming, shepherded by mafia members and people who exploited others solely for profit.

"Trump's stringent policy may seem inhumane, but in fact, it's against the international mafia—the mafia that buys and trades hopes, dreams, and souls. They need to be stopped, not the poor deceived ones who pay with their blood and tears," Xhelo Lakrori would often mutter, neglecting his own tasks.

Returning to his thoughts, as if reflecting on party congresses, he nearly laughed aloud. How many worlds, ideas, memories, and experiences were encompassed within this Xhelo Lakrori! This Albanian American, Xhelo, was a product of the social and political mutation of post-communist Albania. He was both a hero and a victim who remembered, witnessed, and confronted facts and politics, and lived through moments of dreams, disappointments, and beautiful hopes. Xhelo Lakrori was an entirely unique individual who, each day, sought to uncover the truths of life. He strived to discern the similarities and differences between socialism and a free capitalist society, and what made leaders great and glorious in capitalism versus the deceptive appeal of socialism. Through the careful observations Xhelo Lakrori had made, he remained astounded by the fact that Albanian society had always—under every regime, in every era— remained a victim of men lacking virtue. Men who were cowards, deceitful, sycophantic—not akin to the noble snake that protected a pregnancy as beautiful as Ana's, but more like little snakes that hid within the shadows of power. Through this power, they would bite, poison, and bring death, even when God did not yet decree death!

Power, everywhere and always, under all circumstances, possesses a magical recruiting force. However, there is a difference: In a society where freedom serves as the impetus for life, courage exists. Men rise above the moment to speak, confess, and reveal their souls and sins. Such men can only be found in America, never in Albania or Kosova. Although he intended to vote for President Trump, Xhelo admired the civic courage of Trump's personal lawyer, Michael Cohen. He respected the assertiveness of former FBI Director James Comey, whom the president had dismissed via a television announcement. Similarly, many of the president's close aides and advisors, when they found their viewpoints ignored, would resign, and depart as one does from a lofty position—without clinging to their White House offices. Thus, America remained a human marvel. This country continued to thrive because everyone had something they could choose.

Back in Albania, people crawled towards power and those who wielded it, to the point of repelling the power holders themselves. There, they all fawned, laughed, and mingled as though you held their fate in your hand. Meanwhile, in Xhelo Lakrori's homeland, monsters of hypocrisy and human arrogance had been created. While there was a group of people who were fervent supporters of the ruling leader, there was another group staunchly anti-government. This latter group was firmly aligned with the opposition, eagerly awaiting their rise to power to bring about freedom, democracy, and prosperity. "Albania is teeming with a myriad of people and social groups," Xhelo Lakrori would muse. "That country is filled with thousands of 'Enver's bastards!'"

King Zog was correct when he proclaimed himself the "King of a million kings." Albanians remained challenging, a sentiment he'd also gleaned from Ismail Kadare, who himself was as challenging as the nation he originated from. But he viewed Americans as equally challenging, even specifically so in many cases. In America, there existed a vast, boundless expanse where malice and the impossibility of centralized control became indistinct. Here, the best option was freedom of speech, and fearlessness in what was said, a right enshrined in the Constitution as a fundamental individual liberty.

During their years living on this vast continent, Shano, on a weary day, lamented about the ignorance of a coworker who had also attended college for two years. She said, "Thank God, Xhelo that we didn't die without knowing the Americans."

She was right. Few people in the world are aware of the extent of ignorance found in a segment of the American population. Often, this deficiency in knowledge is so repugnant that it's embarrassing to identify oneself as American. Of course, Xhelo and Shano didn't harbor these views about the educated and brilliant elite of this nation. Rather, they directed their sentiments towards those individuals who hadn't even completed two years of high school, where conversations often revolved more around what would be for lunch than around the day's academic subject. Xhelo observed this firsthand among various levels of his clientele.

He believed that even America—with all its impressive development and grandeur, reflected in the gleaming glass of towering skyscrapers, particularly in large city centers—harbored a portion of the population where habit, ignorance, and the community's priest were the prevailing wisdom. It was astonishing that, even in the 21st century, local media still reported someone being the first in their family to graduate from university as a major event. These television chronicles often reminded Xhelo of the propaganda broadcasts of TVSH (Albanian State Television), where graduates would say, "We dedicate it to the honor of the party and Comrade Enver..." Yet, at least in America, these stories showcased parts of the population moving towards civilization and emancipation, which, though available at their doorstep, seemed ignored or rejected. Interestingly, the gratitude wasn't directed towards the White House or Congress, but to the family and community's efforts towards the kind of progress everyone dreams of. "Only freedom, not propaganda, could instill this perspective," Xhelo the veterinarian would think.

Time was moving swiftly. Although the electoral campaign and the worldwide pandemic were the dominant news stories, many local events were overlooked or briefly mentioned. He was aware that murders and crimes in his city were daily occurrences, but during the election season, people paid them little attention. The media often reported these incidents as a daily flash, particularly the cases of violence in the southern part of the city.

A message from Mitch Miller had just arrived, causing his phone to vibrate. Holding a file on a dog exhibiting strange symptoms, Xhelo didn't immediately check the message. The fear that the Covid-19 variant was infiltrating the animal kingdom was unsettling. If confirmed, it could have serious implications for his business. The symptoms the dog presented alarmed him. He quickly noted the need for an urgent test and called the dog's owner to ask some clarifying questions. From his readings thus far, it appeared that small animals were not as severely threatened by the virus as humans were, but circumstances could change abruptly. It was crucial not to underestimate any clinical sign that might warrant his attention. In the meantime, he instructed the secretary to perform a comprehensive blood test in collaboration with the attending veterinarian.

Then he picked up his phone. It was Shano: "Xhelo, they have decided to have the baby shower on October 20th. I don't want to go. Please, help me come up with a strong reason not to offend them..." He replied promptly, "Don't worry, my dear... Just hold on for a moment."

Upon checking his messages, Xhelo noticed that Mitch had also informed him of the same thing. He sent a congratulatory response about the impending big day. Xhelo hadn't yet told Shano, but he'd received a phone call from Albania informing him that Xhaferi, her brother, had been diagnosed with the virus and had been on oxygen for two days. The doctors in Korça presented a bleak prognosis. Knowing he had to inform Shano, he called her without further delay and revealed the news. She was startled; she couldn't understand why they hadn't told her when she had spoken to them that very morning.

"They didn't want to upset you, dear. That's why. They know you are easily shaken. Don't worry; this will pass. Let Mrs. Miller know that due to this, you can't accept her invitation," he said. And that's exactly what she did.

Believing that a short break would bolster Shano's spirits, Xhelo swiftly left the clinic to head home. In times of a pandemic, news travels as swiftly as lightning across a stormy sky. It wasn't the first-time humanity had faced such circumstances, so Xhelo had faith that this challenging period would soon become part of the painful past. When he arrived home, Shano was sipping coffee and seemed calm. He was relieved; any shock to her would affect him as well. They sat in silence, gazing at each other. Xhelo was at a loss for words. This silence felt like a somber family prelude. Deciding to spend the afternoon at home with Shano, he sent a message to his secretary, informing her he wouldn't return to the clinic that day and that the staff could proceed with their scheduled tasks.

The following two days were a whirlwind of activity. Xhelo adhered to his usual routine, arriving at the clinic early to meticulously review the charts for the day's appointments and treatments. Attention to detail was ingrained in him, a habit he couldn't let go of. In the morning, he initiated a $10,000 transfer to Korça through Western Union to assist with his brother-in-law's mounting medical expenses. He promptly emailed the reference number to Shano, requesting her to follow up with her sister-in-law.

Fortunately, the dog suspected of having Covid-19 tested negative, a relief that eased the tension in the clinic. Xhelo directed the attending vet to administer a potent dose of antibiotics, as it appeared they were grappling with a severe case of pneumonia. After meticulously reviewing and annotating all the charts, he left them on the secretary's desk and allowed himself a moment of respite. While sipping his coffee, he delved into a magazine featuring studies on small animals, where he stumbled upon a fascinating exploration of the intricate psychology between small animals and humans. The research illuminated how dogs and cats functioned as intuitive barometers, capable of anticipating their owners' emotional states. It suggested a profound connection forged between these species, a connection that predated the modern era, hinting at an intricate web of intertwined destinies. Humans possessed the vast spectrum of communication and expression, while dogs and cats, with their limited means of expression, internalized everything, often responding with poignant emotions conveyed through their eyes and actions.

Xhelo, driven by a relentless thirst for knowledge in his field, believed that the dynamics between animals and humans were an untapped domain. He anticipated groundbreaking revelations in the 21st century regarding the "diplomatic relations" between humans and the rest of the living world. He felt privileged to have pursued a career in veterinary medicine. In his homeland, this path was often viewed as a last resort, but in America, he found himself amongst a community that not only valued his profession but often regarded him as vital as a family doctor. As he mused about the profession that had unlocked a life far beyond his Devoll roots, his phone interrupted his reverie with its persistent ringing.

"Hello, Dr. Lakrori! It's Mitch on the line. I just wanted to check in after hearing about your brother-in-law's illness. My best wishes for his speedy recovery," the voice on the other end conveyed genuine concern.

"Thank you, Mitch. Your sentiments mean a lot. Shano is quite disappointed about missing the upcoming baby celebration, but I'm sure you understand," Xhelo replied, offering a virtual nod of gratitude.

"No worries at all. Those gatherings are usually women-centric, and it would've been lovely to have Shano there, too. But as you said, everyone has their priorities," Mitch responded, his understanding tone evident. "Are you swamped with work, Xhelo?"

"Busier than ever. Is there anything I can assist you with? Is the enigmatic yellow snake continuing its daily ritual?" Xhelo inquired with a touch of intrigue.

"Absolutely not. They don't call you the miracle worker for

nothing. My wife values your service tremendously. I called because I'm planning a hunting trip to Minnesota soon. There's an incredible hunting spot up north near the Canadian border. Would you care to join?" Mitch's invitation took Xhelo by surprise, prompting him to pause. Again?

If it were a different time, he might have entertained the idea, but given his current workload and his brother-in-law's precarious health, such an adventure seemed extravagant. Furthermore, he wasn't particularly keen on hunting. Xhelo contemplated the best way to decline the offer gracefully.

"I appreciate the kind invitation, Mitch, but I must respectfully decline. When are you planning to embark on this trip? The baby's celebration is approaching, and Shano and I are eagerly looking forward to it," he replied, choosing his words carefully.

"Of course, the celebration will be a grand success, Xhelo! You know we always aim for success, just like our president," Mitch responded with a chuckle. "I'm just quite passionate about hunting, and once the idea takes root, it's hard to resist. It'll only be for a couple of days, and this time, I'm taking my wife along. Please convey our warm regards to Shano," he concluded before ending the call.

What was happening? Here was a man on the verge of becoming a father any day now, and his mind was consumed by the idea of a hunting trip? It left Xhelo baffled, as if he and Mitch were planning to discuss high-stakes investments in China and Hong Kong instead. Lately, this millionaire had reappeared in Xhelo's social sphere, sparking a flurry of questions in the veterinarian's mind. Xhelo couldn't fathom the man's persistent attempts to involve him in so-called "investment opportunities of the century" in China and East Asia. Weren't there plenty of investment prospects right here in America? Even during their last plane journey, Mitch had painted an alluring picture of his financial prowess, narrating how his knack for seizing investment opportunities had earned him the trust of hundreds of investors across America, positioning him as a reliable conduit for investors eyeing opportunities beyond U.S. borders.

Mitch had a way with words, especially when he spoke of the lucrative investment landscape in China. He would imply that even the wealthiest Americans—names like Buffet, Gates, Bezos, and various Trump ventures—had substantial stakes in East Asia. His narratives had the power to make you feel like a millionaire on

Earth. "In China, 100 millionaires are minted every day: in America, just five. Can you see the difference?" he would declare. Xhelo mused, "He's undoubtedly a smooth talker, skilled at making everything appear rosy, but I'm content where I am."

Embarking on a hunting expedition merely two days before their much-awaited baby celebration struck Xhelo as peculiar. If he were as affluent as the millionaire Mitch jested about, the thought of leaving his home or city wouldn't even cross his mind. He'd be anxiously counting down the hours and minutes until he heard the newborn's first cry. He and Shano shared a kindred emotional world and reveled in the life they had chosen. They were immersed in unique emotions because, for the first time, they were experiencing a birth tradition unfamiliar to them, one practiced solely on this continent.

Granted, Shano wouldn't partake in this beautiful American tradition, one that held beauty at its core but also served as a stark reminder of her own circumstances. Nevertheless, her absence during the celebration paled in comparison to the hunting escapade that the soon-to-be parents had in store. Was it jealousy, Xhelo pondered, these irrational thoughts tugging at his consciousness? Was he envious because he didn't know or couldn't do what this couple could? "No, my friend, retract those thoughts," he chided himself. "In America, everyone has their freedom, and remember, here the individual makes the rules, not just customs and traditions. So don't be surprised. Why not view the hunting trip as an auspicious omen? They're heading to the Canadian border for a hunting expedition to usher in prosperity. Hunting is seen as a harbinger of good fortune, unlike how we Albanians perceive it, always finding fault in everything someone does..."

His astonishment deepened when Shano shared similar sentiments upon hearing the news from Ana, who expressed surprise at the couple's excursion on the eve of their forthcoming baby celebration. "We Albanians have a tendency to envision the worst-case scenario, my dear. This is just another adventure for those with means. We fret needlessly. In my eyes, you are and will always be the finest hunter, my dear," Xhelo reassured her over the phone before returning to his daily grind.

His job was growing increasingly demanding, to the point where he had scarcely found time to actively support President Trump's re-election campaign, despite his belief that Trump was destined for a second term at the helm of the great American nation.

Chapter Thirteen

The millionaire couple had chosen October 20, 2020, as the day to celebrate the upcoming birth of their child, conceived in the healthy body of Ana Parroti. This type of ceremony typically gathered a female audience. The timing was perfect, in line with the tradition of holding such ceremonies 4-6 weeks before the expected birth. To Xhelo, however, any celebration or birthday in October seemed adverse. If he held divine power, he would specifically cancel out October 16, marking it as a void, dark, unfavorable date. That was the day the most selfish man, almost to the point of madness, was born. This man had erected his glory and majesty around himself through dubious circumstances, lies, forgeries, ingratitude, murders, and family raids unparalleled in Albania. Yet, regrettably, he remained an idol and beacon of hope for a significant portion of the people.

Xhelo didn't fault those who continued to believe this man was the greatest leader, the true historical figure of the country, the only man who cared for the Albanian people. His real horror was reserved for the entire political class that, with their arrogance, disrespect for law and justice, impunity for evil deeds, and widespread theft, flaunted their powers before the helpless populace. This crowd of politicians, driven by greed for money, profit, power, and business control, deviated from party ideals. It was difficult to pinpoint exactly when Enver Hoxha had died and when dozens of his replicas had been reborn, turning out to be the greatest curse for the Albanian nation.

Xhelo recalled, through memories, as if to heal the wounds of a painful reality for this unfortunate man. He remembered his student days when he had to recite a poem for Hoxha by heart, read a quote, and join in the innocent chorus of children wishing, "Happy birthday, Uncle Enver!" He remembered those October days when leaves fell and winds blew, when grape harvests occurred, and people thought about wine or raki. On those very days, Hoxha's birthday became an obligation. Hoxha, who although proclaimed in speeches to fight against the cult of the individual, had become one with the party he led. So much so that Mayakovsky could not compose a second poem in his famous verse: "When we say Party, we mean Lenin, and when we say Lenin, we mean the Party…"

Enver Hoxha was the sole leader in the Balkans who, after stealing and falsifying everything from history and truth, after all war heroes were either dead or nullified by the party "in the name of the people," began writing his memoirs with his first book "Childhood Years," followed by "Titoists," "With Stalin," "Khrushchevists," etc. Only America could have opened Xhelo's eyes to comprehend all the hypocrisy and falsity of the time, originating from that day of October 16, 1908. How could he erase the past? Impossible. Whether he wanted to or not, the past was the hook where memories hung and dried like pieces of village-made prosciutto prepared for the frigid winter season… Such was life. Harsh and barbaric until death. It could have been worse. He could have died saying, "Long live the party," because, just like thousands of others, he had loved both the party and Comrade Enver, so every outcry about the past was like a blessing for the present...

October 20, 2020. In Chicago, a unique celebration was unfolding. A baby's arrival, the symbol of hope for a luckless couple, was being commemorated. This couple was neither Xhelo nor Shano. Someone else had ordered the baby, much like ordering packages on Amazon; simply pay and wait. That's precisely what the Miller couple had done. They'd ordered a baby from a beauty and were awaiting its birth. A designer baby, which centuries ago the Vatican would have denounced as sinful and haram. No wonder Americans were wary of the Vatican. They understood that Catholic dogmas acted like barbed wire against individual freedom. Wasn't it the Vatican and dogmatic priests who had burned Giordano Bruno at the stake and damned Galileo Galilei? The world feared the Vatican, a tiny state with a colossal presence in people's minds, possessing power more virulent than Covid-19 itself. It was no accident that Americans were hesitant to entrust the White House to a Catholic who might take orders from the Vatican. Didn't some conspiracy theorists suggest that Kennedy, a Catholic, was assassinated by Americans? And was "Sleepy Joe," as Trump called him, as threatening as Kennedy? Had the diverse American nation gleaned any lessons from their history?

Xhelo grappled with an answer to that question. For him, when religious beliefs intertwined with the currents of politics, it sparked a disquieting and perilous collision. Even in the vast expanse of America, where there was a clear separation of church and state by law, it was the evangelists who appeared to predict the outcomes of elections each electoral season. This paradox was so striking that every president, on the day of their inauguration, would place their hand on the Bible and recite a universal prayer echoed in countless courtrooms: "God help me!"

"They do it right," Xhelo thought, "even though I may not believe, there's something deeply sincere about this appeal to the heavens. After all, seeking God's help is a journey back to oneself. God has given every creature the power to govern its own destiny."

It was a day to celebrate the impending arrival of a baby to a couple who had endured a challenging journey. Xhelo needed to put aside the past and experience the day like any regular person. Although he was eager to learn more about the baby soon to be born from Ana's body, he regarded pregnancy primarily as a woman's domain. Even during meetings and walks with Mitch, he refrained from delving into the baby's fate like an overly curious woman would. Men, he believed, had more significant topics to discuss. Shano handled this realm with grace, maintaining contact with Ana, who assured her that all tests, parameters, and developments were entirely normal, and doctors held an optimistic outlook. The connection Shano had forged with the surrogate mother seemed to grant her a unique sensation, allowing her to vicariously experience the baby's movements as if growing within her own body, as if she were the one about to bring joy into the world, as if her grand dream were becoming a reality.

Isn't life a dream that one can only fully grasp when nearing death or standing at the precipice? It's often said that dreamers in the land across the Atlantic live multiple lifetimes. They don't merely experience the fragment of time physically linked to their existence and current era; their minds soar through the countless lives, dramas, and loves woven into their fantasies. This perspective brought a whimsical sense of joy to Shano, the most beautiful girl Devoll's banks had ever seen in her youth.

Since the day Ana had visited him with her boss for that fateful meeting that had become a turning point in his life, their contact had been formal and sporadic. He was prepared to assist in any potential medical emergencies, and Ana had understood his position. She knew how ambitious and assertive men could be, so his distant stance didn't trouble her. Xhelo had his professional reputation as Lakrori, and it was well-respected, but he had not entertained any expectations. Still, something positive had come from his association with Ana. She had introduced them to a family that, according to her, aspired to become American billionaires by the end of their second decade. Xhelo often found amusement in these lofty human ambitions.

Xhelo hadn't shown much interest in the Millers' fate or their impending hunting trip near Canada. During those days, he had become engrossed in following the campaign and had engaged in numerous phone conversations with friends across different states. Biden supporters told him he was wasting his vote, while Republicans cheered him on, suggesting that the more minds he could sway to the right, the better it would be for Republicans and the whole American conservative movement. An intellectual from Shkodra town, had transformed his Albanian café in Detroit into a debating hotbed. As an intellectual teeming with ideas and contributions, he sought to engage people in fruitful debates, though he often struggled to keep things under control. There, Albanian immigrants from various regions, mainly from the north but also from Kolonja, Përmet, Skrapar, and Gjirokastra, congregated. Almost unanimously, they had pledged, with fervent enthusiasm, to vote for Trump.

In their online debates, a multitude of opinions surfaced, labeling Trump's opponent as a communist invention, a socio-communist threat to the continent's freedom, a Sorosian, and an enemy of American glory, among other offensive epithets that echoed the anathemas of the socialist era in Albania. Xhelo held a distinct perspective, free from communist coarseness. He considered voting for Trump, not because his opponent was a socialist or communist—an idea he found laughable—but because, in his view, Trump was a unique socio-political phenomenon unlikely to reappear on the political scene for at least a century. Meanwhile, some Albanians in Detroit, who still lived in two-room apartments and were privy to their neighbors' natural discharges as in olden times, staunchly defended Trump in their analyses. In reality, no one needed that kind of defense. The publicized articles and arguments were reminiscent of those posed by Enver Hoxha's prosecutors, brimming with anger, hatred, hostility toward the adversary, and scant logic. Xhelo Lakrori was amused by the unprecedented love Albanian Americans expressed for President Trump, which occasionally reminded him of Tirana's past official infatuations with Tito, Stalin, Khrushchev, and Comrade Mao.

The wonder of the heated campaign was that many voters were resolute in their beliefs and seemed impervious to other perspectives. Indeed, Xhelo's uncertainty stemmed from broader assessments and comparisons rarely made. Everyone votes in the hope that their chosen candidate will triumph, regardless of the actual final vote count. This is the captivating magic of free voting and the intriguing blindness each side suffers.

Xhelo anticipated this would be the last campaign to which he would mentally commit, for he was contemplating future plans: retirement, fishing, and writing memoirs. It was his dream that, before departing this world, he would publish a book—just one—that he envisioned as a guidebook for anyone seeking to live a happy life, not just in a certain part of the globe, but everywhere. To tether happiness to a specific location is akin to dreaming of marrying the most beautiful woman on earth. Happiness is not a destination in life; it is merely a fleeting moment that, once gone, is gone, and if not seized in time, flutters away like a bird freshly hatched from an egg.

Life is a universe to be lived and digested day by day, and despite the countless lessons imparted by others, mankind remains skeptical. People believe in what they personally experience and live, not in others' tales, which can often be fabrications. Xhelo had already mentally outlined his book, a narrative where numerous currents clashed. His life had evolved from existing under socialism, where a glass of raki, some cheese, and two onions made one feel as if they owned the field of Devoll, to the insatiability manifested in capitalism, where profit is boundless and remains the sole motivation of life. "This book will shake the world, but God willing, I will live that long," Xhelo Lakrori said to himself.

The day before the baby shower, while the Millers were fishing somewhere in northern Minnesota, he was invited to a local television studio, ABC-7, to discuss the precautions that should be taken for small animals during the pandemic. For the first time, he felt the intoxicating power one experiences in front of cameras and when responding to live calls from viewers. He was astounded by the range of questions, some of which even challenged him. Still, he successfully presented himself as a doctor who not only knew his profession but could also entertain and surprise his audience, much like the diverse world of pets, humans keep for companionship.

Dr. Lakrori left an indelible impression during the interview. The host was surprised she hadn't discovered such a professional before. She conjectured that his colleague, who had recently passed away from the virus, must have overshadowed him professionally for some inexplicable reason. As long as he was alive, he had been the sole expert on that TV channel, as everlasting as the members of the political bureau in Albania once were. No one had thought to listen to Xhelo Lakrori, who had quietly built a substantial reputation starting from the underground channels of the great city in the heartland of America. But that wasn't all.

During a live broadcast in that historic American metropolis, the small-animal veterinarian delivered a statement so startling that it left viewers and even the host in a state of shock. With a cool and unflappable demeanor, he concluded his conversation with a Trump-like declaration within the realm of small-animal veterinary medicine. The host on the other side of the studio swooned, teetering on the edge of interrupting the show. But she couldn't bring herself to do it, for her guest had become a virtuoso in front of the cameras, commanding an inexplicable and captivating presence. It was a moment when Xhelo Lakrori, for the first time, perceived himself as an unstoppable force – a tranquil conqueror of the airwaves.

He proclaimed, "I have a simple message for all the pet lovers out there: love and respect your animal companions as you would cherish yourselves. Dogs, cats, parrots, pigeons, birds, turtles, hamsters, fish, worms, and all the others are reflections of our souls in a world where communication thrives more through glances, meows, barks, and chirps than through words. But there is one innocent creature we unfairly revile, curse, and fear as soon as it crosses our minds. This is one of humanity's most misunderstood and understudied perceptions: snakes are our most unfortunate friends. They are more genuine than humans and, despite their small eyes and limbless bodies; they yearn to embrace us with the most unconditional love imaginable – a love that we mistakenly reject and fear. In short, we harbor preconceived notions about these slithering beings, notions that history and human understanding will one day vindicate. As a veterinarian, I implore you to cherish the entire world of animals, where our spirits reside, for they are all innocent, including snakes. No pet, not even our fellow humans, can offer the encompassing embrace that a non-venomous snake can provide. Picture a snake gently encircling your body – a snake that doesn't bite or inject venom, but instead coils around you rib by rib, engaging in the sincerest of animal-human embraces, tenderly caressing you with its flickering tongue. It's the purest form of an animal-human kiss and a therapeutic massage from a cold-blooded creature. Imagine how you might feel beneath such a cold yet profoundly genuine embrace. Do not be frightened or alarmed – the fear of these creatures is an illusion passed down through the centuries. It's time to rehabilitate these innocent beings within our human psyche, and perhaps even discover an untapped business opportunity. For any questions or concerns, our clinic is open for your beloved pets and the kindness you bestow upon them. Thank you."

The journalist was taken aback and broke into applause, as did the cameramen who almost fumbled their equipment. The director's booth buzzed with genuine excitement. The entire ABC-7 television studio reverberated with laughter. A veterinarian had left the audience astounded. Adjusting his loosely knotted snake-head tie, Xhelo Lakrori gazed directly into the eyes of the woman who had invited him to the studio and offered a sincere apology.

"I apologize, madam. I felt compelled to speak my mind. I hope I didn't disappoint you, but I want to express my heartfelt gratitude for granting me this opportunity. Thank you, madam, and thank you to your television network." He then kissed her hand in a manner reminiscent of European gallantry. The journalist was left momentarily speechless, a rarity in her extensive career of live broadcasts. She glanced at her phone, which had been inundated with messages, comments, and likes. Even President Trump and his opponent Joe Biden had engaged with her Twitter account, liking, and retweeting her posts. She could hardly fathom the remarkable success her show had achieved during the peak of the election campaign. Most of the messages echoed a similar sentiment: "You were truly amazing, Dr. Lakrori."

Amidst the flood of messages, two stood out distinctly. Jim Belushi, the renowned actor and the first entrepreneur holding an Albanian passport to own a marijuana farm in California, tweeted, "Our Albania continues to astonish the world with actors like me and geniuses like Xhelo Lakrori. Best of luck to you, my Albanian brother. You spoke with the same fervor as our president; you shook Chicago, much like John and I once did. Keep going, Jimi." In a different vein, Robert De Niro conveyed his thoughts: "Dr. Lakrori, although you may sound like Trump, I doubt you're as mindless as they say in Albania. Congratulations, and keep persevering with that Albanian tenacity. Robert De Niro."

This sudden burst of fame left her in a state of disbelief. He was indeed a unique individual. If Shano had been present, she would have immediately picked up her phone and sent him a heartfelt message: "My love, you are my pride! Thank you for shining brightly as both a doctor and as Xhelo! I love you so much…" He longed for Ana to shower him with similar praise, but all he received from her was a brief yet meaningful text: "Congratulations, Dr. Lakrori!" That was it. He bore no grudge, understanding that her due date was fast approaching, and it's often said that women, before this blessed moment, are consumed by anxiety and delusions. With it being her third pregnancy, Ana's maternal emotions were as predictable as the weight she carried.

He couldn't help but wish that Mitch Miller had been able to witness the interview, but he was likely still engrossed in his game – a passionate hobby known to make one forget themselves, much like he had forgotten everything else while chasing beautiful girls before falling in love with Shano.

The next surprise came courtesy of his colleagues at work. Vasil Myzeqeja, a former teacher of his now residing in Tampa, Florida, and once a prominent figure in the small-animal realm back in Tirana, couldn't resist picking up the phone on the very same day to convey his heartfelt congratulations. "Xhelo," Vasil began, "with that brilliant interview, you've made me a firm believer in the adage that students invariably surpass their teachers. I'll be sure to send a link to Prof. Dr. Nefail Mokra, hailing from your neck of the woods, so he can draw strength in his battle against COVID-19, which I'm confident he'll triumph over…"

Xhelo found himself grappling with a piece of news that had

eluded him previously. As soon as he concluded the call with Vasil, he tried reaching out to the esteemed professor. However, met with no response, he sent a message, expressing his well-wishes for a swift recovery. Overwhelmed by the deluge of messages and phone calls, he powered down his cell phone before heading to the clinic.

Upon arriving at the clinic, he was met with an array of multicolored balloons, each adorned with a prominent inscription: "We're proud of you, Dr. Lakrori. Congratulations!" The sight left him momentarily taken aback. He exchanged pleasantries with everyone, pledging to treat the entire staff to a special lunch from "Pizza Luce" the following day as a token of his appreciation. The thunderous applause gave him pause. While this wasn't the first time, he had been the recipient of such adulation, it marked the first occasion when it felt like a magical wave enveloping him, evoking both a sense of significance and profound emotion. He was known as Xhelo Lakrori, and he was one of a kind. A simple search of his name on Google yielded only one result: Xhelo Lakrori. This filled him with an immense sense of pride, reaffirming his gratitude for not altering the name bestowed upon him by his parents, even when a friend had suggested it be his first order of business upon setting foot on American soil. That friend was none other than the remarkable Shaban Shiroka, to whom he owed a great deal.

The following day arrived with the force of a tidal wave. The moments of glory and public adoration quickly gave way to new challenges. Xhelo had not foreseen that just one day after the interview, his clinic would be inundated with a barrage of requests from reptile owners. One caller asserted ownership of a rattlesnake at home, insisting on house calls and willing to pay any price. Xhelo soon found himself in need of hiring an expert in reptiles to manage the influx of requests. In the meantime, a call came in from PETCO, a pet superstore in the city, offering to cater lunch for all of Dr. Lakrori's staff. The CEO of this multibillion-dollar corporation extended an invitation for him to speak at a national conference on the psychological impact of pet ownership.

However, news from Korça painted a less hopeful picture. His brother-in-law was locked in a life-or-death struggle, and his wife, Mira, had also been admitted to the hospital. He didn't want to burden Shano with these worries, but he promptly sent a substantial sum of dollars to aid the situation. Their children in Greece were barely making ends meet, with four young children to care for. Although he hesitated to share this burden with Shano, he informed her that he had dispatched another substantial sum of dollars to Albania, hoping to alleviate the suffering of those facing poverty.

Their mornings began with coffee, the two of them seated at the kitchen table, rather than tuning into the news. They would engage in conversation about their dreams from the night before and the need for a restful and peaceful start to the day, all while enveloped in the intoxicating aroma of Colombian coffee. Only after they had savored these moments would they finally turn to their phones, a gesture akin to lovers momentarily turning their backs on each other. They weren't alone in this. Across the globe, the ceaseless tide of messages, communications, and surprises transformed the mornings of almost every couple into a peculiar race toward the unknown.

It was Shano who nearly collapsed upon reading the contents of her screen. She had missed ten calls and five messages from Ana.

"Xhelo!" she practically shouted, a note of urgency in her voice. "They weren't there."

"Who?" he inquired, his tone groggy.

"Ana says she was the only one at the baby shower. The couple was absent. How is that possible? It's a bad omen," Shano exclaimed, her astonishment evident.

Xhelo found it hard to fathom. The millionaires had skipped out on the pre-baby celebration, an event they had invested so much in. What could have transpired? How could they have missed such a crucial occasion? If it had been of significance to him, he would have attended without hesitation, irrespective of it being predominantly a women's gathering. But what was the reason behind their absence? He pondered the notion of calling Mitch to verify if everything was all right but refrained, deeming it necessary to first uncover the full story. Amid the multitude of messages, he had received about the show Ana's name finally caught his eye. Almost breathlessly, he opened her message and read: "Dear Xhelo, They didn't show up. I'm bewildered. I don't know what to do. Please call me. Ana."

"This doesn't bode well, Xhelo! Something significant has transpired!" Shano exclaimed, her shock palpable.

He remained silent, feeling as though Ana's message, lost amidst the myriad others, bore an eerie weight. He had wished countless times that Ana would require his assistance, and he, like a devoted knight, eagerly anticipated the chance to rush to her aid, to offer solace during her moments of distress. He would have willingly set off in the dead of night if that's when the message was sent, just to demonstrate that he was a man of his word. Yet here he was, having missed this opportunity, as if it were a form of Balkan retribution. His concern did not stem from what may have happened to the couple, but rather, why he hadn't been there for Ana. He considered dialing her immediately but refrained from doing so in Shano's presence. Instead, he awaited her response.

"Ana's reached out to me as well. What do you think? Should I give her a call?" Xhelo proposed, placing the decision in Shano's hands.

Shano, engrossed in the messages displayed on her screen, found herself lost in their words. They harkened back to the days of yore when New Year's postcards were crafted with care, each letter bearing a piece of the sender's soul—sincere, pure, and undeniably heartfelt. Those were days marked by suffering and deprivation, yet they overflowed with the richness of the soul, of hope, and of emotions expressed through the simplest of gestures. Today, things were as cold as glass. In this age, the art of composing heartfelt wishes or expressing gratitude, fundamental human values, had seemingly been forgotten. In America, businesses offered pre-made cards that could be personalized with any message one desired, printed in beautiful fonts alongside famous quotes, but they were devoid of the soul that once infused Albanian cards. Now, the phone offered countless expressions, all free of charge, yet lacking in spirit, sentiment, freshness, and originality. Everything had become as transparent and icy as glass.

Lost in her reverie, Shano struggled to make sense of the messages filling her screen. Ana appeared deeply perturbed by the couple's absence. She had also called Shano's phone number, but neither of them had been available. Adhering to their personal rule, the couple routinely left their phones charging overnight. With no children or immediate family to tether them to the digital world throughout the night, their sleep represented a time of reprieve—a moment when they would metaphorically return to God, only to be reunited with each other the following morning. What could have occurred with the couple? Had they lost track of time while out hunting, becoming lost in the expansive forests? Or could another unforeseen circumstance have prevented their return to the eagerly awaited, meticulously prepared celebration?

These questions hung in the air, akin to balloons ensnared by the ceiling. What had befallen the couple, who were on the brink of welcoming their first child? Who or what had dashed their dreams? Why had this transpired on the day of the baby shower rather than earlier? What was the enigma shrouding this significant absence? These questions lingered like bunches of grapes poised to tumble from the vine. Shano and Xhelo confronted a profound mystery, one that weighed even heavier on Ana. Burdened by the gravity of the situation and distressed by the couple's conspicuous absence, she sought help, support, courage, and at the very least, a returned phones call. To her astonishment, an eerie silence prevailed, an unsettling tension that suggested some knew the truth but lacked the fortitude to voice it, instead awaiting the intervention of law enforcement, detectives, and FBI agents to conduct investigations, searches, and analyses to unveil a mystery that might ultimately prove to be quite straightforward.

"Shano, perhaps you should be the first to make the call. This silence doesn't feel right. After all, we've been friends for so long, and this hush makes us feel like mere spectators, witnesses to a drama with an uncertain denouement," Xhelo advised Shano. In truth, he was itching to call Ana, to inquire about her well-being, the status of the baby, the couple's absence, and any potential explanations or suspicions she might harbor. He wanted to know who had attended the gathering the previous night, how the couple's nonappearance had been received, and whether Mitch had an undisclosed romantic partner who could have facilitated an alibi. He had a myriad of questions he intended to pose, in his quest to uncover the truth and craft his own narrative.

"You're absolutely right, my love!" Shano conceded. "I'll give her a call right away. But I had the most unsettling dream last night, as though they had perished in a fiery catastrophe in the skies. A plane crash. You know, Xhelo, my dreams often hold kernels of truth. I've told you as much before, though you've never quite believed me."

Xhelo struggled to reconcile the fact that, amidst this unusual situation, Shano was delving into discussions about dreams and nocturnal reveries. They had argued about this many times before, as Shano would often predict events based on her dreams, speculating on what might happen that day or soon. Xhelo consistently countered her, asserting,

"Forget about dreams. They're like visitors in the night, intruding upon our otherwise idle sleep, when we lay there doing nothing. They're a form of entertainment that God grants as a reminder of His presence, though I don't put much stock in them. Dreams are idle fantasies we enjoy when they're pleasant and prefer to forget when they're not. Let's not dwell on these theories."

"Xhelo," Shano interrupted, "your millionaires are no more. They've turned to ashes and dust. I never told Ana, though, especially now that she's about to give birth. My dream is coming true, you see. You've never taken my dreams seriously, not once. Even when you told me you loved me, I cautioned you against it. But you never listened, and here we are, both caught in this web. At least I knew…"

He struggled to grasp why she would occasionally resort to saying, "I hate you," as though it were an attempt to free herself from an impossibility her father had not managed to achieve. He despised this repetition; it harked back to that decision, a choice that could have taken a drastically different turn if only he had heeded her earnest declaration: "I hate you; I'm not meant for you."

"But then, I never would have met Ana, along with the serpent," a voice within him chimed, as if two distinct entities had converged, a reality he had never foreseen. He had never contemplated anyone beyond Shano, yet Ana had become a splinter in his soul, representing an entirely different world he yearned to escape. "Ah, if only I had joined the hunt as well. I could have met the same fate as the millionaires... Then these thoughts wouldn't torment me," he mused like a madman on that morning. He knew it wouldn't be a simple vanishing act or a random engine failure. Ana held more information. She was the only key to unlocking the enigma of that October day. He dismissed what Shano had said, even as she continued to peer into his eyes, as if attempting to decipher his thoughts. Her gaze anchored him back to reality, and he responded with a chuckle.

"Enough of that, Shano. Let's not get superstitious. I've never regretted anything, contrary to what you often remind me. Our fates were sealed long ago, so let's not revisit past decades. Do you understand? If indeed this is an unusual absence or a significant event, it could potentially involve us in trouble... I hope I'm wrong, but it doesn't seem like a mere disappearance or a simple plane crash... Ana might have more information. Please…"

Shano dialed Ana, initiating the call on speakerphone, as if to underscore her transparency and unwavering honesty in her dealings with their millionaire acquaintances. She extended her apologies to Ana for the delay in returning her call and delved into the incident. A stunned Ana revealed her ordeal:

"Thank you, Shano, for finally getting in touch," she began, her voice filled with uncertainty. "I'm at a loss for words, dear. What I thought would be a joyous day has transformed into one of dread and despair. They didn't show up. They promised they'd be here by 2 p.m., and I trusted them. But there was no contact from them after they left. I knew they were off for some hunting adventure in northern Minnesota, a kind of human madness. I'd been there six months ago when they took me, celebrating the early news of my pregnancy as if it were a reward. You lose touch with your origins there. The towering, wild forests, countless lakes, the constant chorus of birds, deer roaming the woods, majestic eagles, pheasants, wild bears, enigmatic snakes—a genuine northern oasis that defies description. I understand how you can lose yourself there, but not a single call to tell me when they'd return, if they were safe, if the weather was favorable, if the cabin was ready... Oh, Shano! I feel like they left with no intention of returning at this critical moment when I need them most, when I was supposed to find my footing and begin anew. I feel cursed, and I don't know what to do. The baby could arrive any day now, and I'm caught in this nightmarish limbo. What if something's happened to them? Where do I go from here? I have no will or any formal documents. Mitch always reassured me, 'Trust me, everything's been taken care of.' I only have a copy of the surrogacy contract, and once the baby's born, I must hand it over to the biological parents. It's a legal obligation, and that's it. I'm terrified, Shano! You're fortunate, dear, not to have children. This moment feels like a tomb to me, and I can't decide whether to bury myself or the child who isn't mine. Can you even fathom what I'm going through, Shano?"

"Calm down, Ana! Everything will be all right. They'll return and lift this strange burden from your shoulders. Have patience, Ana, patience," Shano consoled.

"I have no patience left. Yesterday, twenty-five women came over with gifts, flowers, and kind wishes, along with beautiful cards. But they weren't the baby's parents. I felt like a marionette, even a sex doll of sorts, not knowing whom to appease. I kept saying, 'Look, they're about to arrive. Look, they're here,' but they never showed up. And there's something else, dear Shano, you need to know. All their contracts expire tomorrow, meaning there won't be any cooks, cleaners, or housekeepers. They've all been on the verge of asking for contract renewals, but Mitch would reassure them, 'Don't worry, your job is secure,' without ever putting anything in writing. I'll have to cook for myself and my daughter, do the laundry, and tend to the extensive garden. I feel betrayed, Shano. Can you understand what I'm going through?"

"No, Ana, you haven't been betrayed. You're an angel delivering a legacy to a deserving couple. If I were in your shoes, I'd rise from the grave to be there for them. Don't surrender to despair, please... Let's hope and pray that they're safe."

"Shano, I don't know... This has never happened before. I feel abandoned, dear. You're the only one offering solace with your words... Thank you!" Ana said.

"I refuse to believe it's as dire as you imagine. Please, have faith in the goodness of the situation," Shano urged. However, Ana had already ended the call, overwhelmed by despair.

Xhelo found himself at a loss for words. In some ways, he was relieved that the conversation had unfolded between two women, sparing him from being embroiled in the middle of it all. He understood that this was only the beginning of their troubles. He foresaw a tumultuous autumn ahead and hoped for some resolution to their predicament. He didn't know how to console Shano, and in her eyes, he detected a profound sense of despair. Perhaps Ana's insinuations about the profound misfortune they were experiencing as a couple had left her feeling shaken. Suddenly, a notion struck him: What if the millionaire couple had met with an accident during their hunting expedition? Confronted with such a tragedy, he could potentially be first in line to adopt the millionaires' child, becoming a father, albeit to a child born through surrogacy. But what was wrong with that? Wasn't every person's life a lease from God, a slice of time and space that we eventually relinquish to others when our time is up? From this perspective on life and its enigmas, Xhelo wove a captivating dream. It was undoubtedly a form of madness, but it possessed a unique beauty. With this plan, he'd surmounted societal taboos, and if fate favored him, that baby could gradually change their lives, piece by piece.

Human infants were so innocent that you forged a connection with them through their vulnerability, their infectious laughter, and their tears—they became an integral part of your life. It didn't matter whether they shared your genes or not. Xhelo was aware of cases where it had been incontrovertibly proven that a child was not biologically related to a couple, yet they were loved and seamlessly integrated into the family.

"In the end, it doesn't matter where the first seed originates. What counts is who nurtures you, loves you, invests in you, and educates you. That's where genuine human affection resides. Words and gossip are merely fragments of the morality and hypocrisy that human society has fashioned," Xhelo often contemplated.

It would be a miracle capable of forever altering their lives. Yet he knew it wouldn't be an easy path to tread. Becoming a father at his age was a bitter pill to swallow, albeit a desirable one. In Xhelo's case, it was far from a straightforward endeavor. If he could openly express this sort of paternal yearning for a child—a child with whom he shared no biological connection save for the reproductive fear that plagued him as a human—he might find himself implicated in the enigma of the missing couple. The disappearance remained an unresolved puzzle that might necessitate the intervention of the Federal Bureau of Investigation. All these thoughts loomed in his mind like ominous clouds. He still had no inkling of what had befallen his millionaire friends. Were they alive or deceased? This was a mystery that demanded unraveling.

There was no need to dwell any longer on the bewildering disappearance of the couple who had unexpectedly become a part of his social circle, thanks to Ana's charm and her distinctive role as the surrogate mother of another couple's child. Xhelo informed Shano that he had to head to work and, before doing so, promptly placed an online order for seven specialty pizzas for his dedicated staff using his cellphone, keeping true to his earlier promise. He then composed a brief message to Mitch's phone, hoping for some form of acknowledgment: "We're genuinely concerned about your well-being. If you require assistance, please don't hesitate to reach out. - Xhelo." After bidding Shano farewell with a tender kiss, he set off for the clinic, a place that had seamlessly woven itself into the fabric of his existence.

Chapter Fourteen

The news of the millionaire couple's sudden disappearance had yet to make its way onto television screens. Confirmation of a plane crash or an alleged landing remained elusive, and the absence of any substantial leads via phone calls added to the mystery. In accordance with the law, a minimum of 48 hours had to elapse before an individual could be officially reported as missing and trigger a police search and investigation. This legal provision served a purpose: it allowed room for individuals to temporarily drift away from their usual routines, either for personal amusement or a spontaneous escape from daily life's monotony. A prompt alert to the police would overburden them with cases, making it challenging to address everyday crimes and accidents.

This legal framework offered a glimmer of hope that fueled Xhelo's optimism. Surely, the couple would return, offer their apologies to Ana, and express remorse for their peculiar lapse in memory after a significant party—a situation that, in his mind, could only occur in America. In the event of their reappearance, Xhelo would hasten to their villa, eager to confirm that it had all been a nightmarish illusion and that life would promptly return to normal. Only then could he reconsider the series of business propositions his friend had persistently presented, involving investments in China or Hong Kong. Of course, such a revival would also extinguish his ambitious dream of becoming the child's surrogate father, but such is life—a never-ending cycle of joy and sorrow, where every smile can usher in tears of pain for someone else.

With no time to sift through the multitude of messages and emails that had flooded his inbox following his interview on the local ABC-7 television network, Xhelo counted himself fortunate for having deleted his Facebook account years ago. He had done so to protest the countless insipid posts by individuals lacking character, vision, or progressive aspirations. The images of plates of food and glasses of rakia, accompanied by banal messages, had grown tiresome.

Social media had become akin to agricultural cooperatives, where hordes of laborers and leaders convened to discuss trivial matters and objectives. Although the internet's digital realm was not an exact replica of those gatherings, it seemed like a virtual world where individuals posted everything, regardless of how inane or meaningless it might be.

Xhelo acknowledged that most people utilized social media accounts to stay abreast of life's events—marriages, engagements, births, deaths—but such concerns did not weigh on him. He was different. Had he retained such an account, most of his supposed followers would only remember him upon hearing the news of his passing with a hypocritical outpouring of condolences. These people, who had never spoken to him in person and in some cases, weren't even sure of his existence, would engage in the prevalent hypocrisy of the day, posting messages like "What a tragedy, we've lost a star of Albanian veterinary science," or "We bid farewell to a genius in the service of small animals." Yet none of them would express their true sentiments.

Xhelo understood that he did not shine so brilliantly as to blind others; he merely possessed the ability to remove them from his account as if they had never existed. "It's better this way than to be subjected to people's shamelessness," he would silently muse in his moments of solitude. Nonetheless, he wished he could share the previous day's interview with the few friends he genuinely cared about, allowing them to partake in the unique revelations stemming from his troubled soul. However, due to his deliberate absence from Facebook—an avenue he had willingly abandoned—he had sent the interview to his friend in Tirana, Selfo Muhuri, a distinguished forest engineer. Selfo had shared the interview along with an intriguing note: "A distinctive voice from America. Xhelo Lakrori astounds the audience..." and subsequently relayed all the reactions. Xhelo was taken aback by a comment from his old friend from the Castle of Doda, Meleq Pollogu— a smart, muscular, and robust individual working at a university in Georgia—who had written, "Impressive interview, but tell Xhelo to join this massive arena of human discourse, rather than dispersing these pearls like Mao's speeches." He chuckled, much like he had in the Tirana auditorium where Albanian comedian Vasillaq Vangjeli and Skënder Sallaku once entertained. "People need to laugh, the laughter is the medicine we require even when we lack nothing," he reflected before powering off his phone.

He pondered once more, recognizing that fame was a fickle illusion that even dictators and celebrated leaders couldn't resist chasing. He savored his own moments through the fervor he held for his work. Anything spoken or written about him, or the ideas he shared with the world, lingered somewhere in the digital ether and on small screens. Yet, none of it could tarnish the essence of his daily existence and life's true purpose. Above all, Shano remained his wellspring of beauty and inspiration, an allure that never dimmed. By this, he didn't only mean the enchanting evenings but also the enduring beauty that kept him as youthful and vigorous as the days of his boyhood. "A woman, this vital half of a man, is often comprehended too late. A woman, the missing piece without which one can't truly live, rendering the spirit and body dull," he recited with a mysterious fervor before the mirror, his heart consumed by passion for Shano.

The ordered pizzas had made their grand entrance, and the staff, expressing their gratitude to Xhelo, eagerly reached for plates, drawn in by the tantalizing aroma of the pies. The scent was so enticing that even those who hadn't felt hungry found themselves irresistibly drawn to partake. Xhelo himself didn't particularly relish these peculiar creations; to him, they seemed like a feeble imitation of the hearty pies and pastries that had sustained him in days of yore. Instead of pizza, his thoughts often gravitated towards asking Shano to craft a delectable pie or pastry to his liking. They had come across some delicate sheets of dough at a Greek store, which, under Shano's artful touch, were transformed into a culinary masterpiece. "There's nothing quite like Albanian cuisine," Xhelo would proclaim on occasion. He was meticulous about his diet and physique, maintaining a lean, stallion-like form without the paunch that often-plagued men of his age. What's more, he had invested in a home gym, complete with an array of exercise equipment, to uphold their physical well-being.

As the office settled into a tranquil lull, Xhelo found himself engrossed in the latest news broadcast on the office TV. Unexpectedly, an unannounced visitor materialized at the clinic's doorstep. With most of the staff on their lunch break, Xhelo took it upon himself to open the door and offer his assistance. Standing before him was a man in his sixties, not quite matching Xhelo's stature but coming close in height. The gentleman sported meticulously groomed jet-black hair, a pair of glasses perched on his nose, and a complexion that bore a warm chestnut hue. He appeared slightly taken aback but promptly introduced himself as Frank, the proprietor of a local barbershop that bore his name. This wasn't just any barbershop; it was frequented not only by ordinary folks seeking haircuts but also by a roster of well-known athletes, artists, politicians, and professionals. Frank Mitrushi's enthusiastic visit, inspired by Xhelo's recent television appearance and his call for the conservation of snakes, had led him to the clinic on his day off. Xhelo listened attentively, maintaining a polite detachment, as he simultaneously kept a watchful eye on the TV for any breaking news concerning his missing friends, with the 48-hour mark looming.

"You've become quite the sensation in our city, especially with your unexpected championing of snakes," Frank Mitrushi continued. "I've heard plenty about your reputation as a distinguished veterinarian, but your interview yesterday left me utterly impressed. Although, I must say, you might have been better off praising eagles instead of snakes, for we are a nation of eagles. By advocating for snake conservation, it's almost as if you're turning us into a nation of serpents. Eagles, you see, are the natural foes of snakes and poultry," Frank Mitrushi mused.

"Indeed, it does seem like we've been a nation of snakes for far too long, stagnant for centuries. Haven't you noticed? That's precisely why I made that public appeal! Or, to put it more candidly, my friend, we've been snakes to each other while acting like poultry when dealing with foreigners. Do you catch my drift?" Xhelo replied, his gaze steady and unwavering.

Frank Mitrushi found himself taken aback by the response he received from his fellow countryman. How could someone speak about the Albanian nation in such a manner? Albania, the nation that had endured endless tribulations, the most beleaguered in the Balkans, had always lived under the shadow of injustice and the divisive schemes of its neighbors and great powers. He cast his gaze downward, choosing to listen to this Albanian who seemed to have spoken in a moment of frustration, hoping it was a transient outburst. Following the typical Albanian conversational pattern, he met Xhelo's gaze directly and, with the audacity that only Albanians seemed to possess, offered his response:

"Dear Xhelo! I am as Albanian as you are. We must defend our nation, just as Americans defend theirs. I've spent decades here, and honestly, I've never heard anyone speak of our nation in such a way. I came here to express my gratitude, not to receive such a response from an educated person like yourself. Perhaps I should take my leave before we delve further into this."

In truth, as he encountered the timidity and greed among fellow immigrants, the constant surveillance of one another, and the ceaseless intrigues within their community, he had not only lost hope but also recalled the time, effort, and financial resources he had invested in gathering Albanians for Flag Day celebrations in Chicago. He had organized patriotic songs and displayed a grand flag among the Americans, accompanied by abundant feasts. Yet, from behind their backs, some Albanians had suggested, "You're doing this for profit." His sole intention had been to find joy in it. Eventually, as the hall emptied, leaving him alone amidst scattered beer bottles and glasses of raki, he had cried out: "Albanians, you hollow souls, you have never been fulfilled!" He knew he had paraphrased the words of Faik Bey Konica, but he did so for his own sake, in a somber moment of contemplation. Recalling all of this, he maintained eye contact with Frank Mitrushi, who seemed like a decent individual, perhaps equally wounded by what Xhelo had uttered. With an unspoken sense of remorse, he continued:

"No, dear friend Frank! Those words were not my own. They were spoken by prominent Albanians in the last century, not by an insignificant person like me. Do you know who once declared, perhaps before your time and mine: 'Let all the world know from this day forward, I am no longer an Albanian'? Or the other one: 'Albania, I have mourned you; the baseness never ceases.'" He intentionally borrowed from well-known expressions to infuse their conversation with a touch of familiarity. Frank Mitrushi was one of the few Albanians he had opened up to in a long while, as most had grown resentful of him for publicly disassociating himself from community endeavors, finding more solace in the Serbian club than in Albanian cafes, where conversations seemed to be awash in smoke and verbosity, much like in Albania.

This chance encounter had arrived during a particularly hectic period for him and his business. He knew he wasn't your average immigrant, nor was he one of those who had falsified high school diplomas just to make their way to America with only an eighth-grade education. No, he hadn't fabricated anything, hadn't deceived anyone, hadn't pilfered a single penny in his entire life, yet he felt as if he were cursed by God. He had spoken so fervently in the span of a few minutes that Frank Mitrushi, who claimed to hail from Çërrava of Pogradec and had worked as a surveyor throughout his life, found himself caught in a whirlwind for the very first time.

It seemed as though they had bared their souls to one another, and for the first time, both realized that being Albanian wasn't the issue; the malevolent spirit was the true culprit, a fact that couldn't be expressed more succinctly. Frank, now feeling an inexplicable connection, laid his heart bare. He confided in Xhelo that his real name wasn't Frank but Fevzi Mitrushi. Almost three decades ago, he had come to America with his wife and two children, laboring in various jobs before eventually working with the municipality. There, a compassionate individual had directed him to an office that assisted immigrants in vocational training and English language courses. Frank had randomly chosen to become a barber and had successfully completed his training. He had worked for a remarkable Italian barber, who, upon retiring, had sold him the business and passed down the name "Frank's Barbershop." One day, he had decided to change his name as well, retaining Fevzi as a middle name to demonstrate his continued allegiance to his heritage. But even that had not felt sufficient. Frank Mitrushi divulged so much to Xhelo in those few minutes that his final revelation left Xhelo astounded:

"Xhelo, the years I've spent in America have transformed me profoundly, have been astonishingly generous, and have rejuvenated me both in spirit and vitality. Just five years ago, much like our political prisoner Pjetër Arbnori, the embodiment of political wisdom and became father in his 60th, I too became a father. It's a gift for my later years. When I hold my son's hand, people often remark, 'What a wonderful grandfather,' when, in fact, I am his father. That's the wonder of this country. It has the power to make you fertile even when you believe everything has dried up... This, my dear friend, is America to me."

Doctor Lakrori, to everyone's surprise, did not take this as a provocation. He had listened closely to the whole narrative, which was so genuine, so heartfelt, that it left no room to doubt its authenticity. He chuckled at Fevzi from Çërrava's candidness and, speaking in pure Albanian, recited the old saying, "A friend is better than a farm," emphasizing the value of genuine human connection over material wealth. He realized that what he truly needed was the warmth of people and the sincerity that flowed from the soul— honesty that expressed thoughts without the hypocrisy and flattery often exhibited by sycophants and the multitude of journalists and analysts in Tirana. These individuals poisoned society with their words and deceit, attacking it from all sides, a society that had withered in spirit, character, and entirety. He believed it would take as many years as had passed since Skanderbeg's death to reform and purify the society. From this perspective, the Albanian nation would only truly heal once people like him and Frank Mitrushi were relegated to the annals of history.

"Thank you, Frank, for this genuine conversation, and may your child of old age thrive. Do you know you're the first Albanian visitor to my clinic?" Xhelo inquired, gazing out of the windows where life in all its diversity and complexity unfolded. It felt as though he had finally encountered an Albanian in the big city who shared his sincerity, unburdened by the deceit and pretense that often-accompanied immigrants.

"Don't even get me started on our world, Xhelo! No one shows me any respect in my barbershop. In fact, they all say I'm not the owner but the Italian's servant. To mock me, all those who know me and are familiar with my profession deliberately go to the barbershop across the street.

Xhelo chuckled at the memory. Frank Fevzi Mitrushi, as if he hadn't yet exhausted all his stories, continued:

"I don't need Albanian clients; most of them are headstrong, and you never know where to start with them. I have an excellent clientele, just like you, Xhelo. People appreciate me because I know how to respect them, just as I respect myself. That's the only secret that keeps my business thriving. I'm ready to kiss every hand that extends payment and a tip, especially when I remember that often, this human tip—given freely and willingly by the client—is as much or more than my salary as a surveyor when I toiled between Trebinja and Slabinja. Do you understand, Xhelo? For those of us fortunate enough to find America, life has changed. But, my friend, nothing fell from the sky! Your words in that interview with that American beauty kept me up at night. Not to brag, but I have a diverse array of clients, many of them distinguished figures. I've shaved Robert De Niro, who happened to be friends with my boss. This great Hollywood artist, who has recently become a vocal critic of Trump—whom I admire—visited the barbershop and told Frank he wanted to be shaved by the new Albanian barber. You won't believe it, but with tears in his eyes, he said, 'Frank, let Mitrushi shave me and take a photo.' I've enlarged that photo and displayed it in the shop alongside Mother Teresa's picture. I've also shaved Michael Jordan and Tiger Woods. Only Jim Belushi has never come to me; perhaps he doesn't know I'm Albanian. Before his senatorial career and the presidency, even Barack Obama was a client of mine, not to mention local politicians and Chicago's bigwigs. Buddy, I'm in a business I love. Some Albanians may mock me, but I just laugh because ever since I held my first pair of scissors, I've never been left without money in my pocket."

"Come on, you're not saying you've had Clinton or Trump in your chair, are you?" Xhelo responded, entertained by Frank Fevzi Mitrushi's unabashed and enjoyable boasting. The man's manner of speaking stirred memories of Xhelo's war veteran uncle.

"No, I haven't had the chance to cut their hair. Why would I make up a story like that? It's said President Trump doesn't frequent barbers; he doesn't need to. But to me, he's a man! He's shaken up everyone and left the world in awe."

Their discussion about politics appeared to cement their connection even further. Xhelo was pleased to find another Albanian American who supported Trump—not with the black-and-white judgment of those in Detroit but with an argument that sounded credible, especially from a businessman who desired minimal government interference in his trade. "Look at how fate brings another vote for the man with the raised fist. If this country could endure four years, what's another four? And as for us Albanians, who endured almost 45 years under the rule of the man from Gjirokastra?" Xhelo pondered, offering his guest a slice of the delectable pizza. Yet Frank Fevzi Mitrushi seemed uninterested, yearning for the renowned pies from his region.

Just as the two compatriots appeared to lapse into silence, a torrent of words from the expansive screen in Xhelo Lakrori's office seized their attention:

"Breaking news. A private plane carrying two Americans has vanished in the woods near the Canadian border in the state of Minnesota, where they were believed to be on a seasonal hunting trip. The cause of this perplexing disappearance remains unclear, though weather conditions are not to blame. The aircraft is confirmed to have belonged to the couple Mitch and Gina Miller from Chicago. Additional details may emerge in due course..." The two Albanians stood breathless. Xhelo's visage had turned to stone. The news he had refused to accept had proven true. Profound grief overcame him. His thoughts immediately turned to Ana, who was on the verge of giving birth. He recognized the situation was agonizing, yet it was also a human one. He could commit to the most humane of acts by caring for the child soon to arrive. Who else could do it better than Xhelo Lakrori, who had yearned for an opportunity like this for decades? He knew his longing to become a parent now collided with a harsh reality. According to him, the Albanians had a saying that best fit such situations: "The living stay with the living, and the dead with the dead." Had he been less cautious and joined them on the hunting trip, he would now be on the list of the missing or deceased, as reported on the screen. For the first time, he commended himself for responding with a firm "no," despite the temptation of what he believed was a genuine invitation. Maybe Mitch had extended that invitation as a potential alibi, but the unexpected fate of the private plane had taken all alibis and doubts with it. He felt a profound sadness and was suddenly engulfed in memories of the past, bygone moments. He almost forgot that another Albanian stood beside him, sharing the same shocking news.

"Xhelo, can you hear me? He was my client. Used to get his hair done by me till last year. He was a generous man, Xhelo. Left me a hundred-dollar tip for a haircut. I remember... A real big spender, Xhelo."

The voice belonged to Frank Fevzi Mitrushi, known as the "Barber of Seville," a man caught between the capitalism of his present and the socialism he left behind. Xhelo found himself straddling the line between his past and the words he was hearing now. His friends were presumed lost, somewhere in the wilderness of Minnesota, where the boundaries of capitalist America and socialist Canada converged. Xhelo's return to reality came in the form of the Albanian barber, who had gained fame for his styling skills among Americans.

He was struggling to make sense of the emotions that had overwhelmed him, much like when one Albanian stands by another in moments of shared pain, when Albanians unite in their thoughts like no other people.

"He is my friend Frank. Do you know him as well?" Xhelo asked, finding it hard to believe that his friend might have met his end in the northern Minnesota woods, where the untamed wilderness of Canada met the warm spirit of the Minnesotans—a hospitable people with a touch of Scandinavian kindness, who aligned themselves with both Norway and Sweden, revealing the true essence of humanity without hesitation.

For the first time, Frank Fevzi Mitrushi found himself ensnared in a human dilemma. He didn't know how to decipher the profound surprise that gripped the esteemed doctor, now a household name in Chicago and its surroundings, thanks to his recent interview that had captivated animal lovers even more than a Japanese earthquake. Suddenly, Xhelo had become a beloved hero to the renowned barber, who had once worked as land surveyor in Albania and had spent decades tending to the receding hairlines of Americans. Many of his clients didn't even need a haircut; they came to him for a ritual of rejuvenation and always left generous tips in the capable hands of Frank Mitrushi, who had unexpectedly started trembling like the hands of beleaguered debt collectors in Tirana. Such was life—an irony that could make you laugh at yourself to the point of madness.

Both men appeared to have regained their composure after the initial shock of the news. For Xhelo, this was somewhat expected, as he grappled with the fate of Shano and Ana, both on the cusp of giving birth. But what about the barber? What connected this man to the tragedy beyond a hefty tip? Both men seemed adrift, their faces etched with the drama stirred by the heart-wrenching news. They gazed at each other like two individuals who, believing they had bid farewell to life after a treacherous sea voyage, suddenly found themselves washed ashore by the waves, awakening from the specter of death.

The visitor to the clinic, unfamiliar with this world, felt like an outsider. He didn't own a dog or a cat. He had heard that veterinarians were akin to writers with vivid imaginations, inhabiting a reality where everything human appeared animalistic and everything animalistic seemed human. It was a duality and ambiguity that could never be fully unraveled. Having spent his entire life working with farm animals such as donkeys, goats, cows, and sheep, Frank Mitrushi had drawn a firm line between himself and the animal kingdom. Since his arrival on this continent as an immigrant, he had never felt the urge to own a dog, a cat, a tiger, or a monkey. Frank the barber was already overwhelmed by humans, whose breath, murmurs, whispers, and half-formed words he encountered daily in his work. He was simply content, and when he returned home, he longed to hear only his wife's voice. She had, even in her advanced years, blessed him with a son—a story that seemed plausible only in America.

"Xhelo, this is a well-known wealthy man who's a frequent topic of conversation in my barbershop. You see, my friend, American barbershops function as 'wise councils,' where everything is discussed, and everyone is talked about. Essentially, the Albanian saying, 'What the stomach hides, the beard reveals,' holds true here. In this setting, one hears all the whispers, all the city's tales. So, I've heard about this man. They say he isn't as wealthy as he claims, but rather, he's chasing the almighty dollar. I have many clients who have made fortunes with him, but lately, there's been some discontent brewing. Understand me, these are barbershop conversations, but I've heard just as much truth as fiction there. People even say that Trump isn't as wealthy as he appears. Maybe this man hasn't met his end, God forbid. Barbers are like canaries in coal mines; we're the first to hear things that nobody else believes. May God forgive me if I'm mistaken, but..."

The doctor had had enough of Albanian tales. He felt the urgent need to be with Shano, to speak to her and offer his support. Every minute spent away from her seemed like a curse. He contemplated sending a text of encouragement and solace to Ana, who was surely devastated by the news and likely collapsed on the king-size bed in the Millers' grand villa. However, he couldn't risk compromising his dream. He had abandoned his grandiose ambitions; now, all he longed for was Shano Gërsheta. She alone could understand his loneliness, for even if he had fathered 10 or 15 children, after experiencing the comforting joy they bring with their innocence and lack of guilt, it would still be Shano who could console him if he had been part of the millionaire's ill-fated hunting expedition

"Frank, you've been a delightful Albanian surprise, but I must return home. My wife needs me. Yes, this millionaire couple is in our circle of friends. I apologize, but I have to leave the office."

They couldn't shake hands due to the circumstances, so they exchanged a simple wave of their five fingers, much like distant figures signaling to each other from treetops. Frank Mitrushi was taken aback by the realization that he hadn't recognized such a remarkable figure earlier, a man who had stirred all of Chicago with a single interview. Two individuals who could potentially support Trump had unexpectedly crossed paths, albeit with differing perspectives. Meanwhile, both were left stunned by the news of the tragic fate of the millionaire couple from their city.

Chapter Fifteen

The fate of the Miller couple remained enshrouded in uncertainty. According to reports, their plane had vanished from the radar at Duluth International Airport at 11:52 a.m. on October 20, 2020. The couple had embarked on their return journey to attend a family gathering that day. This detail offered a glimmer of hope to Xhelo, alleviating some of his anxieties. Perhaps they were still alive somewhere awaiting a swift rescue or battling injuries sustained during the plane's calamitous descent. The primal struggle against death was a universal trait of all living beings. What if this malfunction had occurred while Xhelo was inspecting the arch of Saint Louis's famed western gate, with Mitchi at the plane's controls? Just a few days prior, he had been on that very aircraft. He could have met the same fate as his friends. His demise would have made headlines; yet, unlike the quiet, inconspicuous deaths that billions have faced throughout history, his would have been a topic of discussion on TV networks in both America and Albania: "Private Plane Crashes in the USA. Local Millionaire and Veterinarian Xhelo Lakrori, Known for His Campaign to Rehabilitate Terrifying Snakes, Among the Victims..." The snake reference would likely garner more shock than his name itself. He chuckled bitterly. The situation was dire. He had lost two dear and wealthy friends, and yet, details remained elusive. In the meantime, he refrained from reaching out further to Ana, even under these extraordinary circumstances. She didn't need his assistance. The couple must have made contingency plans. On a related note, approximately 150 volunteers continued to scour the presumed crash site, yet their efforts had yielded no results.

According to the latest updates, the aircraft had emitted no distress signals, making it challenging to pinpoint its exact location. Xhelo's gaze remained fixed on the screen, reminiscent of the early days of the pluralist parliament in Albania. It was a period marked by a chorus of diverse voices, where no single voice dominated, and there was no dictatorial tone. It was a captivating time when a nation that had never invaded another but had endured numerous invasions reveled in the animated debates of their parliament—a political spectacle akin to the theatrical productions of the post-communist era.

It was an era marked by the clash of diverse ideas, perspectives, and ideologies. Former diplomats from the days of Enver Hoxha now found themselves addressing the Albanian parliament, quite different from their past appearances at the United Nations. Yet, their attire had undergone a transformation. Simultaneously, descendants of the former National Front, proudly celebrated their forefathers' heroics, while monarchists patiently awaited the day when King Zog's legacy would once again grace the royal palace.

This period witnessed the most tumultuous transformation of Albanian society, a time when the future deputies engaged in the trafficking of drugs, sex, and human lives in the West had yet to emerge. It was a dawn of democratic rejuvenation, marked by frequent misunderstandings and abundant laughter, despite the hardships of the Albanian market.

Xhelo's mind, anchored in the past, was abruptly brought back to the present as he sought more information about the Millers' fate. He wanted to know the status of the search efforts and the level of coordination between local law enforcement and the Federal Investigation Agency. Perhaps the plane had crashed into the dense Canadian woods or submerged in one of the countless lakes in the region, which boasted over ten thousand such bodies of water. Part of him felt the urge to join the search, to call out his friend's name amidst the northern timberlands as a testament to their deep bond. He wasn't sure how else to convey his profound sense of friendship.

Upon sharing this sentiment with Shano, she promptly dismissed it. "We're in America, Xhelo! Our friendship with them, to use an Albanian phrase, was merely 'a dewdrop in morning.' Don't dwell on it. It's tragic, but we shouldn't bear the weight. When will you leave Albania behind, dear Xhelo? You're beyond the Atlantic now; you're in America," Shano asserted. Each day, she manifested a discernment he'd either overlooked before, or perhaps he was just smitten, for every word of hers resonated with wisdom.

The television screen showcased the Trump-Biden electoral battle, relegating other domestic incidents to a ticker at the bottom. They flowed seamlessly, much like the philosophical quotes he'd committed to memory. However, aviation and terrestrial mishaps always gripped the public's attention, ensuring that updates about the plane crash stood out. As he focused on the latest crash-related updates, a reporter appeared onscreen, broadcasting live from International Falls, Minnesota, indicating that the incident had occurred almost 250 kilometers northwest of Duluth. The reporter announced, "New evidence suggests that despite the plane's last known communication with Duluth's control tower, it mysteriously veered northwest, potentially crashing near the U.S.-Canadian border. This is purely speculative, as no eyewitnesses have reported the crash to authorities. Volunteer search efforts from Duluth have ceased, but locals here are rallying to initiate another search, eager for any indication or evidence of the alleged crash. An anonymous aviation expert expressed that this unexpected change in flight path presents the primary mystery, which in turn begets additional questions. The local branch of the Federal Bureau of Investigation has formed a specialized team. We'll provide updates as they come in. Reporting from International Falls in Minnesota, I'm William Washington."

"Shano, why would they deviate from their planned route? What could've prompted such a decision? While guests gathered at their villa for a baby shower, they headed not just west but northwest? What could be happening here?" Xhelo questioned, clearly distraught.

She approached, her gaze sweeping over the ever-changing news reports like the rhythmic ebb and flow of ocean waves. She sensed Xhelo's profound anguish, viewing the incident as a profound tragedy. However, Shano held a unique perspective. To her, life was a fleeting journey, a transient existence destined to fade into obscurity or, worse, misrepresentation. In her eyes, life was meant to be savored—a moment of pure, unadulterated existence where one's essence remained under their sole control. Once that control was relinquished, one became inconsequential. She regarded Xhelo's forlorn expression with sympathy, feeling sorrow for him but shedding no tears. Contrary to his expectations, she remarked:

"Why are you so taken aback, dear? Haven't I told you that a mother's true love for her offspring begins from the moment she feels the kicks in her stomach? That's when it's confirmed that they are two entities, both loving and resisting each other. When the baby kicks for the first time, it's as if it's saying: 'Give me freedom... Let me out.' But you don't offer it the kind of freedom you once dreamt of during that memorable three-month choir tour after graduation. That's precisely when love and the first seeds of resentment take root. It's the onset of an intricate dance of conflict and love that's never been truly deciphered. Isn't the act of intimacy between couples often a mix of passion and dominance, an intense impulse that leads you men to say, 'I had my way with her'? Isn't life, in its essence, a duel? Not the 'Silent Duel' you fondly recall from socialist times, but a continuous tussle between two disparate entities that are nevertheless bound to love each other, share the same bed, reside under one roof, and maintain decorum. It's all a façade. But back to the baby's kicks—the Miller couple might have experienced kicks of a different sort, but not these. And when you don't feel those particular kicks, the ones I can only begin to describe, because men like you remain perpetually clueless, you're essentially a nonentity. Thus, your couple friends, oblivious to the sensation of kicks in a mother's womb, were merely spectators to a responsibility. Perhaps they had a change of heart, much like they seemingly changed their flight direction, as the news suggests."

He had never received such an intense lesson from the woman he adored. Every word resonated deeply, expressed in a manner he had never witnessed before. Not yesterday, not ever. Only today. It felt as though she wanted to blurt out, "Thank God for the plane crash." Yet, she was simultaneously consumed by guilt and concern over their millionaire friends' uncertain fate.

"Dear Shano," Xhelo whispered.

"Immortal Xhelo!" she responded.

After planting a fervent kiss on his lips, she moved to the reading room, a unique space adorned with white leather armchairs, bookshelves, and wine bottles on display. Xhelo had tailored it to her taste, ensuring the room embodied her essence through its colors, artwork, and the few exquisite sculptures that made it feel like a grand showcase. Shano picked up one of the guitars hanging on the wall, and without waiting for another reaction from her lover, she began to voice a song that had been burning inside her, haunting her for decades. She poured her heart out like never before:

"Once, when I was young, I was so naïve/ I yearned for a boy who only knew deceit/ But behold, youth has waned, with it, love's fleeting feat/ Now I sit here, drenched in pain,/lamenting my lost

years, incomplete./ Once, when I was young, I was so naive..."

The strings of the guitar vibrated under her skilled fingers, reminiscent of a snowstorm swirling around a dense pine tree. Xhelo, from beyond the room, absorbed this surge of youthful spirit and hesitated to intrude. He had often attempted to harmonize his voice with hers, but through her fervent strumming, she seemed to convey, "Retreat to the bedroom. That is where we connect, not here... Give me space..." The resonating strings intimidated him, a man capable of alleviating any ailment in mammalian creatures, yet helpless against his wife's impassioned zeal. "To hell with it all," he muttered, aggressively switching off the television, as if affirming that their private universe, composed only of him and her adjacent song, was paramount. Trembling from the melodies, he retreated to the bedroom, awaiting the very cause of his ardor.

He knew his name would surface eventually, prompting inquiries. Fear was foreign to him; he bore no guilt or committed any transgressions. Their brief, delightful encounters reassured him. Moreover, having resisted Mitch's monetary manipulations bolstered his confidence in his financial acumen. Mitrushi the barber's tales bordered on the absurd, but their veracity was inconsequential to him.

He resolved not to burden Shano with Chicago's barber yarns. Such establishments, with their spinning chairs, often gave rise to spiraling gossip, akin to the Albanian barbershops of yore, bustling with chatter and sports enthusiasts. Relieved from the stress surrounding Ana, he acknowledged the quagmire he had narrowly avoided. Had their rendezvous at "Koko" restaurant materialized solo, their discourse could have veered unpredictably. After all, men, despite their intellect, can be effortlessly beguiled by feminine allure.

Shano had procured a few days off to organize the impending Halloween soirée, an event she cherished. Concurrently, Xhelo opted for a brief respite, indulging in domestic chores. His enterprise had matured, now operating seamlessly in his absence, reminiscent of the tranquil flow of Albania's Buna River. Noon ushered in an assertive knock. "They're here," he internally surmised, grateful that Shano remained oblivious to the authoritative knock, akin to an irrefutable government edict. A governmental summons could be onerous. In America, governance was nearly imperceptible, benign until one trespassed the law. Entangled in the web of law enforcement, the dynamics shifted profoundly. Agents, detectives, and police scrutinized, interrogated, and probed. One's tranquility and autonomy evaporated. One became obligated to respond candidly, sidestepping deceit or manipulation, as these could jeopardize one's liberty.

America had sculpted a colossal system, adept at executing law and justice in its combat against crime and potential criminal suspects. Somewhere within its vast offices, his name had undoubtedly been tagged as an associate of the Millers. However, well-aware of the truth, he remained undaunted by this legalistic rite poised at his doorstep. Memories of fellow Albanians haunted him—those who had been subjected to the brutal knocks of a communist regime, signaling terror and potential doom. Fortunately, he had always trodden cautiously, never opposing the government. The age-old clash between the individual and the state eluded him, for he had avoided such turmoil. But why must governance be so heavy-handed? Why, regardless of a dictatorship or democracy, must it oppress the individual, demeaning and belittling him? Who truly is the government, and why does this creation of man seem inherently antagonistic? Is there a more harmonious, compassionate, and logical middle ground?

Over time, he came to understand that governments, by their very nature, possessed the capacity for violence when they perceived an individual as a threat. In dictatorships, this violence often came in the form of ruthless decrees that quashed dissent from the top down. In Western societies, this latent power was dormant until an individual's actions or defiance raised suspicions. If you resisted forcefully, you risked a fatal response. If you became a suspect, the state, armed with court orders and directives from shadowy chambers, would descend upon your home. Whether in a dictatorship or a democracy, the state was ultimately an instrument of force. The only distinction lay in who wielded that force and the methods they employed.

Meanwhile, Shano had switched on the television and immersed herself in the nostalgic melodies of Lepa Brena, a singer from their youth. However, a second, more insistent knock at the door disrupted their tranquility, reminiscent of an authoritarian state's demand for compliance, like a menacing beast ready to pounce on its prey.

"Coming!" Xhelo responded, briefly glancing through the pristine window. Two men, dressed somberly and exuding an air of impatient anticipation, stood on the doorstep. Memories of past invasions during Albania's communist regime rushed back to him, when careless words could lead to imprisonment. Today, while the authority retained its intensity, it approached with more civility, seeking the truth rather than hastily branding individuals.

Xhelo swung the door open to reveal two men, in their forties—one with Asian features and the other Caucasian with Germanic traits. Both were tall and reserved, their professional smiles reminiscent of newscasters. After introducing themselves and requesting entrance as part of their procedure, Xhelo welcomed them into the living area and promptly informed Shano of their presence. Although she had anticipated their arrival, a sense of unease washed over her. Their presence in formal attire reminded her of local operatives from their homeland, who would invade offices unannounced. However, these men appeared more refined.

At first, Shano suggested to Xhelo that they hire a lawyer to preempt potential complications, but he resisted the idea. In his view, the abundance of lawyers in America resembled leeches, draining both individuals and the essence of a free society. They were exorbitantly expensive, charging as if they minted gold with every word, which felt like a stylized repetition of their clients' own words. To him, they were a malevolent element of society, manipulating truths with their intimate knowledge of America's complex laws. Whenever he heard mention of lawyers or legal consultants, his thoughts turned to the communist government, which had ruthlessly dismissed any form of defense for those accused of crimes or treason, particularly after the 1970s. While he hadn't been born when another regime took hold in Albania, his partisan uncle had shared stories of a government that denied any form of advocacy, leaving individuals defenseless against accusations.

In his youth, Xhelo had viewed this system as just. At that time, when the party declared someone an "enemy," that declaration was absolute and beyond dispute. Even if the allegations were baseless, it didn't matter—the party's word was sacred. In stark contrast, America prioritized the defense of every accused individual, even those who were clearly guilty. This intricate system of accusation and defense was the most paradoxical and cherished system ever created by man. Within it, being ensnared in the American legal system was a dire fate.

Shano, more pragmatic than Xhelo, believed in seeking legal counsel. She saw justice as a kind of legal theater where victory depended on the most persuasive interplay of emotion and truth. In her view, Xhelo needed no defense, as he was resolute in his truth, confident that his account would remain unwavering even after a hundred interrogations. Lawyers, he believed, were meant for criminals and felons. Individuals of integrity, those with nothing to hide, had no use for the potentially dubious and certainly costly services of American attorneys.

Xhelo's mind turned to the investigator's question about Ana, sensing a calculated strategy at play. The investigator, with a resemblance to Chinese figures from the 1970s, asked,

"Why did you specifically seek out Ana Parroti?"

"I didn't see the need for an intermediary," Xhelo Lakrori replied. "The meeting was solely to convey our gratitude and clarify that we weren't seeking her services as a surrogate."

"Why wasn't it a joint meeting with your wife? Why was she absent?" the other unfeeling detective.

Xhelo felt caught off guard by the line of questioning. He recognized the direction in which the investigators were heading, yet he was not involved in the couple's mysterious disappearance. Certainly, wild theories had sporadically clouded his mind—mere masculine ruminations, devilish contemplations—but they bore no threat or connection to the actual event. After a momentary hesitation, he decided to respond, fully aware of the detectives' guile that he had witnessed countless times in films.

"We hadn't formalized any joint agreement," he began. "Ana and I had only informally discussed the matter when she visited the clinic to see the snake. Upon sharing this with my wife, she vehemently opposed it. So, I met Ana alone to communicate this." His voice remained steady, and he met the gaze of both men squarely, silently asserting his innocence.

The detectives observed him in silence, jotting down occasional notes before methodically proceeding with their questions.

"Were you taken aback by Mitch's presence during your meet-up?"

"I wasn't anticipating it," Xhelo admitted succinctly.

"Why?" probed the investigator with Chinese features.

"It was a meeting I'd arranged exclusively with Ana."

"Yet, she was carrying Mitch's child," the other detective remarked.

"That's precisely why I held her in high regard and that's where our friendship blossomed," Xhelo responded tersely.

"How did you come to know about the Millers' disappearance?"

"Through a TV news report," Xhelo clarified.

"Were you shocked?"

"Absolutely. They were my friends," Xhelo affirmed with conviction, his unease palpable. This was a type of scrutiny he'd never faced within the confines of his own residence. Fleeting images of Albanians who had endured relentless probes by the dictatorship flashed through his mind. But it wasn't just Albania— similar accounts were rife in Russia, Poland, Romania, Bulgaria, and even East Germany. A system birthed by humanity, revered, and zealously upheld. Even as the presence of the two officers in his opulent abode irked him, he retained a sense of freedom and security. However, an undercurrent of profound apprehension began to stir. It's hardly surprising that many Americans harbor resentment toward their own government. Their most pressing trepidation isn't rooted in fears of foreign adversaries like Russia or China, but rather their domestic governing body. This explains the American affinity for bearing arms, a constitutional right, not as a defense against global threats, but as a bulwark against potential governmental overreach, which they deem the most perilous of all.

"We arm ourselves so that the government fears us, so that the government doesn't overpower us like they did under communism," Xhelo recalled a philosophy teacher once telling him at the clinic. "We Americans view the right to bear arms as essential for governance. The ubiquity of automatic weapons in every household sends a clear message to any governing entity. Hence, always vote for policies that uphold this right. The left desires disarmament to exert unchecked power. If we want our government to fear us, we must be armed, lest we end up like the proletariat of old..." How many insightful remarks had Anderson Fuller, the philosophy professor from the University of Chicago, shared with him? He'd also shown Xhelo astonishing statistics on the arms trade within America. The industry had grown from revenues of $19.1 billion in

2008 to \$60 billion in 2019. A surge in sales typically accompanied presidential election years. Forecasts for 2020 projected a staggering \$63 billion.

Contemplating these numbers, his mind drifted to the socialist policy of "arming the masses." He recalled the weapon depots in his hometown stocked with automatics, Russian rifles, carbines, and even Chinese anti-aircraft guns. But these arms, while touted as belonging to the people, were solely state property. They were never brandished against the government but kept at the ready against perceived external threats. "Had we possessed the audacity of the Americans, we might have toppled the communist regime," he mused, with government detectives present. It bewildered him how his thoughts had strayed to his homeland across the Adriatic, as he braced for the next queries from the pair before him.

"When was your last visit to Minnesota? Ever been to Duluth?" the agents asked in near synchronization.

Their abrupt questioning rattled Xhelo, invoking memories of interrogation methods from his communist past. An urge surged within him, tempting him to retrieve the firearm from his bedroom and chase the detectives out. "What do they care if I've been to Minnesota? Is their implication that I masterminded some plane crash plot? Police everywhere are the same kind of clueless, hence the many jokes about them," he seethed inwardly. For a fleeting moment, he mentally conflated detectives with police officers, but to him, they all symbolized law enforcement. He met their gaze directly and replied:

"I visited Minnesota, specifically Duluth, two years ago. I was there to see my friend, Luftar Korabi, a professor at the University of Minnesota in Duluth. His son had just been accepted to Harvard, a first for our Albanian community. Would you also like to know how many beers we toasted in celebration? Your line of questioning is nonsensical," Xhelo remarked, his disdain evident as he eyed the agents.

"We're simply doing our job, Mr. Lakrori. We ask for your understanding," one investigator responded in a placatory tone. Xhelo was impatient for their departure; their very presence was a source of mounting tension. He was acutely aware of the legal ramifications of misleading or lying in a way that jeopardized a federal investigation. Officials often pounced on such slips, eager to intensify their scrutiny.

The detectives exchanged glances, a silence hanging between them. Finally, seeking a new angle, one ventured, "Should the couple remain missing or, God forbid, be declared dead, have you ever contemplated adopting the expected child? I apologize if this is an insensitive question given your circumstances."

Shano was nearing the end of her tether. To her, the questions felt more like insinuations, almost as though they were trying to implicate Xhelo in a potential crime—a scenario she couldn't fathom. The difficulty lay in the fact that investigators delved into dark places most minds avoided. Crimes and disappearances in America could be so heinous that they defied even the wildest of imaginations. Xhelo caught Shano's gaze and sensed her distress. Meeting the detectives' eyes with a steely resolve, he declared sharply,

"Gentlemen, the absence of an heir is a unique sorrow, known only to those who bear it. My wife and I have never entertained such notions, so my answer is unequivocal: Never!" He rose from his seat, signaling to the detectives that their intrusive line of questioning was over, and it was time for them to depart.

Sensing the palpable tension their inquiry had caused and recognizing the personal struggles of the family they had approached for vital information; the detectives made their exit. But not before leaving their business cards on the table, a customary gesture.

"We appreciate your time. Here are our cards in case you have further questions or additional information to provide," they remarked, their departure reminiscent of a practiced routine. But they were merely two members of law enforcement in plainclothes.

Once certain of their departure, Xhelo returned to the living room, standing before Shano. He saw the anxiety mirrored in her eyes, as solid and looming as a fortress atop a mountain range. Reminded of how Albanians historically sought refuge in the elevated wilds, he sought to comfort her:

"There's no reason to be frightened, my dear," Xhelo reassured, his voice a calming balm. "The story of their disappearance is theirs alone. Americans have a knack for uncovering the truth, and it will surface. You and I have no part in this."

Saying this, he gently cupped her head between his hands, administering a gentle massage that Shano found soothing. He could feel her hands trembling ever so slightly. Was it fear or the oppressive presence of governmental authority? He wasn't sure. But he held her, her head resting against his chest, providing solace during a trying time. Being interrogated by detectives was a first for him.

Shano's perspective differed slightly. While enjoying the comforting touch of Xhelo's hands through her raven-black hair, she voiced her concerns.

"I understand, my love, but why don't you consider hiring a lawyer? These American detectives are intimidating, and their methods remind me of the old dictatorship's tactics. They operate devoid of humanity; to them, you're just another suspect, another case to close. Their sole focus is on their mission. At work, they're unfeeling automatons, devoid of empathy. Such is the nature of detectives everywhere, not just in America."

"Because I don't need one, Shano!" Xhelo asserted firmly. "Lawyers are for those enmeshed in guilt. I am untainted and unafraid."

In the reflective silence that followed, the two of them finished their coffees, half-consumed and now cold. Xhelo promptly discarded the two business cards left by the detectives, their very presence on the table feeling intrusive.

"I don't even want to remember their names," he declared with a hint of a smile, looking at Shano.

Chapter Sixteen

The election campaign surged ahead without pause. To keep himself occupied, Xhelo returned to his work. At times, he felt that Trump might lose; yet, at other moments, he was confident that the President would achieve a resounding victory, astonishing everyone. Xhelo wasn't alone in his admiration; nearly half of America echoed his sentiments. He was particularly drawn to the Republican president's campaign rhetoric. Upon witnessing rallies in various states, he became increasingly assured of Trump's impending win. Amidst the campaign's frenzied information flow, Xhelo sought updates about his friends but was always met with the same refrain: "The search continues."

He couldn't help but notice that since the detectives' visit to his home, a mysterious vehicle seemed to tail him, often parking near his clinic. It was evident he was under surveillance, likely due to the yet-undiscovered bodies. Although this unsettled him, he understood the necessity for the truth. If he were in the detectives' shoes, he would employ the same methods—gathering evidence and facts just as he compiled analyses, information, and pathological signs to diagnose his non-verbal patients.

Every day, Xhelo Lakrori's thoughts oscillated between his missing friends and the intensifying election campaign. Both sides continually emphasized the upcoming "historic election," declaring it as the pivotal juncture that would shape the future of both America and the world. Reports emerged from Texas suggesting that a convoy of Trump supporters had nearly "ambushed" Biden's campaign bus in a show of intimidation, though fortunately, no harm was done. Xhelo awaited a denouncement of this act from the President but heard none. Meanwhile, Trump's advisor, the staunch conservative John Bolton—once an emblem of American conservatism and previously the U.S. ambassador to the U.N., had recently resigned. He was in the process of releasing a book filled with unsettling revelations that could potentially jeopardize Trump's pursuit of victory.

For Xhelo, this ability to challenge even the highest authority in America solidified his love for the continent. In this land, an individual's freedom was sacrosanct, and they remained the bedrock of society. Facts and narratives constantly flooded screens and social media, allowing everyone the freedom to form their own beliefs. The doctor had made up his mind, and he felt assured that a sizable portion of the populace agreed: Trump deserved another four years.

Meanwhile, news regarding the Chicago couple's disappearance in northern Minnesota waned. It seemed intentional that such an event coincided with the elections, diverting the nation's attention away from tragedies. Xhelo had yet to hear from Ana, who was probably grappling with imminent labor pains. He clung to the hope that the couple was alive somewhere, perhaps being held captive. Yet, the absence of any ransom demands was puzzling. What kind of kidnapping occurred without ultimatums or phone calls? Maybe the investigators were onto something and chose to remain discreet? With everything shrouded in ambiguity, the presidential campaign barreled toward its climax as Election Day loomed.

Xhelo and Shano briefly visited Ana to offer her much-needed comfort. She was just as distraught as the rest. Agents from the Federal Bureau had informed her of the plane's continued absence. There were insinuations that the couple might have been killed in the north, though the specifics remained unclear. The aircraft's disappearance added to the mystery. Xhelo found it hard to reconcile the belief that the couple could be dead without the plane being located. To him, the agents were speculating, hoping to gauge reactions and uncover leads. With two weeks gone and no definitive answers, Xhelo was left pondering: Were they alive, dead, or being held captive?

He half-expected the detectives to question him further about the visit they had made to the surrogate mother, but no one approached him. Had they installed surveillance devices in Ana's pregnant form and hence had no questions left? Why this sudden silence? Had they cleared him of any suspicions? It was plausible. After all, he was perhaps the most law-abiding Albanian American citizen. If everyone were like him and Shano, the nation wouldn't need police, detectives, courts, prisons, or the death penalty. If everyone had the same level of civic responsibility as Xhelo Lakrori and Shano Gërsheta, America would lack these crime scenes altogether. However, this was but a beautiful dream. Humanity varied as wildly as the endless spectrum of creatures on land, air, and sea.

Although President Trump had held several campaign events in his state, Xhelo Lakrori hadn't attended any. He viewed such gatherings as mindless mobs, his patience for rallies and parades having worn thin during the socialist years. "Such crowds are for those with time to spare," the veterinarian would muse. "Nothing of substance is discussed, nothing to stimulate intellectual debate. They're just campaign clichés, no different from party congresses," Xhelo reflected. To him, the decision to support one candidate over another wasn't made at these "group events" but came from personal reflection. He often considered himself a complex voter, laden with doubts and considerations.

He discarded all invitations to engage in mail-in voting, or what he termed "lazy voting." "Election Day is monumental! Those who value their voting rights should physically cast their vote, not do it casually over a drink... It's disgraceful how the Democrats encourage such apathy," Xhelo staunchly believed. He still viewed Election Day as a celebratory event and wondered why it wasn't made an official holiday, or at least held on a Sunday, as was the case in Albania—a memory that never ceased to trail him.

November 3, 2020, had arrived. That day, he donned a blue suit, a white shirt, and a red tie, reminiscent of President Trump's attire. To him, Election Day was momentous, deserving appropriate gravitas and respect. He felt elated that, after all these years, he had persuaded Shano, who had never participated in voting, to cast her ballot. "Darling, please come vote. While Biden may have a soft spot for Albanians, he'll raise our taxes. Let's vote for fiscal relief, dear." For the first time, she was convinced. "I'll vote this time, Xhelo. For good fortune!" she declared. He was overwhelmed with joy, thinking, "I've made up for the vote that Bilali couldn't place. Rest easy, Bilal... I've kept my promise!" Xhelo told himself. He regretted that his chosen candidate had potentially lost two additional votes from the enigmatic millionaire couple.

Seeking his prior peace, he had minimized contact with Ana. Shano, however, occasionally conversed with her, lending an ear to Ana's ceaseless expressions of anxiety. Shano, ever the optimist, would reassure her, "They will return. Things will improve. Your day will arrive, bringing relief from the anguish known only to mothers." To alleviate Ana's pain, Shano often shared her own heartbreak over the phone—the one she had endured a decade earlier, even if it was unresolved. "Can you see it? You're still fortunate, dear Ana," she would say. From the other end, Shano could sense that her own painful story served as a balm for Ana Parroti's current anguish.

The Lakrori couple had recently discovered that local investigations had dwindled without significant leads. Meanwhile, the Federal Bureau of Investigation had embarked on a discreet probe away from the media's glare. Ana mentioned frequent visits from the police, detectives, and FBI agents. They had even conducted a house search; the legality of which Ana had confirmed via a copy of the court order. They confiscated every document from Mitch's expansive office. Xhelo and Shano, although intrigued, had come to view their past association with the couple as a closed chapter. They were in a phase of trying to mend the emotional scars inherent in such relationships.

Their respite from the mystery surrounding the millionaire couple was work and the anticipation surrounding President Trump's campaign, now approaching its climax: the voting. Their local voting center was a mere 5-minute walk away. It was a lovely November day; the sun was warm and gentle. Donning masks, they ambled side by side to the center. It was serene, sparsely populated, and orderly. No hint of intimidation or apprehension. Xhelo felt as though everyone perceived him as a Trump-supporting Republican, but he remained unfazed. Voting, to him, was a sacred act that demanded respect. He had little patience for those who took it lightly.

Shano's unique voter registration posed no issue. The electoral officials were adept and clear about their duties. Taking their ballots, they entered the booth together. After confirming Shano's vote, he gestured for her to feed her ballot into the computer located at the room's corner. "Go ahead, the machine will take it just like when we used to process silage in the cooperative," he whispered, chuckling with a hint of pride for securing yet another vote for his favored candidate, Trump.

He then turned his attention to his own ballot, hesitating momentarily. The silver-haired man seemed commendable, but his brunette deputy was a different story. While she appeared intelligent, she wasn't to his liking. A client had once labeled her as a "soulless individual, a ruthless prosecutor who had convicted more of her own race in California than anyone else." This description had left an indelible mark on him. Her behavior throughout the campaign, especially her exchanges with the astute Biden during the Democratic primary debates, seemed like mere political posturing. His decision was made.

He then read the lengthy list. But what if he wrote "Xhelo Lakrori for President"? He could do it, but it would be like a speck in the sky. On the list were not just Trump and Biden. There were many others: socialists, social democrats, members of the marijuana party, and so on. "Inferior media. Compromised media... Why don't they mention all these others? Where's the equality here? Why do all the major media outlets focus solely on the two main parties, the Democrats, and the Republicans? Why are the others kept in the shadows, neglected? Trump is right. The media merely taints perceptions and siphons campaign dollars. He deserves my vote..."

Xhelo marked the box next to candidate Trump's name with a blue circle. For good measure, he circled it again to ensure the computer registered the vote clearly. "How wonderful it would've been if that plane hadn't vanished," Xhelo mused, positioning his ballot into the machine. "The president would've had two more votes. But such is life, unpredictable to its end. Perhaps they're alive, or maybe they mailed their votes, being the busy couple, they were."

The human mind is a complex landscape, teeming with thoughts we often hesitate to voice. Yet this intricacy places humanity atop the ecosystem's hierarchy. Not only does humankind possess the capacity for abstraction, but intriguingly, it becomes ensnared by these thoughts in the most unique ways.

Exiting the voting center, they witnessed someone releasing a flurry of balloons, echoing the colors of the American flag, into the sky. "Long live America!" Xhelo Lakrori whispered, captivated by the balloons' ascent. His spirit seemed to rise with them, filled with newfound gratitude. "Long live America," he repeated, his voice brimming with joy. It was a heartfelt proclamation, starkly contrasting the mindless chants of yesteryears in front of socialist tribunals. He recalled uttering praises for the Party and Comrade Enver, echoing the sentiments of his kin and country. Yet here, in America, it felt distinct. It surged from within, not as a collective roar but as a personal testament. To truly grasp this, one must spend years in this land, as he had. Otherwise, the sentiment remains elusive. Absorbed in these reflections, he gently placed a hand on Shano's shoulder. She seemed even more radiant that November day. Without exchanging words, they journeyed home, their silence speaking volumes.

Back home, they had lunch, silently reflecting on their inexplicably vanished friends. Their spirits were lifted, grateful that the investigators hadn't resurfaced, neither at their home nor their workplace. "They've fulfilled their civic duties," they silently concurred. Later, Xhelo spent a few hours at his clinic. He had cleared his schedule for Election Day and given his staff a day off. "Election Day should be a day of rest," he often proclaimed.

The sole phone call he received was from Shaban Shiroka, a veterinarian friend. Shaban had once conveyed to his children in Albania, "If I pass, lay me to rest in America." For three decades, he'd applied for the green card lottery without success. He had personally aided over two hundred winners in this peculiar American lottery, but fortune had eluded him. "Perhaps I'll win the lottery posthumously," Shaban, with his expansive heart, would jest. It pained Xhelo to see him still ensnared by the American dream in his homeland, while so many less-qualified Albanians had been welcomed. Yet destiny is unpredictable.

"Did you vote or not?" asked his friend from Tirana.

"Yes! I just voted, Shaban Shiroka. My vote is a 'bullet for the enemy,'" Xhelo replied with a chuckle. "I voted for 'our son-in-law...'"

"What? For Trump?!" Shaban Shiroka exclaimed.

"Yes. Free country, man!" Xhelo responded in English. He was aware that Shaban had been an early learner of English, and all his immigration documents translated into English bore Shaban's notarized name and signature.

"You did well, but please don't tell me you voted for him because Ballona Qerrja, the singer leading the pro-Trump campaign of Albanian Americans in America, influenced you. If that's the case, I'll come over, and we'll have a huge argument," Shaban Shiroka responded. Xhelo was aware of his friend's aversion to the American president, but this difference in opinion didn't strain their friendship. He was acutely aware of the division, not just in America between two candidates, but also back in his homeland, even more so. Albanian screens seemed more consumed with American politics than with the issues plaguing their own nation. Albania was caught in a tumultuous political transition, shifting loyalties from one leader to the next, and in 30 years, no new face had risen. As an immigrant, Xhelo had witnessed five different U.S. presidents during that same time frame. Interestingly, renowned analysts in Albania seemed to desire a Trump victory, not out of genuine support, but more as a form of revenge against their prime minister who had publicly decried Trump's candidacy back in 2016. In Albania, freedom wasn't seen as the opportunity to speak one's truth, but more as a mandate to align with the powerful.

Xhelo clarified his reasons for voting for Trump. He was not influenced by the Albanian forums, nor by organizations that to him seemed superfluous and aimless. He valued his autonomy in making decisions, free from the bias of the "political commissars" that dominated Tirana's TV channels, which he likened to ideological morgues. These platforms rarely fostered insightful discussions but rather flattery for leaders. "You're squandering the freedom you've achieved!" Xhelo would often declare, exasperated. Shaban Shiroka concurred, equally disillusioned by the cacophony of voices on their nation's screens.

"Let's hope this voting day goes without a hitch. The world's gaze is fixed on America today." He continued the conversation, recounting to Bane Shiroka—another name he went by—about the episode involving the millionaire, the tale of the snake, the surrogate mother, their mysterious disappearance, and the unsettling visit from the detectives. Shaban Shiroka was taken aback. He couldn't fathom that his respected colleague had found himself entangled in such a predicament. He wasn't sure what advice to offer. It was evident that Xhelo's life now revolved more around his experiences across the Atlantic than in Devoll.

"Tread carefully, Xhelo," Shaban warned during one call. "There's nothing that compares to freedom and peace. You're well aware that the American police are steadfast enforcers of the law, not like Zog's gendarmes or Enver's police from the last century. Be cautious, my friend. May God watch over you." They concluded their heartfelt conversation on the day of the American elections.

Relaying everything to a trusted confidant like Shaban felt therapeutic for Xhelo. In Xhelo's eyes, Shaban epitomized the beauty of Albanian camaraderie. "You made it out, Xhelo, you broke free... Please, take me with you," Shaban would often plead. Xhelo took a moment to reflect, uncertainty clouding his thoughts. However, he took solace in one accomplishment that day: he had convinced Shano to vote for the first time, casting yet another ballot for Donald Trump. In doing so, Xhelo felt as though he had achieved a revolutionary feat, reminiscent of bygone days.

Chapter Seventeen

He had spent six hours poring over the medical records of the animals he was slated to visit the following week. Dialing Shano, he let her know about his impending return, hinting at the possibility of sharing dinner together. She had prepared a mouthwatering fish casserole. As they uncorked a bottle of white wine, they raised their glasses in a toast, sending well-wishes for peace and prosperity, not only to America but also to the wider world. For them, wine had become a customary French tradition, as familiar as a glass of water. Yet, as a couple, they sipped just enough to aid digestion. He often recalled a quote by Galileo that likened wine to sunlight diluted in water.

His plan for the evening included watching the election results at the Serbian club, knowing that Aleksi would be there, adding excitement to this historic night. Near the Serbian club, he had reserved a hotel room for the night. Although it was only twenty kilometers from home, he was reluctant to drive after indulging in a few drinks, a decision that Shano approved of. Her evenings were typically dominated by movies, with politics and election results barely registering on her radar. "Regardless of who occupies the White House, the bills still need to be paid. People get all worked up over minor things," she would often remark during heated political discussions.

At the Serbian club, the crowd consisted of Americans and Serbs, with only a handful of Albanians in attendance. Xhelo Lakrori was a frequent visitor, especially when he met up with Aleksi. Their lengthy conversations covered politics, history, and traditions, defying conventional wisdom. Xhelo considered Aleksi to be his best friend, despite the envy his success in Chicago stirred among many Albanians, who would snidely comment on his lack of offspring. Such gossip irritated Xhelo, taking him back to the days of Korçë and Devoll, where gossip was as common as the air they breathed. However, Aleks Petrović never slighted him; he had emerged as

Xhelo's closest friend. Family dinners were a regular occurrence, and Aleksi's American wife, with her Irish roots, often brought their three children along, who loved spending time with Xhelo's two cats. They were particularly drawn to the large aquarium, where they would watch the fish swim with delight. Xhelo cherished his bond with his "enemy" Serb, and he often thought of a saying by the Pogradec writer Niko Nikolla, which emphasized the familial connections among all Balkan people. Xhelo lived this truth every day, wondering, "Who sowed the seeds of this hatred?"

By 10 o'clock, preliminary election results began to trickle in, and it appeared that President Trump was in the lead. This lifted Xhelo's spirits, and the rakia tasted even better.

"To the true sanctity of free voting," he toasted with Aleksi.

"Hold on, the final verdict is still out. Be patient," Aleksi responded.

As they continued their discussion, they realized they had both voted the same way, sparking Xhelo's curiosity. When asked, Aleksi explained, "I'm no fan of the Democrats' constant tax hikes."

They both belonged to the demographic directly impacted by the Democratic candidate's proposed tax increases for those earning over $400,000 annually. This stance had played a significant role in swaying many, including Xhelo, toward Trump, who had promised tax cuts for businesses. Although his goal of simplifying the complex tax code into something as brief as a "greeting card" remained unfulfilled, he had brought about transformative tax reform. Many, including Xhelo, saw this as a boon for the affluent. Xhelo, on the other hand, simply yearned for a uniform tax rate, believing that the convoluted tax laws favored the wealthy, who had the means to navigate the American legal labyrinth to their advantage.

Election night in America resembled a tense football match, with each side uncertain of when the game-changing goal or decisive penalty might come. Xhelo had decided to watch the election results in a slightly inebriated state. He knew that, given the Democrats' election practices, which he saw as akin to freely handing out candy to voters, the final results would likely be shrouded in uncertainty for days, if not weeks. This frustrated him. It seemed that the system had been disrupted by this "voting indulgence," exacerbated by the infamous virus.

"Another plate of meatballs, please!" Xhelo beckoned the waiter as a barrage of updates flooded in. Suddenly, Aleksi introduced another Trump supporter to the table: Vllanica. She proudly identified herself as the granddaughter of a former Serbian American governor of Illinois—a man whose political career had ended in disgrace due to corruption. Without hesitation, she declared that her vote for President Trump was partly driven by the hope that he would pardon her unjustly incarcerated uncle. Vllanica, a professional translator who had established her own successful translation agency, had golden hair that reminded Xhelo of Lepa Brena, whom Shano adored, adding a touch of femininity to the evening. Aleksi mentioned that she had expressed a keen interest in meeting Xhelo after watching his interview about small animals, particularly intrigued by the on-screen discussion about snakes.

Reflecting on it, Xhelo made a connection: advocating for a better understanding of snakes paralleled a plea for Albanians to view their perceived Serbian adversaries in a new light. Vllanica concurred.

"You've found a profound allegory, Xhelo," she observed. "I've dated two Albanians and found them delightful. In fact, I might marry the latest one. Why not? This is America. I hold no animosity toward Albanians; they certainly don't match the negative depiction some Serbian nationalists insist upon."

That single interview, which Xhelo might have brushed off, had not only resonated with animal enthusiasts but also seemed to bridge broader divides. His debut public appearance had inadvertently positioned him as a champion of harmony, channeled through the love for animals. He decided to keep from Aleksi his encounter with the millionaire and the subsequent run-in with detectives. "A Serb is a Serb. Why give him ammunition?" he mused, marveling at how vast America seemed—vast enough to allow infinite possibilities. "Perhaps this expanse is why madness manifests here first before it engulfs other parts of the world," he pondered, sipping his rakia. He remained cautious, heeding his mother's age-old wisdom: "Rakia's true container is its bottle."

Approaching midnight, his phone buzzed to life. Recognizing Shano's number, he answered promptly.

"I'm good, love. How about you? Which movie has caught your attention tonight?"

A distraught sob met his ears. Something was amiss. Shano managed to relay between sobs,

"The cat isn't well. He's been vomiting and can barely breathe! I think he might be poisoned."

This news rattled Xhelo. On such a momentous day, the last thing he wanted was harm befalling their cherished feline companion. Glancing at his drink, he noted he'd consumed little. His sobriety and the urgency of the situation emboldened him to decide his next course of action.

"Have you been drinking?" Shano inquired. "If so, don't drive. Please, take an Uber."

"No, I'm fine. I'm on my way."

He quickly settled the bill and left a generous tip for the waiter. After a brief apology to Aleksi, he exited. In truth, he felt remarkably clear-headed. The alcohol hadn't dulled his senses, and he believed a brief drive would maintain his clarity. He swiftly headed to the hotel to retrieve his emergency equipment bag, then to the clinic for antidotes. Mindful of the potential consequences, he kept his speed in check to avoid attracting any police attention.

Nearing home, he approached the last traffic signal. As the light shifted to yellow, he tried to accelerate past but realized he couldn't beat it. With the red now glaring, he muttered, "Damn it!" Hoping no officers had noticed his misjudgment, he continued, internally celebrating his perceived evasion. But that relief was short-lived. Soon, flashing red and blue lights illuminated his rearview mirror. "Oh no!" he exclaimed, gently braking to pull over.

The glaring spotlight from the police cruiser brought back memories of the border spotlights on Lake Pogradec. Back then, watching from a hotel room, those lights seemed more curious than menacing, especially after intimate moments with Shano. But now, the circumstances were vastly different.

Throughout his time in the country, the police had never pulled him over so late. The single traffic citation in his history was for a minor infraction at a stop sign. He was grateful Shano wasn't with him now; she would've been petrified. As two officers emerged from the cruiser behind him, their hands hovered near their holstered weapons, anticipation evident in their posture. Panic welled up in him. Memories of the evening's brandy resurfaced. Was it too much? "Only two doubles," he reassured himself, "I'm coherent."

As the officers closed in, his mind raced. Recollections of countless movies watched with Shano played in his mind. Suddenly, he felt caught between being the protagonist and the victim. He kept his hands visibly on the steering wheel, awaiting their approach. With every passing second, the gravity of the situation intensified. The lingering scent of alcohol could betray him. Hastily, he donned a mask, hoping it might mask the raki's aroma. If subjected to a test, the results could land him behind bars, irrespective of how clear-headed he felt. He observed the two officers closely. The lead was a tall man of color, his finger dangerously close to his gun's trigger. His partner, in his mid-twenties, exuded the jitteriness of a rookie fresh out of training, evident from his awkward handling of the weapon.

Xhelo tried to remain calm, fully aware that any unnecessary movement could cost him his life. "Police are professional killers," he recalled a client remarking during a discussion on police violence in America. Moments stretched out, feeling more like hours. He felt besieged by legions of police, their gun barrels trained on him, reminiscent of the menacing snakes from his nightmares. A reckless urge tempted him to seize the revolver from the glove box and attempt a daring escape. For a fleeting moment, he felt as though he were the protagonist of a thrilling movie. The tall officer of color appeared exceptionally trained, and Xhelo surmised he would be swiftly neutralized if he tried anything rash. Another wild thought crossed his mind: he could scribble "Long live President Trump" and ensure posthumous fame. The media would undoubtedly spotlight him, labeling him "the first hero for Trump's second term." He would captivate global attention, if only momentarily, before the world's fickle attention span moved on.

Xhelo pondered the racial dynamics at play. If he were unjustly killed, would there be mass protests, as had been the case following the death of African Americans? Would Albanians rally for him? What about the Serbs, or even Ana, who would likely be preoccupied with childbirth? He reflected on an incident where a white Australian woman was fatally shot by a Somali American officer in Minneapolis, with minimal public outcry in its wake. Who, then, would champion justice for Xhelo Lakrori? The Albanians who begrudged his wealth? The Serbs who waited on him for generous gratuities? And how would news of his untimely demise be received in Albania? He could already envision the sensational headlines alleging conspiracy.

The weight of these contemplations nearly pushed him to the brink of laughter, but he stifled the urge, aware of the watchful officers, their fingers hovering near their triggers. Struggling with the emotions stirred up by alcohol, he opted for silence, choosing not to draw attention to himself.

The two officers approached cautiously, clearly ready for any signs of resistance or suspicious behavior. Xhelo found himself enveloped in a chilling apprehension, seeing the holstered weapons on their hips as menacing as the mouth of a cannon. For reasons unknown to him, his thoughts wandered back to an old Albania, when Enver Hoxha had made a declaration, he never quite comprehended, bragging about having the upper hand against their enemies. In his intoxicated state, he couldn't help but entertain hallucinations of having a formidable weapon by his side, one that would make the police officers flee in terror.

As he rolled down his car window, anticipating the officer's questions, the tall officer with a deep African American accent broke the silence.

"Good evening, sir. Do you know why we pulled you over?"

"I'm unaware. I'm dealing with a family emergency," Xhelo responded tersely.

"May I see your identification and vehicle insurance, please?" the officer requested.

He handed over his license and insurance card, trying to appear composed. The scent of alcohol seemed to hang in the air around him. "Maybe they have Covid and can't smell," he muttered under his breath, thinking, "I'd rather have Covid-19 than end up in jail." He wished the intersection had been a roundabout; perhaps that would have spared him this predicament. As he waited, he couldn't help but recall a radio show discussion about the exorbitant cost of American intersections with traffic lights—millions of dollars each. The entire United States had 350,000 such intersections, each costing between $250,000 to $1 million, not including maintenance and other services. "Wasting your own tax dollars," Xhelo mused. The cost of these traffic lights alone dwarfed the entire budget of the Albanian state. "Oh, Albania, you're so small. Just the size of a few American intersections, yet you manage to create such a commotion... What luck I have on this election day," he lamented to himself.

While the officer from the Southern U.S. remained vigilant, his finger poised on the trigger, the taller officer returned swiftly. For a moment, Xhelo dared to hope they might let him go with a fine or a warning, considering his clean record. "Please, let it be," he silently prayed. But sometimes prayers go unanswered.

"You ran a red light. Driving like that endangers both you and others. Please, step out of the car," the tall officer commanded, her tone curt and devoid of sympathy. To Xhelo, her words sounded like a death sentence. They would surely test him for alcohol. A DUI charge would be a personal catastrophe.

"Please, officer, I'm in the middle of a family emergency. Can you simply fine me? I'll even pay double if it means I can get back to my family," Xhelo pleaded, knowing the gravity of being asked to exit the vehicle. Once more, his mind raced with thoughts of drawing his weapon, defiantly declaring his political allegiance. But the stern command interrupted his thoughts:

"Sir, step out of the vehicle." Reluctantly, he complied, his legs feeling unsteady as he did so. He hoped the officer wouldn't notice. She instructed him to stand upright, then moved her fingers from left to right before his eyes, to assess his sobriety. He struggled to focus, feeling himself spiraling. When they ordered an alcohol test, he weakly protested, "No, please, just let me pay the fine."

Xhelo clung to a fragile hope: another crime, a sudden act of violence on the south side, or even a terrorist incident, would distract the police and grant him a lucky escape. But no such event occurred. The alcohol test confirmed his intoxication. He had known, of course; he had been drinking in celebration of the president. Now what? The other officer stood ready, revolver in hand.

"Sir, you're driving under the influence. We need you to come with us to the station," the policewoman declared without a hint of leniency.

"I've done nothing wrong! Just one glass of tequila. You're only doing this because I voted for President Trump. This is a travesty!" Xhelo protested vehemently.

"Sir! You are under arrest for operating a vehicle on a public road under the influence of alcohol. Anything you say can and will be used against you in court," the officer intoned.

"I voted for Trump! That's why you're arresting me. Let me go free!" Xhelo Lakrori asserted loudly.

The tall policewoman acted swiftly. She forcefully twisted his arms and clamped the handcuffs on him. For the first time in six decades, Xhelo Lakrori felt the biting chill of the American police's handcuffs. He had never been arrested before, neither during the dictatorship nor the transition. Was it really possible? Arrested in the land of freedom? In America? He wondered who was behind this unforeseen fate: Biden or Obama, whom he hadn't voted for, or Trump, for whom he hadn't secured enough votes?

The two officers guided him towards their patrol car, its headlights piercing the darkness and its red and blue lights flashing hypnotically. He was on the verge of shouting again, but who would hear? The policewoman, once more, informed him of his right to remain silent and, with some force, pushed him into the back seat, behind the crossed bars. He quickly declared that he had a gun in the car and presented the license that legally allowed him to carry it. The other officer efficiently secured and cataloged the weapon according to procedure. The cuffs seemed to grow colder, binding him like constricting snakes, inhibiting the flow of blood.

Memories of George Floyd, the man killed by the police in Minneapolis, surfaced. Xhelo felt a deep pang of sorrow for Floyd and yearned to be a symbol, a beacon for all immigrants. However, he lacked the strength and the means. Floyd's demise had been public, witnessed by the world. But Xhelo was alone on this dark night, save for the imposing presence of the officers. Military drills from his past came back to him, making his obedience almost automatic. Other tragic tales, like that of the Australian woman killed by police, haunted him. "These people can kill... There's no jesting with them," he inwardly acknowledged and silenced himself.

As he glanced sideways, a tow truck began relocating his black Benz. The police car, in which he was confined, set its course towards the nearby station. Xhelo felt sharp, not the least inebriated. Why were they detaining him? Paranoia set in. Memories of the long-standing enmity between the Albanians and Serbs consumed him. Words from a retired Albanian academic living in Vancouver resonated: "There's no Albanian nation without the extermination of the Serbs." While Xhelo always viewed his Serbian friend, Aleks, as an emblem of unity, doubts started to creep in. Could a Serb have indeed betrayed him to the police, hinting, "A drunk driver. Follow the black ML 550 Benz..."? History had shown that such treacheries were possible.

Bane Shiroka was right. Before America acted as the world's international gendarme, it boasted the most heavy-handed domestic police force that rarely gave its citizens any latitude. Seated in the back of an American police car, with crossed bars reminiscent of a fragmented Nazi cross, Xhelo Lakrori understood the weight of American policing. He sat quietly, handcuffed. Life felt empty. His hard-earned legacy, the act of voting—once seen as an educated person's duty—now seemed trivial. In the backseat of an American police car, everything felt inconsequential.

Could this be a trap set by the detectives who had earlier interrogated him at his residence? His responses to them had been sharp, even caustic. Were they marking him, just as past enemies had been labeled by the party and the people in Albania? If only he had his cellphone to call Shaban Shiroka and relay his arrest, to share that the America he had once dreamt of was merely a veneer hiding violence and tyranny. He wished he could tell his old friend that the grass wasn't greener here, that it was perhaps better to meet one's end freely in Albania than while bound in America. For the first time, he found himself hoping that the missing millionaire couple was still alive; it might save him from further accusations. An American citizen surely wouldn't be incarcerated for merely indulging in a glass or two of raki.

Such a misfortune. Who had hexed him? Was a burdensome heritage life's gravest curse? Or were there even darker fates, as they whispered in Devoll? How he wished he had met his end in Bilal Eshka's grand pool in Denver. At least he would have departed with dignity. No dream offered solace. Xhelo Lakrori was, plainly, under arrest.

The station bustled with detainees from various backgrounds. Seeing others in his situation did offer a sliver of comfort, although he was the sole detainee from Devoll on voting day in America.

"God bless America! Amen," Xhelo Lakrori murmured.

"Has the winner been announced yet? I voted for Trump! He'll win!" he declared. However, amid the commotion of the precinct, no one heeded the words of a handcuffed detainee. The environment was frenetic. Everywhere he looked, he saw others, like himself, handcuffed, ensnared by the system. They were all part of this collective, those who had faltered in the eyes of the law. After this realization, uncertainty and anxiety took hold.

The police car's blinding lights had dimmed, and his intoxication began to subside. A blonde policewoman, following protocol, released him from his cuffs and led him to a holding cell that felt oppressively ominous.

"Jemi lindur senatorë/Jemi votuar kongresmenë/Të gjithë në garë për Shtëpinë e Bardhë" *- he recited in Albanian. Lost in the bleak ambiance of the police station, he slumped onto the cold ground, consciousness slipping away.

----

* *"We are born senators/ We are voted for congressmen/ Our race towards the White House,"*

Chapter Eighteen

Shano Lakrori waited in vain, the eerie silence of the night shrouding her like a thick fog. The man she had leaned on for everything, from life's very essence to dreams, beauty, spirit, and energy, was conspicuously absent from her doorstep. This absence was a stark aberration, an unsettling departure from the norm. A sense of guilt gnawed at her core for interrupting Xhelo's tranquility on that pivotal electoral night. Should she have allowed him to immerse himself in the Serbian whispers and political fervor of the club? She knew that politics was his second heartbeat, a realm alive with fervent debates, passionate arguments, and spirited banter. What had driven her to make that fateful phone call?

Cats, those resilient creatures, had always held a special place in her heart. Her grandmother used to say that tomcats possessed seven lives. Driven by mounting concern, Shano turned to her instincts, drawing on age-old remedies. She delicately fed the cat sugary water, one drop at a time, as if invoking the wisdom of ancient healers. "Home remedies have stood the test of time, even before the days of Hippocrates," she whispered to herself, as her hands moved with purpose, coaxing life back into the creature.

Was this a moment for sorrow? What if gangsters had crossed paths with Xhelo that night, draining his life away like siphoning gas from a tank? Alone in America, with two cats and a pile of unfamiliar banked dollars, how would she find her footing in this unforgiving land? But then again, did one truly need money? Life's unpredictable twists demanded a readiness for whatever might come. Every euphoric phase, no matter how long it lingered, eventually met its conclusion. The final curtain, no matter how much one wished to avoid it, had to fall someday.

In the place she once called home, contemplating such grim eventualities was a rarity. "It's all in God's hands. Do not dwell on mortality," were the words she often heard. Within the tapestry of Albanian culture, death was a subject that left behind regrets for the living. But had anyone ever pondered the agony experienced by those who bid farewell to the still-breathing? Such debates were seldom entertained. Life and death, in their eyes, were distinct realms, and any attempt to blur the lines was seen as sacrilege. Yet Shano had possessed the foresight to prepare for every possible outcome concerning Xhelo. Their meticulously documented will, crafted with the assistance of a lawyer, left no stone unturned, from burial rites to financial allocations and protocols for potential incapacitation. Every instruction was precisely laid out in English. She would only have to grapple with the emotional toll of his absence.

"No, Xhelo doesn't fade into oblivion easily. He still has much to accomplish in this world," ruminated Shano Lakrori, who, on occasion, fondly embraced her maiden name, Shano Gërsheta. The name evoked a distant past, yet Xhelo was unperturbed by her choice. He held liberal views, once telling her, "Keep whichever name you hold dear. Some people eagerly assume their husband's name, only to betray them shortly thereafter. To me, you are irreplaceable." The passage of years had fused them together as inseparably as elements in an alloy. Their bond was unbreakable.

Shano couldn't envision a life without him, yet his prolonged absence sent shivers down her spine. She yearned for the comforting ring of the telephone, but the silence in the room remained unnervingly unbroken.

What could have transpired with Xhelo on that fateful election night? She turned on the television, tuning in to the local station, the harbinger of breaking news in the area. There were no reports of murders, accidents, or kidnappings, providing her with a fleeting sense of relief. Her thoughts then veered toward the detectives who had paid her a visit. Could they have concocted some ruse, detaining him for further questioning, attempting to tie him to the enigmatic disappearances of the affluent? In this land, everything seemed possible.

"God, watch over us," she murmured, seeking to redirect her thoughts. To her, Xhelo was unassailable, and she clung to the hope that she might be the one to depart this world first, freeing him to remarry should he choose. But if she lost him, would she ever consider remarrying? "Never! Never another man around me! Never!" Shano Gërsheta exclaimed, her voice quivering. Such notions had never entered her mind.

Suddenly, a wave of fear swept over her. The detectives' unexpected visit, though anticipated, had shaken her to the core. In America, dealings with law enforcement – be it the police, investigators, or lawyers – often felt like navigating treacherous waters. Evading their clutches could cost a fortune, countless hours spent in government and legal offices, and never-ending trials. "Why am I letting my thoughts wander? We have broken no laws. In this land, if you're law-abiding, you're untouchable," she whispered, as if trying to convince herself in the face of mounting anxiety.

This was, without a doubt, the most harrowing night of Shano Gërsheta's life. What if Xhelo had accidentally struck someone with his car? Hadn't a similar fate befallen Senator Kennedy in Boston in the '70s? Hadn't he, in a drunken stupor, caused the tragic death of a young woman? "Such tragedies occur more often than we know," she recalled her mother saying. Perhaps a despondent soul had thrown themselves in front of Xhelo's car? Some, rather than silently ending their own lives, chose this grim path. Lurking in wait for a luxury car – a symbol of opulence – they would fling themselves into its path, hoping their families might sue and extract a fortune from the affluent driver. The relentless pursuit of wealth in America struck her as inexplicably bizarre.

Each morbid scenario she imagined deepened her dread. Never had she experienced such a prolonged separation from Xhelo. In their 35 years together, their bond had been unparalleled. From intimate moments at home to journeys as far as the Great Wall of China, they had been inseparable. His unexplained absence, the stifling silence, and the absence of communication were driving her to the brink of despair.

She needed to brace herself for any outcome. "If something were to happen to me, I would want you to find love again," Xhelo had whispered to her after sharing many a bottle of wine. She would respond with a wistful smile, "If you were to leave me – which you won't – not only would I never remarry, but I wouldn't even admit to anyone that you were gone. I would carry myself with pride, as if you were forever by my side. Marriage, my love, can be a double-edged sword."

Had she possessed the wisdom she now held, she might never have walked down the aisle, never have surrendered her freedom to any man. Marriage, to the young, was a snare. It astounded her how people rejoiced at weddings. Marriage, she had come to realize, was a spiritual prison, a looming monotony that the young failed to comprehend until they found themselves ensnared within its suffocating grasp.

Once more, she closed her eyes, straining to hear the soft sound at the door that always heralded Xhelo's return. His arrival felt like the breaking of dawn, a moment of pure radiance. Her love for him knew no bounds, and their bond remained unbreakable. This disquieting silence, his inexplicable absence, defied all understanding. She clung to hope, while the plaintive 'meows' of the cats served as stark reminders of his absence. Her mind raced, envisioning a knock on the door, a stranger wearing a black mask, delivering a grim message: "Xhelo is in our custody. Deliver two million dollars for his safe return. Alert the authorities, and both you and he will meet a dire fate."

Chilling possibilities haunted her. Xhelo's recent television fame might have attracted unwanted attention. Anything was plausible in this land. Yet the silence of the phone brought her a strange sense of relief. She had just received heartwarming news of Ana Parroti safely giving birth to a son. Stress had expedited the delivery, but it had been a normal birth, save for the mystery surrounding the biological parents. Shano eagerly awaited sharing this joy with Xhelo, knowing it would bring him elation. The situation had become deeply personal to them, a journey filled with emotions. But to Shano, beyond the profound moment of a new life's arrival, it held little other significance. "People should reconsider marriage! Preserve your genetic material in banks to ensure humanity's future. Live freely, savor life's pleasures, indulge in your fleeting desires – desires that often reveal themselves too late," such musings surged within her, an outcry deemed improper by tradition for a woman from Devoll.

"Meow... Meow..." The revitalized cat stirred, invoking sensations akin to the aftermath of a passionate tryst with Xhelo. Freed from worry, she basked in the serenity and contentment that coursed through her, much like a desert oasis after a long drought. In that moment, she felt the vibrancy of life beside her, affirming that she was more than a desolate twig in a barren wasteland. She was a woman dedicated to the multifaceted dimensions of life, transcending mere genetic legacies that often represented the zenith of human self-importance.

The lingering echo of a phone ring jolted her from her reverie. Could it be the captors of Xhelo? She hesitated to answer, her heart racing. Quickly, she checked her voicemail. Nothing. Her pulse quickened further. It had to be them. Clutching her phone tightly, she held her breath, awaiting a message on WhatsApp. Meanwhile, the cats had settled down, slumbering peacefully. She envisioned herself as a veterinarian, a soothing presence to calm their frayed nerves. If only she hadn't made that call about the cats, she wouldn't be wrestling with this anxiety now. Self-recrimination was futile, though. She looked at the two cats, sprawled lazily one after another on their plush bed. They were like her own offspring, and her heart swelled with affection for them. Quietly, she covered each one with a small blanket and moved into the living room.

The television flickered to life, bombarding her with updates about the election campaign and the intricate electoral vote system. The American voting process left her baffled. It astounded her how a majority vote might not guarantee a presidential victory, all due to these enigmatic "electoral votes," a concept she neither grasped nor had the inclination to delve into. The numbers on the screen shifted back and forth between Trump and Biden, resembling the capricious symbols on Las Vegas slot machines—machines that had devoured her money with the false promise of elusive fortunes.

Switching to a local channel, she found the same political fervor prevailing. However, a breaking news bulletin seized her attention: "State Senator of Illinois, Jim Forest, Apprehended for Driving Under the Influence of Alcohol." She couldn't help but smirk. Even the mighty were subject to the law's reach here. In Albania, such an incident would spark public outrage, decried as a political maneuver, or equated with dictatorial oppression. The comparison struck her as amusing. What if Xhelo had been detained for a similar offense? "When even a state senator isn't immune, what chance does a veterinarian stand, no matter how renowned?" she pondered.

The tranquil presence of the cats momentarily distracted her from Xhelo's absence. Glancing at her phone, there was still no call, aside from that anonymous one. "No news is good news," she recited an American adage she had grown fond of, echoing the Albanian proverb, "Bad news flies." Her mother's wisdom echoed in her mind: "Misfortune strikes swiftly. Stay vigilant, my child! Being a woman comes with its own set of trials and tribulations. Keep your eyes open..." It felt as if her mother's spirit stood before her, and she longed to confide in her, to share her anxieties about Xhelo's mysterious disappearance. Her beloved mother, a tireless worker perpetually besieged by hardships, had been a pillar of strength. Raising four children while caring for her in-laws was no small feat. Those endearing grandparents had spun countless fairy tales for her, despite having six grown children, each with their own families. None had stepped up to care for the elderly couple who had given them life. Tradition dictated it was the youngest child's duty, as they constantly reminded her father: "You're the youngest. The elders are your responsibility." But why the youngest? Was it rooted in the Albanian belief that "The youngest reaps all"?

To her, it seemed an unjust family burden, a form of exploitation. Yet, she remained silent; she was too young. Her hardworking father had pleaded with his siblings, "They'll stay with me. All I ask is for you to take them for a week, just once a month, to give my wife a break." His pleas were ignored. Her mother often succumbed to despair, mourning vociferously in front of a small photograph of her deceased mother, "Oh, Mother, when will it be my turn? Such an unfair life..."

Shano had witnessed these breakdowns countless times. On several occasions, during her mother's late-onset menopause, she had discovered her mother in the attic, desperately attempting to hang herself. The rope would be entwined around her hands and neck, and in fear, Shano would rush to intervene. Her mother, like a tragic actress on a gloomy stage, would cry out, "I want to die! My husband's family treated me like a mule... Let me go!" Shano would wrest the rope away and cast it aside. Her often-half-intoxicated father would then barge in, exclaiming, "Enough of this! Let me hand you a gun if this is what you want, but not this way. You will terrify the children!"

With his strength, he would pull her back inside. Preparing her an egg coffee with a spoonful of honey, he would weep alongside her, gently scolding, "Your constant grief has plunged our lives into misery. You've scared the children enough. Stop this madness." Slowly, due to the coffee or the crushed garlic he mixed in as an old remedy, her mother would regain her senses. With remorse in her eyes, she would murmur, "I don't know where I was, what I said... The village gossips, the demons... They took over me. Forgive me."

Shano had silently borne witness to this recurring family tragedy. They lived in an isolated house, ensuring the village remained oblivious to the sporadic crises within their walls. When Shano first discovered the enchantment of love—a world of stars, light, hope, and embraces, especially those from Beni—she realized she had been imprisoned by her family's troubles. She had lived in the shadow of her mother's tormented memories, always rushing to her side to hush her, fearing that the village would overhear. But the reality had been grimmer.

Nafija of Tele Dushi, a villager with two sons and two daughters, met a tragic end during her own feminine crisis. Employed at the village poultry farm, it appeared that amidst the ceaseless clucking of the hens, her anguished cries had gone unnoticed. One day, she brought her husband's shotgun to work and, amid the cacophony of the birds, had taken her own life. The hens had scattered in panic, attracting eagles that preyed on them. When the guards finally noticed, they realized something was amiss. They discovered Nafija's lifeless body, giving birth to countless rumors. Shano, however, remained skeptical. After this incident, the men in Hoçisht began to show more empathy toward the women, especially when they faced similar emotional turmoil.

"Family crisis or global crisis, we unknowingly welcome horror into our lives," young Shano often mused. However, those reflections momentarily faded into the recesses of her mind when she experienced her first kiss from Ben Kapshtica, a pivotal moment that altered the course of her life. On that serene election night, she couldn't comprehend why she found herself ensnared in this whirlpool of memories and past traumas. Why were thoughts of her deceased mother, the tragic Nafija, and the events that had scarred her lineage resurfacing now? Was this a form of telepathy hinting at ominous news regarding Xhelo amidst the prolonged silence? Never had she been trapped in such a labyrinth of memories. It was akin to the lanterns from her village in the past, whose feeble light struggled to dispel the encroaching darkness. "We were so impoverished, yet so unaware," she whispered to herself.

In America, a woman's position had evolved significantly over time, in stark contrast to the circumstances of two centuries ago, marked by widespread oppression. Back then, men wielded dominion, relegating women to the realm of household chores. They toiled under the dim glow of lamps and candles, hauling water in buckets and stowing away belongings in wooden crates. This bore little resemblance to the modern America she now knew. Such historical realities could be daunting, especially to those who failed to comprehend or make comparisons. America had once been a land of slavery, where a man's wealth was measured by the number of slaves he owned. An individual with a single slave was considered affluent, while those with multiple slaves were even wealthier. Those who possessed an entire army of slaves were deemed the wealthiest and were labeled as slave masters. She often thought, "Thank God I wasn't born in that era. I could've been a slave... Time has ushered in changes, and for this immense transformation, we should be grateful."

Her mind fondly drifted back to her early years in America. Every experience had felt like an awakening, as if she had landed on a different planet rather than merely another continent. In the year 2000, when Al Gore announced his presidential candidacy, she had learned that his wife, Tipper Gore, would be visiting Rochelle, a town west of Chicago, as part of the campaign against Republican George Bush. Eagerly, she and a few friends had attended the event and taken photographs. The wife of the man who had sponsored their visa was astonished, remarking, "You've acclimated so quickly, dear Shano! I've been in America for 30 years and yet I've never had a photograph with politicians of such stature. Congratulations on achieving this so soon after your arrival."

However, when she later heard that the political couple she had met and admired had separated after 40 years and four children, Shano dismissed it as tabloid gossip. She struggled to believe in their divorce, as they had seemed genuinely happy during their encounter. Tipper could have been the First Lady of America, thanks to Al. "Some intricacies of a relationship are known only to the couple involved," a work colleague had once told her. From that point on, she distanced herself from politics. Even if Melania Trump had extended an invitation for a photograph, she would have declined. Many things that had once seemed miraculous in her youth now appeared trivial.

Her reverie was interrupted by the vibration of her phone on the table. Her heart raced, hoping it was Xhelo. However, it was an unknown number. Could it be the kidnappers of her husband, demanding ransom? With a mix of trepidation and eagerness, she answered:

"Shano Gërsheta speaking. Xhelo, is that you?"

Silence followed. She initially suspected it might be one of those robocalls from India that threatened jail for supposed tax evasion, but this felt different. Such calls typically came during the day, not late at night.

Reluctant to end the call, she spoke up, "Hello! Who's this, calling at such a late hour? It's 1 a.m. here."

"Shano, it's Liza. How are you? Liza from Bilisht. Do you remember? I had to hear your voice. I'm sorry if I woke you."

"Liza!?..."

"Yes, from school. I wanted to wish you well for the elections. We're all hoping for peace in America. We in Albania are on tenterhooks for the results. It feels like we're more connected to that continent than our own... Your husband's TV interview has gone viral here. Everyone's talking about both of you. Did you know? Even President Ilir Meta mentioned Xhelo's interview in a press conference. Thanks to the 'Devolli' association's proposal, he's been awarded the title 'Great Master.' All of Albania is abuzz. But you know us; we often call without regard for time zones. It's home for you and me."

Shano recognized the voice; it was Liza. They had navigated their youth together, sharing heartaches and laughter. Liza's call was like a balm, a brief respite from the weight of her worries. Liza sounded fatigued but unmistakably joyful. Shano didn't have the heart to tell her about the potential connection between that interview and her husband's possible abduction.

Their conversation drifted to other topics. Liza was elated, having secured a spot for her autistic son to study in the U.S. through an American church. The joy in her voice was palpable. They had overcome numerous hurdles, but the journey was worth it. She hoped the move would take place after the American presidential inauguration.

"I feel rejuvenated. In Albania, even those without conditions are often treated as if they're lacking. And when there's a genuine ailment, the stigma is even worse. Long live America," Liza remarked. Shano shared in her friend's happiness. America often embodied hope for many, a salve for wounds life doled out.

That phone call breathed new life into her, reminding her that someone out there might still remember her. So, she didn't feel entirely alone. Sleep would have been a welcome respite, perhaps hastening Xhelo's return, but it eluded her. After managing some orders on Poshmark and Amazon, she realized she hadn't checked her Yahoo email account in a while. Curious, she logged in and found almost 150 unread emails awaiting her attention. She tried to prioritize them based on subject lines and senders. One email stood out, reminiscent of a ghost she wished to avoid. After all these years, what gave him the audacity to reach out? She toyed with the idea of deleting it, but a nagging feeling told her he'd persist. She knew him all too well. To her, he was an unparalleled monster. Why should she read a monster's words? "Forget it," an inner voice whispered. She almost heeded the voice, but the subject line caught her eye: "Please, read it. Please, hear me...." Could there be a connection between Liza's call and this email? The timing was uncanny. A sleepless night seemed inevitable. But before opening the email, she made herself a fresh cup of coffee to stay awake, to await Xhelo.

How did this email find its way to her? Who had divulged her address to him? And why now, particularly when she was already consumed by distress over her husband's mysterious disappearance? Could it be that someone, perhaps that malevolent figure from her youth, had connections with global criminal organizations, Mexican cartels, or the ruthless gangs of Chicago? Were they intentionally targeting her and Xhelo, a grim hint that their fates were inextricably bound, even in the face of death? The subject line, with its plea, didn't carry an overt threat; instead, it resonated with remorse and supplication. She decided to open it, hoping it might offer clues to the enigma of Xhelo's absence.

With trembling hands, she summoned the fortitude she had gained from her newfound resilience. She was no longer the vulnerable Shano of the past; she was now an American citizen. If she were threatened, she could rely on the protection of her adopted country. America had not only granted her citizenship but also an assurance of safety. She didn't require glasses; her vision remained sharp. With a mixture of anticipation and trepidation, she clicked to open the email. In that moment, as she followed the cursor's path with her eyes, she found herself reflecting on the beauty of her native language. She noticed the cursor linger on the word "abrogated," and she silently paid tribute to those who had preserved and enriched the linguistic treasures of her culture, even as they faced the ceaseless assault of modern media. Oh, how she wished Xhelo were by her side to confront this relic from their shared past. With the cursor hovering over the email, she clicked and began to read:

"Shano, the sin of my soul! Forgive me. I am Ben Kapshtica, the man who shattered your youth and life. My anguish won't cease until I have your forgiveness. I admit, I have been cruel, thoughtless, and barbaric. I still don't comprehend why I was that way, yet I also know I couldn't have been any different. The past is irreversible; no matter how ardently we wish, we can't relive it and undo my deeds. Please forgive me, beautiful Shano, for all the pain, anguish, and torment I inflicted upon you. It's only now, as life's tumult has thrust me into despair, making me wish for death over life, that I truly grasp the cruelty of causing another being such pain. It wasn't just youthful folly, nor the times or the circumstances. The blame lies solely with me for all the suffering I caused to you, Shano, and your Xhelo. Forgive me for both our sakes. Now, I am limbless. A mere torso, aimlessly drifting. In essence, I am nothing. Even as an immigrant in Greece, I never reflected on my actions. After what I did to you, Shano, there were many others, but none haunt me as profoundly as the tragedy I imposed on you. Please, release me from your curses and perhaps pray for a swift end for me; it might be that only your plea reaches the heavens. For over a year, I've been a mere shell of a man. While working on a farm near Thessaloniki, I accidentally fell into a combine harvester, which mutilated my limbs. It's a miracle I survived. I write this to convey that I'm paying for my sins against you. Again, please forgive my youthful transgressions.

Shano, the gem of Hoçisht! That's how you will always linger in my memories. I wouldn't have bared my soul in this message had life not dealt me another cruel hand. It seems as though the divine heeded your curses and remembered that slap you gifted me when I said 'No,' thus becoming an accomplice in a grievous act. You were an angel, and I was too blind to cherish you. Forgive me. It seems I lost you only to let Xhelo Lakrori in, but there is no atoning for my wrongs. Years later, as a father of three daughters, I received the gravest punishment: they disowned me. My wife, Donika, tolerated two decades of my sins and debauchery before she couldn't endure any longer and divorced me using a Greek ad. Alone in Thessaloniki, to add to my misery, my daughters, when I yearned just to glimpse their smiles, publicly renounced me. The Greek media was astounded by their decision, which was later legally validated. This has been the harshest punishment any father could bear, and I assure you, its sting was profound, even more so than my reckless acts that denied you your legacy. Reeling from the blow dealt by my family, I lost all hope and met with that accident. Maybe my time wasn't up yet; perhaps I had to return to seek your absolution. I'm wracked with guilt, and even if it seems irrational, maybe it's yet another facet of my pitiable state.

Forgive me, Shano. I understand it might be futile, perhaps even too late. Every word I utter may seem as fleeting as the wind that escapes into the Gorge of Cangonj, but I crave your forgiveness for the transgressions I committed against you. I long for your prayer, asking God to grant me a swift end. Please! I couldn't bear not expressing my remorse and informing you of the torment I endure. I have metamorphosed into the snake Dr. Lakrori mentioned in a widely discussed television interview that resonated even in Thessaloniki and Athens. I am a penitent snake, a mere husk of a man, bedridden, dependent on others to move me to a chair. In essence, I am the living dead.

Please absolve me of the cruelties and impetuosities of my youth, and of my mad choice to murder an innocent. Pray to God for my swift departure.

"With the most profound remorse, Ben Kapshtica Thessaloniki, November 3, 2020.

"P.S. I'm incapable of writing, Shano. I relayed this to my nurse via a recorder, and she transcribed it for me as a plea for my soul's salvation. There are still kind souls in the world."

As Shano absorbed the words on the screen, her breath grew heavy, palpable, as if it pressed against the very ceiling above her. She felt as if she had been transported to a realm of sins seeking redemption. She never would have believed that she could harbor any sentiment for the man who had marred her youth. Yet, as she finished reading the message, tears flowed freely down her cheeks. She struggled to identify the source of her tears—whether they were for Ben's tragic plight, Xhelo's inexplicable absence, or her own unyielding barrenness. For the first time, she found herself torn between two men, each at opposite extremes, both in body and soul. The mere thought of Xhelo enduring such a harrowing fate sent shivers down her spine. Despite the passing years, her core remained unaltered: a tender heart in a delicate world, recoiling from ill will towards anyone. In her heart, she felt an unshakable connection with Xhelo. The other man, audacious enough to pen this plea for absolution, was a ghost from her past, punished by the hand of fate itself. The rejection of his own daughters, their renunciation of his paternal legacy, was a punishment that eclipsed any earthly judgment—let alone his physical afflictions. These thoughts raced through her mind, plunging her back into the anguish of yesteryears.

Without further delay, she composed a brief response: *"I have forgiven you. May God assist you..."* And in that act of forgiveness, she found a measure of solace. To her, it felt like constructing a bridge—one she hoped would lead Xhelo back to her.

Caught in a whirlpool of emotions, she felt adrift, her mind inundated with a myriad of thoughts, imaginings, and inexplicable resentments. This unfamiliar emotion weighed on her, and even the perceived curse in her gaze felt like an emptiness of spirit. But from where did this curse spring? And to whom was it directed? It delved deeper than mere cursing; it harbored a bitter animosity towards the concept of repentance as a way out for the wicked.

"Why doesn't remorse precede the sin?" she pondered. "Why must individuals seek atonement only after they've wreaked havoc upon others? Why does an evildoer eventually find the need to repent, to beseech forgiveness, to yearn for solace? Why doesn't this internal battle take place prior to the act, serving as a moral anchor to prevent wrongdoing? Wouldn't the world be a more genuine, upright place? What does it truly signify when one says, 'Forgive me, for I took your life. Forgive me, for I shattered you'?"

In the heart of America, she had witnessed cold-blooded killers, those who, in the wake of unleashing mayhem upon unsuspecting souls—children, women, the elderly, and young men—would later stand before the unforgiving lens, wearing masks of remorse and pleading for redemption. Wasn't this remorse merely a charade, an empty performance, bereft of sincerity? How could both the doctrines of faith and the standards of society lend their approval to such brazen audacity?

She wasn't a philosopher by any stretch of the imagination. Her calling was rooted in healthcare, a path leading her steadily towards the realm of licensed doctors. Yet, her thoughts often meandered, delving into contemplations that bore an uncanny resemblance to the political musings of her husband, Xhelo.

The soft, muted meows of the two feline companions disrupted her reverie. They stirred from their slumber; their gentle cries reminiscent of the pre-dawn moments of sustenance during the sacred nights of Ramadan. As she popped open a can of nourishment for her feline friends, the faint hiss of escaping air evoked haunting memories of explosives being detonated in the depths of the Zvezda quarry. Anxiously, she awaited Xhelo's return, yearning for that fleeting relief, praying that he would soon cross the threshold, just as he always had.

Chapter Nineteen

Xhelo sat in the cell, awaiting his fate. Ever since that staggering moment, sleep had eluded him. An unshakable feeling of shame enveloped him due to a momentary lapse in judgment. He recalled having had only two doubles of raki. Perhaps the breathalyzer used by the statuesque brunette officer—whom he might have approached at a nightclub—was faulty. How could he have been arrested so abruptly without committing a crime? Was this the America that championed universal human rights, yet treated a man who'd had a mere two doubles of raki the same as a violent criminal? "This is a disgrace... This is a disgrace," he thought, echoing Sulo's cry from a beloved socialist realism film. He felt a surge of defiance, almost ready to shout for all of Chicago to hear.

"It seems to me you cursed the senators and congressmen of this bastion of democracy. What language did you use to curse? I'm in the same boat as you, arrested on this historic voting day. Can you see the tyranny in our America?"

Jolted from his reverie by the voice, Xhelo realized he wasn't alone. This election night was exceptional; the Chicago police station cells housed multiple detainees. Apart from those held for graver crimes, the police dealt with countless inebriates who sought comfort in alcohol. Xhelo, whose knowledge of incarceration was limited to films and cozy nights with Shano, felt like a pawn in a twisted game that evening. Another person shared his cell, a man of ambiguous ethnicity who seemed more intoxicated than Xhelo and mumbled,

"What language did you use to curse our senators? Tell me..."

"I don't know. I speak five languages—Albanian, English, Greek, Italian, Russian. Which did I use?" Xhelo replied, feigning innocence.

"I only speak English, sir. America speaks English, not five languages. You're overqualified. We only speak English here.

Explain yourself. I represent the people, and you've insulted me—someone elected by the diverse American populace!"

"Your words are pure drivel. Representatives of the people lead; they don't sit in jail like me. I represent the people, and I don't recall voting for you. I voted for Trump, championing the idea that America can be great again—MAGA! I'll say it in Albanian: 'We produce senators, congressmen, and propel them towards the White House.' Understand, sir? I hail from Skanderbeg's lineage. They call me Albanian. Do you know where you stand?" Xhelo shot back, challenging the man who was, for the first time, his cellmate.

"How could I not know?! I'm a senator of this great state! I have an office in our state's capital, Springfield, where our legendary president, Abraham Lincoln, lived. Albania, aligned and friendly with communist China, is an avowed adversary of America. I feel threatened sharing a cell with an enemy of this champion of human rights and freedom. Down with China! Long live my America! I must protest; I'm a senator of this state!"

"You're either intoxicated or what we'd term 'foolish.' Compared to you, Senator, I'm a mere bloom. I'll protest this baseless arrest. You're the genuine inebriate here, not me, the immigrant who voted conservatively. What's your name, sir? I'm Dr. Xhelo Lakrori, a veterinarian."

"Wait, aren't you that doctor who venerates the world's snakes? That Chicago eccentric who even managed to baffle the forthcoming president, Joe Biden, with your odd comparisons? You, to whom America granted freedom and a chance at prosperity—rather than lauding this great beacon of democracy and individual liberty—you revere snakes? Creatures that bite and bring death? This is nothing short of a betrayal to America, warranting an FBI investigation. They call me Enver Hoxha! Do you recognize me? I am Enver Hoxha..."

As Xhelo listened to the state senator's diatribe, he realized the gravity of his unfair arrest. If only he could show a video clip of their current confinement, proving their contrasting states of inebriation. Had he his phone, capturing this senator's absurdities would ensure an unconditional release by any judge. Yet, in the isolation cell, he was stripped of all personal belongings. America, a land that can grant you everything, can also, without warning, take it all away—just as it had taken Xhelo's wallet, phone, and revolver.

His thoughts drifted to Shano, who was undoubtedly awaiting his return, cradling their kitten with tearful eyes. He felt an overwhelming despair. He wished he could end it all right there, leaving the mysteries to investigative journalists. Why had this happened? Could two doubles of raki truly be the undoing of a life? He was certain he wasn't as intoxicated as the law assumed. The raving man beside him, proclaiming himself a senator, was the evident inebriate. Even in Xhelo's tipsiest moments, his hands were steady enough to skillfully castrate a tomcat or a bull. He was merely euphoric from the alcohol and the anticipated Trump triumph. His thoughts and instincts remained so pristine that, when juxtaposed with the senator, Xhelo felt as pure as what Albanians term as "chickpeas."

He turned his head to the camera, rage blazing in his eyes, and with an impassioned Albanian fervor like never before, began addressing the camera in his native tongue:

"This is an outrage... This is the injustice of the free world. Consider the two of us: I, a veterinarian who has had two doubles of raki, and this state senator elected by the people who have downed an entire crate of 'Modelo' beers from Mexico. We're both victims here, but I am Xhelo Lakrori, a polyglot even in custody, while this man can barely pronounce his own name... I protest this American injustice... Release me. I need to be with my wife and kittens... I demand justice."

The newly appointed chief of the 20th police district in Chicago never expected to contend with an eloquent Albanian, educated during a dictatorship era. Reviewing the recorded footage, he confirmed that it was indeed Xhelo Lakrori. Having been transferred only six months prior from his position as an inspector in the family crime division in Cleveland, Ohio, he was now the chief in a city that evoked memories of bygone May Day parades.

Chicago, this urban heart of America, is also notorious for its vast array of shocking crimes. He was now grappling with a predicament he hadn't anticipated. Throughout his tenure as a police officer, he had sworn fealty to the law, the Constitution, and the unvarnished truth. He understood his background society leaned heavily on connections; interventions, political sway, and veiled threats. However, in his years serving in America, he learned that the immutable truths were facts, reality, and accountability—not fleeting emotions or sensitivities.

He had never considered that in America, the role of a policeman would be the most daunting: the individual who wakes each morning, bids farewell to his family, and steps out of his mortgaged home to combat evil, crime, and drug syndicates, armed only with the guiding light of his vow to uphold the American Constitution and laws. He vividly remembered the words imparted by the police academy director upon his graduation: "The law is your sole beacon, guiding your responsibilities in any capacity. This is the most arduous job in a free society. Each dawn might seem like the end, but never yield to fate. As you embark on your duty, smile for yourself and your family, for it's through our efforts that citizens feel liberated and secure." Those words resonated with him, embodying the honor and sanctity of his chosen profession.

In the eyes of the seasoned law enforcement chief, America teetered on the precipice of chaos, held steady only by the dedicated men and women who wore the badge. These officers were the sentinels, the last line of defense against the descent of freedom into anarchy and lawlessness. It was this precarious balance that fueled the twisted satisfaction of certain deranged individuals who delighted in sowing chaos, attacking unsuspecting crowds, taking the lives of police officers, and reveling in the ensuing pandemonium and media frenzy. To him, these malefactors were driven by a desire for infamy, to dominate the headlines and seize the spotlight.

In his view, America's core principles needed a reevaluation. Freedom, as it stood, was not an inherent right, but rather an overindulgence of the visual and written media. He believed that if criminal activities could be shielded from the media glare, kept within the purview of crime experts, and stripped of their publicity, crime rates would inevitably plummet. This approach would render crimes inconspicuous, shrouded in profound silence, leading to the self-effacement of criminal acts themselves. After all, most criminals were propelled by a perverse hunger for attention, recognition, and fleeting, senseless acclaim.

He marveled at how a nation as advanced as America, steeped in emancipation, progress, and vision, could still find itself ensnared by crime. It wasn't just the crime itself that troubled him, but the sensationalism surrounding it—placing notoriety not on the root causes but on the perpetrators often driven to madness by substance abuse. He believed that crime should remain faceless, free from the public limelight. As an experiment, he considered that if this approach were adopted in even a single district and yielded positive results, he would be willing to stake his career on it. But he had to tread carefully, knowing that hailing from a communist nation could easily label him as a "police officer tainted by communist ideals." Every lost life weighed heavily on his conscience, as did every individual detained, even if only for a few hours.

"Boss, is everything okay?" His secretary's voice broke him from his reverie, a gentle reminder that she had often played the role of grounding him when he drifted into deep thought. He contemplated his next steps carefully, aware that the station's cells were full, and a looming protest from the current president's supporters could strain the facility's holding capacity. Thinking on his feet, he decided that those booked for minor, non-violent offenses with no prior criminal history should be released first, though penalties would still apply.

He reflected on the vast difference between his homeland, where individuals often remained oblivious to the content of their dossiers—files that passed through countless hands, each adding or erasing details—and America, where every action, from a minor traffic violation to public indecency, left an indelible mark on one's record, following them to the grave. He then ordered a retest for the two individuals in room 22. The initial results for Xhelo Lakrori had indicated a blood alcohol level of 0.085, just slightly over the legal limit. Both men cooperated when asked for fresh samples. As he waited for the results, the chief whispered to himself, "Ah, Xhelo Lakrori, I never imagined our paths would cross under such circumstances." He summoned the legal advisor.

A statuesque blonde woman, her greenish eyes exuding a blend of mischief and sharp intelligence, entered his office. After formal introductions, she awaited his query. He slid the dossier detailing Xhelo Lakrori's arrest across the desk and inquired, "What legal grounds do we have concerning this individual? Our records show no prior infractions, so he has a clean record. If the lab results confirm the initial alcohol reading or show a lower concentration, can I authorize his release?"

She examined the digital file displayed on the screen, while the chief noticed the two officers involved in Dr. Lakrori's arrest standing near his office door. He motioned for them to enter. In moments of tough decisions, he often sought input from colleagues across various ranks. As the officers entered, his deputy arrived with a report on the arrest of a state senator who had shared the same isolation room as the Albanian man. The analysis results flashed on the screen: Xhelo Lakrori's blood alcohol level was 0.077, while the state senator's registered at 0.085. The chief let out a deep sigh.

With a hint of vulnerability, he acknowledged his shared nationality with the detained man. "This squarely falls within your jurisdiction, Chief. Based on the facts, you're acting within your legal rights," the legal expert chimed in. "By the book, we should involve legal representation, and the cost should be borne by the arrestee." The officers noted that Dr. Lakrori had been cooperative, though in his inebriated state, he would occasionally lapse into his native tongue. They couldn't discern whether his words were slurs against the police or simply emotional outbursts.

In what felt like a collective decision, they opted to vacate isolation room number 22. They had other cases to review, aiming to free up as many holding cells as possible. That night, America was restless, with the dawn ushering in unforeseen challenges. Reports were pouring in about hundreds of protesters gathering in downtown Minneapolis, Minnesota, brandishing a prominent black banner that declared, "America falls..." Police departments across states and regions stood poised for a massive trial.

"Thank you for your guidance and support. Those who need rest should take it," the Albanian-American chief murmured, settling back in his chair, and savoring the aroma of freshly brewed coffee that filled his office. The clock ticked past 3 a.m.

Xhelo Lakrori couldn't believe his luck. From the confines of an isolation cell—an experience he had managed to avoid even during Enver Hoxha's dictatorship—he now stood outside the police station, the crisp night air filling his lungs. An officer directed him to a waiting car.

"This is for you, Doctor Lakrori," the officer said, pointing to a sleek black limousine parked nearby.

A passing thought crossed Xhelo's mind—maybe the car had been intended for the state senator who was still engrossed in paperwork inside.

"All the better," he thought inwardly. He had no desire to disturb Shano.

As he approached the luxurious vehicle, its opulence was evident, although it lacked the ostentation of the car Ana had arrived in with that box of snake. A whimsical notion crossed his mind—could this be another playful gesture from the fortunate Ana? But then a harsh dose of reality hit him; she could very well be in labor. In his mind's eye, he pictured himself in a delivery room for the first time, gazing through a glass window at Ana, in the throes of labor. He imagined himself speaking softly, like a character from a movie, offering words of encouragement as if he could absorb her pain, whispering, "Hold on... Hold on... Stay strong, Ana..."

His thoughts spiraled into a vivid daydream, one that echoed the scenes of war he had heard from his uncle, tales of partisan resistance. Somehow, the imagery of partisan warfare became entangled with the cries of a woman in labor. This surreal blend, a hallucination unlike any other he had experienced, left him perplexed. The battle cries against the German invaders had been filled with anger and determination. But how did that connect with the soothing voice urging, "Stay strong, Ana"? What linked these two worlds? Ana was neither a German soldier nor a partisan fighter. Yet, both scenarios were pleas for freedom—Ana and her unborn child seeking separation, much like the partisans yearning for a liberated Albania. Xhelo's mind, disoriented, still felt the cold touch of the handcuffs. The few hours spent in the precinct seemed to have unraveled his sanity. If he felt this way after such a brief stint in a free society's holding cell, what must it be like for those imprisoned for decades in Albania's jails?

He was a veterinarian, a man who had rescued countless animals from the brink. Xhelo believed that only in death would his true essence be understood.

In his heightened state, he half-expected to find Ana cradling a newborn inside the limousine, whispering, "The baby is born, Xhelo... Will you take it in? It's without family... Born amidst celestial realms... Disappeared as if cursed by the divine." The idea had always fascinated him, as if a recurring dream had merged with reality. Even if the Millers were lost in the dense woods of Canada or northern Minnesota, he would gladly embrace fatherhood for a brief moment, cherish the child as his own, and then accept his fate. He entertained thoughts of the potential consequences, even if it meant being branded a child abductor from Albania, a nation notorious for crime and narcotics.

The long limousine came to a stop before him, yet no one emerged—neither Ana nor Shano. The door slid open as if guided by unseen hands, revealing lavish interiors—plush black seats, sparkling champagne flutes resembling precious gems, and the soft tunes of Michael Jackson, an icon he had revered since his youth.

"Welcome to the free world, Doctor Lakrori," a voice resonated from impeccably tuned speakers. The expansive limo was eerily empty, save for him and the voice of Jackson, a talent he believed had been tragically victimized by the relentless media. Tentatively, he stepped into the luxurious space, feeling as though he was being carried by a legion of supporters. Not just Black supporters, but individuals of all races—white, Asian, Greek, and Turkish—all orchestrating his every move. Again, the speakers announced, "Welcome to the free world, Doctor Lakrori!"

Xhelo had rediscovered a sense of freedom that felt more precious than ever before, a freedom he had failed to fully appreciate until it was temporarily taken away. It was true that people often longed for what they didn't possess. Never had he imagined that his liberty could be curtailed in the "land of freedom," yet it had been, even if only for a few harrowing hours. Upon regaining it, he was elated, almost giddy, teetering on the edge of another lapse in judgment, much like the time he had run a red light.

Surrounded by his personal belongings that symbolized his identity, he thought of the lines penned by the Russian poet Mayakovsky: "One, zero, and null... One..." He took a deep breath, contemplating. Was he, Xhelo, the zero and null? Was this esteemed doctor, who had celebrated snakes, nothing more than a "zero and null"? Certainly not. Anyone could be considered insignificant, even great leaders, but not Xhelo Lakrori. He saw himself as a linchpin, a man destined for greatness had he perished in prison. Yet, death was not his desire. He longed to live, to one day enlighten future generations about a time when society placed unwavering faith in a singular entity: the "zero and null."

His thoughts straddled the realms of East and West. It wasn't his fault that during his formative years, an era marked by unquenchable curiosity and voracious reading, only literature from Lenin's Russia had been accessible. Back then, venturing into modern Western literature was considered political sacrilege and dangerous decadence. Even the choice of foreign language study had been dictated, with no room for personal preference. Had he been exposed to English back then, Xhelo might be lecturing at Harvard today.

His uncertainties mirrored the broader dilemmas of the 21st century: to live or not, to vote or abstain, to believe or doubt. Was the pandemic real or a fabrication? Did the virus truly exist? Trump or America, capitalism, or socialism? The continent had not seen such turbulence since the last British soldier had retreated. He had underestimated the significance of voting day and Shano's fervent inaugural vote for President Trump. From the limousine's speakers, a voice announced his impending arrival home in twenty minutes.

Relieved and truly liberated, he didn't bother counting the cash to ensure it was the exact amount he had handed to the police during his detainment. Could anything go missing within the precinct? Everything was in order, except for an envelope bearing the police station's insignia and address. It rested on top of his revolver, which he secured firmly to his belt for a sense of security. His attention returned to the envelope. A message from the police chief, perhaps? Unfamiliar with the protocols of detainment, he wondered if it was customary for the police chief to release someone with a letter, reminiscent of the old days when commendations were penned for commendable actions in one's youth.

Without hesitation, he tore the envelope open with a fervor that seemed as though he wanted to send it all the way to Istanbul. He read quickly, each word drawing him in:

"Dr. Lakrori,

You may not remember me, but I remember you. We may not share the same fortunes, but as they say in Albania: 'Fate is fate; one's luck doesn't resemble another's.' I regret our meeting under these circumstances, but I'm grateful that the law has given me a way to assist you. Please, I implore you, never drink and drive again. This is America, with laws that can devastate lives. I don't wish for a fellow countryman to suffer under the strict rule of law here. It can be a nightmare. Enjoy your regained freedom.

I found a minor loophole to aid you, not out of weakness but in recognition of the hope and vision you've radiated. You, Xhelo, reintroduced me to America. I was desolate, without hope, and had returned to Albania. Yet, you never faltered in your unwavering belief in the vast freedoms here, and your rallying cry: 'Return if you've left. America is not just about sustenance but boundless freedom, not just for you but for subsequent generations.' You brought me back, Xhelo. I'm thankful I can reciprocate your kindness. My father always said: 'When you do honorable deeds, inscribe them in beach sand. When good is done unto you, etch it in stone.' So, please, avoid alcohol, especially behind the wheel. It can dynamite even the strongest bonds. Thank you for ensuring I didn't squander an opportunity for me and the generations following.

Kristo, who traveled with you from Albania to America. Chicago, November 4, 2020."

Emotions welled up within him, choking his breath. He was acutely aware of the far-reaching Albanian diaspora and their influence across the globe, a stark contrast to their limited impact within their homeland. He understood how historical figures like Skanderbeg had gained renown in foreign lands, such as Turkey, rather than in Albania itself. Ismail Qemali had made a name for himself in Istanbul before his iconic return to Vlora in 1912. Xhelo pondered the concept of true glory, whether it resided in the East or West, on Earth or in the heavens.

Despite the anticipation of receiving a flood of messages on his phone, related to his recent local television interview, Xhelo wasn't hungry for acclaim. He realized that those considered "great men," whether presidents, dictators, or monarchs, often succumbed to the allure of glory. Whether it was artificially manufactured, bestowed by adoring masses, immortalized in history, or broadcast on screens, this glorification created a deceptive illusion. It whispered temptingly to those in power, convincing them of their irreplaceability. Xhelo, having narrowly escaped confinement, which felt like a manifestation of dictatorship within a free society, was now poised to declare, "Beware, people! Your freedom teeters on a precipice daily. Guard against the insidious slide into tyranny that any government can undergo."

As news alerts flashed across the screen, he reached for some bottles of imported Pellegrino sparkling water from Italy, each with its distinctive red star seal. CNN was broadcasting President Trump live from the White House. Xhelo lit a cigarette, listening intently, although he had an overwhelming urge to shout, "Even Shano, who has never voted before, cast her ballot for you this time... Stay firm,

Trump..." However, the news took precedence over Xhelo's fleeting thoughts. Addressing the nation at that late hour, Trump proclaimed, "We've won, we will prevail. All these numbers are false. I am president once more..." It felt like a divine message. Still reeling from his recent ordeal, Xhelo fixated on the screen, pleadingly thinking, "No, no... Hold on. Pause... Show patience. Shano and I supported you... Just wait until all the votes are counted."

However, the world wasn't tuned into Xhelo Lakrori. He had never seen an American president so swiftly claim triumph or acknowledge defeat from the Oval Office. Ballots were still being tallied nationwide, and observers diligently documented the process. In his heart, he wished he could directly advise Trump, saying, "Stay composed, Mr. President! Many still hold affection for you... My wife and I, we backed you. Wait for the complete tally... Hold your ground..." His earnest desire was for Trump to emerge victorious in that election. Not merely because he had chosen him, but primarily to make Americans grasp what life felt like in a regime where "The One is infallible, visionary, just, and the beacon..." Essentially, he was conveying that if Albanians could endure their "One" for half a century, what harm would another four years under Trump do, after which he'd inevitably politically "fade." It was only this second term that would truly enlighten Americans about the omnipotence akin to the one Xhelo had fled from.

A realization dawned upon him: engaging with American politics seemed like the grand farce of the century. To him, it was a colossal ruse, a vast enticement. He perceived voting as a cynical play where most vested their belief, but which eventually turned out facetious. He wished he could vehemently decry from his plush limousine, bellowing, "Folks, trust in yourselves! Political parties are a cruel illusion, the pinnacle of insincerity played upon humanity's intellect and spirit. Beware of politicians..."

In that moment, he made a firm decision never to engage in voting again. Just like Shano, whom he had persuaded to support Trump— the man in whom he had placed his electoral trust. Hadn't enduring Enver Hoxha's rule for nearly five decades been enough? He regretted his sincere investment in the outcome. He wondered if America might fare better under the British Crown than with the unpredictability of White House occupants. "They're all cut from the same cloth, all consumed by fame, ambition, power, and the allure of televised charisma... Presidents are like two sides of the same coin," he pondered. As he expressed this, he felt a sharp pang, a sorrow for those who steadfastly believed in global justice, champions of human rights, paragons of integrity... "It doesn't exist and never will. Life is but a stage for human egoism. There is no righteousness, just mirages, like the utopian dream that 'All shall dine using golden cutlery'... Folks, have faith in yourselves! Leaders are the grand deception of the 21st century or mankind's greatest delusion..."

Lost in his own political fervor, pondering the fate of Trump, and resenting the media's apparent bias toward his rival, Xhelo Lakrori found himself freshly released from police custody. It was the first time he truly grasped the deceptive nature of the electoral process on the world stage of so-called freedom. Lies pervaded every corner, and people celebrated these falsehoods as victories, successes, and promises of a brighter tomorrow. Silenced, without a platform to voice his thoughts after his Facebook ban, he felt overwhelmed by the mainstream media's narratives. Ignored and marginalized, he wondered why there was no mention of a renowned veterinarian in Chicago, an Albanian American potentially related to the likes of Mother Teresa or Skanderbeg, who had been unjustly arrested over two servings of rakia. The silence was deafening. Where was the justice for the common person?

If Trump had made any outrageous gesture during a speech, every camera in the country would be focused on him. Yet not a single lens captured Xhelo's release from undeserved imprisonment. Would the media have swarmed around him if he had assaulted a police officer? Would CNN have broadcast it live? In a moment of frustration, he wanted to shout, "Down with sensationalist media! Trump is right, labeling you 'enemies of the people.' You only appear when there's tragedy, blood, and chaos. Long live Dr. Lakrori, the beacon of honesty from Devoll!"

If he had been in a secluded location, away from prying eyes and ears, Xhelo would have smashed every screen and speaker in sight, seeking solitude akin to Mato Gruda an Albanian hero of WWII, who lived with a cannonball embedded in his hangar. Xhelo's frustration didn't solely stem from Trump's premature victory declaration; it also sprouted from the agonizingly slow vote count that would be leaving the nation in limbo for weeks, testing the patience of political enthusiasts. In this vast world, individuals often felt insignificant, manipulated by the media, with politicians acknowledging them only during elections.

As his limousine approached home, he realized he had forgotten to inform Shano of his return and that he was on his way to deal with her ailing cats. Six hours had passed since her urgent call. Burdened by guilt, he wondered whether she had learned of his arrest or if she had sent the limousine. Yet, he dismissed these notions, envisioning her anxiously waiting with her cats, the fireplace aglow with three candles, as she preferred.

He recognized the paradise he had briefly forsaken—his home—for a political figure who was unaware of his existence, let alone his unique name, Xhelo Lakrori. Such recklessness was foreign to him, even during the days of dictatorship. Entrusting his fate to a limousine whose driver remained a mystery, and blindly following a police officer's instructions, he felt like a naive fool. What if this ride was simply a transition from one prison to another? In this vulnerable state, he empathized with clients who placed their trust in him. Reflecting on his current predicament, he was reminded of Dostoevsky's "The Idiot" and its modern reinterpretation titled "The Idiot Travels to America." He mused, "Indeed, I am the very 'idiot' that Albanian writer Lazër Stani wrote about. This writer has an uncanny ability to breathe life into his characters. If he were privy to my plight, he might be inspired to pen a novel." With this, Xhelo fondly recalled the writer who had spoken so eloquently of their mutual friend, Bilal Eshka, during their school days.

As the world's attention remained fixated on the election results, Xhelo's thoughts teetered precariously amidst recent events. Despite being confined for several hours, he had received no added information about the search for the Millers. He scanned the news headlines, and soon enough, fresh updates emerged. CNN, amid its vote-count reports, reported, "The Millers' private plane discovered burned near the Canadian border. Biological evidence in the wreckage suggests the presence of two hunting dogs. The couple's phones were found, but there's no conclusive evidence to confirm their fate." Another source added, "Forensic suggests the plane didn't crash but was intentionally set ablaze after landing, taking the dogs with it. The mystery deepens. The whereabouts of the American couple remain unknown."

He grappled with trying to fathom their fate. He recalled Gina

Miller's dog allergy, as Ana had informed him during her first visit. Why were there dogs on the plane? Why were the dogs found burned, yet there was no trace of the couple? Were they held hostage somewhere, awaiting rescue or a ransom? Why hadn't they called for help? The flurry of information confounded him. Torn between the electoral fate of President Trump and the enigmatic disappearance of the Millers, Xhelo felt an unparalleled psychological turmoil. He yearned to escape this overwhelming flood of information and find solace in Shano's embrace.

Relieved, he couldn't fathom that he was nearing his home, finally unshackled, and liberated from his unforeseen incarceration, along with the haunting regret of not having children. This ordeal had crystallized one thing for him: his freedom was paramount. The election updates streamed endlessly, "Trump leads with electoral votes..." "Joe Biden takes the lead in California..." The coverage was relentless.

But after President Trump's brazen victory proclamation from the White House, new headlines emerged. A burgeoning movement, even more aggressive than "Black Lives Matter," had taken root. Dubbed "Stop the Steal," it saw irate crowds in Arizona and Detroit demanding an immediate halt to the vote count. America, long considered a paragon of democracy, was unveiling a hitherto unseen facet. In the mere twenty-minute ride from the police precinct to his home, Xhelo had witnessed such bizarre and unsettling events that he felt compelled to exclaim, "No more politics!" But his voice was drowned in the void.

He lamented the hours wasted on political debates, dissecting candidates, and scrutinizing congress members. To him, they were all deceptive, mere illusions of trust. Politicians, in his eyes, valued you only for your votes, support, and applause. Once they achieved their goals, you faded into obscurity. As he rode back in the limousine, he made a solemn vow to distance himself from politics forever. Furthermore, he pledged to give up alcohol. His new mission was clear: to devote himself entirely to animals. He dreamed of pioneering research that could enable animals to converse in human language. Such a breakthrough would alleviate humanity's profound loneliness and despair. If animals could communicate, people would never long for other companionship or face desolation. This became Xhelo's ultimate aspiration: giving a voice to animals.

"You have reached your destination," the computerized voice announced. Suddenly, all visuals on the screen disappeared, replaced by shimmering lights on the floor, guiding his way.

"Dr. Lakrori, thank you for choosing our service. I apologize for any unintended offense. If you need a good laugh, visit my barber shop. My brother-in-law, Kristo, who witnessed your release, is immensely grateful. You convinced him to return to America, something I couldn't achieve. This limousine service is our joint venture. Thank you, my friend! It's an honor to serve individuals like you. Your first ride is on the house!"

The limousine's driver appeared on the screen: Frank Mitrushi, or Fevzi Mitrushi, the renowned barber who had once spent two hours in his clinic. Xhelo was taken aback. How had this happened? Who had sent him to prison? Why him and not someone else? Why hadn't Ana sent her own driver? Could this have been a twist of fate, a testament to the adage, "Save the bone, though the meat is gone"? Kristo had returned without a word to him. What fortunate star had led him straight to an Albanian police station chief with such an immigration background?

Overwhelmed, he watched as the man on the screen waved goodbye and faded. The door opened, revealing a mock advertisement: "Thank you for traveling with 'Poradeci Limousine.' Always at your service." Xhelo marveled at the indomitable spirit of Albanians, who seemed to have made their mark globally.

The grand façade of his house loomed ahead, Halloween decorations resting under the moonlight. He was no longer the same Xhelo, freed from doubts and fears. He had evolved, yearning only for the company of Shano and the cats who softly meowed, awaiting his return. He realized that life was simpler than the human mind made it out to be, more beautiful than any television portrayal. Life was a miraculous wave of emotion to be experienced without prejudice or grudges.

As the limousine glided away, Xhelo felt a pang of nostalgia for the slice of Albania it represented. He regretted his skepticism and occasional disdain toward Albanians, his own kin. He pondered the words often spoken by Albanians: "The greatest enemy of Albanians is the Albanian."

The cold touch of the handcuffs seemed to have jolted him back to reality. He realized the age-old struggle between good and evil persisted across all societies, both forces bearing a human visage. Much like the snake in his dream had hinted, humanity was both its own beacon of hope and a vessel of fear. Xhelo resolved to devote himself to animals; in them, he found unconditional companionship. He let go of his previous anxieties about Ana and the elusive millionaires. Climbing the steps of his home, he wondered if Shano awaited him, anxious and fraught with nightmares during his mysterious absence.

Approaching the door, intending to use his fingerprint as the biological key he usually did, bypassing the need to depress the black handle. But there was no need. The hefty door began to swing open, reminiscent of those expansive screens that depict imagined paradises. Shano awaited him on the threshold, clad in a white nightgown that flowed down to her feet. Her face bore a mix of relief and reproach for his prolonged absence, and in her arms, she cradled two cats that looked like silent twins, unable to speak in either Albanian or English. The entirety of the world, with the moon in tow, felt as if it were present in that very moment, all awaiting his return. The cats murmured soft meows, communicating their desire for rest, signaling that his very presence was the comfort they sought. Shano moved closer, pressing her lips to his in a kiss that harked back to their initial electrifying connection.

"Thank God you're back. I hadn't realized how deeply, how fervently I loved you," she whispered gently into his ear. Her dry lips delicately grazed the edge of his earlobe, sending exhilarating shivers down his spine. It felt like a profound reawakening of two souls, entwined in the embrace of love. Tears welled up in his eyes, the weight of emotions threatening to submerge him in a pool of remorse. He was finally home.

Chapter Twenty

The following day, Xhelo had little interest in discovering the election's outcome. The premature victory declaration from the White House didn't sit well with him, but he was just a voter. He and Shano had cast their ballots in favor of the towering figure, Trump, echoing the sentiments of millions of other Americans. At that moment, he cared less about the perplexing numbers pouring in from every state and more about the fate of his millionaire acquaintances. Xhelo Lakrori felt liberated from the frenzy of political fervor. To him, America had spoken. He awaited the official results, seeking confirmation. He resisted the urge to check his phone. However, one piece of news had already reached him: Ana had given birth to a son at the stroke of midnight on Election Day for the 46th American president. Shano had shared this information while he was overwhelmed with emotion. The birth, which occurred in the prestigious city's central hospital, was peculiar due to the absence of the biological parents. It was yet another enigma that marked Election Day in the USA. The significance of the event was further accentuated for him because, on that same day, Xhelo Lakrori had been handcuffed by American law enforcement. These were two pivotal moments, like guideposts in his tumultuous life of aspirations.

As Shano busied herself with breakfast preparations, an unusual news segment was broadcast live from the Federal Bureau of Investigation's central office on CNN. The reporter began by detailing the search for the enigmatic disappearance of the Millers from Chicago. He then read the FBI's statement aloud: "We regret our failure to prevent their escape from America. Despite being on our watch list, the millionaire couple, the Millers from Chicago, eluded our agents. Through a clever ruse involving a staged plane crash in northern Minnesota, they successfully used counterfeit Canadian passports to enter Venezuela. They boarded a direct flight from Toronto to Caracas, after having previously transferred several million dollars there. The Central Bank of Venezuela (BCV) has verified this transaction. Organized crime groups in Canada played a role in aiding their escape, prompting the FBI to collaborate with Canadian officials to uncover the whole truth. Mitch Miller stands accused of running a pyramid scheme that potentially defrauded over 550 Americans across twenty-five states. Victims were lured with promises of a 17-25% return on investments in Hong Kong and China. The estimated loss stands at around two hundred million dollars. The U.S. government will now seek the extradition of its citizens to face justice..." concluded the statement from the Federal Bureau of Investigation.

Xhelo Lakrori felt a tightness in his chest. Immersed in the freshly aired news, memories of his conversations with Mitch Miller came rushing back. Miller had an uncanny talent for delving into an individual's psyche, masterfully and convincingly painting the allure of financial domination and its potential to secure one's freedom. Simply put, Mitch Miller was the most persuasive individual Xhelo Lakrori had encountered on either continent. Thus, it didn't shock him that Miller had duped so many.

Struggling to capture Shano's attention, who was engrossed in her culinary pursuits, a passion she pursued with a devotion few could fathom, let alone emulate, he whispered to himself, "Stay calm, stay calm." Though he had fleeting doubts about the effectiveness of their vote for the president's re-election, he felt relief for not succumbing to the millionaire's seductive investment promises. "The almighty dollar is king!" A thought intruded, only to be countered by a distant echo: "Ideals above all... For the party's ideal..."

America had finally attributed tangible weight to what was once an abstract ideal. Donald Trump, with his unequivocal four-year tenure unlike any of his predecessors, had fractured the once cohesive union of states more than anyone before him. Votes were being tallied amid unprecedented scrutiny and pressure. While victory proclamations echoed from high offices, state-level officials on the ground—funded by the electorate and undeterred thus far—remained committed to accuracy and truth, as mandated by a remarkable document: the American Constitution. Rarely had this foundational script of a nation been as challenged as during these pandemic-ridden elections. America grappled with a timeless conundrum: materialism versus idealism. Historically, society oscillated between these poles, believing it had struck equilibrium in America. Yet, in 2020, this balance—between personal ambitions and the might of the dollar—was profoundly disrupted. Xhelo Lakrori stood as a witness to this monumental struggle in a land where freedom was cherished—a freedom weighed in both dollars and radical ideologies, which despite nearing calamity, persisted. As he grappled with the startling revelations about the Millers' mysterious escape, the two kittens curled upon his shoulders, nuzzling his short blond hair, as if expressing gratitude for the warmth they found in the expansive house. "Soon, I'll teach you Albanian, then English," Xhelo murmured, caressing them. Their presence imbued him with an almost transcendent comfort.

It was beyond Xhelo's comprehension that the events unfolding onscreen were real. He felt a tumult within, paradoxically soothed by the kittens' company. A man he had revered for his achievements, envied for his American birthright and revolutionary ideas, a man who seemed to have it all—including an anticipated heir and even the world's priciest snake, a couple he had assumed held sway over half of Chicago and tragically perished in a plane crash—was now alive, evading capture in a socialist country like Venezuela.

"Unbelievable! Impossible!" murmured Xhelo Lakrori, reveling in the freshness of the morning after his unexpected encounter with the American police. "Beyond the Atlantic, anything can happen, Xhelo! This is the land of wonders, after all," a voice seemed to echo from deep within him. It was reminiscent of tales from his uncle who spoke of wars against the Germans and fervent cries of, "Forward, partisans!" He couldn't decipher why that voice had trailed him to America, whispering cautionary phrases like, "Open your eyes, Xhelo!... Be wary, Xhelo!"

It felt like timeless wisdom passed between generations: to be vigilant, understanding that life, in all its beauty, was vulnerable at every global corner. Never be ensnared by illusions; trust should be bestowed cautiously. True life is a journey within, understanding the intricate balance that encompasses existence: birth, joy, dreams, desires, legacy, barrenness, delirium, and the inevitability of death. This seemed most vivid in America, where liberty could lead to self-chosen obsession or madness. Wasn't the bizarre disappearance of the millionaire couple, anticipating a surrogate-born child, a testament to this continental wildness?

How could he articulate this tale to Shano, who approached him bearing breakfast on a plate, as pure as her soul, abundant with love—a love both profound and timeless? He considered himself fortunate to have married her and not someone from his past; not the ones who'd bunk in cramped 8-person dormitory rooms, reminiscent of cigarette packs jumbled in the bustling corners of old Tirana's markets. Such memories now felt as distant as the UFO footage the American government had been revealing. Amidst his reflections, he felt blessed to have Shano Gërsheta by his side, the enchanting woman who never ceased to mesmerize him, constantly exuding youth, and a profound love he struggled to verbalize. "My great fortune... My great fortune," he'd often whisper, seemingly entranced by her captivating allure.

Maybe those swindled by the fraudulent millionaire were now rallying for protests, chanting demands like the deceived Albanians from years past. Maybe they echoed cries of "We want our money back." Perhaps news of this deceit hadn't yet reached these victims, while elsewhere, fervent supporters brandishing slogans like "Stop the steal" and "Enough counting, Donald Trump won" began their dissent. The imagery of armed individuals converging on polling stations eerily mirrored guerrilla units from Tirana's yesteryears. These chilling scenes, broadcast across American televisions, were a sign of tumultuous times.

The late autumn of 2020 hinted at a looming, frigid American winter. Albanian American Xhelo Lakrori had noted his first brush with American law enforcement in his personal chronicles, symbolic of an impending political chill on a continent already shaking with fever from the pandemic. "How is this winter going to be for me and my America?" whispered the Albanian immigrant. Now, one could be uncertain if even this winter would prove to be an unusual one.

December 2020, Minneapols, MN, USA

About the Author

Shefqet Meko is an Albanian-American author. He was born in 1959 in Pogradec, Albania. As a student, he was involved in writing and became the editor-in-chief of "The Student of Agriculture" newspaper. Meko graduated successfully from the Higher Institute of Agriculture as a veterinarian doctor in 1983 but kept working as a journalist. He finished a master's in journalism & communication from the University of Tirana in 1985.

After the collapse of communism, he became involved in journalism and civic activities. He worked for Radio-Tirana, Albania's national radio station. Meko is one of Albania's founders and first President of the Albanian Agricultural Journalist Association (AAJA) and the founder and executive director of RCRD (Research Center for Rural Development). He moved to Minnesota in 1999 to start life from scratch with his wife and their two children. As a green card holder, he worked hard to build a new life by testing and challenging American freedom. He became a US citizen in 2005. Shefqet Meko has been and remains an intellectual bridge between his homeland (Albania) and the US.

Living the American dream, he translated and published "The Wonder of America" by Derric Johnson in Albania, a collection of remarkable stories of the US nation. In Minneapolis, he worked to organize and bring together the Albanian community. He is the President and founder of the Albanian-American Institute of Relations & Contributions (AAIRC). Shefqet Meko is an independent entrepreneur in the real estate business in Minneapolis. Meko has published several books in Albania. "The American Visa" was his first book in English. "Saga across the Atlantic" is his second one.

www.ingramcontent.com/pod-product-compliance
Lightning Source LLC
Chambersburg PA
CBHW021952170726
47994CB00020B/200